Christmas 2008

Enjoy Tull's

Love Maine + Ned

MW00488548

To John and Sandy —
thank you for your service to
our country! All the best!

OWN
THE NIGHT

Paul Evancoe

mon rêve
MEDIA

Copyright © Paul Evancoe 2008

All rights reserved. No part of this book may be used or reproduced in any manner without written permission of the author

This book is fiction. All names, characters, places and incidents are products of the author's imagination or are used fictitiously. Any resemblance to actual events or locales or persons, living or dead, is coincidental.

Printed in the United States of America.

Published by Mon Reve Media, Gaithersburg, MD.

ISBN 978-1-59594-273-9
First Edition 2008

Library of Congress Control Number – 2008928420

Visit the author's Website at www.paulevancoe.com

Cover designed by Michelle Cronin Shroyer, monrevemedia.com

DEDICATION

To my mentor and author of nine best selling novels, Vince Flynn. Thank you, Vince. Your sage writing advice and bottom line helped make this book possible. It is a privilege to have you as my friend.

ACKNOWLEDGMENTS

To my manuscript readers, critics and editorial advisors – Robb Evancoe, Paul S. Evancoe, Missy Clark, Kay Good, Sara Moline and Bruce Riley. I am especially grateful to Jill Russell, Alberta S. Evancoe, Elaine Bullington, and Bruce Duncil. This diverse group of family and friends read my draft manuscripts and provided invaluable story continuity and editing recommendations. To my editor, Geri McCarthy, thanks for all your red ink. To Larry Johnson, a loyal friend and excellent story critic. To Mike Subelsky, former Naval officer and electronic warfare expert. The Navy will never know what they lost when you left. To Jay Cook, retired USAF Special Operations MH-53 Pavelow pilot-extraordinaire and Tennessean (just a reminder—the North won). Thank you for all the flyboy help. To Chief of Police Barry Subelsky, retired FBI Supervisory Special Agent, counterterrorism expert, a great friend and the best all-around pistol shot I know. I promise I won't speed in Charles Town. Thank you for your technical assistance and for always making me laugh.

To my three best cheerleaders: Jeremy Ward, a former Hercules shipmate and loyal American; Ann R. Evancoe, the love of my life; retired Navy Commander Jon Roark, former Hercules and SBU-20 shipmate and a man with whom I would trust my life (and have). Your constant encouragement made all the difference and got me over the hump to finish this book. To Paul Schneeburger, screen writer, director, and my screenplay-writing partner. Your critique of this story was nothing less than superb. I value our "odd couple" friendship. To Professor Harold Wise, historian, author of *Inside the Danger Zone* and a most helpful friend in getting this novel published. To Ben Small, author of *Alibi on Ice* and *The Olive Horseshoe*. Thanks for your brutal honesty and for being my publishing mentor.

To Doug Waller, writer for Time magazine, author of *The Commandos* and the man who got me started writing magazine articles back in the early 90's. Doug told me then, "It's probably easier to turn a SEAL into a writer than turn a writer into a SEAL." I'm not sure I agree, but thanks for patiently taking the time those many years ago to help me get started writing. I am afraid you may have created a monster.

And most importantly, to the warriors who serve –
you know who you are.

Book One

CHAPTER 1

Tan Son Nhut Airbase, Saigon, January 1968

Two Air America C-130 cargo planes sat wing tip to wing tip outside the revetment in a high-security exclusion zone known as the "Red Label Area." Situated well to the far east end of the parking ramp that the South Vietnamese and U.S. war planes used, each C-130 had its gaping, tail-end cargo ramp extended to the full-down position. Two dozen men wearing a mixture of civilian clothes and battle dress uniforms were rushing to complete a variety of tasks, both onboard and outside the planes. The Red Label Area was normally brightly illuminated. Only dim, red lights were operating this night, providing just enough glow for the ground crew to see without spoiling their night vision. In the middle of a very dark, rainy night, this scene was most unusual.

Six all-terrain forklifts, each carrying a fully-loaded aircraft pallet, growled toward the planes. The crew chiefs onboard retracted the planes' cargo ramps to the horizontal position, level with the tarmac. A man quickly placed a "milk stool" jacking device under the end of each plane's tail ramp to help support the heavy load that was about to be placed upon them. Another man, wearing an olive-drab, military rain poncho, directed the first two forklifts to the waiting tail ramp of each plane.

The forklifts were eased up to the open tail ramps and their heavy pallets carefully loaded. Men inside pushed the pallets forward to just the right spot and tightly secured them to the planes' cargo decks using chains and locking grips. The other forklifts followed in turn. A fueling truck drove up to the first plane and went to work. As the last plane's tanks were topped off, the rain intensified. The men scrambled to finish up.

As the fueling truck was leaving, the first enemy rocket streaked in, crashing into the tarmac about six-hundred feet from the two C-130s. The initial blast was followed by the arrival of five more rockets that seemed to walk their way to the east and then back to the west with an impact spacing of less than seventy-five yards. Men working nearby the C-130s dove for cover, but cover was scarce on the flat, concrete tarmac. Searing hot, high-velocity shrapnel hissed its way toward flesh and metal with every explosion. Miraculously, neither of the C-130s sustained a major hit save a few minor fragment perforations of the planes' skin that didn't affect air-worthiness.

At the moment of the attack a panel truck, moving with its headlights off, made its way through the driving rain across the dark tarmac toward the two C-130s. It stopped at the first plane, just forward of the portside wing. Six crewmembers hurried from the truck into the open portside door, disappearing into the plane's dark interior. The truck again began to move forward, semi-circling the nose of the second C-130. A bright flash engulfed the small truck as a lethal 106mm rocket detonated only yards from its side, raking it with hot shrapnel and shredding its right side. The truck heaved upward, bursting into bright, gasoline-fueled flames, and tumbled on its side. No one emerged from inside. Emergency crews were there in seconds, pulling the injured men from the burning vehicle. All but one was carried from the inferno.

But the Viet Cong were not through with their deadly attack. Following the initial rocket barrage, they began dropping mortars on the airfield from three different launch points well beyond the base's perimeter fence. There was a delay of fifteen to twenty seconds between the muffled thud of each mortar launch and the resulting impact explosion on the airfield. The enemy mortar location was not far, and they probably had spotters somewhere close by—perhaps even on the airbase—directing the murderous barrage.

U.S. and Republic of Vietnam (RVN) artillery batteries were returning fire in the direction of the attack. The U.S. had prototype radar that could detect incoming artillery and provide a return-fire solution in a matter of minutes. One of these experimental systems was deployed to Tonsonute because it was key to the defense of Saigon. The only problem was that it took time to do the triangulation calculations. Tonight was no different. Fate always seems to play its role, especially in the fog of war.

The crew of the first C-130 made it into their aircraft unscathed. Their plane suffered some minor scarring and non-critical frag perforations to the rear fuselage and tail, but nothing serious. Weather permitting, they would be able to fly. The other crew was not so lucky. Five of six crewmembers sustained fragmentation wounds from the rocket's deadly impact, as well as burns from the ensuing fire. The backup crew would now have to fly the mission.

James Ray had been the mission commander. Sitting along the sidewall of the panel van, he was suffering from frag wounds in his ass, left shoulder and left leg. His wounds were not life threatening, but they were painful and would require surgery. His backup, CIA pilot Josh Miller, was now the mission commander.

The Parrot's Beak, Cambodia, the same time

A deluge of rain angrily pelted the jungle canopy above, covering the sound of the Navy SEALs as they methodically moved through the dense jungle. They were deep inside bad-guy country and on their own. That was why Boucher had his entire twelve-man SEAL platoon with him—for the added firepower. Large drops streamed down Lieutenant Jake Boucher's water-soaked flop-hat, glistening across his black-and-green, camouflage-painted face. Undistracted, Boucher squinted into the darkness along the muddy, jungle trail as he and his fellow SEALs quietly patrolled north from the Mekong River.

The SEALs' objective for this mission was to insert themselves into enemy territory from a riverine gunboat and patrol through the jungle, undetected, about eight-thousand yards, to a designated ambush position at a canal intersection. There they intended to "body snatch" a North Vietnamese senator-level kingpin ("thuqng nghi si") from his bodyguards.

The SEALs refer to this kind of operation as a "body snatch" because it sounds so much better than calling it what it really is—a combat kidnapping.

Two days earlier, the SEALs paid a North Vietnamese agent for some detailed intelligence on the area and the *thuqng nghi si*'s movements. They expected to encounter trip-wire booby traps along the trail they were now walking, and to be outnumbered by the *thuqng nghi si*'s bodyguards—possibly by as much as two-to-one. Neither prospect was particularly disturbing to Boucher, or his SEAL platoon, because they knew how to efficiently neutralize both threats.

This night's mission took Boucher and his men to an area north of the Cambodia-Vietnam border—to a point where the Mekong River made a sharp turn east, then north, then back to the south, creating the shape of a parrot's beak, as it was so nicknamed. The North Vietnamese Army was amassing there to strike deep into the south. It was a risky attempt to penetrate well into an area that military intelligence proclaimed to be "extremely hostile." Earlier, the SEALs had penetrated these enemy-controlled waters along a thick, mangrove tree line that bordered a shallow irrigation canal about twenty-three miles up the Mekong River. Their transportation was a mini-armored transport craft (mini-ATC), a water-jet-powered, lightly-armored, flat-bottom boat, designed explicitly to support SEAL riverine operations.

The mini-ATC can carry a fully combat-loaded, twelve-man SEAL platoon at speeds up to thirty knots and then quietly idle into a shallow waterway with little engine noise or fear of grounding.

The SEALs were operating precisely where President Lyndon B. Johnson insisted no American troops had ventured—but that was a cover story that almost everyone fighting in Vietnam knew was a lie, including the enemy.

The Parrot's Beak was a hot-bed of enemy activity because it was where the Ho Chi Min Trail, which ran along the highland border from North Vietnam down through Laos and Cambodia, turned southward into South Vietnam. This route followed the Mekong River toward Saigon and beyond, and was used to re-supply the Viet Cong fighting in the Mekong Delta. The SEALs always had good hunting in this area and it could be reliably counted upon to yield a high enemy body count. Boucher hoped this night would be no different.

Johnny Yellowhorse was on point, leading the patrol. Suddenly, he crouched and then froze, dead in his tracks. Boucher, following a yard or so behind Yellowhorse, did the same thing. Holding up his clenched fist for the SEALs behind him, Boucher signaled the patrol to stop and take up a defensive position. He slowly knelt down on one knee as he quietly flipped his M-16's selector lever off safe, down to full automatic-fire position. Carefully pressing the fleshy part of his right index finger against the trigger, Boucher made ready to fire.

The other ten SEALs behind Boucher instinctively followed, each taking up a position that allowed them to project their deadly firepower forward or to either flank. Gabe Ramirez, the last man in the patrol, was responsible for the platoon's rear security. His job was to prevent people from sneaking up behind the SEAL patrol and to immediately assume the duties of point man should the platoon have to reverse its direction in a hasty retreat. Yellowhorse checked his compass and sighted it on a heading a few degrees to the left of the muddy trail the SEALs were following. It was raining so hard that he had to skim the water off the glass face to see the luminescent numbers of the compass. This operation required precise navigation so the SEAL platoon could position itself at exactly the right place at the right time. To do otherwise would put the entire SEAL patrol in jeopardy of becoming the ambushees instead of the ambushers. Yellowhorse estimated the target location was approximately 1,500 yards ahead and about three degrees to the left of the platoon's current position and heading. Holding up five fingers for Boucher to see, he opened and closed his hand three times and then pointed in the direction he was going to lead the patrol. Boucher acknowledged and nodded in the same direction.

Tan Son Nhut Airbase, Saigon, the same time

Miller and his crew were brought from the ready-room to the C-130 in a panel truck like the one that carried Ray and his crew to their near demise minutes earlier. They dashed from the truck to the plane and took their places inside. Miller strapped into the pilot's seat and began his pre-flight checklist. Looking over at his co-pilot, Ron Tener, he shouted above the noise of the rain beating the cockpit's thin aluminum outer skin, "Button up the cargo ramp."

Tener acknowledged his boss with a thumbs-up gesture and spoke into his helmet mic, passing the order to the crew chief in the rear of the plane. As they worked through the checklist, a second, unforgiving barrage of mortars rolled in, along with the relentless, monsoon-like rain. Bright, exploding strobes of light flashed through the rain-covered cockpit windows every fifteen to twenty seconds. Some detonated right in front of the aircraft, while others were hundreds of yards away.

"Shit that was close!" said Tener.

"Come on crew, we gotta get moving!" Miller said into his mic. "Speed it up!"

Miller and Tener coolly began the engine start procedure and, one at a time, the powerful C-130 turbo-prop engines whined up to power.

Ground support crewman pulled the chalks from the main gear and Miller eased two of the four engine throttles forward. The massive plane began to creep along the tarmac toward the runway. Tener only used the plane's taxi lights at intersections so the enemy attackers would not have a clear target. Visibility was next to impossible in the driving rain. Miller and Tener strained to see through the watery streams on the windshield in order to follow the taxiway out to the runway. Neither man spoke, but each hoped they would not drive their plane into a flooded shell crater.

The second C-130 followed close behind. Both planes approached the active runway and turned at a thirty-degree angle to do an engine full-power run-up. Miller and Tener continued the pre-flight checklist and got the clearance to take off. Miller swung his C-130 onto the end of the runway and powered up all four turbo props to full power while holding the plane's brakes. Tener placed his left hand behind the throttle levers, as a safety backup should Miller do the wrong thing. Both men looked at each other without speaking and nodded. Miller released the brakes and uttered a single word into his mic, "Rolling."

In training, a pilot practices zero visibility take-off while wearing a hood. Like blinders on a horse, the pilot must steer the plane on a straight heading down the runway using the gyrocompass on the instrument cluster in front of him. When the plane reaches take-off speed, the pilot rotates the yoke and closely monitors his air speed and angle of ascent to keep from stalling and crashing. Of course in training there is an instructor sitting in the co-pilot's seat, ready to take the controls. But tonight was the real thing. Miller's hands were sweating so profusely that he had trouble gripping the yoke. As the plane picked up speed, Tener began to call out, "V-one...V-two...", and finally "Rotate," as the lumbering plane hit take-off speed.

Miller skillfully coaxed his heavily laden Air America C-130 into the rainy, night sky, slowly banking toward the northeast. His destination was Utapao Air Base in Thailand, where he would deliver his cargo and receive further orders. The second C-130 followed about a thousand yards behind Miller, but it turned toward the southwest moments after take-off, heading straight toward the South China Sea. In minutes the ground support crew disappeared into the drizzly darkness and left no trace of what had just occurred. The enemy rocket and mortar attack had actually served to cover up both planes' load-out and departure.

CHAPTER 2

The Parrot's Beak, Cambodia

Over the last hour the rain had steadily intensified. The drops had grown in size to the point that their impact onto the surrounding jungle foliage was almost deafening. The heavy torrent kept the foliage moving, which served the SEALs well by helping to camouflage their movement. Of course it served the enemy equally well, but the SEALs would not hesitate to pull the trigger if a target presented itself. They didn't need a command to open fire. They knew there was a standing order from Boucher they needed to follow—"See the target and shoot it!" Their survival depended on this simple principle of fire discipline.

The SEALs had progressed another thirty minutes down the trail towards their ambush objective. Even though he was only a few feet behind Yellowhorse, Boucher squinted into the wet darkness as he saw his point man sidestep off the trail and melt into the surrounding foliage. He instinctively did the same, as did the rest of the SEALs behind Boucher. Within seconds a man exploded into view, splashing blindly along the muddy trail, past Yellowhorse toward Boucher. A woman followed closely behind. Both were wearing classic, black, Viet Cong pajama uniforms and coolie hats. The man carried an AK-47, slung over his left shoulder, and wore a khaki-colored canvas magazine pouch on his chest. The woman carried a small green-colored bag, slung over her right shoulder, and wore what appeared to be a pistol in a brown leather shoulder holster. They never noticed either Yellowhorse or Boucher, who were only a few feet beside them in the rain-soaked darkness.

Boucher let the man pass, watching him from the corner of his eye. He didn't look directly at him because a full frontal view could expose the whites of his eyes. As the woman passed by, Boucher, in a single fluid motion, swiftly rose from the side of the trail. With one hand around her throat to keep her from screaming, he tackled her with all his strength, lifting her off her feet and slamming her, face first, into the muddy trail. Simultaneously, LeFever used the same assault on the man. Risser Jackson assisted LeFever, snatching the man's AK-47 away from him as he struggled. The fight was over before it started. The SEALs now had two prisoners.

In the event more enemy blundered into their patrol, the SEALs quickly set up a hasty ambush on the trail. Yellowhorse remained on point, as Boucher and Jackson pressed gun barrels into the ear of each prisoner to keep them from struggling. Boucher knelt with his full weight on the woman's shoulders, pressing her face down in the mud. As the pressure he exerted pushed the breath out of her, she gasped in a soft moan. He could barely make out her features in the darkness, but she appeared to be in her early thirties. Her long, jet-black hair was now mud-soaked. He quickly searched her body for weapons, but found only a banana knife, a towel, and some rice in her canvas bag. What appeared to be a shoulder holster was actually a well-weathered canvas pouch that contained a number of various bandages and other medical supplies.

"A first aid pouch?" Boucher questioned in a whisper.

Boucher couldn't speak much Vietnamese, but he did know the word for "medic." Leaning down next to her ear he whispered, "Bac si?"

She nodded yes, too frightened to reply otherwise.

The man was a different story. He was clearly an armed, enemy soldier. The SEALs quickly removed his magazine pouch and found two fragmentation grenades and three fully-loaded, thirty-round AK-47 magazines. He was also carrying a loaded, American-made Colt 45 pistol concealed inside a small fanny pack. Jackson held up the pistol for Boucher to see. He acknowledged it, as he released some of his weight from the woman's back.

Now Boucher was faced with a decision. He couldn't allow the two enemy prisoners to go free for fear that they would bring back reinforcements and attack the SEALs. He couldn't take them along on the patrol and continue the mission for fear of additional compromise. He needed every man he had to successfully complete the mission. He couldn't tie them up and leave them behind because, if they were discovered, they could provide a description of the SEAL platoon's size and weaponry and aid in an ambush attempt. And, he couldn't abort the mission and take the prisoners with him because his task was to snatch an enemy dignitary who possessed plans for the impending Tet offensive against Saigon. Boucher glared at Jackson and LeFever. No matter what else, the safety of his men came first. It was his job to make the hard calls and they all knew what had to be done.

The two SEALs holding the prisoners withdrew their razor-sharp K-bar knives. Boucher grabbed the woman's hair and pulled her head back exposing her throat. Even though he had experienced this before, it still sickened him. While still holding her firmly on the ground with his knee, he nodded to the other SEAL who quickly pulled the sharp blade across her throat, severing the trachea and the jugular veins on both sides of her neck. Boucher heard a bubbling gasp and felt her shudder beneath his knee from the pain of the knife, then slowly relax as her life flowed out through the wound, creating a black-looking puddle in the mud. He glanced over at Jackson, who had similarly slain the soldier. Both prisoners were dead in less than thirty seconds. The SEALs quietly dragged the two lifeless bodies into the dense jungle and covered them with foliage. The rain instantaneously washed away any evidence of what had just taken place.

Boucher took a moment to refocus as he fought back the revulsion of what he had just done. He didn't feel any guilt. This was a war zone and his job was to kill as many of the enemy as he could while preserving the lives of his own men. Clearly, both those people were enemy combatants operating deep inside Viet Cong-held territory. But for Boucher, it all just seemed so counterproductive to the human race. He was not a religious man, but he was a man of honor. And somehow, even though killing these two enemy soldiers was unquestionably necessary and completely justifiable under the rules of engagement, cutting people's throats didn't seem honorable to him.

Boucher stood and looked up into the driving rain, as if to wash away the pain he felt. He slowly lowered his head and opened his eyes. Turning to Yellowhorse, he nodded and passed the hand signal to move out. As he looked forward, Yellowhorse nodded back at him and returned the signal, confirming that he understood. The SEALs had lost some valuable time, but they were again patrolling toward their objective where they all knew the real fight would occur later this drenching night.

Onboard the C-130 enroute to Utapao, Thailand

Miller was piloting his C-130, flying in the soupy clouds on instruments while observing strict radio silence, and he was lost. It was a lousy night to be flying the otherwise reliable C-130 on instruments, but this was a priority mission. The tactical air navigation (TACAN) beacon was not working properly and his primary horizontal indicator was bouncing around wildly from a gyro malfunction. His altimeter indicated he was flying at about twenty-five-hundred feet. His magnetic compass indicated a northerly heading of three-hundred-fifty degrees, but he couldn't be sure. The sky above was too black to take a sextant fix on a star and he couldn't climb above the rain clouds anyway because he was losing fuel from the right wing tank at an alarming rate.

Miller glanced over at Tener, his co-pilot, and adjusted his helmet-mounted mic closer to his lips. "Status?" he asked calmly.

Tener leaned forward and tapped some of the gauges on the instrument cluster in front of him before replying. "We're leaking like a sieve from both wings! I guess we must have had frag perforation in the wing tanks from the rocket attack, and we missed it in all the rain during preflight."

Miller grunted aloud. Tener took a moment to work a fuel consumption problem on his flight computer, and then continued. "I estimate we have maybe one to one-and-a-half hours of fuel left and we're off course by at least two hundred miles. If we are where I think we are, we got mountains dead ahead. Josh, I don't think we're going to make it."

Miller shifted nervously in his seat. "Yeah, that's kinda how I see it too. Jeez, this weather sucks!"

Miller adjusted his mic again. "Pilot to crew. We've sprung a catastrophic fuel leak in both our port and starboard wing tanks. We have a fifty-knot head wind and we're several hundred miles off course. I'm going to drop down lower and try to get under the clouds. If we can find a suitable landing site, I'm going to give it a try."

The crew each clicked their transmit buttons twice, signaling without words that they understood Miller's message. All of them knew how dangerous it would be to attempt to fly beneath the clouds to find an emergency landing site. It was raining, there was turbulence, it was very dark and there was only jungle below. The odds of surviving an emergency landing were stacked against them.

CHAPTER 3

The Parrot's Beak, Cambodia, one hour later

The SEALs patrolled about three miles and finally arrived at their objective—a bamboo bridge at a canal crossroads. The plan was to kill the *thuqng nghi si*'s bodyguards as they crossed a flimsy, bamboo bridge that spanned a relatively narrow irrigation canal.

The bridge was constructed using a lashed bundle of six pieces of bamboo for the walkway, supported by larger-diameter, pile-like, bamboo supports driven into the mud of the canal bottom. Bamboo handrails were tied to the piles that protruded about four feet above the walkway. This crude, fragile-looking structure allowed one person at a time to pass across its length. While it only spanned about twenty-five feet, arching six feet above the water at its highest point, it provided a better alternative than wading through the dirty, leech-infested, neck-deep, canal water and fighting the sticky, knee-deep mud beneath its surface.

The SEALs count on human nature to catch their prey. What sane person would prefer to wade across foul-smelling, chocolate-colored water of the canal rather than use the bridge? This is especially true for the enemy, because they are in the security of their own backyard where the likelihood of encountering any Americans is remote, if not outright impossible. And the Parrot's Beak is definitely the enemy's backyard.

The SEALs knew the *thuqng nghi si*'s bodyguards would organize their patrol with approximately an equal number of troops in front and in back, sandwiching the VIP they were protecting. That meant the enemy procession would probably patrol single file along the narrow jungle trail leading up to the bridge with the VIP safely guarded somewhere in the middle. They would stop there, and the rear security element behind the *thuqng nghi si* would likely set up a defensive perimeter around their VIP as the lead element crossed the bridge single file. After crossing, the lead element would set up a defensive position on the other side of the bridge. As soon as the defensive positions were in place on each side of the bridge, they would have the *thuqng nghi si* cross, followed by the rear defensive element. When they were all on the opposite side of the bridge, they would again reorganize into patrol formation and continue on.

When planning this operation, Boucher and his fellow SEALs figured the only time the *thuqng nghi si* would be vulnerable was when he was crossing the bridge. It was the only time that he would be out of the line of fire and separated from his bodyguards. The SEALs intended to simultaneously attack both bodyguard elements, while they were separated on each side of the canal bridge, when the VIP was at the middle of the bridge. The only problem was that the SEALs would likely be outnumbered at least two-to-one and maybe more. But outnumbered doesn't mean outgunned, and the SEALs knew they would have the element of surprise. After all, the President of the United States, himself, attested to the fact that no U.S. forces were operating in Cambodia, in front of both the American people and the world media. Boucher smiled when he thought of the President making that statement, knowing full well it was a well-preserved secret. He couldn't help but wonder what else the President might be lying about.

As previously planned, Boucher divided his twelve-man SEAL platoon into three four-man, fire team elements. Billy Reilly, the platoon's Leading Petty Officer, led Fire Team Blue. Reilly's element consisted of Cherry Klum, who carried an M-60 machine gun; Dick Llina, the platoon's medic, who carried an M-16 with a grenade launcher; and Bad Bob Barns, a Stoner machine gunner. Fire Team Gold was led by the platoon's Chief Petty Officer, Senior Chief Haus Quicklinsky. The Chief's fire team consisted of Jack Doyle, an M-60 machine gunner, and Gabe Ramirez and Mojo Lavender, each a Stoner man. Boucher led Fire Team Green, positioning his team between Blue and Gold, who were now quietly taking their ambush positions—one on the left flank, one on the right—along the main canal, directly across from and parallel to the target bridge.

Boucher, Yellowhorse, LeFever and Jackson were now settling into position in the center of the ambush line between the two fire team elements. This way the chain of command is divided for survivability, as is the platoon's formidable firepower, should the worst happen. If Boucher bought the farm, Senior Chief Quicklinsky would take command from the right flank. If both Boucher and Quicklinsky were killed, then Reilly would take command. If all three were taken out, the next senior SEAL Petty Officer would lead the platoon and so on down the chain of command.

Under the vigilant cover of the team gunners, one SEAL slowly entered the canal from each flank. Both men pulled out the oral inflation tube from their life jackets and puffed several lungfuls of air into them. This provided them additional buoyancy so they could swim across the canal while still wearing all their combat equipment. Now with only the heads of the two men showing above the water, they were each handed two Claymore mines. The two men cradled the pouches containing the mines and hellbox clickers on their chests, as they silently half-stroked and half-waded across the muddy canal, heading toward the end of the bridge opposite their respective flanks.

As the men cautiously moved through the water, their teammates carefully spooled out the electrical firing wire used to remotely detonate the mines. Several minutes later, each man crawled from the water beneath his particular bridge end. There, they proceeded to set up the mines in some low weeds at the foot ends of the bridge. They carefully aimed the mines down the dark trail covering the bridge approach and departure routes.

SEALs almost always employ Claymore mines when they set up an ambush against a numerically superior enemy force. It is a simple tactic of waiting until the enemy patrol is evenly distributed on either side of the mines before exploding them. This assures that any enemy on either flank, out to at least one-hundred yards, will be cut down by the deadly, high-velocity fragmentation. The mines brutally slice and dice their way through anything in their path. The result is never pretty when Claymores hit human targets.

The two SEALs completed their task and made the return swim to their respective fire team element on the opposite side of the canal. As they arrived, their fellow SEALs eased into the shoulder-deep water, backing themselves into the overhanging foliage along the canal's steep bank. From this concealed ambush location, each SEAL had a field of fire directly in line with the enemy bodyguard on both sides of the bridge. This position allowed the SEAL fire team on either the left or right flank to engage the other's target with a grazing crossfire.

Boucher and the Green Fire Team, consisting of Yellowhorse, LeFever and Jackson, settled in behind a small, bamboo stand surrounded by some low, broad-leaf, wild banana trees. This location provided them concealment on the intersecting corner of the canal, only a short distance from the middle of the bridge. As Boucher's element slipped into the foliage along the canal bank, blending in perfectly with their surroundings, they carefully pushed the weeds and leaves down in front of them to provide an unobstructed view of the bridge. The purpose for this was to give him a full tactical view of all his men. It also provided for speedy movement in the event they had to react to any enemy flanking movement, or counter-attack coming from another axis.

The SEALs' discipline enables them to sit motionless in the knee-deep mud and neck-high water for hours waiting for their prey, while leeches and mosquitoes feed upon their blood. Boucher lay, flat on his belly, straining to see the bridge through the relentless rain and dark. He could feel the mosquitoes' needle-like stabs penetrating through his camouflage battle dress as they fed on his back and neck. For a second, he tried to remember if he had taken his malaria pill before leaving on this mission.

About forty minutes passed. The rain continued to pound the jungle, causing continuous movement of the surrounding leafy foliage and at the canal's water surface that served to camouflage the SEALs even more. Boucher wished that he could ease into the warm mud, like his men on the left and right flanks. He shivered for a moment before his well-disciplined mind took over, disallowing any further shuddering. *Cold is a state of mind,* he thought to himself. He slowly raised the night vision scope, carefully removed the protective lens caps, and flicked its switch to the ON position. He could barely hear its high frequency whine over the noise of the rain, as the scope's electronics warmed up.

Boucher had two night vision scopes assigned to his platoon, but he rarely used them because viewing their bright green, illuminated, monocular screen ruined your night vision. Having to wait five to ten minutes, until the eye readjusted to the darkness, was the price you paid to use the starlight scope. To reduce the effect, the SEALs use their non-target eye so only one eye is affected. Boucher likened this phenomenon to walking into a darkened room from bright sunlight and trying to see. No matter how hard he strained into the darkness after looking through the starlight scope, it was always impossible to see from the exposed eye for three or four minutes until that eye readjusted to the darkness. But he needed to be able to identify the *thuqng nghi si* when he crossed the bridge, so on this murky night he carried it for just that purpose. He had to be sure they got the right man.

Boucher slowly raised his left wrist near his eyes and peeled the green duct tape off the face of his Rolex diver's watch. The SEALs covered the watch face with a strip of green duct tape so an observant enemy couldn't see the dull, luminous glow of the numbers.

It was now 0310.

Good! Boucher thought. "Not long now," he whispered to himself. He replaced the tape on his watch face and moved his thumb back to the fire selector on his M-16.

The SEALs carried specially modified M-16s with holes drilled into the recoil buffer spring housing that allowed water to freely drain from the gun. That way, it could be reliably fired immediately as the SEALs emerged from the water.

The rest of Boucher's SEAL platoon carried a hodgepodge of modified weapons. Four of his eleven men carried M-60 machine guns that had been stripped down to lighten their weight by removing the butt stocks and bi-pods. The barrels were also cut down to about sixteen inches, making them unlike any other U.S. weapon in Vietnam. In addition to the magazine box hanging from each M-60, each machine gunner also carried six hundred rounds of linked ammunition beneath his camouflage, criss-cross over his chest and shoulders. This not only serves to quiet the metallic sound of the cartridges rubbing together, but it also hides the glint of shiny brass from sight and keeps it clean for increased reliability. Some of the other SEALs also carried extra ammunition for the machine gunners on their web gear, coiled inside canteen pouches. This unorthodox means provides ample ammunition to sustain a firepower advantage against a numerically superior force, as long as the ammunition supply lasts.

There were four other machine gunners in the platoon that carried Stoner machine guns. The "Stoner," named after its inventor, Gene Stoner, is the fastest firing, man-carried machine gun available. The Stoner gun barrels are usually cut 10 inches in length to help lighten the gun and make it easier to carry through the dense jungle and mangrove-lined river. The SEALs are the only force using the Stoner. When a Stoner man opens fire, his machine gun's report is so loud and voracious that the sound alone will, many times, cause the enemy to disengage and run. This night the Stoner gunners each carried between eight and ten one-hundred-round bandoleers of linked ammunition beneath their camouflage, in addition to the one-hundred-twenty rounds coiled in the gun's drum magazine.

Yellowhorse carried a 12-gauge shotgun with a choke that looked like a duck's bill, functionally designed to spread the shot pattern horizontally. The remaining three SEALs, Boucher included, carried shortened M-16s with a newly-developed, 40mm grenade launcher mounted beneath the barrel. Each SEAL M-16 rifleman/grenadier carried about 140 rounds of ammo along with ten to fifteen rounds of fragmentation grenades in a pouch-covered flotation vest. In addition, many of the SEALs, no matter what gun they carried, occasionally carried a rocket propelled light antitank weapon (LAW rocket) slung across their backs. Some always carried a few Claymore mines they jokingly referred to as a "force multiplier" for when the going gets rough.

About the only common equipment of the SEALs is a first aid kit with the contents distributed throughout their pockets, two or three hand grenades, a couple of smoke grenades, a strobe light to mark their position for air support, and several canteens of water. Few carried pistols, simply because the weight tradeoff meant less ammunition or water. This didn't apply to Boucher. Standing at six feet four inches tall and weighing two-hundred-five pounds, his sheer size and strength allowed him to easily carry a 9mm Browning Highpower in a shoulder holster, in addition to everything else. He did so just because he could.

Fully combat-outfitted, each man carries forty-five to sixty pounds of guns, bullets, grenades and water. They rarely take food along. They can't afford the risk of letting their guard down to eat. Most carry a candy bar, which they snack on when their energy levels wane.

In most cases, the SEALs will immediately withdraw in the initial twenty to thirty seconds following a firefight they can't win. They expertly employ the age-old tactics of surprise, strike with overwhelming firepower, and disappear again before their opponent knows what hit them. They can then regroup to counterattack. Every SEAL knows that, no matter what, no one will ever be left behind, this night or any other. There will either be twelve dead SEALs or everyone is coming out. This understanding provides them with an unspoken, psychological edge.

The SEALs reduce the chances of their detection by going barefoot. Since the enemy doesn't wear shoes, the clearly unique footprint made by the welted soles of GI jungle boots stand out in the soft mud and earth of the jungle trails. By not wearing any foot protection, unlike the rest of the American troops in Vietnam, the SEALs are impossible to track. This works so well for them that they find it almost amusing when they observe the enemy, walking along a trail, searching for jungle boot tracks instead of looking for signs of an impending ambush.

Boucher detected movement coming from the jungle trail across the canal to his right. He strained to see through his starlight scope in the rain. First one…then two…then three dark, menacing shapes appeared, all carrying AK-47 assault rifles. Their dark-green uniforms and leaf-covered helmets looked black through the starlight scope.

North Vietnamese Army... NVA, he thought, *perfect!*

He slowly squeezed LeFever's arm, then Jackson's, signaling to them the enemy had arrived. Six additional soldiers came into view and, as he had anticipated, they dispersed around the foot of the bamboo bridge setting up a defensive position. Boucher judged that the first soldier to appear was the enemy point man, and watched as he cautiously mounted the bridge's flimsy walkway and slowly teetered across to the far side. Immediately after stepping off the bridge, he knelt down momentarily and carefully surveyed the soft, muddy trail for telltale GI boot prints. Satisfied there were none, he rose to a low crouch and searched the surrounding jungle for signs of anything threatening.

More uniformed troops faded in and out of view, to the point where Boucher was unsure of their numbers. He estimated perhaps ten, maybe twelve, but wasn't sure. At any rate, he judged that he had his enemy opponents outgunned, even if the SEALs were outnumbered. The key to any successful ambush was patience. Every instinct was to initiate the ambush and kick some enemy ass, but the Commander knew he had to maintain compromise discipline. The two SEAL fire team elements positioned on either flank will not detonate the deadly Claymore mines and open fire with their machine guns, unless Boucher or the enemy initiated the ambush by firing first.

A second enemy soldier cautiously made his way across the shaky bamboo bridge and knelt beside his point man on the other side. Another followed, then another, until a total of eight soldiers had crossed the bridge. Boucher could see still more enemy soldiers arriving on the near side of the bridge. He estimated there were about twenty enemy soldiers, eight of which had already crossed. Without relying on the starlight scope, he couldn't discern any difference in their dress, which he knew would make it difficult, if not impossible, to identify the *thuợng nghi si* as he crossed the bridge. Boucher knew if he fired the Claymores and initiated the ambush while the VIP was on either side of the bridge, he would certainly kill the very man he was there to capture. The SEALs needed to capture him alive to gain critical military intelligence from his interrogations.

Boucher continued to peer through the blurring rain at his foe, now only about twenty yards away. *Just as soon as the senator climbs on that bridge, it is sure going to suck to be him*, he thought to himself.

What the Commander saw next almost made him gasp aloud. An enemy soldier went to the foot of the bridge and mounted the narrow bamboo walkway, crossing about two-thirds of the way, where he stopped and turned around. A man clearly much larger in stature than any of the others was led to the foot of the bridge by two guards. Boucher quickly brought the starlight scope up to his eye, straining to confirm the man's status. He appeared to be a prisoner. Boucher now saw the man's hands were lashed together in front of him and one of the guards held the end of a rope leash that was looped around his neck. The soldier standing on the far side of the bridge motioned for the prisoner to come to him. Using the muzzle-ends of their AK-47s, the guards pushed him over to the foot of the bridge. Boucher caught a glimpse of the prisoner's face. He was a black man wearing a flight suit. *A downed pilot?* He looked American. *He was a POW.*

"Shit!" Boucher whispered.

CHAPTER 4

Above the Parrot's Beak, Cambodia, the same time

Miller eased the yoke forward and pulled back all four throttles. Gradually, the C-130 descended through the thick, soupy clouds, breaking out of them at barely two-hundred-fifty feet above ground level. He couldn't make out any horizon through all the rain, and there wasn't enough ambient light to give him a view of any terrain features below. As he and Tener struggled to see the dark ground below, occasional lightning flashes illuminated it in surreal shadows and highlights. All of a sudden, four strings of orange tracers raced skyward out of the blackness, snaking their way directly toward the limping C-130. Miller couldn't react fast enough to turn the lumbering plane away from the incoming bullets.

"ZU23!" he shouted over the intercom.

"Oh shit!" Tener swore, pressing himself back into his seat as if he could hide from the deadly, anti-aircraft machine gunner who had them in his sights below.

The Ambush Site, the same time

As the *thuqng nghi si* stepped onto the bridge, one of the guards slammed the POW between his shoulder blades using the butt of his AK-47. The prisoner collapsed onto the muddy path at the foot of the bridge. The guards pulled him back up and dragged him onto the bridge.

Boucher heard the man groan, then utter one word in perfect English.

"Fuckers!"

Showing obvious pain, the prisoner began to feel his way across. Boucher knew the stakes had just been raised by several magnitudes.

Screw the enemy VIP, he thought, *this guy is one of ours.*

Boucher quickly evaluated the situation and his options. He knew when he fired the mines, the VIP—now on the bridge, only a couple of yards away from one of them—would be blown off from the blast, neutralizing him as a threat to the POW. Also, the guards at the other end of the bridge were nearly standing on top of the two mines positioned there.

He anticipated that the explosion from the first barrage of Claymores would kill most of the enemy soldiers, but he was concerned that some of them might be out of the line of fire and survive. If he went for the POW, who would certainly end up in the water beneath the bridge, and waited to detonate the second barrage of mines, he might inadvertently lose the POW. Should the unseen enemy numbers be larger than he expected, the SEALs would be forced to break contact and extract themselves. If he fired both barrages simultaneously, he would surely kill more enemy soldiers at first, but might also injure the POW from the blast effects. Boucher didn't like the hand he was just dealt, but he made his decision.

The POW approached the center of the bridge. Boucher held two Claymore detonators, one in each hand. He peered over at Yellowhorse, who was holding the other two firing clickers, and nodded three times. The four mines exploded, in a single, white-hot flash, at each end of the bridge. The SEALs instinctively closed their eyes to keep from losing their night vision from the bright flash.

Boucher had anticipated the Claymores' effects correctly. The guards on both ends of the bridge were dismembered. Body parts splashed into the canal. The enemy in the path of the deadly mines was cut to shreds. Those not hit by the shrapnel were disoriented by the blast.

The SEAL machine gunners opened fire, devastating the main body of soldiers directly in front of them. It was all over in a matter of seconds. The SEAL fire teams on the flanks easily finished off the remaining enemy. Each fire team moved forward in the canal, alternately wading and swimming. They advanced, shoulder to shoulder, in a firing line across the canal intersection toward both ends of the bridge, raking anything suspicious with short bursts of machine gun fire. As fast as he could, Boucher plowed his way through the water and mud to the point beneath the bridge where he thought the POW had hit the water. He anxiously probed the bottom with his feet in search of his fellow American. Yellowhorse remained ready on the near shore to provide covering fire.

Chief Quicklinsky and Reilly directed their fire team elements to set up a hasty ambush for any additional enemy, using two machine gunners who faced down each direction of the trail. The rest of the SEALs began the grisly process of searching the bodies for documents.

Boucher continued to use his feet, frantically searching the canal bottom for the POW. Suddenly, he hit two bodies. He took a deep breath and submerged beneath the muddy canal water, popping back up a few seconds later holding the VIP's lifeless body by the collar of his shirt.

"Shit!"

He pushed the corpse in the direction of Quicklinsky, who was waiting on the canal bank where the bridge once stood. "Search him!" Boucher ordered.

Quicklinsky grabbed the corpse and pulled it ashore. He quickly removed a canvas document pouch the man had strapped over his shoulder. He emptied everything from the dead man's pockets and put it inside the pouch.

After submerging again, Boucher returned to the surface clutching an unconscious man in his arms. The Commander began mouth-to-mouth resuscitation as he dragged the man to the canal's muddy bank where the bridge used to stand. Reilly and Quicklinsky pulled the man up onto the path and continued to resuscitate him. The other SEALs continued their grim task of searching the enemy bodies, some of which were little more than torsos. No one spoke. The only sound was the rain thrashing the jungle leaves and canal water. Remarkably, the rain slowed—almost stopped—as if someone above had turned off the spigot.

Abruptly, the two right-flank M-60 machine gunners guarding the trail opened fire in a sustained volley. Boucher could see their red tracers, snaking out along the trail in the direction from which the enemy patrol had come. Two Stoner machine gunners rushed over to support the M-60 gunners and opened fire. The SEAL machine gunners unleashed four streams of red-hot tracers that tore through the jungle fabric at high-velocity to find their marks. In retaliation, two orange tracer strings were returned from the indefinable black. They were directly followed by at least six more bursts of AK-47 automatic weapons' fire.

Boucher knew what that meant; an enemy counterattack was underway. Without hesitation, he shouted orders to his men. "We're outta here! Fall back!"

Two SEALs rushed over to the machine gunners that couldn't hear Boucher's order over the shooting and pulled them away. They peeled back, one at a time, maintaining the volley of fire to make it suicide for the enemy to advance.

Bob Barns, the platoon's designated booby trap man, quickly dropped a hand grenade and a Kodak Instamatic camera along the trail leading to the bridge. The grenade was armed with a special fuse that would detonate instantaneously if the user attempted to pull the pin and throw it, or if he attempted to defuse it. The camera was filled with plastic explosive lined with ball bearings. It could be set to detonate if moved, a picture was snapped, or if the back of the camera was opened to change film.

The SEALs have a variety of "give-aways" as they refer to them, that they will drop at the scene of an engagement for the unsuspecting enemy who thinks the items were lost in the confusion of battle. When the enemy attempts to use these devices, it results in their wounding or death.

Boucher pointed to the American POW, who was still unconscious, directing Doyle to help hoist the man over his shoulder. He and Boucher effortlessly picked up the unconscious man and draped him over Boucher's shoulder. Cradling his dangling arms and head with his left arm, Boucher turned and ran to the muddy bank, clumsily splashing into the water and heading toward the opposite side of the canal. While the first SEAL fire team re-crossed the canal, the remaining fire team suppressed the enemy fire, covering their teammates' escape to the far bank.

On the other side, that fire team took up the volley of suppressing fire to cover the others as they crossed. Two of the SEAL grenadiers began to lob their deadly 40mm grenades at the source of the orange tracers. When they fired, the sound was unmistakable. It was like a loud bop, rather than a gunshot. It took six to eight seconds before the egg-size grenade reached its target. An orange flash reflected off the rain clouds above, followed by the unmistakable, high-explosive thud, as it detonated on impact.

Half swimming and half wading through the thick mud of the canal bottom, Boucher slowly made his way back across the canal intersection to his men. The unconscious man he was carrying hindered his progress. Then Boucher heard the first two mortar tubes report as the enemy launched their deadly warheads in his direction. Judging from the sound, he estimated the first mortar was probably a 60mm and not that threatening, unless it exploded next to him. The second report was much louder. Boucher knew that meant a larger 81mm mortar with a fragmentation kill-radius which covers the area of a basketball court—serious stuff!

Boucher quickly shifted his rescued POW around to his front. He clutched the man against his chest to provide him some protection against what was to surely follow. The small mortar exploded harmlessly in the treetops, well on the other side of the canal intersection. The bigger mortar exploded on impact with the canal water, twenty-five yards behind him. Hot shrapnel hissed by the SEALs. They had all taken cover, knowing what was to come. Boucher felt a hot, searing slice above his right ear as a razor-sharp fragment slashed along three inches of his scalp. At the same time, a stabbing pain pierced his right triceps and shoulder blade.

Nonetheless he continued on, holding the unconscious man's face above the water. The SEAL grenadiers continued to pound away in the direction of the attack, but the NVA's mortar launch points were beyond the range of the small grenades being lobbed their way. The second NVA mortar barrage was even more accurately placed. A mortar exploded within feet of the far end of the bridge, ripping what was left of it off the bamboo supports like straw blowing in a thunderstorm. Pieces of the bridge splashed into the canal around Boucher. Another one detonated on the canal bank in front of him, into the middle of his fire teams. The blast threw mud high into the air as its deadly shrapnel hissed outward. Somehow, no one was hit. As he reached the canal bank, Jackson and Lavender scurried to help drag him and the unconscious man from the water.

A third salvo of enemy mortars streaked in. Boucher fell on top of his charge to shield him. One mortar exploded in the treetops about seventy-five feet behind the SEALs and another blasted the surface of the canal about forty feet from his position. He felt another burning stab, this time on his right thigh. Two fragments hit Yellowhorse in his left calf. Lavender took a piece in his right forearm. Miraculously, no one else was hit. Yellowhorse had already been awarded two Purple Hearts and knew that as long as the wound wasn't fatal, the SEALs counted on each other to continue on and do their jobs.

CHAPTER 5

Above the ambush site

From Miller's point of view, it looked as if his C-130 flew right in-between the four parallel strings of tracers racing up to them from the black unknown below. For a moment, both he and Tener thought they had gone unscathed. Then a second tracer burst rose out of the darkness in front of them and walked right through the starboard wing, instantly igniting the leaking fuel and starting fires on both starboard engines. As Miller and Tener each pulled the levers activating the engine fire extinguishers and fuel feed cut-off on the right wing, a third engine fire warning light began to flash on the left wing. Miller immediately hit the fuel cut-off switch, shutting it down, and Tener pulled the fire extinguisher for that engine. The fire was out on the portside engine, but it restarted on the starboard wing.

Miller got on the intercom to his four-man crew in the plane's rear cargo area. "Crew Chief! Status?"

"Got some new holes in the fuselage we didn't have five minutes ago, otherwise we're all pretty much okay back here. Problem is we have one hell of a campfire burning on the starboard wing."

"Yeah, Chief, I know." Miller replied calmly.

Miller searched the blackness below for any sign of terrain, but could see nothing. Then suddenly, flashes from exploding shells and tracer strings appeared, wildly streaming back and forth in an apparent ground exchange.

Miller keyed his mic. "You see that firefight below?"

"Yeah, looks nasty," Tener replied. "We're not going to make it are we?"

"We're going down," Miller coolly warned. "Get everybody ready."

Tener peered over at Miller with a look of disbelief. "It's been a pleasure flying with you, Sir."

"Likewise. Steer away from that firefight!"

Each man tightened his grip on the yoke and tried, in vain, to keep the limping C-130 flying. While it was a gallant effort to save the airplane, they both knew it was a useless attempt with only a single engine running. The law of gravity was now dominating. Gravity always wins in the end. They knew if they walked away from this, it would not be a result of their airmanship. It would be a miracle.

The ambush site

As Boucher prepared to drag the rescued POW toward the tree line, he noted the unmistakable engine drone of a low-flying, C-130 cargo plane. It seemed to be approaching his position in this jungle battlefield. The unconscious man sputtered, coughed, and momentarily opened his eyes, just as the C-130 streaked overhead trailing bright orange flames. Boucher estimated the plane was heading due west at an altitude of no more than one-hundred feet. Several strings of orange tracers streaked upward and seemed to pass directly through the plane. The mortally-wounded aircraft shuddered as it banked slightly to the right before disappearing from sight. A muffled explosion ensued that briefly flashed like lightning across the bottom of the clouds.

Boucher lifted the semiconscious man over his shoulder and quickly organized his platoon into patrol order. The SEALs melted into the dense jungle, just as the unmistakable thud of two additional mortar launches occurred. Boucher hustled his platoon along the pre-planned extraction route, heading southwest. This trail would take them back to the Mekong River and their waiting gunboat.

The two mortars impacted within yards of the SEALs' previous location. The men could hear the snap of hot shrapnel hitting the trees behind them, but they were now out of its lethal range. Boucher kept the platoon's pace up for the first click, just to put distance between them and any pursuing enemy. Even though the sweating men showed no noticeable fatigue, he realized they needed a rest. He raised his fist, signaling the platoon to stop. He then gave the signal to circle wagons, which meant the SEALs would set a defensive security perimeter and take a rest break.

Using his sleeve to wipe the blood from his eye and cheek, Boucher carefully placed the semiconscious POW on the ground. Dick Llina, the platoon's corpsman, unzipped the man's flight suit and examined him for wounds. He appeared to have a broken left arm and a dozen or so third-degree burns that looked like brands on his chest. Beyond those injuries, plus multiple bruises on his face, arms, and legs, he appeared okay.

"He seems okay," Llina whispered to Boucher.

Boucher nodded.

"How are you making out, Sir? You look like shit!" Llina added.

"I'm okay. I just took some frag."

"We need to get him on his feet," Llina whispered, nodding at the man.

Boucher turned the man's face toward him and carefully pulled one of his eyelids up. "He had the shit knocked out of him by those four Claymores we fired. Then he almost drowned."

Llina again checked the man's pulse. "Probably in some shock, but otherwise I think he's alright."

"Stay with him," Boucher whispered.

As Boucher turned to check on his men, the POW groaned. His eyes fluttered open and he attempted to struggle. Llina quickly put his hand over the man's mouth. Boucher helped Llina hold the struggling man down.

"We're Americans," Boucher whispered to the man. "You understand... we're Americans."

The man relaxed slightly.

"We're United States Navy SEALs...we're taking you home," Llina added.

The man looked wildly confused.

"What's your name?" Boucher asked in an almost inaudibly low voice.

The man attempted to sit up. Llina and Boucher pulled him up to a sitting position. The man shook his head as though he was trying to grasp his circumstances.

"Patterson," the man sputtered. "Lieutenant Leon Patterson off the Kitty Hawk. I got shot down ten days ago. You guys are Navy SEALs?"

"Yeah. I'm Lieutenant Junior Grade Jake Boucher and these are my guys." Boucher swept his hand through the darkness as though Patterson could see them. "Look Lieutenant, we got into one hell of a fire fight back there with the NVA and they may be chasing us. We need to move out. Can you walk?"

Patterson attempted to stand but fell back on his butt. Boucher and Llina lifted Patterson to his feet and a shaky balance.

"Yeah, I think I can walk okay," he replied grasping Boucher by the shoulder to steady himself.

"Alrighty then," Boucher nodded. "Lets head 'em up and move 'em out. It's gonna get daylight in a few hours and I want us to be as far away from here as we can be by then. I want you to walk behind me. Stay close!" he added, looking back over his shoulder at Patterson.

Patterson stopped Boucher with a quick, grasping hand on his arm.

"Thanks," he said. "Thanks for rescuing me."

Except for his white teeth, Boucher's smile was concealed by his green and black camouflage face paint. "The pleasure was all ours, Lieutenant." Boucher withdrew his Browning Highpower pistol from his shoulder holster and offered it to Patterson. "Here. There's a round in the chamber and fourteen more in the magazine. It's ready to shoot. I hope you won't need to use it."

Boucher turned back to Risser Jackson, who carried the radio. "Call NAVFOR-V and tell 'em we're bringing a U.S. POW back out with us and his name is Lieutenant Leon Patterson from the Kitty Hawk. Tell 'em Lieutenant Patterson is alive and well."

Jackson nodded and began to speak into the radio's handset.

"Risser," Boucher added, "tell 'em to get a B-52 strike diverted here ASAP and tell 'em to drop everything they have around that canal intersection. There has to be at least a fucking NVA reinforced rifle company back there judging by the firepower they just demonstrated."

Boucher looked at the man he had just rescued then turned back towards the ambush site mumbling aloud, "Sons of bitches!"

The SEALs once again assembled into single column patrol order behind Yellowhorse and began disappearing into the jungle darkness, one by one. Gabe Ramirez was still kneeling on one knee facing backwards, his Stoner machine gun at the ready, maintaining his rear security vigil. As Jack Doyle, the M-60 machine gunner who was second to last in the patrol, turned away from Gabe to follow his platoon, Gabe slowly rose from his knee into a low, crouching position. Stepping slowly backwards, he melted into the dark jungle behind his teammates. He didn't know if they were being followed or not. If they were, he would kill those pursuing before they could sneak up on the SEAL patrol. If they weren't being followed, it didn't matter. Either way, he was ever-vigilant and ready to unleash his Stoner's deadly 900-round-per-minute volley on the enemy.

The SEALs had not slowed their pace for nearly forty-five minutes. By that time, Boucher's platoon had distanced itself from the ambush site by about a mile. The commander judged that they were out of immediate danger from the enemy force they had just engaged and an opportunity to rest for a few minutes was in order. He snapped his fingers to get Yellowhorse's attention, held up his fist and then his index finger, and waived it in a circle. The SEALs silently passed the order along the patrol and the men quickly circled wagons around Boucher, Quicklinsky, Jackson and Patterson.

Jackson was listening to the radio handset. "BUF inbound," he reported to Boucher.

"Roger. Tell 'em we're clear of target area." Boucher always found poetic justice in the B-52's nickname, "BUF." Anyone who ever saw one knew it truly was a big ugly fucker.

Moments later, a high-flying B-52 began dropping its payload of bombs on the coordinates of the ambush site. Even though the SEALs were more than a mile away, the ground shook like an unrelenting earthquake and the sky flashed with surreal brightness.

Boucher pulled Patterson over next to him. Both men sat down a few feet off the side of the trail. Boucher yanked his canteen from his webbing pouch and passed it to Patterson.

The bomb flashes provided quick, strobing glimpses of Boucher. Even in the rain-soaked darkness, his powerful frame was an ominous sight. Patterson could see that Boucher's hair and cheek were streaming with blood. He also noted Boucher was favoring his right side.

"You okay?" he asked Boucher.

"Yeah."

"You don't look okay."

Boucher gave him a stern look before responding. "Lieutenant, I'll be sure to let you know when I'm not okay. Let's cut the chitchat. We're still deep in bad guy country and we have a couple more miles to go."

"Yeah, sure, but I just can't imagine why you did what you did to rescue me. You and your men could have ended up on the end of a leash, like I was."

Boucher contemplated Patterson's words for a few seconds before replying. "Don't take this the wrong way, but there ain't no fucking way a SEAL is going to allow himself to be taken alive. And there ain't no way a SEAL platoon will ever allow any of their own, including flyboys, to remain behind—dead or alive—as long as any of them are alive to fight." Boucher sat back and clutched the wound on his right arm. "I suppose we all got lucky tonight."

"Luck isn't the word for it," Patterson replied.

Boucher wiped the blood from his face with his sleeve. "What were you doing when you got shot down, Lieutenant?"

"Ahh, I was conducting close air support for a Marine outpost that was under attack and at risk of being overrun."

"Exactly! You put your ass on the line for our brothers in arms because they needed your help. Did you have any second thoughts about why you were helping them out when you were making your bomb runs? Of course not! You knew some dumbass fellow Americans needed your help to survive, so you did what you did because you could. You know what, Lieutenant? I was just starting to like you when you started into this line of bullshit. So knock it off! We have a lot of ground to cover before daylight and there will be plenty of time to debate the warrior code later."

As if God was listening, Boucher's declaration seemed to trigger even heavier rain from above. He held out his open hand in the rain and smiled as he raised his face towards the downpour from above. "Hooyah!" he said aloud.

Book Two

CHAPTER 6

Yakura Restaurant, McLean, Virginia, today

The lights flickered following a loud thunder clap. Neither man seemed to notice.

Jake Boucher and Pat Patterson had just ordered the sushi lunch special. They tried to meet for lunch somewhere in the Washington, DC, Metro area on a weekly basis.

"So, how's my short-timer buddy?" Boucher asked.

"I gotta tell you Jake, I can't wait to retire. The FBI has been a great career, but I'm ready to retire and try something else. Friday will be the first day of my new life."

Patterson's cell phone rang. "Patterson," he answered in monotone brevity.

Boucher could tell by his friend's facial expression that the call brought bad news. Patterson closed the phone's cover with a snap and shoved it into his shirt pocket.

"Sorry Jake, I gotta run. Got a hostage barricade situation at Sidwell Friends School. They have the President's daughter."

"Oh shit! Let me come with you!"

"Sorry Jake, this is an FBI matter. Besides, you aren't in the government anymore."

"Yeah, so what? I can still…."

"No, Jake!" Patterson sternly replied, stopping any further debate.

Boucher grabbed Patterson by both shoulders. "Well then, keep your head down, Pat. I don't want to have to go through the nut roll of rescuing your dumb ass again."

Patterson smiled at his long time friend. "Don't worry, Jake, once is enough for me too. I'll give you a call when it's over."

Sidwell Friends School, Washington, DC, an hour later

FBI Critical Incident Response Group's Special Agent in Charge (S.A.C.), Leon "Pat" Patterson, pulled his Suburban onto the private campus of Sidwell Friends School, splashing through a deep puddle. A loud rumble of thunder that sounded more like an exploding mortar shell momentarily drowned out the excited voices on his police radio. At that instant, his mind carried him back to the canal intersection of thirty-some years earlier—the Claymore mines and mortar rounds exploding and the torrential rain. Patterson quickly re-focused his thoughts back to the present as he stepped out into the deluge.

The hostage barricade situation inside the new middle school building was deteriorating by the minute. Heavily armed terrorists had forced their way inside this exclusive private school where the rich and famous sent their children to gain an early advantage towards an Ivy League education. As S.A.C., it was Patterson's job to resolve this hostage situation.

"What you got?" Patterson asked Les Hager, the FBI Hostage Rescue Team (HRT) on-scene commander.

"As best as we can determine, they are holding forty-eight kids and five staff members hostage. They placed kids in front of all the windows and doors! Pat, it's gonna get ugly!"

"Any ID on the T's?"

"The only thing we know is they all appear to be Middle Eastern. CIA says no known direct al-Qa'ida link. I guess nobody saw this one coming."

Patterson and Hager stepped inside the brightly-lighted mobile command post and went immediately to the cramped briefing room filled with law enforcement officials. Hager began the briefing.

"Gentlemen, I believe you all know S.A.C. Pat Patterson, who heads the CIRG. Please feel free to interrupt me at any point if you have anything to add to this briefing. Pat, about two hours ago a group of at least six heavily armed terrorists entered the main school building here," Hager said, pointing to a real-time, video picture of the building displayed on a large, flat-screen, wall-mounted monitor.

"They were reportedly all armed with AK-47s and carried heavy equipment bags. They entered here," Hager said, again pointing on the monitor. "They shot and killed an unarmed building security guard on the way inside and barricaded the doors. As you know the Secret Service has a protectee in that school. Apparently the Secret Service agent attempted to evacuate the President's daughter. He was able to radio his headquarters, notifying them of the situation, and report that he was attempting to evacuate his protectee. Shots were reported and we have not heard from him since.

We can only assume that he has been killed. We do not know the status of the President's daughter."

Hager indicated various points on the monitor. "We got snipers out here, here, and here. Washington Metro SWAT is covering this end, here. They have also established a perimeter outside the school grounds."

A Secret Service agent sitting in the back row interrupted Hager.

"Pat, this operation falls under our jurisdiction and we need to get the President's daughter out of there now!"

"I disagree and I say we wait!" a young man insisted as he stood up. "I'm the Department of Homeland Security, Director for Infrastructure Protection and this operation falls under DHS jurisdiction and, in case you don't know, the Secret Service works for DHS. I want to bring in my people and..."

Patterson stopped the argument in mid sentence. "Gentlemen, this is an FBI operation. It is not about who has the biggest dick! We have a bunch of school kids that are being held hostage by terrorists who have already demonstrated they will not hesitate to kill. If you or any of your people get in the way, I will have you arrested for obstruction! Is that clear?"

"But DHS has the authority to..."

"Stop right there!" Patterson demanded loudly. "What's your name, son?"

"Ahhh, James Lockbourne."

"Mr. Lockbourne, in just a moment I am going to make a call to Director Freeman. I am going to apprise him of the situation here on-scene. Would you like me to mention that DHS is attempting to take charge of a domestic hostage-taking incident? I'm sure he would be happy to pass that along to the Attorney General for action. I mean, I really don't give a shit! My retirement is already set for next Friday!"

"You call anybody you like, Agent Patterson! The Secretary of Homeland Security is my reporting senior, not the Director of the FBI or the Attorney General!"

Patterson blistered for a moment before speaking. "Get this asshole out of my sight!" he ordered.

"You can't make me leave!" Lockbourne yelled. "I represent the Secretary of the Department of Homeland Security! I have jurisdictional authority here!"

Two FBI HRT agents, decked out in full tactical gear, grabbed Lockbourne by his arms and escorted him out of the command post.

"If he comes back, arrest him!" Patterson ordered as the two agents passed by with Lockbourne in tow.

Hager continued the briefing the moment the door closed.

"Alright everyone, give me your attention. Pat, here's the tactical situation.

We have a security officer confirmed dead, maybe another dead assuming the worst for our Secret Service brother. We have forty-eight kids and five staff members being held hostage. The terrorists have placed kids in front of every window and door which, as you know, will prevent us from entering at those points or from getting a clean sniper shot. The terrorists have not made any demands and have so far refused to take any calls. We have three breaching teams on-scene. We have a twenty-five man HRT assault element ready to go. The armored vehicle is on its way here and should arrive within the next hour. An eight-man Secret Service Counter Assault Team just arrived and they're suiting up. What are your orders, Pat?"

Patterson slowly rose to his feet and stepped to the front of the cramped room. "We're not going to wait until they start killing kids. We'll breach the building's walls at three points and hope we don't have any kids standing next to the breach. I want the Secret Service CAT to follow us through the breach. They'll secure the President's daughter. We need to end this *now*! The longer we wait, the more time the T's will have to put their plan in place and manipulate our options."

At that moment an FBI agent burst through the door of the conference room.

"Pat, the terrorists just answered the phone. They claim to have most of the kids, including the President's daughter, in the common area. They are going to start executing a kid every hour until the President goes on national television and apologizes for waging war against Islam, and agrees to immediately cease all military operations in the Middle East, and withdraw all U.S. forces. They say they will begin the executions with his daughter! We have less than an hour."

Patterson turned to the monitor, which was still displaying a live picture of the middle school building that contained the hostages. "Les, get everyone together. I want a word with them before we do this."

Ten minutes later, Patterson entered a large, military-style tent where the FBI and Secret Service assault team was assembled. Patterson flashed a determined smile at them. Many returned the smile.

"Director Freemen just gave us assault authority. We're going in. But before we do, I want to share my thoughts with you. We all know the risk involved here. We all know some of us may not walk back out of this. Worse yet, we all know some of those kids in there may not make it either." Patterson swallowed hard. "Most of you know I was a POW and Navy SEALs rescued me from my captors. The SEALs were outnumbered three-to-one. As things turned out, there was probably another thirty or forty enemy behind those escorting me we never saw, but who wasted no time counterattacking the SEALs."

Patterson swallowed hard again, fighting back the strong emotions from the memories that were surging through his mind.

"It was a desperate move by those who rescued me. They didn't have to take it on, but they had courage. Their Officer in Charge bravely pulled me from the bottom of a canal as I lay there drowning and unconscious. He and his men showed me that SEALs never leave a man behind—dead or alive. They either all come out together or they all stay behind and die fighting, but they never leave a man behind. I know for many folks that sounds very bold, perhaps even Hollywood, but it isn't. It's courageous! In all these years since, I have always remembered that you must be courageous to win, not bold, and I have adopted this philosophy as my own. Bold men lose battles. Bold men die young. Bold men seek recognition. Boldness is non-directional. Courage has aim with a rightful and virtuous purpose. You may wonder if one needs to have a degree of boldness to achieve a courageous act. Perhaps…but I believe boldness is more often a defense, while courage is always an offense. So, if I have any words of wisdom to pass along to you who follow me, it is simply this: Be not bold. Be courageous. Allow your opponent to be bold and see that for what it is…weakness."

Hager slowly nodded in silent agreement.

With some effort, Patterson transformed his raw emotions into a resolute determination. He set his jaw, sucked in a deep breath and scanned the solemn faces in room. "Now, let's go get those kids back from those bold fuckers!"

Everyone applauded.

Washington, DC, the next day.

Patterson was summoned to Director Freeman's office in the FBI's Hoover building in downtown Washington, DC for a 10:00 AM meeting. He arrived a few minutes early and was surprised to find the building crawling with Secret Service agents. He was ushered inside Director Freeman's opulent office and seated on the overstuffed sofa in front of the Director's desk. Moments later Freeman entered the office with the President of the United States by his side.

"Pat, President Knight would like to shake your hand," Freeman announced.

Patterson bounded to his feet. "Mr. President, I am honored."

"Agent Patterson, the honor is mine," the President said smiling. "Jim was just telling me all about you. May I call you 'Pat'?"

"Yes Sir. Please do."

"Pat, I am truly grateful for the rescue of my daughter yesterday and I just wanted to tell you that personally. You are an American hero and I, for one, am deeply proud of you and your service to our country. Tell me what I can do for you and it's yours."

"Thank you Mr. President, but the true heroes are the FBI and Secret Service agents who took down those terrorists yesterday. And Sir, all I want is to retire on Friday."

The President laughed as he continued to shake Patterson's hand.

"Retire? You can't retire until I say you can retire."

"I'm afraid you're wrong, Sir," Patterson countered with a chuckle. "I can retire without your permission and I intend to do it on Friday."

"Well, you've certainly earned it, Pat. Can I ask you a question about the hostage rescue?"

"Of course. You're the President."

"Well, how did you know the terrorists were wiring the gymnasium with explosives? I mean, what was it that prompted you to authorize the takedown. I understand that all the other agencies involved wanted you to wait, but you didn't. That was a bold move."

Patterson thought for a second before responding. "No Sir, it was not us who made a bold move. It was the terrorists who were bold. I knew the terrorists had explosives with them because our evidence response team did some explosive detection swipes on the vehicle they left in the parking lot. Why carry explosives if you're not going to use them? When we breached the common area walls we risked killing some of the kids. Cutting their explosives' firing circuit from the breach was sheer luck. I sort of took a lesson from Mayor Giuliani during the 9/11 attack. You know, they evacuated about fifty thousand folks from certain death or injury before the towers fell, but they ran out of time. If the towers hadn't collapsed when they did, perhaps several thousand more may have been saved. I guess we were lucky yesterday. I figured we needed to seize the initiative and fight those terrorists on our terms rather than wait for a traditional negotiating technique like they used at Columbine and see it all sour, leaving us no alternatives. You know three of the kids and two of my agents were wounded yesterday?"

"Yes, I know. But your assault was brilliant and I'm told that none of the injuries is life threatening. Besides, you killed all six terrorists—end of story for them!"

"Sir, I wish it could have turned out better for the security guard and the Secret Service Agent protecting your daughter. We did the best we could under the circumstances."

"Pat, your performance was splendid. I want to thank you on behalf of a grateful nation. My wife and I will always be personally indebted to you for saving our daughter's life."

"Thank you, Sir. I am honored. By the way, I voted for you."

The President laughed and slapped Patterson on the shoulder.

"You're a good man, Pat. What are your plans after you retire?"

"I'm going to work for a friend's security firm, sell everything I own that doesn't float and buy a big-ass bass boat, hunt for buried treasure, jump feet first into a bottle of single malt, and find out what I've been missing all these years!"

Only the President and Patterson laughed. Director Freeman silently glared at Patterson for his irreverence in front of the President.

...

Patterson left the Hoover Building and drove back to his apartment in Alexandria, Virginia. After changing from his business suit to blue jeans and a T-shirt, he called Jake Boucher. "Jake, you still riding with me to my retirement party at the FBI Academy on Friday? Great! Hey, you'll never guess who I talked to an hour ago."

CHAPTER 7

I-95 North, Friday

Following Patterson's retirement party at the FBI Academy in Quantico, Virginia, he and Boucher drove north on I-95 toward Boucher's home in Laytonsville, Maryland. Patterson turned the radio volume down and looked over at his dozing friend.

"Jake," he said in a low voice, "we're going to get rich."

Boucher readjusted himself in the seat without opening his eyes. "Yeah?"

"We're going to get rich. You hear me?"

"Yeah, sure Pat, whatever," Boucher replied uninterested, still not opening his eyes.

"No shit, Jake! I mean it! We're going to get rich!"

Patterson glanced over at his friend momentarily before speaking. "I couldn't tell you this while I was still an FBI agent, so I've waited a long time for this day to arrive."

Boucher sat up and fixed his gaze on his best friend. "What the hell could possibly be so damn compromising that it would make you wait to tell me? For Christ's sake, we have shared everything from women, to cars, to advice, since the day we met! You're the brother I never had. What could possibly be so damn important that you had to protect me from myself?"

Patterson snickered. "Our retirement plan, dickhead!"

Boucher acted indigent. "Who the hell are you calling a dickhead, flyboy?"

Both men laughed.

Patterson, now very sober, began to speak slowly and methodically. "I said 'retirement plan,' Jake. That means we have one more recovery operation to do together before we can retire."

Boucher smiled. "What kind of operation are you talking about? You wanna rob a bank or something stupid like that?"

"No, it's a little bigger than that!"

"Well then, what the hell?"

"You remember telling me about a C-130 that passed overhead in flames and crashed during the firefight that night you rescued me from the NVA?"

"Yeah. What about it?"

Patterson concentrated on his driving for a few seconds before continuing.

"Well, after I joined the Bureau in 1970, I ran across a guy who told me what the deal was with that C-130."

Boucher laughed at his friend. "Some guy told you the deal on that plane, did he? And that's what you couldn't tell me for the past thirty years? Ya know what buddy? You are a dickhead with a capital 'D'!"

"Hold on Jake! I'm serious as a heart attack. The guy told me on his death bed."

"On his freaking death bed, huh?" Boucher chuckled. "You know what Pat? You're not just a dickhead, you're a dickhead moron!"

Patterson again glanced over, this time grinning from ear to ear. "Well here's the deal. That was an Air America plane on a secret mission. It was carrying South Vietnam's gold reserves out of Saigon because the CIA thought Saigon was going to fall to the NVA during the Tet Offensive. No one knew where the plane went down, because it was so far off course in the storm and flying too low to be tracked by radar. As far as any records show, the plane was never found and the gold was never recovered. You might be the only sorry ass alive who knows the rough location of that plane crash. So," Patterson snickered, "am I still a dickhead or do you want to help me go find that crash site?"

Boucher sat staring straight ahead as the car's windshield wipers pushed the blinding rain from side to side. His mind drifted back to that rainy night years earlier. He visualized the C-130, its right wing trailing orange flames as it passed overhead, banking to the right, then seconds later the bright flash from the crash that illuminated the bottom of the clouds. Boucher's thoughts returned to the present.

"Yeah. I remember it like it was last night. I could probably go back to that canal intersection and walk on the heading the plane took that night and find the crash site. But what makes you think the NVA never found the gold?"

Patterson smiled at his friend again. "Jake, the gold ingots were stacked in cubes and solid concrete was cast around them encasing the gold. That way if the plane went down, the concrete blocks would easily survive the crash and no one would be the wiser. The Japanese did the same kind of thing with the gold they collected all over Asia during World War II. I'll bet you the gold is still there. All we have to do is find the crash site, dig the concrete blocks up, break 'em open, and the gold is ours. Whadda ya think?"

"You definitely have my attention. So who exactly was this guy you talked to?"

"There's something else, Jake. Remember when I did that three-year detail at the CIA Counterterrorism Center?"

"Yeah. I remember you told me they were some of the most competent people you ever worked with."

"Well, I'm kinda embarrassed to tell you this but..." Patterson hesitated.

"But what? Let me guess. You turned queer and married a fellow aviator?"

"Damn it, Jake! Please be serious for once!"

"Sorry to sound so homophobic. Anyway, it's good to know you haven't turned queer. Okay seriously, what's the skinny?"

Patterson scowled at his friend. "I got my hands on some NSA overhead imagery of the area around the canal intersection, had the analysts crank in terrain evaluation data and do a geospatial intelligence analysis looking for potential crash sights and..." Patterson hesitated again.

Boucher sat up. "And what? Damn it, Pat! What?"

"Ahhh, after we added that data, I had the National Geospatial-Intelligence Agency build a CADRG digital map of the local area and there appears to be a crater located on the side of a densely-foliated hill about a mile north of the canal intersection. The analysts couldn't say for sure, because the imagery resolution was only one-to-twenty-thousand and it wasn't that sharp, but they said it was a likely location based on the anomaly of the shape compared to the rest of the terrain features in the surrounding area."

"Holy shit, Pat! You used classified NSA overhead, CIA and NGA analysts to take a look at it, and you didn't get caught? You must be the biggest dumbass I ever met! You're damned lucky you're not making big rocks into little ones in some federal penitentiary!"

"Yeah, I suppose you're right. But what the hell. You woulda done the same for me."

"Okay old buddy," Boucher chided, "who was your source?"

"He was a former Air America pilot who was supposed to fly the mission that night. He said Tan Son Nhut Airbase was being rocketed and he caught a piece of frag in his side on the way out to the plane. It turned out that it probably saved his life."

Boucher grunted. "Yeah, but who was he and why did he tell *you* about that mission?" Patterson looked over at his friend. "You remember my first wife's father?"

"Yeah."

"Well, he was the guy."

"He was a CIA Air America dick?"

"Yep," Patterson replied, "and when he was dying from bone cancer he told me the C-130 story the day before he checked out. Since I was already in the Bureau, I couldn't risk telling anyone...even you."

Boucher nodded. "Did he tell you anything else about the crash?"

"Yeah. He told me who his co-pilot was and gave me the name of one other guy who he said would be able to help. He said the guy knew the whole deal. I've kept tabs on his whereabouts over the years and I ran a background on him last week. Apparently, he's living in an Orlando retirement community."

Boucher grumbled under his breath as he rubbed his eyes. "So you wanna go find that gold, huh? You know, even today the U.S. isn't exactly in bed with Cambodia. We're gonna need some serious help."

Patterson slapped the car's steering wheel with both hands. "Yeah, I know. Ain't this great!"

Boucher snorted in acknowledgment. "Okay. I'll make some calls to my old platoon and see what kind of interest I can generate. I have a feeling that one last hooyah might appeal to them. Can you search the web and pull off any current overhead of the general location of the intersecting canal? I still have the map I used that night somewhere in my SEAL-shit cruise box out in the garage. I'll get you a ballpark lat-long."

Boucher sat quietly for several minutes, watching the car's wipers sweep the rain from the windshield. "I guess we ought to go visit the guy in Orlando too. He might have some information we could use. You have his name?"

Patterson put a dip of snuff inside his lower lip before continuing. "Yeah, I got his name. It's James Ray, CIA retired. He's gotta be in his late seventies by now. But what the hell. He might know something we need to know too."

"Okay. We need to watch what we say and to whom we say it. That includes your girlfriends."

Patterson nodded agreement.

"Pat, you have a feel for how much gold we're talking here?"

"My father-in law told me that they were four-by-four concrete blocks, stacked on four standard eight-by-eight pallets that the plane was carrying. He figured there were probably about two-hundred-fifty pounds of gold bars inside each cube. So, two-hundred-fifty pounds, times eight cubes per pallet, times four pallets is...eight-thousand pounds of gold. That's four tons of gold!"

"Holy shit!" Boucher gasped. "How the hell do we carry *that* out of country?"

Patterson rolled his eyes. "You're the Penn State engineer and fucking Navy SEAL super commando from the Mekong Delta...you tell me! I'm just an old, broke-dick, fighter pilot who you happened upon one rainy night."

Both men chuckled.

"Yeah, I got your broke dick dangling, flyboy! Hey Pat, you thirsty?"

"Does Howdy Doody have a wooden dick?"

"*Turn right now!*" Boucher shouted.

Patterson instantly pulled the steering wheel right, veering off I-270 onto the Clarksburg exit, cutting two cars off in the process. As they approached the light, Boucher told him to turn north onto Route 355.

"There's a great little restaurant a few miles up the road with a good bar. It's on the left, just before you cross the Monocacy River. I'll buy the first five rounds."

As they drove along the winding, wet road, Boucher suddenly burst out with a chuckle.

"Hey Pat, who would have ever thought thirty years ago, that we'd be sitting here planning a treasure hunt?"

"Yeah. It's kinda freaky. I guess we're both still just as stupid as we used to be."

Boucher didn't laugh. "Pat, you suppose you can bullshit your main squeeze into letting you disappear for a few months?"

Patterson nodded, "Hell yes! I've been bullshitting Barbara since the day I met her. I told her I'm just joining your little security consulting business after retirement so I don't get bored. How about your latest girlfriend?"

Boucher smiled at his friend. "Annette is a way-smart lady, but she has no clue what I really do for a living. Besides, we're just good friends—nothing more or less."

"I think Barbara could help us if we cut her in on our plans."

Boucher locked eyes momentarily with Patterson. "Pat, she's your call in the bedroom, but the chicks stay out of this. The potential danger is just too great. If the shit hits the fan, we'll need seasoned SEAL operators."

"Okay, no chicks."

Patterson understood the grief Boucher still bore for his deceased wife, Sophie. She died in a fiery car accident twenty-four years earlier and he had never gotten over it. His five-year-old son, Doug, survived the crash, but as he got older he blamed Boucher for never being around when he needed him. Boucher immersed himself in his job as a SEAL officer and volunteered for every Joint Task Unit he could deploy with. Doug grew up in Valley Forge Military Academy and he and his father grew further and further apart. In fact, Boucher hadn't talked with his son since he graduated from USC with a PhD in biology and joined the Peace Corps.

Boucher told Patterson to slow the car. "We're coming up on it—Monocacy Crossing—here on the left."

Patterson turned into the gravel parking lot and stopped, shutting off the engine. The two men sat in silence as the rain hammered the car's roof, making a metallic rattle.

"I've stayed in contact with a Thai SEAL officer by the name of Thanite," Boucher explained. "He was the CO of the Thai SEAL Team back in the early eighties. I worked closely with him over a period of about four years, doing everything from counter-drug ops along the Burmese border highlands to intelligence gathering against the Russian Navy in Camron Bay. I think we can trust him to help us."

Patterson raised his eyebrows. "So you're thinking we'll have to launch from Thailand?"

Boucher shrugged. "Perhaps...but I need to see what we're up against. Terrain, weather, hostilities...you know, the kind of stuff that can get us seriously killed."

"Yeah, I know," Patterson, responded. "Let's go inside before somebody sees us sitting out here and thinks we're a couple of fag boys on a date."

Boucher and Patterson left the car and hurried through the chilling rain in through the bar entrance, taking station on two stools at the bar's far end—well away from the other three men sitting at the bar.

The woman bartender, a gorgeous blond, approached them. "What can I get you gentlemen to drink?"

"How about a Blue Sapphire gin martini straight up? Make it very dry, shake the hell out of it, and put three olives in it," Patterson replied while staring at her breasts, which overflowed from her tank top.

"Sure. And you Sir?" she said, fixing her gaze on Boucher.

Boucher always kidded his friend about the way he liked his martinis. "I'll have a beer-tini, please," Boucher replied to the young woman as if a beer-tini was a common request.

Naturally, she had no clue. "A beer-tini?" she questioned.

Keeping a straight face, Boucher added, "Why yes, ma'am, that would be a draft with four olives and don't bother shaking it."

The young women rolled her eyes, clearly not seeing the humor in his request. "Certainly," she answered, as she turned away.

Boucher pulled his cell phone from his jacket pocket, pushed a string of numbers, and put it to his ear. "Reilly, this is Boucher.... Oh, I'm doing just fine, Billy. How about you?" Boucher listened intently. "Hey Billy, I'm sitting here with Pat Patterson having a beer. We're going to have one last hooyah. You interested?"

Boucher looked at Patterson and nodded, pointing to the phone. "Okay, would you please contact the old platoon and see who's up for an OCONUS job...say, a couple of months overseas... really big bucks if we can pull it off." Boucher listened for a moment to Billy's reply. "Good! You remember the canal intersection where we met Patterson? Well, we're going to visit our old stomping ground. I'll need everyone's help planning this event. Call me on my cell when you get the gouge...Yeah, I still love you too. See ya soon. Out here."

Boucher pressed the red "end" button on his cell phone and put it back into his pocket. "That ought to get the shit moving." He picked up his beer glass and held it out in front of Patterson. The four large, green olives on the toothpick at the bottom of the glass looked gross.

"Here's to the breezes that blows through the treezes and lifts the girls' dresses above their kneezes."

Patterson picked up his martini by the stem of the glass. "To the breezes."

The men clicked their glasses together and took a sip. Boucher looked over at the blond beauty tending the bar. She was bending over, scooping some ice into a glass at the other end of the bar. Her attributes were well accented by her tight-fitting, designer jeans. Boucher snorted and repeated the toast in a low whisper. "To the breezes."

"You know what, Jake?" Patterson contemplated his friend, who was staring at the young woman's butt with obvious target fixation. "This adventure could get real ugly if we're not careful."

"Yeah," Boucher whispered, "I know."

CHAPTER 8

Orlando, Florida, one week later

"Turn *here!*"

Boucher was driving while Patterson navigated.

"Damn it Pat! Would you just give me a little warning before you tell me to turn? You fast-mover flyboys never could read a frickin' map!"

"Ahhh-haaa, like you slow swimmin' bubbleheads ever could either. Turn left *now!*"

Boucher braked the car into a swerving turn with all four tires squealing for traction. "You asshole! That's exactly what I mean!"

Patterson chuckled as he pretended to study the map. "The home ought to be ahead on the right, two…no…make that three blocks."

Boucher snorted. "Oh, that's just freaking wonderful. You're finally giving me a rudder order and we're almost there!"

Boucher turned into the parking lot in front of the Crystal Bay Nursing Home and parked in the shade under a large cypress tree that hung over the parking space. In unison, the two exited the car and followed the brick walkway into the reception area.

"May I help you?" an elderly lady wearing a nurse's uniform asked.

Patterson idly noted that her hair was almost as white as her uniform. "Yes ma'am," Patterson replied. "I called yesterday about one of your occupants by the name of James Ray. Would it be possible for us to visit Mr. Ray?"

The nurse quickly evaluated the two men standing in front of her before answering Patterson's question. "Yes, I suppose Mr. Ray would like some company. As I'm sure you know, he suffers from Alzheimer's and has been in his own little world for sometime."

Patterson winced as Boucher stared down at the floor, emotionless.

"Follow me please," the nurse said as she led them down the hallway toward Ray's location.

She pushed open an extra wide door and entered a large room. There were rows of couches and chairs, all facing a television. Only three of the chairs were empty. Some of the occupants were clearly younger than the other seniors, but all had Alzheimer's in common.

Jerry Springer was interviewing several men and women on the TV screen. Most of the people stared at it wistfully. Others babbled and laughed loudly at each other without a clue about the world around them. Boucher felt uncomfortable in this confined space, surrounded by hopeless people.

The nurse led them to a frail old man sitting in a soft chair at the rear of the room. "Gentlemen, this is Mr. Ray. I will leave you with him. Please see me if you need anything. Also, be sure to see me before you leave the home."

Patterson and Boucher thanked the nurse and knelt beside the old man who was staring intently at the television.

"Mr. Ray," Patterson began gently, "would you please talk with us about flying?"

Slowly the old man turned toward Patterson. "Flying? I used to fly."

"Yes, we know. That's what we would like to talk with you about."

The old man turned back to the television.

"Mr. Ray," Boucher said, "you flew C-130s for Air America."

The elderly man turned back toward Boucher and Patterson and nodded as he tried to speak, but couldn't manage the words. Patterson placed his hand on top of the old man's hand.

"It's okay. Just listen. I want you to remember a mission you were supposed to fly during Tet in 1968. You were supposed to fly the gold reserves from Saigon to Utapao, Thailand, but you were wounded as you were trying to get to the plane. You knew a guy by the name of Chase Woods. Chase later became my father-in-law and told me about you and that mission."

The old gentleman's eyes welled up as the pain of those memories surfaced. "Chase?" he whispered, "Chase."

"Do you remember him?" Patterson whispered.

Tears streamed down the deep creases in his cheeks as he forced out the name. "Chase."

Patterson pressed for more. "Do you remember the operation to move the gold from Saigon?"

He nodded again but couldn't make the words come out. "Lost," he strained.

Patterson quickly glanced over at Boucher who was watching intently.

"Mr. Ray," Patterson said, "we think we know where that plane crashed. We think we might be able to find the crash site. Can you help us?"

He feebly tried to stand, but couldn't. Boucher put his arm around the old man's lower back and attempted to lift him up to his feet, but the old man couldn't quite make it.

"Mr. Ray," Boucher said, "let's put you in this wheelchair and we'll get you out of here."

Ray seemed to understand and helped Boucher and Patterson place him in a wheelchair. Boucher grabbed the handles and looked up at Patterson. "Take point," he whispered.

Patterson snapped around to the front of the wheelchair and held the door open. They went down a long hallway until they found a vacant room with the door halfway open.

"In here," Patterson said.

Boucher rolled the man inside. Patterson quickly surveyed up and down the hallway, then quietly pulled the door closed. Boucher wasted no time. He already had positioned the old man between two chairs next to a hospital bed.

Boucher began the interview. "Mr. Ray, you were a CIA operative. During Tet of 1968, you were part of an operation named 'Eldest Child'. You were transporting the gold reserves out of South Vietnam so the NVA wouldn't capture them in the event that Saigon fell. But the plane, an Air America C-130 cargo plane, went down in a storm somewhere in southern Cambodia and the gold was never recovered. The crew was never found and presumed dead. The crash site was never located."

The elderly man acted as though he understood Boucher, but couldn't speak.

"Can you tell us about that operation?"

He kept trying to speak, but couldn't get the words out.

Boucher leaned over beside the wheelchair. "You remember, don't you?"

He was now snorting and almost squealing like a farm animal as he attempted to speak. The memories were flooding into his infected mind, churning back and forth between eddies of calm and turbulence.

Boucher looked over at Patterson and winced. "The poor old son-of-a-bitch can't get the words out. I say we leave him alone."

"Okay, Jake. Let's let him be."

As they began to turn the wheelchair back towards the door, the old man seemed to suddenly cycle in on reality. "Wait," he pleaded, raising a trembling hand. "The mission wasn't to take the gold to Thailand."

Boucher and Patterson caught each other's dumbfounded gaze.

"We were going to take it to the Philippines."

"The Philippines?" Boucher and Patterson questioned simultaneously.

Ray nodded. "Yes, we were going to launder it there so we could equip and pay the Khymer Rouge in Cambodia to invade Laos."

Boucher sat down on the edge of the bed. "But the Khymer Rouge was not friendly to the U.S. In fact, they were hostile as hell! What was the goal? To stop the North from using the Ho Chi Min Trail to resupply their offensive in the South?"

"No," Ray gasped, "to defeat the Soviets. That's why we fought the Vietnam War. It's in five-thousand; you need to see five-thousand. Ask Jackson. He'll tell ya."

Boucher studied the deep sadness lodged in his eyes. "The damn Soviets? You mean that you were part of a conspiracy way back then to kick their Commie asses?"

The old man did not seem to understand Boucher's last comment. He looked back down at the floor, once again oblivious to his surroundings. "Five-thousand," he uttered in a weak whisper.

"Pat," Boucher mumbled, "we better get him back to the other room before nurse Cratchet misses him."

"Yeah. I'll take point."

Patterson slowly opened the door and then signaled Boucher to follow. They returned Ray to his couch in the television room and left him mindlessly staring at Jerry Springer.

Boucher looked at the TV and snarled. "That dumbass TV show is enough to make anybody go brain-dead!"

They thanked the white-haired nurse at the nurses' station on the way out. They walked slowly to their car without speaking. After what seemed like hours, Boucher finally spoke. "Pat, I don't believe that shit."

Patterson shook his head. "I do. We need to check it out sometime and find out who that Jackson guy is."

"Yeah, but not now. We have an operation to plan. Agreed?"

"Agreed," Patterson said smiling over at him.

Boucher started the car engine. "What do you suppose he meant by five-thousand?"

Patterson shrugged, "Beats the livin' shit outta me."

Boucher put the car in reverse and backed out of the parking space. "Airport," he declared. Patterson nodded in agreement.

What they didn't see was the beat-up, white Chevy van that followed them. The two men driving in the front maintained their distance, well behind Boucher's rental car.

"Pat...use my cell phone and dial up Bill Reilly. He's on the menu. Ask him who he's come up with."

Patterson put the phone to his ear. "Billy, this is Pat. How the heck are ya?" Patterson paused to listen to Reilly's response. "Hey, I'm on Boucher's cell phone calling you from Florida. I'm sitting here next to him in a rental car. Jake wants to know what you've come up with."

Patterson quickly pulled a small note pad and pen from his shirt pocket and began to write as he repeated the information. "Yellowhorse, Ramirez, Jackson."

Boucher interrupted, "Ask him about Bad Bob Barns."

Patterson waved at Boucher to be quiet. "Doyle and LeFever. How about

45

Bad Bob Barns?" Patterson was listening intently. "So Bad Bob can't leave the country until his divorce is final? How long is that gonna take?" He scribbled notes and repeated the details back to Reilly to ensure that he got it right. "Barns thinks about another month."

Patterson looked over at Boucher. "You want Bad Bob in on this?"

Boucher didn't hesitate a second. "Hell yes, I want him!"

"Yeah, Boucher wants him anyway," Patterson relayed and paused again to listen. "Okay, wait one." Patterson covered the phone's mouthpiece. "Jake, your boys want to know what's up. When you gonna tell them?"

Boucher considered the question before replying. "Tell them we'll arrange a meeting next week. I'll be in touch."

Patterson passed on the information to Reilly and ended the call quickly, shifting his attention to Boucher. "Jake, that's still only nine. Aren't we going to need more help?"

"You stupid flyboy! You wanna cut the whole freaking carrier battle group in on this, or keep it need-to-know? We'll bring in more help as needed. This is the core group; the trusted ones who get the full briefing and have a full vote."

Boucher turned the rental car onto the airport access road. Patterson, stone-faced, glanced over. "Hey Jake, you sure we really don't want to bring my lady friend along on this? She's smart, she's trustworthy, she's a P.A., and we could probably use another medical tech."

Boucher laughed. "Yeah, and she's used to taking orders from you, right? You wanna know what buddy? You're still a fricking hound dog!" Boucher sneered. "You're so damn pussy-whipped it's pitiful!"

"Okay, okay, don't go off the deep end. I was just messing with you. Where's your sense of humor?"

"You know what? Sometimes you're one big asshole, but I still love you."

"Yeah, but I truly believe that she could contribute and she's easy to look at too."

Boucher smiled nodding in agreement. "Yes she is…but no chicks! By the way, does she have a sister with big tits?"

Patterson sat back, acting insulted. "You're an asshole, Jake!"

Boucher shrugged his shoulders. "Yeah, but I work at it."

Patterson sat silently, staring straight ahead for about twenty seconds, then glanced at Boucher. "Huge tits."

CHAPTER 9

Virginia Beach, Virginia, the following morning

The sun was high and hot and it was only ten in the morning. September in Virginia Beach always brought sweltering heat, high humidity and huge air conditioning bills.

Boucher and Reilly sat at the kitchen table in Reilly's "Thoroughgood Manors" house. The house was located about four blocks from the historical site of Adam Thoroughgood's colonial home, now a museum. This quiet neighborhood sprawled between Independence Avenue, Shore Drive, the Lynnhaven Inlet, and the Naval Amphibious Base at Little Creek, which happened to be the main, east coast SEAL Team base. This ideal location provided its residents superb access to the beachfront, the SEAL base, and some great bars that both Reilly and Boucher had spent years of their lives staggering into and out of. If one could tally all the hours they spent slamming back oyster shooters together, it would have probably added up to years.

Boucher and Reilly had each just taken a swallow of beer when Boucher's cell phone chimed.

"Boucher... Yeah, thanks Pat. Hey, could you get the GPS lat-long gouge on the canal intersection? We need the overhead on that, the topo maps, and the navigation charts for the river. Also, get the latest dope on the order of battle for Cambodia, and all the other cats and dogs in the Mekong...from Cambodia down through the Delta."

Boucher looked up at Reilly.

"Billy, you have anything for Pat?"

Reilly momentarily contemplated the question before taking the cell phone in hand.

"Pat, we need the Mekong's current navigational data and tide tables. You also might want to get the latest info on U.S. posture with regard to Thailand, Vietnam, Malaysia, Singapore, Indonesia, the Philippines, and the South China Sea Theater as a whole."

Reilly listened to Patterson's reply as he read back the tasker.

"Yeah, the Spratlys too. Good idea." He shifted the phone to his other ear. "Okay, I'll tell 'im. Out here."

Reilly returned the cell phone and scribbled some additions to his notes as he briefed Boucher.

"Pat thinks that we need to look at the Spratlys as a potential escape and evasion lay-up point. I know that China, Vietnam, and Philippines have all disputed the ownership of those islands since the end of the Vietnam War. In fact, I remember something about the Chinese building fortifications on one of the larger islands in the chain. I guess the Spratlys are certainly a potential E and E point if things sour on us."

"Yeah. He's probably right," Boucher replied. "Those islands are nothing more than small coral atolls that barely make it above the surface of the sea at high tide. They're important to all those countries because they're floating on top of huge oil reserves. Well, anyway, they're only a few hundred miles from Luzon and Palawan if we need a stepping-stone. They might come in handy if things turn to shit."

Boucher took a long swallow of beer, emptying the can. He crumbled it in one hand and tossed it into the open trashcan a few feet away.

"So what's the status on Yellowhorse, Ramirez and Jackson?"

Reilly followed Boucher's lead, tossing his empty beer can into the trash.

"Yellowhorse has been living in a cave outside Santa Fe ever since he got out. Doesn't have a phone, never got married, says he's never been in any trouble with the law, so he's good to go. He's a gardener for some yuppie-scum-fuck that has more money than brains. Since Yellowhorse doesn't have a phone of his own, I can only leave messages for him at the estate where he works. He returns my calls a few days later. I guess all the killing got to him and he just wanted to drop out."

Concern flooded over Boucher's face.

"Is he still onboard? Can we rely on him?"

"I don't see why not. He's no more fucked up than any of the rest of us. And, for sure, nobody's going to miss him."

"Okay, he's in…but I want you to keep a close eye on him. How about Ramirez?"

Reilly thumbed to the next page of his small notebook and quickly reviewed his notes before speaking.

"As you probably remember, Gabe Ramirez retired as a Senior Chief from SEAL Team Six back in the mid-eighties. He moved back to Puerto Rico with his old lady and teenage son, Josy. Josy enlisted in the Navy after graduation from high school and made it through BUDS, class 255. He's really a good kid—respectable and polite. I watched him grow up. Ramirez's old lady shit-canned him shortly after he retired. Now, he lives on Vieques. He bought a small dive shop there about two years ago where he's been spending his time drinking, diving and drinking. He's definitely available."

Boucher snorted, "Which team is Josy serving on?"

"Team One," Reilly answered.

"Isn't Jim Thomas the CO of One?"

"Yes. I'm not sure who the XO is. All I know is that he's an F.N.G." Reilly smiled.

Boucher thought for a second.

"Okay. Get Ramirez onboard. Be sure to tell him not to tell his kid what we're up to. Make sure he understands that."

Reilly nodded and made a note before continuing.

"Risser Jackson got out in '75. He went to work with Dan Summers, a former Team One guy, as a government consultant in D.C. He left that job in '98 and went to work for Norwegian Cruise Line as a security officer and has been there ever since. He says he's available on short notice with no strings attached."

Boucher smiled. "What a guy! One of the best SEAL operators I ever knew and the biggest fucking liberty risk in the entire Naval Special Warfare Command! And he's now maintaining order and discipline on cruise ships? Is that funny or what?"

Reilly shared Boucher's smile.

"I'd say, more like ironic, but we need him."

Both men chuckled.

"Yeah, I know," said Boucher. "Tell him to muster. Tell me about Jack Doyle and Thane LeFever."

"Jack lives here in Virginia Beach. He's a full-time pilot instructor at Norfolk airport. Got out in '72 and went to college. Majored in aeronautical engineering and became a certified flight instructor. Got his CFI and has ratings in multi-engine, jet, and rotary wing. He flew black operations for the Agency and retired a few years ago. Says he's been through three wives and is paying more in alimony than he earns teaching people how to fly. He wants to escape and has no strings. Says he's ready, willing, and able. He'd be a valuable asset to us on this operation."

Boucher nodded, "Check!"

"LeFever retired in '89 with thirty-one years in the Teams, currently lives in Seminole, Florida and drives an eighteen-wheeler for a living. He has nothing to keep him there. No kids, no relatives, no commitments. Claims he's ready for a change of hemisphere. Who am I missing?"

"Bad Bob Barns," Boucher answered.

"Oh yeah," Reilly said as he flipped backwards a few pages in his notepad. "Bad Bob's old lady is divorcing him. His legal address is in Mount Vernon, Virginia, but he's been living on a sailboat at the Fort Belvoir marina for the past seven months. He works as a consultant with EXTEC—some explosives technology company located along I-66, close to Dulles International Airport in Northern Virginia. Says he has to wait until his divorce is final before making the break with us because of all the lawyer and settlement bullshit."

"How long?"

"Bad Bob figures maybe a month to six weeks at the most."

"Okay. Let's read him in so he can hit the deck running."

"Roger. I'll call him back and tell him the good news."

"Okay Billy, I'd like to get everyone together as soon as we can for the warning order. I want to ensure that we're all still able to do our respective jobs. Just like the old days, we're still only as fast as our slowest man, so it's important that we don't overlook any liabilities. For those who need financial help with the airfare, I'll leave three credit card numbers with you. Let's shoot for next week…say, Thursday afternoon, here."

"Got it, Boss."

Boucher stood up from the table. "I want to tap my kidneys before I drive north. Where's your head?"

Reilly pointed down the hall. "Port side. Don't forget to wash your hands."

Minutes later the two men exchanged goodbyes. Boucher started his car and slowly backed out of Reilly's driveway. As he proceeded down the street, he dialed Patterson on his cell phone.

He didn't notice the black Monte Carlo following cautiously from a block behind.

"Hey Pat, I just left Billy's house and I'm heading back on I-64 towards Richmond. The meeting went well. Billy thinks we can pull the bubbas together by next Thursday. How's it coming on your end?"

Boucher pressed the cell phone tightly against his left ear—his "good" ear. Almost all hearing in his right ear was lost as a result of numerous combat firefights. He had a hearing aid but never wore it.

Boucher stopped Patterson in mid-sentence. "Say all again, Pat. I can't understand you." He quickly increased the phone's volume with a click of the button under his forefinger. "Okay, I hear ya lima charlie. I copy. You got the overhead and the charts. What else?" Boucher put a small notepad on the seat beside him and began to write. "You got a lead on Jackson? He what? Son of a bitch! You're shittin' me, aren't you?"

Boucher pulled the phone away from his ear momentarily as if to question what he was hearing. "He's in jail on Bimini Island for disorderly conduct?"

Boucher was half laughing and half pissed off as he repeated Patterson's report. "Let me get this straight. He got caught balling two women off the cruise ship under an overturned fishing boat on the beach? He was drunk and beat the shit out of the three cops who tried to arrest him? He says they were disturbing his 'piece' when they tried to drag him off in the middle of the short stroke. Oh that's great! Just fucking great! After all these years the dumb ass still has his brains in his dick!"

Boucher patiently listened to the rest of Patterson's status report, but interrupted. "So if we pay his fine and court costs and promise that he'll never be seen screwing tourists on Bimini Island again, they won't press charges and they'll let him go?"

Boucher turned left onto the on ramp for I-64 west.

"Alright, if he wasn't so damn good in the field I'd let the dumb ass sweat it out until his time was up, but we need him. See what you can do to get him out, ASAP. Call me later. Out here."

Boucher sped up to sixty-seven miles per hour and set the cruise control. The black Monte Carlo followed, remaining well behind, barely in sight. He drove for about an hour, passing by the Camp Perry-Williamsburg exit without even noticing. He was thinking about a variety of issues that he knew must be resolved before conducting this mission. They would probably have to fly into Thailand or Singapore and launch the mission from one of those locations, using it as an intermediate staging base. He would need to identify a forward staging base (FSB) as well. The FSB would have to be in range of the crash site and it would need to be secure enough to provide sanctuary, both on the way in and on the way out. Boucher didn't see the small black and white sign along the interstate highway that read, "Entering New Kent Township." He didn't notice passing the Virginia State Police car hidden in the trees between the lanes of the divided highway, waiting for speeders. The policeman slowly pulled out onto the highway and sped up to catch Boucher. Boucher was so deep in thought he didn't realize the police car had approached him from behind. He was cruising in the right lane behind several other cars, keeping up with traffic. The State Police car pulled in behind him and followed for a minute or so, then turned on its red and blue flashing lights. Boucher looked up in his rear view mirror and, for the first time, saw the police car that was now tailgating him.

Asshole, Boucher thought to himself as he put on his right turn signal and slowed to pull off onto the highway's asphalt apron. As he came to a stop the police car pulled up directly behind him, positioning his car slightly toward the highway. Boucher rolled the window down so the officer wouldn't get nervous, then leaned over to the glove box to find the car's registration. As he sat back up with the registration in his hand he turned towards the open window and looked straight into the barrel of a .357 Glock pistol.

"Get out of the car and keep your hands where I can see them!"

Boucher's surprise was obvious. "Officer," he said calmly, "don't point your gun at me."

The cop appeared irritated. "I said get out of the car, asshole!"

Boucher flinched as his blood pressure skyrocketed. "Why did you stop me and why are you pointing your gun at me?"

The cop nervously adjusted his grip on the pistol. "I said get out of the car! Do it now!"

Boucher looked up at the boyish face of the policeman and then into his eyes. He quickly evaluated this scared young man for a moment before speaking.

"Alright, my hands are in full view. I am going to slowly open the door with my left hand. I will exit with my hands on the top of the door. Do you understand me officer?"

The young cop stepped back without relaxing his posture or lowering his pistol. "Get out of the car!" he again demanded.

Boucher slowly exited the car, using the exact procedure he said he would. "Why have you stopped me and what is this all about?"

"Put your hands on top of your head and get down on your knees!" the cop ordered.

Boucher complied. The officer quickly handcuffed him and then searched for weapons. The cop removed Boucher's wallet from his hip pocket and led him back to the police car. Boucher glanced down the road as he was led to the police car and noticed that a black vehicle had pulled off the road about a quarter of a mile behind.

"Get in!" the cop ordered as he shoved Boucher into the back seat. Boucher complied without protest.

The policeman got into the front seat and began to go through Boucher's wallet. Boucher was getting angry.

"I want to know why you have stopped me and why you are treating me like a criminal!"

"You're wanted on a warrant for armed robbery!"

"No way! I haven't even had a parking ticket since 1979 and I paid my twenty dollar fine the same day."

"I pulled you over for speeding and ran the tags." The cop still seemed irate.

Boucher was now pissed. "No way! I had my cruise control set at sixty-seven and I was going exactly the same speed as the cars in front of me."

The cop showed a faint smile as he glanced into the rear view mirror at Boucher. "You can tell that to the judge."

"Get your supervisor out here now! This is bullshit!"

The cop was reading the name on Boucher's driver's license. "Don't you worry, Mr. Boucher. After we search your car, we're going to take good care of you."

Boucher leaned forward and put his face near the metal cage separating the front and back seat.

"You hear this, officer? This is bullshit and we both know it! You can't search my car without cause and there *isn't* any! I don't have any outstanding warrants and I wasn't speeding. So why don't you get your supervisor out here, now!"

"Shut up!" the cop shouted back at Boucher as he picked up the radio mic. "Headquarters, six three four, my suspect is 10-15 at this time, slow down any assistance. I am 10-4 and open channel. I need a 10-29 on the following subject."

The cop read from Boucher's driver's license.

"Boucher, Jake, white male, two-hundred-five pounds, blue, brown, Maryland ..."

The officer proceeded to transmit the rest of the information as Boucher sat quietly and calmly, watching the drama unfold.

A lady's voice crackled over the radio. "Six three four, headquarters, your twenty-eight comes back to W...M, negative on the white male. Suspect is black male, not Caucasian."

The cop replied, "Six three four."

The cop turned and glanced back at Boucher in surprise. "This guy is white, over."

Boucher sat there shaking his head in disgust. "You don't even know the difference between black and white? Some cop you are."

The lady's voice replied, "Repeat, suspect is black male, not Caucasian."

"Ahh, copy," the cop responded, "Six three four, out."

"Okay officer," Boucher growled, "it appears you got a case of mistaken identity. Now how about letting me out of this fucking car so I can go about my *legal* business!"

The young cop sat quietly for a few seconds and then turned around to Boucher. "You were speeding. That's why I stopped you."

Boucher almost came out of the seat. "Horse shit and you know it! Now get me out of this back seat and get your supervisor out here because I want a piece of your unprofessional ass!"

The cop slowly got out of the car and opened the rear door.

Boucher got out and turned so the cop could remove the handcuffs. "Get these fucking cuffs off me!"

The cop removed the cuffs and stepped back.

Boucher was clearly angry. "Now it's my turn officer. What's your name and badge number?"

The cop pointed to his name tag pinned over his pocket. "Corporal Charles Trusty Lavender the second."

Boucher's jaw dropped in surprise. "No way!" he whispered. "You wouldn't happen to be related to a retired Navy SEAL who goes by the nickname of 'Mojo,' would you?"

The officer nodded. "Yeah. He's my dad."

Boucher laughed aloud. "Well son-of-a-bitch! I served with Mojo in Vietnam. How the hell did he end up with such an asshole for a kid? That's what I want to know! So tell me," Boucher asked chuckling, "Do you go by Chuck, or Trusty, or Asshole?"

The young cop stared down at the asphalt shamefully. "I go by Chuck Lavender. I'm sorry about this. I honestly thought you were somebody else."

By now Boucher's anger had disappeared. "Okay kid," Boucher replied. "Where's your dad hanging his hat these days? I lost track of him. After he retired in '93, he seemed to fall off the face of the earth."

The young officer looked up at Boucher with a painful grimace.

"He's living by himself in a hunting cabin outside of Renovo, Pennsylvania. Doesn't even have a phone or electricity. Mom died in '95 and he took it really hard. He said all he wanted to do was fish and hunt and not have anybody mess with him."

Boucher clapped the young man on the arm. "Well kid, you sure got Mojo's blue eyes and your mom's red hair. Janice was a beauty. You have your old man's address?"

"Sure," Lavender replied, "but it's just a post office box in Renovo, Pennsylvania."

Boucher waited as the young policeman scribbled directions to his father's hunting cabin onto the page of a small pocket notebook. Boucher glanced back down the highway and noticed the black car was still parked along the apron as Lavender tore the page from the notebook and handed it to him.

"Chuck," Boucher smiled, "no harm done here. I gotta get back on the road. Keep your head down."

The two men shook hands.

"Thanks, Mr. Boucher," Lavender said humbly. "You know, I'm very proud of my father."

"You ought to be. He's one brave son-of-a-bitch! He saved my bacon and took a bullet that should have been mine."

Lavender smiled knowingly at Boucher. "That must be the time he got shot in the shoulder?"

"Nah, that happened almost a year later. It was the time he got shot in the ass."

Boucher grinned as he got back into his car and closed the door.

Lavender looked puzzled. "He never told me about that one."

Snickering, Boucher looked back out the window at Lavender. "Ask him about it the next time you see him. I bet he'll lie, even though the truth is a better story."

Lavender smiled in acknowledgment as he tapped Boucher's car roof with his open hand. Boucher pulled away, tires squealing.

As the young officer returned to his car, the black Monte Carlo sped past.

CHAPTER 10

Laytonsville, Maryland, later the same day

The old, shingle-sided house was built in 1935 and the sagging barn behind the house, now in dire need of a fresh coat of red paint and a new tin roof, was built about a year later. During the summer Boucher used the barn as a garage for his pickup truck, but in the winter he usually stored his John Deere tractor and bass boat to keep them out of the weather. The second floor of the barn was inhabited by barn owls, field mice, and spiders.

Boucher looked out onto Maryland's rolling farmland from his kitchen window and noticed movement near a tree line that bordered one end of the soybean field behind his house. He strained his eyes to identify three deer that were feeding along the field's tree line as he filled a glass of water. Without taking his eyes off the deer, Boucher took several swallows of water. Glancing away, he wandered into the small, adjoining living room where there stood a beat-up, deeply-gouged, executive-style walnut desk. Pushing several history books aside, he picked up the phone and dialed Reilly's number as he sat down on the well worn, brown leather desk chair.

"Billy? Boucher here. Hey, you remember Mojo Lavender? Well, I bumped into his kid today on the drive back up here. The kid says Mojo is living in Renovo, Pennsylvania. I thought I might just see if I can locate him tomorrow. Mojo was one of the best surreptitious entry guys the Teams ever had. He could pick the lock off a sleeping lion's balls and crawl up its ass without waking him. I think he might be available."

Boucher sipped his water as he paused to listen.

"Yeah. I'll drive up there in the morning. Renovo is right up I-81 about five hours from here." Boucher paused as Reilly replied. "Okay. Please ensure that everyone has a current passport. Yep, press on. Out here."

Boucher replaced the phone on the desktop and sat back in his chair. With pen and lined notebook paper in hand, he began to develop an outline. He divided the page into six sections: 1. Situation, 2. Mission, 3. Execution / Coordinating Instructions, 4. Administration and Logistics, 5. Command and Signal, and 6. Tasks. This was standard format for an operations order—one that he knew the men would be familiar with and would readily understand.

Boucher worked several hours drafting the operations order before realizing that the sun was now low in the sky and he was hungry. He closed the notebook with the pen inside and strolled to the kitchen. After a quick search through the pantry, he grabbed a box of macaroni and cheese and placed it on the kitchen counter next to the sink. He then hand washed a small pot in the sink. He casually glanced out the window to the tree line where he had seen the deer earlier and scanned the area for the familiar brown shapes feeding along its edge. There were none to be seen. He absent-mindedly filled the pot half full of water and put it on the stove. In the process he glanced out the window again, only this time his eye caught movement. Years of SEAL Team surveillance operations taught Boucher to unconsciously key on anything abnormal.

He focused on the tree line, trying to identify colors and shapes. The object of his scrutiny slowly moved a few feet inside the area. Without thinking, Boucher leaned toward the window, staring at the trees. He now saw the movement from two separate objects concealed behind the thick foliage.

Animals don't wear camouflage, he thought to himself. Boucher knew it wasn't archery season—a time when the deer hunters would use camouflage—and he knew the property behind his house was privately owned. Whoever it was had no permission. He grabbed the binoculars that he kept handy on top of the refrigerator so he could watch the deer, and peered through them at the area where he saw the movement. He continued to study the activity for several minutes until it disappeared into the dense foliage beyond his field of vision. *Very strange, but it doesn't look human...can't make out human form. It's just barely in view. No, it comes in and out of view. Probably kids building a tree fort or something.*

Boucher turned away from the window and sat down at his small kitchen table, clicked the TV remote onto the evening news and began writing additional details into the operations order. The water soon boiled and he poured a cup of macaroni noodles into the pot. The evening news was doing a special report on the National Security Agency and the reporter was explaining how the NSA eavesdrops on the radio and telephone conversations of average American citizens for intelligence purposes. The reporter closed her broadcast by suggesting that Big Brother was watching. Boucher was tired of the news and tired from writing. It was time to turn in.

...

Boucher got up at 4:00 AM and left the house by 5:30 AM. He headed north on Route 15 to Harrisburg, Pennsylvania where he got onto I-81. Four hours later, he turned off I-81 toward Lockhaven. The drive from Lockhaven alongside the Susquehanna River to Renovo was scenic. Lavender's hunting camp, located at the foot of a rough, single-lane, dirt road where the headwaters of Bakers Run bubbled from a hillside spring, was very remote and hard to find. At the top of the mountain, Boucher turned his vehicle onto the road leading to Lavender's camp and disappeared in a cloud of brown dust as he sped along, bouncing in and out of the numerous potholes. Four miles later, he turned right onto a narrow lane that was poorly maintained. Between the areas that had been washed out and the protruding rocks that cropped up everywhere else, it was difficult for Boucher to negotiate his way down the steep grade.

The deep ruts and steepness of the mountain road made it treacherous to navigate. Wild huckleberry and blueberry bushes lined the overgrown roadside, fighting the other vegetation for the nurturing sunlight which was at a premium under the canopy of this northeastern hardwood forest. Boucher chuckled to himself as he made mental comparisons between this North American forest and the jungles of Southeast Asia that he knew so well.

About a hundred yards ahead the lane gradually began to level. Boucher could make out the black asphalt, shingle roof of a small hunting camp, nestled between some hemlock trees that towered eighty feet above it. A metal gate, fabricated from steel pipe and angle iron, blocked the road about fifty yards before the camp's small, grassy parking area. A faded, blue Chevy 4X4 pick-up truck was parked between some trees, apparently without regard for the need to turn around easily. To the right of the parking area was a white, well-weathered outhouse. Boucher pulled up to the gate and saw that it was secured with a heavy chain and a massive padlock. He got out and walked around the gate heading for the cabin. As he walked into the open, grassy parking area adjacent to the camp, he called out.

"Mojo Lavender, you here? It's Jake Boucher."

Boucher's voice echoed back and forth, only to be lost in the tall forest surrounding the camp. He walked around the cabin peering into the windows, but there was no sign of life. Nature was now calling as Boucher suddenly felt as though he was ready to explode from the thermos jug of coffee and two sandwiches he had downed on the drive north. His full attention shifted to the outhouse and he cut a beeline straight to it. Pausing at the door, he glanced around, sweeping the general area for signs of movement. He observed none and opened the door to find himself staring into the business end of a Colt .45, Government-model, automatic pistol.

Instinctively he jumped backward, almost pissing in his pants. The man on the other end was sitting on the outhouse toilet with his pants down around his ankles. He had a long white beard and mustache that flowed well down over his flannel-clad chest. His long, white hair was tied back in a ponytail. The man's squinting, steel blue eyes seemed to penetrate through Boucher, sending a menacing message. Boucher read that message loud and clear—
Fuck with me and you die!

Boucher quickly raised his hands in the open position and stood facing the man who had now leveled the pistol at Boucher's center of mass.

"What da ya want?" the man growled.

"I'm looking for Mojo Lavender," Boucher calmly replied.

"Whatdaya want with him?"

Boucher smiled. "He's an old SEAL Team buddy who I haven't seen for a long time. I ran into his state cop kid a few days ago and he said Mojo lived up here. Mojo?"

The man still hadn't moved his pistol away from the center of Boucher's chest. "Maybe I am, maybe I ain't. Who the fuck are you?"

"I'm Jake Boucher."

The man lowered the pistol slightly as he reached into his shirt pocket to withdraw a pair of glasses. Without taking his eyes off Boucher he put the glasses on, then began to laugh. "Sorry, Commander. I'm suffer'n from a bad case of anal glaucoma. I can't see shit anymore without my fucking glasses and I don't need to be wear'n 'em to take a dump. How about closing the shithouse door fer me and I'll be through in a minute."

Boucher began to laugh as he closed the door. "Hey, Mojo, when did you become so damn shy about having a teammate see you with your pants down?"

"I ain't shy, Commander," came a muffled voice from inside. "I just don't want you get'n jealous when I stand up and you see how much bigger my enlisted dick is than your officer dick."

"Yeah, yeah, yeah...you've been telling the whole SEAL community that for over forty years and now I think you actually believe your own bullshit."

He could hear Mojo chuckle inside.

Boucher banged on the wooden outhouse door. "Hey, Mojo, don't be taking your good old time in there. I just drove for five hours to find your dumb ass, and I'm percolating some serious butt coffee of my own...so hurry up."

Mojo knocked back on the door from the inside. "Okay Commander, this turd was only a one wiper anyway. Been eating a lot of red meat and fish lately."

Lavender slammed the door open and exited the outhouse.

"Hey Commander, don't forget to wash your hands."

Boucher extended his hand and the two old warriors shook hands, and then hugged.

"I'm glad I found you, Mojo. Your kid told me about Janice. I'm sorry; she was truly a lovely lady. We have a lot to talk about."

Lavender nodded. "You over Sophie yet?"

Boucher winced at the sound of his deceased wife's name and looked down without answering. Lavender knew the answer to his question had still not changed.

"I'll be wait'n at the cabin fer you with a cold one."

Boucher entered the dark two-room cabin. "Mojo?"

He could easily understand the simplistic, hermit-like life that Lavender had chosen. The substitutes for electric lights were coal oil and gasoline lanterns that seemed to hang everywhere. A wood-burning, potbelly stove that also served as a cooking stove heated the cabin. All the fresh meat and fish a person could eat was available in the forest and streams in the surrounding area. The cabin overlooked a small springhouse that provided both potable water and limited refrigeration as it flowed out from deep inside the mountain at a chilly fifty-two degrees. The springhouse was also the headwaters of Bakers Run, one of the best native brook trout streams in north central Pennsylvania.

Boucher exited the back door to the porch where he found Lavender sitting on a weathered, wooden rocking chair.

"Sit," Lavender said, pointing to a second rocker next to his.

Lavender popped the caps on two beers and handed one to Boucher. "Latrobe."

"Latrobe what?" Boucher asked as he grabbed the beer.

"Latrobe, Pennsylvania. It's God's country, Commander. It's where this here beer comes from. So what brings you here today?" he asked, raising his beer in a toast.

Boucher took a long swallow before replying. "Man, this is some good stuff, Mojo."

"Hell yeah, Commander. You think us Pennsylvania boys drink panther piss?"

Boucher gave him a sobering glance. "I'm putting together an operation and I could use your expertise."

Lavender nodded affirmatively. "Okay, what's the gouge?"

"I'm putting together an operation to go back to Cambodia."

Lavender sat up in surprise nearly spitting out his mouthful of beer.

"Cambodia? What kinda wacky shit have you been smoking, Commander?"

Boucher laughed. "You remember the flyboy we rescued during Tet? Well, he's provided some reliable intel that a billion or so in gold bullion is lying under a crash site close by that canal ambush location where we rescued him."

"No shit! What's the deal?"

"We're putting our old platoon together and we're going back there, Mojo. We're going back to recover that gold. It's equal shares for all of us.

It'll be dangerous and it won't be easy, but I believe we can pull it off. One last hooyah. You interested?"

Lavender sat quietly for a moment, staring out into the forest. "I don't need the money...but one more hooyah...?"

He seemed to be silently torn between giving up a simple life and being with his old team mates again. Maybe he was saying goodbye. Boucher couldn't tell.

Lavender slowly looked up at the treetops, then over at Boucher. "When we leave'n, Sir?"

Boucher took another swig of beer before answering. "You can come back to Maryland with me today if you like. Otherwise, I'll come back here in two weeks if you need some time to get your shit together. So far, most of our old platoon is in. We need to execute this operation before the rainy season sets in full force, so we only have a little more than two months to get ready, get there, get the gold, and get out."

Lavender upended his beer bottle and drained it. Without taking his eyes off the forest, he provided the exact answer Boucher had hoped for. "Ahh, what the fuck Commander. It's too damn quiet around here and I could use a change of scenery. Give me five minutes to pack. I'm goin' back with ya today. You can brief me on the plan during the drive."

Boucher stood and slapped Lavender on the shoulder. "I'll help you pack."

"Nah. I ain't got much to bring. Sit here and have another beer and enjoy the quiet."

Lavender went inside and Boucher popped open another beer. As he sat there he smiled, remembering how Mojo got his nickname. During Lavender's early days in SEAL Team Two, he was quite a ladies' man and chased anything that wore a skirt. One particular Saturday morning, SEAL Team Two was having an all-hands personnel inspection by the commanding officer. Every single man in the team was wearing his dress uniform and they were assembled in ranked formation on the asphalt parking area across the street from the team's main headquarters building, awaiting the CO. Muster had been taken and reported to the executive officer. Mojo was missing and reported as an unauthorized absence. Minutes before the CO's appearance, Mojo arrived in the company of three gorgeous, young girls with whom he had apparently spent the previous night. He ran from their car to take his place in the formation. As he did, the girls yelled, "Hey, you got any *mojo* left, come back and see us again tonight." Of course, every man standing there was a witness and heard what they said. The name stuck.

Boucher and Lavender arrived back in Laytonsville after midnight. Boucher showed his old teammate to the spare bedroom and helped him carry in four kitbags and a backpack containing his operational gear and personal items. After making a bathroom call, both men ended up in the kitchen for a nightcap. Boucher brought out a bottle of sixteen-year-old, single-malt scotch and poured a three-finger shot for each of them. The two men toasted the future over some shared war stories and hit the sack by 1:00 AM. Boucher stretched back in his bed and couldn't get the canal ambush site off his mind. He relived every detail, as sleep slowly overtook his consciousness.

Boucher awakened to the sound of his cell phone playing the chorus from the song "Bootylicious." He absolutely hated that ring tone, but still hadn't figured out how to change it.

"Damn, pussy-sounding phone!" he whispered to himself.

It was still dark outside and he fumbled for the alarm clock to see what time it was. He finally saw the red LED read-out on the digital alarm clock and it was 4:30 AM.

"What the fuck," he grumbled as he reached for the phone. "Hello... What?"

He immediately recognized the voice of his closest neighbor.

"Yeah, I hear your dog barking but…you saw two at my barn? Okay, thanks. I'll check it out."

The next door neighbor had called to tell him that they were awakened by their dog and had observed two men enter Boucher's backyard barn. Boucher was instantly out of bed and on his feet. He quickly pulled on a pair of shorts and a black sweatshirt. He reached under the upper right corner of his mattress and withdrew his custom Novak .45 pistol. He conducted a quick press check of the slide to ensure that he had a round chambered before putting the pistol inside the front waistband of his pants. Now a man on a mission, he headed downstairs. To both preserve his night vision and to keep from alerting the potential burglars, he didn't turn on any lights.

He slowly slipped out the side door and crouched next to a low hedge, straining his eyes to detect movement at his barn which was about fifty feet behind the house. Like a cat on the hunt, he cautiously moved toward the barn using the shrubs in the yard for cover, being careful to stay within the shadows. He was stalking them.

His eyes had not yet adjusted to the darkness. He cautiously approached the side of the barn and slowly worked his way to the partially-open barn door, where he stood slightly crouched, concentrating on detecting any noise from within. After a moment, he slipped inside the barn and knelt down on one knee. It was even darker inside. The only starlight penetrating the barn came through the slightly open door behind him, and through two very dirty, cobweb-laced windows that opposed each other on the walls to his left and right. He could make out both his Ford pick-up truck, parked directly in front of him, and the door on the far wall in front of his truck that led into the stable area.

Boucher slowly stood and crept beside his truck, heading to the door leading into the stable. He carefully placed his left hand on the door handle and slowly unlatched it. He then eased the creaking door open and stepped inside. That was the last thing he remembered. A smashing blow hit him on the head from behind, driving him onto the barn's dirt floor.

...

Struggling to regain consciousness while peering into a bright light, Boucher realized that someone was holding him. Boucher took a wild swing at the man, only to hear Lavender's voice next to him.

"Dang it, Commander! You need to stop trying to punch me!"

Boucher was confused, but suddenly realized that he was back inside his house. "What the hell? You...Mojo?"

Lavender winced. "Damn it, Jake! I'm trying to put some ice on your head. Now hold still!"

Boucher was now painfully aware of his splitting headache.

"I heard you go outside," Mojo explained. "Figured you were havin' a flashback or someth'n. When you didn't come back after twenty or so minutes, I went looking fer ya. Found ya in the barn, tits up. I get the feeling you got some neighbors who really don't like ya."

Boucher sat up. "Somebody sure as hell doesn't. That's for damn sure! Thanks for the help, Mojo."

"My pleasure, Commander. Kinda like old times. Me bailing your dumb ass out of tight spots."

Boucher forced a painful smile as his fingers fumbled to feel the lump on the back of his head. "See anybody?"

"Nope, but there was definitely some activity inside your barn. I saw a bunch of tracks around your truck and on the steps going up to the second deck."

Boucher winced as Lavender pressed the ice pack against Boucher's neck. "Tracks? What tracks?"

"I saw there was a bag of lime broken on the floor, just inside the back door. Whoever whacked you must have come in there and unknowingly stepped in it. They left real nice tracks."

Boucher pushed Lavender's ice pack away. "They? You think there was more than one?"

"Oh hell yeah. You wanna go take a look?"

"Yeah, first thing in the morning. I gotta pop some aspirin and get horizontal for a few hours first. My head is killing me!"

...

After coffee the next morning, Boucher and Lavender went to the barn. Boucher retraced his footsteps from the night before. He opened both barn doors in the front and switched the lights on inside. The telltale, white, lime dust detailed the extent of the tracks. Lavender was right. The tracks encircled the truck.

Lavender walked to the stairs leading up to the second floor. "Check this out."

Boucher began climbing the steep, wooden steps, looking for anything unusual that might help him figure out why he was attacked. At the top of the stairs the tracks disappeared behind the trap door that he always kept locked. Before unlocking it, he examined the lock for damage. The lock looked fine.

"Hey Mojo, how hard is it to pick a lock like this?"

Mojo snickered. "About twenty seconds, maybe less, if you know what you're doing."

Boucher nodded, then swung the door upward and open, peering along the floor in the direction of the tracks. He slowly finished climbing the stairs and stepped onto the wooden floor. Reaching upward, he pulled on an overhead string that switched the lights on.

The second floor of the barn was where Boucher had his shotgun and rifle reloading equipment set up. His ten-foot-long reloading bench was cluttered with empty shell casings, wads, bags of shot, and various small boxes containing bullets of assorted calibers and weights. The shelf on the wall behind the bench was crowded with one-pound cans of rifle and pistol powder. Boucher spent countless hours reloading ammunition, which he consumed in competition shooting almost faster than he could reload it.

He traced the tracks that led along the reloading bench and could not detect any tampering. Everything was as he had left it the last time he was there, a few days earlier. Looking back at his friend, Boucher shook his head. "So what were they looking for?"

Mojo shrugged. "Maybe they weren't looking for anything. Let's go outside."

Mojo pointed back down the stairs and put a finger up to his lips, cautioning Boucher not to speak. At the bottom of the stairs they walked through the door leading into the old stable area where the assault on Boucher had taken place. There were clear, telltale tracks leading outside through the stable into the field behind the barn. Boucher peered at the tree line about one-hundred yards in front of him. Looking at Lavender, he rolled his eyes toward the tree line. Lavender understood and nodded.

The two men left the barn and walked toward the house. Lavender glanced back at the barn before speaking. "These guys were pros. They probably whacked you because you caught them in the act."

"The act of what?"

"I'll betcha' a beer they were bugging your shit."

"Bugging me?"

"Hell yeah. You said you went to Florida to talk to that old Air America guy and you've been asking around for imagery and other shit. These guys are probably feds, or somebody who works fer 'em, and they're looking to grab the loot before we do."

Boucher grabbed his friend's arm to silence him. When they were well clear of the barn, Boucher continued. "I can't imagine who would be watching us. We have to assume that they bugged my truck and maybe even my house. Max OPSEC is in effect. We're going to feed 'em some misinformation and see if we can draw them out. We can't afford the risk of compromise."

"Gotcha, Boss."

Boucher and Lavender continued their stroll back to the house.

"We need to call Reilly and let him and the guys know."

"Yeah," Lavender whispered. "I reckon so."

Boucher opened his cell phone and dialed. As it began to ring, he heard a strange clicking sound that seemed to echo behind the normal ringer tone. He pressed the cancel button and opened the line again to dial. Again, he heard the same clicking sound in the background. Now suspicious, he ended the call and went to the land-line phone in his bedroom. He slowly put the phone to his ear and listened for the dial tone as he released the button on the phone. The phone clicked and echoed again just like his cell had done. He wasted no time dialing Reilly.

"Billy this is Jake. You been noticing anything weird with your phone?"

"Well there's definitely some weird shit going on, but so far my phone's been working fine. What's up?"

"Maybe it's just me, but it seems every time I pick up the phone I hear weird clicking sounds like somebody is on my line. Billy, remember Eldest Brother?"

"Sure do."

"Good," Boucher replied. "Eldest Brother in effect. Pass the word to ALCON. Mojo my posit."

"Roger Boss, WILCO."

"Rosemary, twenty-one. Sierra, tango twenty-three."

Reilly repeated the code back to Boucher.

"Roger Rosemary, twenty-one. Sierra, tango twenty-three. Out here."

Boucher pushed the end call button on his phone and carefully placed it back on its charger. The commands he just gave Reilly were thirty years old and well known to SEALs from that era. Rosemary was the old call sign for Underwater Demolition Teams. UDT's were the famed Navy frogmen from which, in 1963, the first SEAL Teams—Team One and Team Two—were born. Boucher's use of that old UDT call sign, followed by his use of the number twenty-one, meant that he would contact Reilly again at 9:00 PM. His reference to sierra twenty-three meant that, if for some reason he was unable to make the primary contact time, he would make a second attempt at 11:00 PM. Eldest Brother was a reference to an operation the SEALs ran in Cambodia and the Mekong Delta area during and following Tet. It really had no other significance besides providing a frame of reference, and Reilly understood perfectly.

Boucher looked over at Lavender, who was sitting next to the bedroom window sipping a beer and staring outside at the rising sun. "What do you think?"

"I reckon we all know the deal."

"Yeah," Boucher whispered. "We need to visit Patterson."

Lavender nodded in silent acknowledgment. Both men stood. Lavender headed toward his room to grab his pack.

...

At that time of night, the drive from Laytonsville to Patterson's apartment in Leesburg, Virginia only took about fifty minutes. Boucher kept checking his mirrors for anyone tailing him, but couldn't identify anything suspicious. Lavender continuously surveyed the surrounding landscape in an active effort to detect anything abnormal. He saw nothing.

"You think Big Brother is watching?" Lavender asked Boucher.

"You know Mojo, at this point I really don't know, but we can't afford to take any chances. To be sure, there seems to be some weird shit going on."

"Yeah, I hear you Jake. I just can't help but wonder who would give a shit?"

Boucher frowned. "That's exactly what I was thinking."

CHAPTER 11

Washington, DC METRO area

S ir," the man said into his radio, "they're on the move."
A distinguished-looking man in his early sixties sat up in bed and depressed the send key. The radio chirped a quick e-tone beep signifying that it was secure.

"Details?"

"Two, Sir. Subject Alpha, plus one. They seem to be headed toward Leesburg. Destination unknown."

"Stay on them and don't lose them! You got that?"

"Yes Sir. We're on them."

The white 1999 Buick followed, unobserved, about a quarter mile behind Boucher's diesel pick-up truck.

"Unit three," the man said into his radio.

"Unit three, roger," the voice on the other end replied.

"Unit three, be ready to assume tail as the suspect gray, Ford F-250 pick-up truck passes your posit. ETA five mikes."

"Five mikes, Unit three, roger out."

Unit three's white Dodge van was positioned next to the parking lot exit ramp outside the Leesburg outlet mall along Route 15 north. The van had the Verizon Cable TV logo painted on its sides. A man wearing a yellow hard hat and orange safety vest appeared to be working on a cable junction box next to the Route 15 on ramp.

As Boucher's F-250 growled past, the man closed the box and returned to the van. He quickly closed the van's rear doors and climbed into the passenger side front seat. The driver started the van and turned on the headlights. After waiting for several other cars to pass, he eased it onto Route 15 about four hundred yards behind Boucher's pickup truck.

"Control, Unit three," the man in the hard hat said into his radio, "we're on them."

The Verizon van's driver was careful not to approach Boucher's truck too closely. The man wearing the hard hat on the passenger side reached down between the front seats and withdrew a laptop computer. The computer was already running, with a GPS road map on the monitor. It showed a real-time display of two dots moving along the map. The leading dot was displayed in red and the following dot was displayed in green. Both dots seemed to move in unison.

67

"Drop back a few hundred," the man with the laptop told the driver.

The pickup truck they were following quickly disappeared ahead of them as they wound north on Route 15, past the road to White's Ferry.

"Any audio?"

"No. They're either not talking or these hills are blocking the line-of-sight reception. I have the recorder running. We can analyze the audio later."

The man studied the laptop display intently.

"They turned left. Turn left at the next intersection."

The driver nodded just as the traffic light came into view a few hundred yards ahead.

"They're speeding up. I don't like it."

The van's driver sped up in an attempt to close some of the distance.

"They're turning right! They're turning right, but I don't show a road where they're turning! Slow down, slow down! I don't want to overshoot the turning point. Okay, we're almost there… another hundred yards. Slow it down! Slow it down. Turn right! Turn right now!"

As the van stopped, both men peered into a dark cornfield along the right side of the road. There was no sign of a vehicle having entered the field. The man with the laptop gazed intently into the display, trying to make sense of the data.

"I still show movement here in this field. I'm guessing four to five-hundred yards into that field on our right. Go, go, go!"

The driver turned into the cornfield and began to slowly blaze a path through the seven-foot-high cornstalks.

"Movement has stopped. Turn five degrees to the right."

The driver adjusted the steering wheel, estimating the new direction he was given.

"There, straight ahead…three-hundred yards. Stop! We'll go on foot from here."

The driver stopped the van and turned off the engine. Both men exited and put on night vision goggles. Giving each other a thumbs-up, they slowly began walking through the cornfield in the direction of the pickup truck's estimated location.

It was slow going as they cautiously crossed corn row after corn row, peering left, then right, down each row so they wouldn't miss anything or be ambushed by those they were following. After ten minutes they arrived at the estimated position of the last contact reported on the laptop. They quickly did a circle search of the area but could find nothing. Not even a footprint.

The man in the hard hat raised the radio to his cheek.

"Control, Unit three, we lost contact. Our current position is last known contact."

"That is unacceptable Unit three. Reacquire contact and resume surveillance."

"Ahh, that may be impossible Control. We believe the locator beacon has been removed and placed at our current location. There is no sign of vehicle presence here. We believe that we may have been compromised."

There was a long pause before the radio crackled. "Unit three, abort mission and return."

"Okay. Unit three will can-x and return."

The two men looked at each other through their NVGs and began the walk back through the cornfield toward their van.

As they arrived at their van, they realized they indeed were compromised and were no match for those they had been following. All four of the van's tires were slashed. The van was now sitting on the wheel rims. The passenger side door was open and the GPS tracking laptop was missing. The van's hood was open and the sparkplug wires had all been cut. There was a business card on the driver's seat that simply read, "Where the bullet meets the bone."

At that point, as if orchestrated, they saw the glint of blue flashing lights coming from the direction of the street. The men looked at each other through their NVGs.

"We're had! Torch the van!"

The driver quickly retrieved a small backpack located behind his seat. He reached inside a side pouch and withdrew a willy-peter grenade. The men nodded at one another as one of them pulled the pin on the grenade and threw it inside the van. The eight-second countdown seemed more like two. The grenade detonated with a bright flash as the white phosphors embers raced to umbrella outward, like a Fourth of July fireworks display, barely missing the two escaping men. The van and the surrounding cornfield out to a radius of about twenty yards, instantaneously burst into white-hot flame. The two men ran as fast as they could.

· · ·

The county sheriff arrived at the point where the van had entered the cornfield and immediately called the fire company along with back-up deputies. In what seemed to be a matter of minutes, there were fire trucks and police cruisers on the scene. A Virginia State Police helicopter arrived, circling above, illuminating the area with its powerful searchlight.

· · ·

The two men made their way as fast and as far as they could from the scene. After running and walking for almost an hour, the two sweat-soaked men stopped for a rest break and to report in.

"Control, this is Unit three," the man said, panting so hard he could barely speak into his radio mic.

"Control," the reply crackled back.

"Ahh, we were compromised and had to destroy the van. We've been E and E for the past hour."

"Roger all, Unit three. Keep your radio keyed thirty count for position DF, then standby for instructions."

"Roger, Control, thirty count starts now."

The man held the transmit key down and put his hand over the mic. He looked at his partner.

"Who the hell were those guys?"

CHAPTER 12

Naval Amphibious Base, Little Creek, Virginia, one week later

The annual UDT/SEAL reunion is held the third weekend of July at the Naval Amphibious Base (NAB) in Little Creek, Virginia. NAB Little Creek has been the main SEAL base on the east coast of the U.S. since the 1950s and a fitting place to hold the annual reunion. Boucher chose this event to bring his old SEAL platoon together because it provided both an excellent cover and good operational security, as it took place onboard the naval base.

The reunion events are always the same from year to year. Friday begins with an all- hands get-together at the old Officers Club. Hundreds of former and active duty SEALs show up. They reunite, drink together, and tell war stories. Saturday morning, distance swimming and running races are held for various age groups. There are also golf and shooting competitions. In the afternoon, the active duty SEALs conduct the infamous "demonstration" on the sea, air, and land at Fort Story, thrilling the families. Today's SEALs demonstrate their tradecraft to a well-scripted scenario that begins with the original World War II frogman up to current-day SEALs dressed in desert camouflage. The SEALs swim and parachute onto the beach before the excited onlookers, set off explosives, hold mock gun fights, and put on a very impressive war capabilities demonstration.

On Saturday evening, there is a dinner dance at the Chief's Club and a beach party that truly rocks on the Officer's Beach. The party usually lasts into the early hours of Sunday morning. Sunday afternoon they hold a family picnic with some additional live demonstrations for the children and provide just about anything one could want to eat. It's a three-day party that can only be appreciated in person. Both old and young warriors come together and share a common brotherhood. The dead are honored; never forgotten. Everyone, active duty or retired, is given a sense of history and family.

Boucher had a sun canopy set up in the picnic area which displayed a banner in large block letters: "ST-2, 8ᵗʰ plt, 1968." He was settled in a lawn chair under the canopy. Seated around him were Pat Patterson, Billy Reilly, Jack Doyle, Cherry Klum, Bad Bob Barns, Mojo Lavender, Risser Jackson, Thane LeFever, Dick Llina and Johnny Yellowhorse. Only Gabe Ramirez and Chief Haus Quicklinsky were not present. The men were all engaged in multiple conversations that ranged from personal updates to war stories.

Boucher smiled as he looked around at these old warriors he knew so well. All in their fifties and early sixties and still fit, they looked ten to fifteen years younger. Boucher raised his beer bottle in a toast.

"Gentlemen, thank you for coming here with me today. By now, Billy has contacted you and read you into what Pat Patterson and I are up to. We still have a few holes to fill, but I think this operation is doable with an acceptable level of risk. As I told some of you in my room at the bachelor officer quarters last evening, we may all be a bunch of old broke dick frogmen, but all that does is even the odds a little bit more for the opposition should we have to use force. In addition to Jack, we still need another good air guy who can fly anything. I think I may have such a man, and I'm waiting for his answer as I speak. Do you have any questions?"

"Bouch, what happened to Gabe and Haus?" Doyle asked.

"Gabe told us he had some family issues that he just couldn't neglect. He said he's pretty sure he'll get it all behind him in time to make the mission deadline, but no promises. I figure he'll make it. Haus said he just isn't interested in going back over there on the ground again, no matter what the bounty. I consider that an honorable position and I wish him well. He did tell me we should give him a call if we need support."

The men all nodded in agreement.

"Okay. From this moment on we will refer to this operation only as 'Just Reward'. By now you should all have the target folder and have had a chance to study it. As you know, this won't be a cakewalk. If any of you want to pull out, now would be a good time. None of us will think any less of you."

The men stared back at Boucher impassively.

"Okay then, we go forward and execute 'Just Reward' as planned. Let's all enjoy today's picnic and go on from here. I will be in touch."

About an hour later, Boucher's cell phone chirped. He checked the number and walked over by the swimming pool, located across the street from the picnic area, where there was a pay phone. He dialed the number and waited. "Mossman, it's me!"

Boucher listened intently. "Great! It's going to be the last hooyah for all of us. I'm glad you're in. Code name is 'Just Reward.'" Boucher listened again. "No problem, I'll have Reilly overnight the target folder to you first thing tomorrow. We launch per the plan's time line. I'll see you later, Mossman." Boucher hung up the phone and grinned.

"Hooyah!"

Boucher was clearly tickled that another old friend from his Vietnam days had agreed to join "Just Reward." Frank Moss was one of the hottest sticks Boucher had ever flown with. Moss was gifted with a natural ability to fly anything, from any rotary wing aircraft to most every fixed wing single or multi-engine plane ever built. He seemed to be able to adapt to any plane under any circumstance in a matter of seconds. He had amassed thousands of hours of stick time and was still flying today as a hunting and fishing guide in the Great Northwest. As Boucher walked back toward the picnic area, he relived the first time he met Mossman during the Tet Offensive in 1968. Moss was a Navy Seawolf gunship pilot who bailed Boucher and his SEAL platoon out of a number of tight jams. The first was the worst, and Boucher remembered it like it was yesterday.

...

Boucher and his men were operating in the Rung Sat "Secret Zone" where no Americans dared to set foot. They had blundered, unknowingly, between an NVA base camp and fortified NVA field hospital while searching for a POW camp. Several Americans were reportedly being held at the camp awaiting transfer north to Hanoi. Intel hadn't provided any warning about the fortified NVA positions hidden deep under the thick, jungle foliage. Boucher and his 8th platoon were pinned down between the two enemy strongholds by heavy machine gun crossfire.

The machine gun fire was so intense they couldn't break contact, and daylight was fast approaching. Doyle and Yellowhorse had been wounded and required medical evacuation. When Boucher called for helicopter gunship support and a medievac dust-off, two Army gunship helicopters arrived on scene about fifteen minutes later, but refused to provide the badly needed close air support two-thousand feet below because of the intense ground fire coming up at them.

The 8th platoon was now running critically low on ammunition and first light had arrived. Escape by fighting their way out was out of the question. They were pinned down and completely encircled by a superior NVA enemy force. Boucher had Jackson radio an emergency call for any aircraft available to come in low and slow to suppress the enemy fire to give him and his fellow SEALs an avenue of escape.

Boucher's frantic call for help was answered by a Navy Seawolf gunship detachment onboard a Navy amphibious ship anchored in the Mekong River about thirty miles away. In response, Moss immediately took off, followed by his wingman in a second Seawolf. Moss came in at treetop level and hovered over the point where the SEALs had marked their position with red and purple smoke. He fired his deadly rockets in all directions while his 50-caliber door gunner suppressed enemy fire. Moss was so low that his gunner's hot machine gun brass rained down on the SEALs below. Moss directed Boucher and his men to a flooded rice paddy a few clicks away and remained hovering above them to provide covering fire. His wingman, in the second Seawolf, picked up the volley of fire as the guns and rockets in Moss's Seawolf were expended to the last round.

Moss headed his UH-1 to the edge of the open rice paddy and hovered at treetop level. His two door gunners were now using their M-16s to fire at the enemy. As the SEALs ran toward the waiting Seawolf, Moss ordered his crew to throw their machine guns, ammo cans, and anything else heavy overboard in an effort to lighten the helicopter to the point where he could get all of Boucher's SEALs onboard and still be able to take off.

On the ground below, Moss's helicopter, Boucher, and his men were engaged in a running gunfight with the enemy in hot pursuit. As Moss landed his Seawolf on the edge of the rice paddy next to the SEAL platoon he was trying to rescue, his helicopter was laced by AK-47 fire coming from the tree line opposing his landing site. The SEALs jumped onboard, still firing their guns out of the open helicopter doors. But even at full power the helicopter was too heavy to make a vertical take off. Moss literally bounced the Seawolf along the soft ground on its skids until he had enough forward airspeed to take off and then coaxed his overloaded helicopter through a slow climb at stall speed, barely clearing the tree line on the other side of the rice paddy.

Moss's wingman followed slightly above and behind Moss's Seawolf, flying backwards so he could bring all his remaining rockets and guns to bear against the heavily-armed enemy forces. Moss's Seawolf took thirteen rounds through the tail cowling and fuselage on the way out. Moss, himself, took a round in his right calf. His co-pilot lost two fingers from a stray round that also shattered the cockpit canopy. Leaking hydraulic fluid from nearly every control line that counts, as well as the engine transmission, Moss nursed his dying Seawolf nearly four miles to a flooded rice paddy. As the engine died, he auto-rotored the overloaded helicopter into the rice paddy below. It was a skillful attempt at a controlled crash. The force of the impact buried the Seawolf in the mud up to its belly.

The engine immediately burst into flames from the overheated transmission. Miraculously, no one was seriously injured from the crash landing. The second Navy Seawolf landed beside Moss. Two Army UH-1 gunships arrived on scene in response to Moss's mayday call and landed to assist with evacuating the SEALs, along with Moss and his crew. All the SEALs and Moss's crew divided themselves among the three waiting helicopters to distribute the added weight. On the way out, Moss's wingman turned his Seawolf back toward Moss's smoldering crash and fired his remaining two rockets into the downed Seawolf, destroying it completely.

Boucher remembered looking at Moss sitting there beside him on the deck of the second Seawolf. The right leg of Moss's shredded flight suit was blood-soaked. Moss pulled off his flight helmet and placed it next to him on the helicopter's aluminum deck. He unzipped a leg pocket on his flight suite and withdrew a black baseball cap, which he put on. The hat had DILLIGAFF embroidered in dirty white letters above the brim. Boucher extended his hand in gratitude.

"Jake Boucher, SEAL Team Two. Thanks for saving our bacon back there."

He remembered Moss's piercing eyes and his toothy grin. He also remembered Moss shaking his hand with his powerful grip and his reply.

"Wouldn't have missed it for anything. Hey, you know where I can get a cold beer?"

...

Boucher smiled as he neared the picnic area. Those were Moss's exact words during their phone call just now. Boucher knew he had just successfully recruited another old friend and an extraordinary pilot he could count on.

CHAPTER 13

Bongserrie, Thailand, several days later

Departing the United States from a variety of locations and at different times, Boucher and his team independently made their way to Bangkok. Some flew to Singapore and Butterworth and then took the train north to Bangkok. There they took the bus to Pattya Beach where they immediately boarded a taxi to Bongserrie. Bongserrie is a small fishing village on the northeast panhandle of Thailand, about fifteen miles south of the Thai-Vietnam border. An expatriate by the name of Paul Goodman lived there with his Thai wife, Tu. Goodman and Tu ran a small hotel which catered mostly to foreign oilmen who worked out of the nearby port, just a few miles north.

Boucher had initially met Goodman and his wife in the early eighties while cross-training with the Thai SEALs. He and his platoon had roomed at Goodman's hotel numerous times over a period of eight years. Boucher and Goodman gradually became trusted friends to the point where Boucher would rely on him to logistically support some of the counter-drug operations he and his Thai SEAL counterparts were running along the Thai-Burmese border area in Thailand's northwestern highlands.

Boucher liked Goodman because he was a former Vietnam-vintage, Army warrant officer, helicopter gunship pilot. He liked staying at Goodman's hotel for a number of reasons. First and foremost, Goodman knew how to keep his mouth shut. Secondly, Bongserrie was about fifteen miles from Pattya Beach and the Thai Navy SEAL headquarters. That also made access to the best bars and night spots in Thailand close, but not too close, allowing him and his men to keep a low profile. Boucher also loved Tu's cooking and she treated him and his men like an extended family. Even though he had not stayed with Goodman and Tu in nearly nine years, he had remained in touch via the Internet. He knew this visit would be no different than any of his previous ones as far as hospitality went.

Boucher, with Frank Moss at his side, was the last to arrive. The men eagerly awaited Boucher's entry in the open-air cabana bar, located directly across the access street in front of the hotel. Goodman, or "Goodie" as everyone knew him, was tending bar. Casablanca fans hung beneath the crest of the thatched roof, spinning lazily, some wobbling out of balance, some buzzing like they were going to burst into flames, and some doing both. A tapioca field, fifty yards wide and a quarter of a mile long, abutted the rear wall behind the small bar providing a lush, green backdrop. The eight-foot-tall tapioca plants were nearly mature and would soon be ready to harvest. Across the street, Goodman's small, two-floor, cinderblock hotel was flanked by numerous, flimsy, plywood–covered, bamboo-frame houses, with thickly thatched roofs that served as lodgings for the local fishermen and their families.

Immediately behind the small village was the Sea of Siam. In the bright sunlight the shallow sea appeared a dark, brownish-blue color. At night it was as black as the ace of spades. Goodman always said the reason he never left Thailand at the end of the Vietnam War was because Bongserrie was as near to Paradise as he felt he could get in this lifetime. While Goodman no longer had any political ties to the United States or family there, he was no less a patriot.

As Boucher entered the cabana bar, his men began to cheer and applaud. He burst into a wide grin and raised his left hand to quiet them. Patterson was the first to shake his hand, followed by the rest of those present from his former SEAL platoon. The enthusiastic reunion took a few minutes to die down, but gradually the men took seats in front of Boucher. Patterson and Moss flanked his sides. Boucher cleared his throat and hesitated a moment, as if he was searching for just the right words. The room was silent.

"Just like the many years when we worked together before, we all know what we're here for. We know the risks involved. We have accepted embarking upon this mission, not because we must, but because we want to. We have always relied upon each other through thick and thin. This operation will be no different."

Some of the men hooted and a few clapped. Boucher held up his hand to quiet them.

"However, there are some differences this time around. You all, of course, remember the two men standing beside me. Pat Patterson has been gracious enough to share his crash site secret with us. Providing we are successful, none of us will ever have to work again. The briefing book that Billy gave you to study should have made our objective and tactics clear. The key will be to get to our objective undetected, recover the precious cargo, and get back out before anyone else can intervene. We will rely on another trusted friend standing here on my left."

Boucher placed his hand on Moss's shoulder. He was wearing his infamous, well-worn, black ball cap with DILLIGAFF embroidered in grungy, white letters above the brim, a wrinkled Hawaiian shirt, and cargo shorts with torn pockets. His hair was uncombed and he hadn't shaved in three days. He looked more like a homeless man than a seasoned, professional pilot.

Boucher grabbed Moss behind the neck and pulled him closer.

"Frank Moss, who I'm sure you all remember, saved our asses countless times. Mossman is the hottest stick I have ever known. He and Jack will provide the infil and exfil transportation for us via a Boeing 234 heavy-lift helicopter he leased from an oil exploration company a few miles up the coast. For those of you who might have forgotten what a Boeing 234 is, it's basically the civilian equivalent of a CH-47 Chinook. It has both adequate cargo payload capability and range to get us to the objective and back again."

The men nodded approvingly. Some raised their beers in a silent toast.

"Goodie will provide logistics support, communications, and deception. The only player who is not present is our old friend Tahnite. Tahnite has long since retired as the commander of the Royal Thai SEALs, but I have remained in contact with him. Tahnite now runs his family's rice exporting business in Bangkok. He is providing the explosives, guns, and the other tools we need. Any questions?"

The men sat silently. Some were nodding, some were smiling, and some showed no emotion at all. Johnny Yellowhorse raised his hand. Boucher pointed at him.

"Jake, where's Haus?"

"Senior Chief Quicklinsky won't be on the ground with us on this op. However, I briefed him in and he is onboard so he can help us if we need him. He's our plan B backstop and also heads the home team."

Yellowhorse nodded quietly. "How about Ramirez?"

"I have great news! He'll be here in the morning."

Boucher surveyed his trusted crew and nodded approvingly. "Okay. If anyone comes up with any last minute shit, you know how to reach me. We launch tomorrow evening. Remember, max OPSEC. I want you all to check your field kit today and have it laid out for me by 1600. Goodie and I will swing by each of your rooms to ensure you have everything you need. We'll hook up with Tahnite in the morning before we infil. Billy, we'll need you and Bad Bob to prep the ops gear. Everyone, get some rest and don't forget to hydrate."

The men nodded acknowledgment.

Before an operation like this, the SEALs always tried to jam as much liquid into their bodies as they could to help prevent dehydration in the sweltering heat, and to eliminate the need to carry more than one canteen of water. Once they consumed the first canteen, they would refill it by scooping up water from any freshwater source they could find and drop a couple of heliozoan water purification tablets into it to kill the biologicals. Unfortunately, the water source available was usually a canal or rice paddy. The water's odor and taste was always horrible, but at least it was wet, safe to drink after the heliozoan treatment, and it kept them going.

Boucher, Goodman, Moss and Patterson left the cabana bar and headed for the hotel across the street.

"Mossman, you got the helo ready to go?"

"Sure do, Jake. Goodie has her leased for one week. Got the auxiliary fuel tank in her so range won't be an issue. We can shitcan the aux-tank later if we need the cargo deck space. Doyle and I will pilot. Pat will assist with navigation."

"Goodie, you have the boats lined up?"

"Yeah. Two large motor sampans for the river in Dong Tam and a blue water junk on stand-by at Thani and Palawan, in case you need them."

"Pat, is Tahnite ready for us?"

"I spoke with him this morning, Jake. I'm in my comfort zone. He has the demo and the weapons pre-positioned at the rendezvous point. All Mossman and Jack should have to do is land us next to the truck and we'll load our stuff onboard."

"Okay, it's a go for tomorrow. Mossman, I'll see you and Jack on the helo."

...

A few hours before sunset the next day, a heavy-lift, twin-rotor Boeing 243 made an uneventful, low-level approach and landed behind the cabana bar inside a small clearing the men had cut in the tapioca field. The men quickly loaded the helicopter with their equipment and two Zodiac inflatable boats. Boucher conducted a communications check with Goodman using both Iridium satellite phones and regular cell phones. He followed that by checking each man's individual squad radio. Even though everything checked out okay, Boucher was secretly concerned because all the communications equipment they were using was commercially available, off-the-shelf stuff that Goodman had either leased or purchased.

This communications equipment was incapable of secure scrambled transmission, unlike what the military used. Boucher realized that if someone wanted to, they could listen in on the conversation and he wouldn't know they were listening. That led Boucher to use a verification system of code words and brevity codes to pass information in the clear. If all went according to plan, they would be in and out before being detected. Even if they were detected it would take some time for any opposition force to react and mount a counter-operation. Boucher felt the risk was acceptable.Moss pushed the throttles forward to full power and slowly pulled up on the collective with his left hand. The powerful helicopter gradually rose off the ground and climbed straight up before pivoting onto a seaward heading. Moss pushed the stick forward. As the helicopter's nose tilted down a few degrees it seemed to almost instantaneously shoot forward, quickly picking up speed. Moss held the helicopter at an altitude of about fifty feet above the sea and maintained level flight out over the horizon before banking to a northeasterly heading.

...

Back in Bongserrie, Goodman checked his watch and made the first phone call. "Play one now."

About forty-five minutes passed when Goodman's phone rang. "Yeah," he answered curtly. "Roger, WILCO." Goodman ended that call, dialed a number, and left a message similar to his first. "Play two."

Again, he waited anxiously until his phone rang. "Yeah," he answered. "Confirm feet dry."

Boucher, Patterson, Moss and Doyle had scripted a deception flight. This employed a series of pre-scripted radio calls made along the aircraft's fake flight path that reported position. In reality the aircraft was in another location not even close to that being reported. This technique was commonly used by the Air Force's Special Operations Squadron to deceive the enemy. While this deception certainly wasn't as elaborate as the kind the Air Force employed, it was good enough to throw off the uneducated and unsuspecting. Goodman glanced through the windshield outside, relieved to see that it was almost dark.

...

Sitting in the co-pilot's seat on Moss's right, Doyle refolded a map that showed the flight path they were following. Using a pencil, he circled the point where the line crossed over land.

"Feet dry at twenty one ten," he reported to Moss.

Doyle continued running the point of his pencil about an inch along the line, stopping at a waypoint marked sierra papa. He again checked his watch.

It was about twenty-five minutes after dusk. Moss was now flying with night vision goggles, keeping the truculent helicopter about one-hundred feet above the ground, which really meant that he was only a few yards above some of the treetops. He would occasionally dive and then abruptly pull up to take advantage of terrain masking. He was flying well below any radar's ability to detect the helicopter. Additionally, he had turned off the aircraft's external red and white flashing marker lights and was flying blacked out. As the mammoth helicopter skimmed the treetops, it presented a near ghostly image against the dark sky above.

Patterson was sitting in the Crew Chief's jump seat that folded down behind the center instrument cluster between the pilot and co-pilot's seat. From this position he could see everything that was going on in the cockpit and he could help Doyle and Moss navigate. He keyed his mic as he raised his Rolex watch into full view. "Pilot, point bravo on my mark…five, four, three, two, one, mark!"

"Roger," Moss replied as he banked the helo sharply to the north.

Patterson and Doyle checked the navigation chart against the GPS computer lat/long coordinates display in the center console. "Point Charlie, eleven minutes," Patterson announced.

"Ah, roger," Moss replied.

Boucher sat silently in the noisy cargo compartment, his mind drifting back to the canal crossroads and the night he first met Patterson. He couldn't help but wonder what this night would bring.

Patterson raised his watch again and keyed his mic. "Pilot, point Charlie on my mark…five, four, three, two, one, mark!"

In classic military pilot efficiency, Moss responded with a simple, "Roger," as he banked the powerful helicopter back to the northeast.

This process of employing predetermined waypoints that were calculated as part of the flight plan was designed to take maximum advantage of the terrain for the purpose of masking this unauthorized intrusion that followed the Mekong River into Cambodia. Moss and Doyle were flying a path that kept them well clear of any populated areas where they might be compromised. It also kept them below radar detection in Cambodia, Thailand, and Vietnam. While terrain-following wasn't a ride to be enjoyed, especially for those in the back of the aircraft, it was the only way to provide sufficient cover to get an aircraft of this size to the objective without detection.

After several more waypoints and thirty-five additional minutes of flight, Patterson finally announced his final navigational point. "Pilot, cast zone five miles, heading two niner five."

"Roger, five at two niner five."

Using steady pressure, Moss pulled back on the stick, slowing the helo's air speed while at the same time trimming the helo's nose to maintain the proper angle of attack.

Doyle began reading the radar altimeter and air speed to Moss. "Ninety feet, ninety knots. Cast zone, straight ahead. Check heading."

"Heading two niner four. I see cast zone clear," Moss reported. "Cast zone clear."

"Roger, clear," Doyle confirmed. "Tail ramp going down."

Moss quickly scanned his instrument cluster on the dash in front of him and then focused on the path ahead of the helicopter.

"Stand ready to cast. All clear."

Moss pulled the collective upward and flared the helicopter, bringing it to a hover. The helo began to sink into the blackness below. Boucher had no idea how high they were or if they were about to land on the river or in the jungle. He marveled at Moss's piloting skill and iron nerves.

Doyle was glancing between the altimeter and the side cockpit window counting off the altitude to Moss. "Fifty, thirty, twenty, ten, hold, hold, hold!"

Moss skillfully worked the helo's controls. There was a brief feeling of weightlessness, and then the belly of the helo lightly splashed onto the surface of the Mekong River. Doyle nodded back at Patterson, who promptly left his jump seat for the rear of the helicopter. The SEALs in the back of the helo were ready to go. They quickly pushed the two Zodiac inflatable boats off the open tail ramp into the water behind the helo.

The boats were now positioned directly behind the open tail ramp and being held by their bowlines. The SEALs wasted no time climbing onboard. Boucher and Patterson were the last to board, casting off their bowline. The men started the outboard motors and headed around to the front of the helicopter.

Even in the spray of the rotor wash, Boucher could see Moss and Doyle sitting at the controls in the nearly dark cockpit peering out at him. Boucher smiled and gave Moss a thumbs-up. Moss returned the gesture with a nod as Doyle closed the rear cargo ramp remotely from the cockpit.

Boucher looked around at all his men and gave the thumbs-up. He pointed toward shore and they motored away from the low, hovering helicopter. As they approached a smaller estuary, Boucher heard the helo's powerful jet engines strain as Moss climbed vertically at maximum power. Within minutes the sound of its engines and clatter of its rotors had nearly disappeared into the black, night sky. Boucher's two boats quietly slipped into the estuary canal and the surrounding darkness.

Boucher pointed ahead and motioned to Reilly, who was acting as coxswain, to head closer to the canal bank. This particular part of the canal was bordered by heavy jungle. Their plan was to try to navigate up this canal to the intersection where they had rescued Patterson. From there they would follow the smaller canal that headed in the direction of the plane crash site and go as far as they could go by boat to get as close as they could without having to walk. Once there, they would hide their boats and hike it to the crash site. Boucher and his men felt this would give them the reference points they needed, using dead reckoning navigation as a backup should their hand-held GPS fail.

Boucher noted that heavy clouds had moved in since Moss dropped them off, and the ambient illumination required for efficient NVG use was diminishing rapidly. Moreover, an almost fog-like drizzle had begun which further deteriorated the NVG's ability to magnify the available light.

Boucher made the decision and keyed his squad radio. "Discontinue NVGs."

The men all removed their NVGs and stowed them in their carrying cases.

Boucher turned around and whispered back at Bill Reilly, "Just like old times."

Reilly nodded agreement.

The boats continued for about another mile, winding their way deeper into the countryside.

Patterson finally broke radio silence. "I make point India two-hundred yards ahead."

Boucher clicked his radio mic twice, signifying that he received and understood the message.

Reilly slowed the boat as they approached the scene of the vicious battle that they had taken part in over thirty years earlier. The bamboo walkway had been rebuilt across the small canal. Otherwise, it looked almost as it had before the SEALs had detonated their deadly Claymore mines.

Boucher waved the boats under the bamboo walkway at the canal intersection and into the mouth of the smaller canal. They proceeded another half-mile before the canal narrowed to the point that it became impassable. This natural choke point was also a densely foliated area that would provide excellent cover to hide their boats. Boucher and his boat crew quietly pulled the boat out of the water and hid it in the dense vegetation. The SEALs crewing the boat behind him did the same thing.

Once ashore, they quickly unloaded their equipment and haversacks of explosives from the boats,and partially deflated one of them. Ramirez and Jackson cut small tree branches and used them like brooms to brush all traces of the landing from the canal's muddy bank. They carefully raised any trampled grass and underbrush back into place, working their way from the canal bank inward to where the others had painstakingly concealed the boats and motors in the dense undergrowth.

The men quietly put on their backpacks and other equipment and created a security perimeter. Boucher motioned to Yellowhorse to move out on point. Yellowhorse got on his feet and stepped forward into the dense jungle. The rest silently followed in patrol order.

After slowly advancing about a hundred yards, they came upon the muddy jungle trail they were searching for. Yellowhorse crouched on one knee at the edge of the thick undergrowth, cautiously surveying up and down the trail before exposing himself. Steadily, the men followed Yellowhorse, as they had over thirty years earlier, not far from this spot. Also as before, the rain began to pour down in sheets, completely covering their movement. They progressed methodically, much older now and perhaps a lot slower, but they had not lost their edge.

The overhead imagery and maps that Patterson had provided for navigating to the crash site were incredibly detailed and accurate. Even so, Boucher and his men did a detailed map study and committed this terrain to memory. It was as if they had all been down this trail before. With the aid of Boucher's hand-held GPS, he had no difficulty determining exactly where he and his men were and how far they still had to go. This was a cakewalk compared to the last time they visited this location during the Tet Offensive.

Boucher passed the hand signal to stop and circle wagons. While they had not gone far, Boucher judged it was time to take a ten-minute rest break. Boucher checked his watch. It was 2341 and he was relieved to know that they were well within their pre-planned time schedule.

NSA Headquarters, Fort Meade, Maryland, the same time

Deputy Director Cunningham answered on the second ring. "Cunningham."

The call was from Wayne Dunn, the Chief of the Intercept Branch.

"Sir, we have Cane Pebble ELINT activity. It's primarily limited to Iridium and cell phone intercepts, but we believe there may be two related radio calls from a helicopter registered to a Thai aviation charter service. We're on it and I'll keep you informed."

"Thank you, Wayne," Cunningham replied. "Is it our boys?" he asked.

"It's too soon to say with any acceptable level of confidence, but it could be. All the calls have been made in English using a brevity code that we haven't been able to make sense of."

"Very well. I want to know the second you can say for sure."

"Yes Sir," Dunn obediently snapped back.

Cunningham leaned forward in his leather-bound, executive chair and gazed at a large world map mounted on the wall of his office. His eyes focused on southern Cambodia and the Parrot's Beak. He slowly reached for his secure telephone and punched in a six digit number string. "Linda, please get Mike Lawson over at NGA on the phone. I need to talk to him... secure. Thank you, Linda."

Sitting back in his overstuffed, executive chair, he again fixed his eyes on the Parrot's Beak. Moments later his STE rang, startling him out of his daydream trance. He quickly sat forward, striking his left elbow on the sharp edge of his desk as he snatched the phone with his right hand.

"Cunningham," he announced in a strained voice. "Thank you, Linda. Go ahead and transfer me."

Cunningham relaxed slightly as he briskly rubbed his left elbow with his right hand.

"Mike, Greg Cunningham. How you doin' today?" Cunningham again leaned back into his chair. "Good. I'm glad to hear it. Mike, the reason I called is to ask for your help. We've been tracking some suspicious activity in the Thailand-Cambodia area. We haven't yet confirmed what they're up to, but it could be terrorism-related. At any rate, I need your help to narrow it down."

Cunningham was listening intently as he carefully leaned forward on his desk, propping himself up on both elbows. "Well thank you, Mike. I knew I could count on you. Here's what I would like you to put together for me. I need a geospatial intel analysis done on the vicinity of the Parrot's Beak in Cambodia. I want you to specifically look for an airplane crash site. I'll e-mail the coordinates to you on the SIPRNET after we get off the phone. Yeah, I know there isn't any commercial imagery available for that region. I'm going to see if I can get a one-meter resolution LIDAR flyover and some current multi-spec imagery over the next several days. When I get the data, I'll send it over to you for inclusion into the vector fusion. How's that sound?"

Cunningham was doodling on a steno pad, outlining the words "Cane Pebble" several times as he patiently listened to Lawson's reply. "Okay, Mike. Sorry for the short fuse but I'll need a quick turnaround on this. And one more thing. This has to stay in Cane Pebble special category channels. It's strictly need-to-know." Cunningham drew a solid arrow through the words he had outlined as he listened. "Many thanks, Mike. Hope I can return the favor."

Cunningham hung up and sat at his desk again, staring up at the wall map of Southeast Asia.

CHAPTER 14

The Crash Site

Boucher signaled Yellowhorse to move out. The men naturally fell into patrol order behind Yellowhorse. Boucher checked his GPS and signaled Yellowhorse to continue along the trail on his current heading. They patrolled for another fifteen minutes. The rain continued to pound down on them. Boucher's GPS showed that they were only about fifty yards west of the crash site. Boucher signaled Yellowhorse to turn right, off the muddy trail, and penetrate the dense jungle. It would now be an arduous pace as they picked their way through the trees and vegetation.

They patrolled for another grueling ten minutes.

Boucher continued to check his GPS. "Bingo," he announced loud enough for all to hear.

The men quickly huddled under Boucher's poncho, stretching it above them, creating a makeshift roof.

"Okay, we're on top of it, or at least close enough to find the point of impact. Let's get to work. It will be daylight in about four hours."

The men fanned out and began clearing a small area, using the sharpened edge of their collapsible entrenching tools like machetes.

The Vietnam-vintage SEALs often carried this tool, not to dig foxholes, but rather as an effective close combat weapon. By sharpening the edges of the shovel, the tool could clear vegetation, chop down undergrowth, or hack the limbs off an enemy attacker. It could also be used for the purpose it was designed—to dig.

Lavender, Klum and Ramirez pulled foot long sections of steel rod from their backpacks and threaded the rods together, making them each about eight feet long. Each following behind one of their teammates who was clearing a path, they began to probe the soft jungle floor by pressing the rods down into the soil as far as they could. It wasn't long until Mojo hit something about three feet below the surface, making an unmistakable, dull-sounding, metallic thud. Mojo grabbed his entrenching tool and began digging.

The others continued to chop and probe, using a circular search pattern similar to what divers use when searching the sea floor. This process employs walking concentric circles that radiate out from a central point. It is highly effective, especially in a debris field. Klum's probe hit an object and he began to dig. Shortly after that, Ramirez located something as well. Boucher took Mojo's probe and continued the circle search.

Boucher considered the situation as he searched. It all seemed to be going too well. They had penetrated into Cambodia undetected. They had found the crash site exactly where Patterson's intel predicted it would be. They had easily located several objects buried only a few feet beneath the jungle floor. The rain was letting up and everyone was healthy. In a couple hours it would be daylight. Then he would have time to walk and mark the debris field and develop a recovery strategy. He also knew they were pushing the human endurance envelope for men their age and their adrenaline would not last indefinitely. They would all need rest and a meal.

Boucher's probe struck a hard object about a foot beneath the soft, humus surface of the jungle floor. Holding his small, red lens flashlight in his mouth, he scraped the earth from what appeared to be a concrete block with a top that was about three feet square. He could hardly believe it. It seemed that they had found what they came here for. Boucher continued to dig until he had scraped the composted, sour-smelling soil from the sides of the block. It was exactly what Patterson's former father-in-law had described.

Boucher checked his watch. It would be daylight in about an hour. The rain had slowed to a fine drizzle. He gathered his men.

"It will be daylight in another hour. We've been going way too long without sleep and a meal. Let's take a break and hit it hard again in the morning. We'll set reveille for zero nine thirty. Don't forget to brush."

The men quietly found individual locations to sleep. Most didn't even bother to erect their ponchos to shield them from the rain. They just wrapped themselves in their ponchos, found a small tree to rest against, and settled back on their backpacks.

...

The morning came way too fast. The sky was partly cloudy with small patches of blue showing through and the sun was characteristically hot—in fact, sweltering hot. Boucher opened his eyes and leisurely pulled his flop hat back above his eyes so he could see. For some reason, he immediately focused on a small branch located directly above him.

There was a small, bright green snake, slightly larger in diameter than a pencil and about twice as long, hanging about a foot above Boucher's face. It was a Bamboo Viper, one of the most lethally venomous snakes in the jungle. One bite from that snake causes its victim to go into nearly instantaneous anaphylactic shock. Fifteen seconds later death occurs.

Boucher cautiously eased away, then grabbed his entrenching tool and sliced the green snake into numerous smaller pieces.

"I fucking *hate* snakes," he mumbled aloud.

His mind wandered to the Thailand highlands along the Thai-Burmese border, where he and Tahnite, his Thai SEAL counterpart, had conducted months of grueling counter-drug operations fifteen years earlier. It was there that he developed his hatred for snakes. The densely-forested rubber plantations seemed to act like magnets for the King Cobra. Boucher remembered one particular night when he came eye-to-eye with one while on patrol. The snake stood over six feet tall.

Cobras don't spring like most other venomous snakes and their height is measured by their length. Cobras coil and stand up at half their length. One that stands six feet tall is twelve feet long. When they strike they fall forward, catching their prey with a downward strike. So, if you're outside of a six-foot radius, you're safe from being bitten by a Cobra standing six feet tall. However, anything inside that radius is either toast, faster than the snake, or lucky.

Boucher knew that a snake that was equal to his height was one big, badass snake. He remembered how he stopped, startled, eye-to eye just a few feet in front of the Cobra, and the speed at which the snake struck at him. He instinctively jumped sideways, parrying the snake's downward strike with his gun barrel. He barely avoided its three-inch-long fangs as its head passed by his torso. He was carrying an MP-5 sub-machine gun and he emptied the entire thirty-round magazine into the snake. He followed that with his Beretta pistol and put another eighteen rounds into the snake, just to make sure it was dead. As might be expected, the sound of the gunfire compromised the SEAL patrol's location and they had to abort the mission. When later asked what happened, Boucher never apologized. He just mumbled, "I fucking *hate* snakes."

Boucher could feel his heart pounding again, exactly the way it had the night he faced the cobra. He checked his watch. The time was 0900. He knew he would not fall back to sleep now, so he tore open a Meal Ready to Eat (MRE) and began to munch on it as he slowly strolled around the small, variously sized clearings the men had cut a few hours earlier. He returned to the concrete block he had excavated and tried to decide on the best way to break it open, using the plastic explosives they'd brought along, without destroying the contents.

Reilly joined him.

"So what do you think, Boss?"

Boucher swallowed a mouthful of cold MRE beef stew.

"I'm thinking we'll build a linear shape charge and see if we can surgically crack it open. If we use two-inch diameter bamboo, split it in half, then mold a half-inch layer of C-4 over the outside of the bamboo, it should make an effective linear shape charge. We'll fire it with electric blasting caps. How's that sound, Billy?"

"Sounds like a plan. How many blocks do you figure there are?"

"I don't know for sure but, according to our intel source, there were supposed to be two pallets of them. I guess there could be about ten or so."

"I don't like it, but we'll have to risk a test shot on this block to make sure the charge will cut it the way we want."

Boucher checked his watch again. "Let's get everyone up and working. We need to uncover as many blocks as we can before we do the test shot."

Reilly smiled. "Roger, Boss."

A short while later all the men were up and working. By noon they had found and uncovered six more blocks. They now had a total of nine. Boucher halted the work and gathered the men around him.

"Alright, listen up! So far we have been very lucky. I don't think anyone knows we're here and I'd like to keep it that way, but as every one of you knows, there is just no quiet way to detonate high explosives. By my count we have uncovered nine blocks so far. It is now time to attempt a breaching charge to test our method. Make sure you all take a look at the linear shape charge Billy built using a bamboo standoff. I think, if we place one charge on all four sides of this block so each charge opposes the other on a different face of the block, we should be able to split this puppy neatly in half without messing up the contents. Providing it works, we'll build enough charges to shoot the other eight blocks. If there truly is gold inside these blocks, we'll have more than we can carry with us right here in these. Any questions?"

Ramirez raised his hand. "I reckon I can carry about sixty pounds. What do you figure sixty pounds of gold is worth?"

Some of the men chuckled.

Boucher considered before replying. "Well Gabe, I'd guess a million or two."

"Holy shit!" Mojo exclaimed. "That means if we all carry that much out we'll easily end up with more money than any of us could spend, and that's after taxes!"

General amusement ensued. Boucher waved his hand in the air. "Alrighty then, we got the talk'n done. Let's do it! Hooyah!"

Reilly jumped down next to the block in the narrow hole. Jackson handed him the first of four shape charges. Reilly carefully slid the charge under the block in a hole that Boucher had carved just for that purpose. Reilly took the second charge and propped it vertically along the middle of the block's side. He did the same with the third charge on the other side. He laid the fourth charge on top of the block, in line with the other three charges. Next, he took a length of detonating cord and stretched it around all four charges so that the cord was in contact with the plastic explosives on each. Finally, he took an electric blasting cap and placed it inside a loop he made in the det cord. Jackson handed him a roll of black electrical tape. Reilly wound a short length of tape tightly around the blasting cap and the junction loop in the det cord, securing both in a single union. He stepped up out of the hole and carefully attached the two wires of the blasting cap to a fifty-foot-long, electrical trunk line that they had run along the ground over to another hole that had been excavated around a block. Except for a cursory electrical continuity check, and connecting the trunk wires to the blasting machine or "hellbox," as the SEALs called it, the shot was ready to fire.

Boucher was waiting as Reilly joined him in the makeshift bunker. Reilly pulled the ten-cap blasting machine from his pants' cargo pocket and attached the two trunk line wires to its electrical connection terminals on top.

Reilly looked over at Boucher with a nod of approval. "Say when."

Boucher stood up and quickly scanned the surrounding area to ensure none of his men were exposed, and then ducked behind the block beside Reilly.

"Fire in the hole!"

Reilly clicked the firing trigger on the hellbox as the instantaneous crack of a high explosives detonation echoed through the jungle. Reilly and Boucher covered their heads with their hands as small chunks of concrete and smoldering dirt rained down upon them. The noise of concrete fragments and dirt falling back through the jungle foliage lasted about ten seconds. Then everything went quiet. There was no sound at all. A light breeze swept the smoke from the blast site into the jungle.

The blast crater was still smoking as Reilly and Boucher approached it. The explosives had done their job. The block lay broken, exposing a plywood interior and the glint of gold bars.

"Holy shit," Boucher whispered.

"No, Jake! Holy fucking shit!" Reilly bellowed.

The rest of the men ran over to the crater and just stood there, staring at the gold in disbelief.

Patterson slapped Boucher on the back. "Like I told you, old buddy, it's our retirement plan!"

Boucher slid down into the crater next to the gold bars. He slowly picked one up and passed it up to Patterson, then another to Reilly and another to Lavender. They passed the heavy gold bars around to the rest.

"Alright, let's get to work building enough charges to shoot the other eight blocks. I want to fire them simultaneously. One big shot and we're done. Risser, call Mossman and Doyle on the Iridium and tell him we have joy and that the exfil plan is good to go."

Jackson nodded and went to his backpack to get the Iridium satellite phone.

Boucher raised his voice for all his men to hear. "One more thing. Let's get these boxes emptied and the gold packed away as quickly as possible. If we have to make a run for it, at least we'll have some spending money."

Some of the men went about building the linear shape charges and digging the charge access hole beneath the midsection of each block. Several others unloaded the gold from the fractured block and repacked the bars into rigid frame rucksacks that they humped into the jungle toward the boats they had earlier hidden by the canal.

It was now mid-afternoon. The sun was high and hot. Boucher wished for rain to cool things off and provide some relief from the sweltering heat. He was almost finished inspecting the explosives on the eighth block when he heard the faint, but unmistakable sound of a jet aircraft engine in the distance. It seemed to be getting closer. Boucher stood and looked around at his men, then up through the thick jungle canopy. There was only one hole in the canopy, and that was the one they had blasted through earlier in the morning. But it was not large enough to make much of a difference unless someone was searching for it.

Boucher still took precautions.

"Got a plane headed our way," he yelled. "Let's take cover just in case."

The men quickly stepped into the dense foliage and disappeared beneath it. Only Boucher remained partially uncovered so he could watch the plane. To his surprise, it was smaller than he expected. Once he saw it, he immediately knew what it was—a Global Hawk remotely-piloted surveillance plane. He couldn't help but think how curious it was to have a spy plane like that flying around this particular spot.

"Pat," Boucher yelled at Patterson who was under cover about twenty feet away.

"Yeah Jake, what's up?"

"What do you suppose a Global Hawk is doing flying around this part of the world?"

"A Global Hawk?" Patterson was astonished. "You sure?"

"About as sure as I can be without standing on its wing. The damn thing looks like it's flying lines on a serpentine grid. It's searching for something... but for what?"

"So what do you wanna do about it?" Patterson asked. "You wanna try to shoot it down?"

Boucher stepped out from behind his partial cover and faced Patterson.

"We can't continue to hide. We're burning daylight. If we explode the boxes now, it will still take us three or four hours to be ready to move out. The longer we wait, the higher the risk of compromise. I say we shoot the boxes now and get the hell out of here as fast as we can."

"Concur," Patterson replied.

"Billy," Boucher shouted. "Get the shot ready to go. We're going to shoot, grab the loot and run. Pass the word."

Reilly was already moving as he answered, "Roger, Boss."

Patterson and Boucher stepped out of the foliage, as did the other men, and immediately returned to the task of readying the demolition charges for firing. The Global Hawk remained above them, flying a tight racetrack pattern for nearly an hour. Boucher reasoned that if the small, unmanned reconnaissance plane was searching for him and his men, it was doing so without the permission of the Cambodian government. Otherwise, there would be manned airplanes above instead of the Global Hawk. He surmised the Global Hawk would have a slim chance of actually seeing them through the dense jungle canopy and even if it did, the reaction time between the analysis of the plane's imagery and the arrival of a response force would take hours. In a few hours it would be nightfall and he and his men would once again disappear into the jungle darkness. Only this time, they would all be very rich. All they needed was a few more hours.

Reilly pulled the men back with him as he reeled out the firing wire. They selected an area approximately one-hundred feet from the closest block where there were some large palm trees they could use for cover. Reilly returned to the det cord end and taped the blasting cap to it. He carefully twisted the blasting cap wires to the main trunk wire ends, making sure the splice was secure and then cautiously returned to the safety site with the rest of the men. He hooked the blasting machine to the firing wire after running an electrical continuity check, and handed the blasting machine to Boucher. He conducted a quick muster to ensure everyone was at the safety site and then knelt down next to Boucher.

"Ready to fire, Sir," he pronounced.

Boucher passed the blasting machine over to Patterson. "I think we owe you this one, Pat."

Patterson wrapped his meaty fingers around the trigger mechanism and yelled, "Fire in the hole!" As he squeezed, the jungle floor instantaneously erupted.

The blast was horrendously loud. Each block had been loaded with ten pounds of C-4 plastic explosive formed into a linear shape charge. The explosives performed as planned. The men were pelted by chunks of concrete as it rained down from above. The jungle above the blocks had been ripped to shreds. The sun radiated through the gaping hole in the jungle canopy as it never had before—at least not since man inhabited the planet. The smoke slowly thinned and then cleared, revealing a surface that looked more like that of the moon than something terrestrial.

"Now that's what I like," Yellowhorse roared. "The only thing better than the smell of high explosives is pussy!"

LeFever laughed nervously and shook hands with Ramirez. Boucher and Patterson stepped away from the tree they had used for cover.

"Everyone okay?" Boucher questioned.

"I need to change my tampon," Jackson said sheepishly in a falsetto voice.

Boucher laughed. "Okay Risser, I'll help you just as soon as we move the gold."

The men charged forward toward the craters. Boucher noticed one of the craters was strewn with smoldering paper and what appeared to be one-hundred dollar bills. That block was different. It did not contain gold, as all the others had. Rather, its encased plywood box contained two 20 mm. ammunition cans surrounded by one-hundred dollar bills in neatly wrapped bundles. One of the cans had been partially breeched by the explosives and its contents, along with hundreds of dollars, were strewn around the edge of the crater. The other can remained intact. Boucher saw the unmistakable "Top Secret" markings all over the strewn pages. He reached down and picked several up.

He had seen this kind of document many times during his SEAL career. The header at the top of the page read, "TOP SECRET - OPLAN 5000." The document was dated 20 February, 1954. Boucher pulled the undamaged metal box out of the crater and opened it. It contained two more volumes of OPLAN 5000 and Boucher noted that they were all dated differently. He realized at that moment that he was looking at an historical progression of updated OPLAN 5000s.

OPLAN 5000 was the detailed strategic plan for how the United States and its allies would fight World War III against the Soviet Union in the Pacific theater. It detailed how many forces would be used, what the main objectives were, and the basic order of battle. Boucher had actually only read OPLAN 5000 once, while he was deployed to Naval Special Warfare Unit One in Subic Bay in 1983. While he remembered the basic importance of the plan, he had forgotten the overarching strategy. He quickly scanned a few pages of the 1954 version of the plan.

Patterson walked up on Boucher, startling him. "Whatcha' got there, Jake?"

"I got a rich-ass flyboy sneaking up on me from behind."

Both men laughed as Patterson reached down to snatch several one hundred dollar bills strewn along the side of the crater.

"It seems we have a bunch of old war plans here, starting in 1954, leading up to 1967."

"So what are they doing in a box encased in concrete, on the same plane carrying Vietnam's gold reserves?"

"Who knows? Well, actually, those who do know are either dead or in the nuthouse suffering from Alzheimer's. Remember the old guy we visited in Florida?"

"Yeah, I remember him. James Ray, the Air America pilot. He was the guy who was supposed to fly this bird the night it went down."

"Do you remember him repeating the words 'five thousand'?"

"Yeah, I do, now that you reminded me."

"Well I figure he knew about this and was trying to tell us. I just don't understand the significance. Give me a hand recovering this stuff. I want to take a closer look when we get a moment."

Boucher and Patterson pulled the two cans that contained the plans out of the crater and set them side-by-side. Boucher counted three bound volumes perfectly intact. The fourth, a volume dated 1954, was damaged from the blast, but most of it was readable. Boucher closed the undamaged can and sat down on it, using it as a stool. He employed the other can as a reading table, laying the 1954 volume on top of it.

Patterson watched his friend before speaking.

"I'm gonna get back to work with the other guys. I'll pack up this cask. I figure we can be ready to roll out of here around dark, say... 2100."

Boucher was already absorbed in what he was reading. "Thanks Pat," he mumbled. "I'll be right with you."

Darkness was close upon them. Patterson held up an open MRE. "Jake, you hungry?"

Boucher looked up for the first time. "Jeez, this OPLAN is some really scary shit!"

Patterson smiled at his friend and asked again. "You hungry?"

"I could eat the ass out of a skunk! Thanks, Pat."

"How's beef stew...okay?"

Patterson handed him the MRE.

"Jake, we should be ready to move in about another fifty minutes."

Boucher nodded as he gulped down the MRE.

American Embassy, Bangkok, Thailand, the same time

Melvin Lewis Brown, the CIA's Chief of Station at the American Embassy in Bangkok, was being briefed in his office by his Deputy, Dwight Howe. There were two other CIA operatives in attendance, Richard Gunn and Tom Stowell. Brown, or ML as he preferred to be called, was sitting at the head of a small table. Gunn and Stowell flanked his sides. Howe was standing in front of a flat, plasma screen at the foot of the table, facing the other three men.

"Now, if you take a closer look at the overhead from the Global Hawk here," Howe indicated using a short metal pointer, "you can plainly see our subjects have cleared some foliage using explosives. Now, if we merge the radar ground mapping and LIDAR images and overlay that into a CADRG map marking the boundaries of the flight path, we get this."

Howe stepped closer to the flat screen and circled an area about six inches in diameter, as it appeared on the screen.

"Now, I'll advance the imagery by an hour and....wow! They have now cleared an area large enough for a helicopter to land and have blasted eight more craters."

Brown leaned back in his chair before speaking. "Alright Dwight. We're going to move on these guys now. Do you have any intercepts?"

"It's the darnedest thing ML. These guys are either real pros or they're real stupid. They seemed to be aware of our Hawk flying above them, but they went on working as if it didn't matter. They only communicated one time, as far as we can tell, and that was by Iridium. All they passed was that they 'have joy.' We traced the number on the receiving end and it went to a phone booth located in a small village called Thanai, a few miles west of the Thai-Vietnamese border. So far, we're at a loss to figure out the relationship."

Brown eased forward in his chair. "They sure don't seem stupid. Are these guys the same guys that Homeland and the FBI identified?"

"While we can't be one-hundred percent sure, I think we can be ninety-five percent sure they are."

Brown scowled. "Okay, can anyone tell me what their next move is going to be?"

Gunn turned toward Brown. "Sir, my guess is they're treasure hunters and are only interested in the gold. They'll take it and run."

Brown buried his head in his hands before looking over at Gunn. "We can't take that chance, Dick. If they have the plans and they put it all together, it could jeopardize national security. Hell, it could become a constitutional crisis! No!" he said pausing momentarily. "We can't risk it. Get your people and run the operation yourself. Oh... and Dick, this stays with us. No one else has a need to know."

"Got it, ML."

Gunn and Stowell stood, nodded at one another, and departed the room.

"Dwight," Brown appealed, "you know what we have to do. I'll close the loop with Cunningham at NSA."

Howe shook his head in acknowledgment and left the room, carefully closing the door behind him.

Brown returned to his desk and keyed in a number string on his STE. He watched as the LCD window on his secure phone automatically linked with a similar phone on the other end of the call. After a few seconds the display read "US GOV - Top Secret" and the secure line was established.

"Greg, its ML. We got 'em located, thanks to your help. It's my action now and time for you to look away." Brown listened intently. "Okay, read them out. Thanks Greg. Talk to you again soon."

Brown keyed a new number into his STE and waited as the secure line was established. "Admiral, Melvin Brown here. We're in motion." Brown listened. "Yes Sir," he replied. I'll keep you fully informed through codeword channels. Good day to you as well, Sir." Brown replaced the hand set on the phone and sighed. He sank back into his desk chair and sipped his coffee. *Why now, after all these years?* he thought to himself. *Why now?*

...

Forty minutes later Gunn and Stowell arrived at a small Thai military airfield located on the east side of Bangkok's city limits. This airfield better resembled a dark, rural street lined with small hangers than a runway. The largest hanger, located on the south end of the runway, had its door retracted. There were two B-105 helicopters inside the dimly lit hanger. Four heavily-armed men dressed in jungle camouflage waited nearby as the pilots and ground crews conducted their pre-flight checks. Gunn and Stowell parked their car beside the hanger and went inside, joining the four men. It was obvious they all knew one another.

"Let's do a quick equipment check and get going," Gunn ordered.

The men immediately began checking each other's equipment to ensure nothing was loose or missing. After a few minutes the hanger lights were turned off and each man checked his night vision goggles to make certain they were working properly. The ground crews towed the two B-105s outside with a riding lawnmower and untied the small helicopters from their transport platforms. The pilots started the jet engines and soon both the small helicopters had their rotors turning. The pilots gave the six men a thumbs-up and three men climbed into each helicopter. The agile B-105s rapidly disappeared into the darkness on a southeasterly heading.

CHAPTER 15

The Crash Site

The clouds thickened and gradually filled the sky above, eliminating all ambient starlight and making the night vision goggles less efficient. Boucher was now reading the OPLAN through his NVGs using the active infrared, or "IR" mode. Patterson was quietly sitting beside him, counting the hundred dollar bills in one of the cash bundles.

Boucher strained his ears to hear the faint sound of the Boeing 234's twin rotors beating the air into submission as it approached from the west, with Moss and Doyle at the controls. He checked his Rolex. The huge helicopter would be overhead in two minutes. Boucher reasoned Moss was flying at treetop level since the approaching helicopter could still not be heard clearly. He estimated they had recovered about two-hundred-twenty one-pound bars of gold bullion. He did the math in his head and roughly calculated the value at around sixty to seventy million dollars. That would sufficiently cover the expenses and still put several million in everyone's pocket—and that didn't include the cash they had found.

Boucher was jolted away from his thoughts as the Boeing 234 seemed to explode overhead without warning, clattering noisily above in ghostly silhouette. The absence of its marker lights and landing lights made it even more ominous.

Boucher yelled to Patterson, pointing at the OPLAN. "I'll tell you about it later!"

Patterson gave Boucher a thumbs-up and both men hurried over to the rest of the crew.

Moss positioned the large helicopter just above the treetops and landed it, dead center, in the clearing the men had blasted open for that purpose earlier in the day. He immediately lowered the helicopter's rear cargo ramp, keeping the engines running and rotors spinning. The men wasted no time. They quickly formed a line from the edge of the small clearing where they had pre-positioned the gold to the rear of the helicopter, and began feverishly passing the bars into the helicopter's open cargo bay as fast as they could.

It took only twenty minutes to load all the gold and cans full of cash. In the helicopter's cockpit, Moss was sitting in the left seat at the controls. Except for the dim instrument lights, the helicopter was completely dark.

Reilly took a head count as the men entered the cargo bay. Boucher was missing. He ran forward to the cockpit and shouted to Moss, "Hold for Boucher!" Moss acknowledged with a thumbs-up signal back to Reilly. Returning back to the cargo bay, Reilly sought out Patterson.

"Where the fuck is Jake?" he yelled at Patterson above the whining jet engines.

Patterson unbuckled his seat belt and made his way to the tail ramp. In the dim light, amplified a hundred-thousand times by his night vision goggles, he saw Boucher running toward the waiting helicopter, clutching the four volumes of OPLAN 5000 against his chest.

At that moment, Patterson's NVGs flashed so brightly it looked like a lightning bolt had struck the trees near the helicopter. He instantly recognized the reverberating thud from a high-explosive detonation.

Boucher fell face down and didn't move.

Reilly ran to the tail ramp and witnessed the unfolding drama. He fully realized they were under attack. He checked the open cockpit and saw Moss, turned around in his seat, looking to him for the signal to take off. Reilly held up a clenched fist signaling Moss to hold. Moss acknowledged with a nod and held up his fist so Reilly knew he understood the signal. The other SEALs had by now unbuckled their seat belts and were poised at the back of the cargo bay, guns at the ready, prepared to defend or counterattack.

Patterson ran to Boucher and rolled him over onto his back. He could see black-tinted blood oozing from Boucher's forehead above his NVGs.

A second explosion hit the treetops, well above the helicopter, on the far side of the small clearing. Patterson could hear the hot shrapnel hiss past him as he lay on top of his friend, trying to protect him from further injury. Reilly and Lavender were now at his side. The other men had set up a defensive perimeter around the rear of the helicopter.

"Come on," Reilly shouted as he and Lavender grabbed Boucher's shoulders and began to drag him toward the waiting helicopter.

Patterson grabbed the OPLANs and followed them into the helicopter. As they crossed the tail ramp, a third explosion flashed in the treetops about fifty feet behind the helicopter. Hot shrapnel hissed by, well in advance of the chunks of treetops and branches that followed. Miraculously, except for the helicopter's rear fuselage section, nothing and no one was hit.

Suddenly they appeared. Two B-105 helicopters flew overhead just above the treetops and split up as they passed by. There was no time to even take a shot. Reilly waved the order for all the men to follow him onto the helicopter. He gave Moss a thumbs-up, holding one hand out as he counted all the men. Moss rammed the helicopter's throttles to full power for a maximum performance take off. When Reilly had a firm muster count that everyone was onboard, he gave Moss a two thumbs-up signal. Moss pulled up hard on the collective, milking one-hundred-ten percent of all the horsepower the Boeing 234's powerful jet engines had available for take off.

The B-105s were now bearing down on the Boeing 234, directly in front and below them. The first of two missiles impacted the trees in front of Moss's cockpit, illuminating the jungle for a split second and spraying shrapnel fragments across the Boeing 234's nose and windshield. Moss felt a sharp jab on his left hand and knee. The second missile detonated harmlessly in the treetops about seventy-five feet to the right of the first.

The massive Boeing seemed to hesitate for a second, as if it was tensing its muscles, before making a vertical leap one-hundred feet straight up. At the top of the ascent Moss dropped the helicopter's nose and set it forward, almost putting it into the treetops.

Reilly was on the helicopter's cargo bay headphone using the intercom. "Mossman, Boucher is down. Everyone else is okay. Who the fuck is shooting at us?"

"I only got a quick glimpse, but it looks like two B-105s are attacking."

"Are they Cambodian?"

"No, I don't think so! They don't have any ID markings. I don't know where they came from!"

"Can you get us out of here?"

"I can if I can lose them. I don't think they have guns. All I saw were rockets on their pylons. I'll keep the top of the tail ramp open for you. If you guys get a shot, take it and hold the fuck on!"

"Roger!"

Patterson was sitting on the cargo bay's metal deck, supporting Boucher's upper body on his lap. Dick Llina was putting a compress bandage over Boucher's head while trying to keep from being thrown against the helicopter's bulkhead from Moss's radical maneuvering.

Fortunately, Moss and Boucher had planned for the worst and had secured four heavily-constructed, large, wooden crates to the cargo deck. Those boxes now contained the gold and cash.

Moss was flying a roller coaster-like track, doing everything he could to evade the smaller, more agile B-105s that were in hot pursuit. The B-105s remained far enough behind to remain out of effective small arms range, but still close enough to maintain visual contact and missile range.

Patterson slipped on an intercom head set. "Mossman, this is Patterson. Boucher took some frag in the temple. He's conscious. We got the bleeding stopped. Doesn't appear to be life-threatening, but he might need medical care. What's your status?"

"Got power, got gas! Don't see how these guys behind us are going to last much longer. They don't have the legs. If we can keep 'em off us just a little longer we're gonna be home free."

"Roger. Reilly and the boys are taking shots every opportunity they get, but they're staying on the limits of our rifle range."

"Roger. Hold 'em off as long as you can!"

As Moss crossed the tree line of the Mekong River, he dove the powerful, twin-rotor helicopter toward the water, ninety feet below, just as the lead B-105 fired a rocket. The warhead detonated in the treetops slightly above and behind them, spewing hot shell fragments across the rear fuselage and engine housing.

Boucher suddenly clutched Patterson and pulled himself up next to the crate beside him. He yanked his NVGs back over his eyes. He quickly glanced back at his three men laying on the tail ramp, trying to get a shot at the pursuing B-105s, then at the cash in the open crate. He grabbed as many bundles of the one-hundred dollar bills as he could hold, tore off the paper bands binding them together, then rushed toward the open tail ramp.

"Fod! Fod!" he shouted.

Patterson immediately understood. He pressed the intercom mic against his lips. "Mossman, we're gonna chaff on my mark, be ready to do something really brilliant!"

"Roger. Got a bend in the river coming up just ahead."

Patterson clasped Boucher's shoulder and held on to him. "Mossman, in three, two, one, mark."

As Boucher threw his armful of cash out of the open tail ramp into the wind stream, Moss banked right so hard that his rotor tips barely missed the water below. Boucher was nearly thrown out of the helicopter by Moss's maneuver, but Patterson somehow held on to him. The B-105 boldly sped past the open cargo ramp, trying to avoid the cloud of one-hundred dollar bills cluttering the air in front of him. Reilly, Lavender, Jackson and LeFever opened fire, spewing several deadly strings of their AK-47 armor-piercing bullets into the side of the B-105.

The B-105 rose slightly skyward, then pitched down into a death spiral, crashing into the river at over one-hundred knots. There wasn't even an explosion. The small helicopter just disappeared in a splash, triggering a resounding geyser that briefly plumed upward. The B-105 was gone without a trace.

The second B-105 broke off and headed toward the crash site. Moss was now flying about twenty feet above the water at one-hundred-forty knots. With Patterson's help, Boucher stumbled forward toward the cockpit and put on an intercom headset.

"Mossman," he growled. "Status?"

"We're thirty out from Point Echo. Got enough gas to make it, but I'm getting some fluctuations in hydraulic pressure. Might have taken a frag hit back there on one of the lines. I'll keep us flying as long as I can. Probably need to climb some, just in case I need the extra reaction time."

"Do whatever it takes!"

"Hey, old buddy?" Moss asked. "You alright?"

"Not bad for a Monday...considering the alternative. Keep me updated, Mossman. I'm going aft."

"Roger that!"

Boucher and Patterson returned to the helicopter cargo bay.

"Let's button up and go red," Boucher said to Patterson.

Patterson switched on the helicopter's interior red lights. This was the first artificial light the men had seen in days. Boucher signaled his men on the tail ramp to move back inside. Patterson hit the switch and lowered the tailgate's top half, closing the gaping rear end of the Boeing 234. Boucher pulled off his NVGs, as did the rest of his men. He looked around admiringly at his tired men. Smiling, he gave them a thumbs-up. One by one they all returned the gesture and began to relax. It had been a long forty hours. It would not be much longer now. They would land, refuel, and disappear once again into the night.

Suddenly the helicopter lurched, nearly throwing Boucher onto the deck.

Moss's voice blared through the intercom. "We're losing hydraulic pressure!"

"How long?" Boucher demanded.

"Five minutes, maybe less," Moss calmly replied.

"Can you make Point Echo?"

"Got an island in sight up ahead. Doesn't look inhabited."

"No, Mossman, Point Echo." Boucher calmly insisted.

Everyone's eyes were now on Boucher.

"Ahh, the navigation computer says we still have nine miles. You want to risk it?"

"If it can be done, you can do it, Mossman."

"Okay, here we go!"

Boucher surveyed his men. All eyes were glued on him. "Strap in! We're going down!"

Everyone quickly buckled in and prepared for the worst. Moss climbed slightly and slowed the helicopter's forward speed.

Moss opened his mic again. "Jake, we're five out. Hydraulic pressure is almost off the gauge. I'm doing my damnedest to wrestle the controls!"

"You can do it, Mossman!"

"Three out. I'm losing it! Controls are going!"

"Mossman, you remember when you pulled my ass out of that hot LZ during Tet?"

"Yeah, dumbest thing I ever did. Kinda like now! One out. Open the tail just in case we splash and you gotta get out fast."

"Come on Mossman, you can keep this thing flying."

Patterson flicked the switch on the tail ramp control box next to his seat and opened the top half of the tail ramp.

"Got the LZ in sight," Moss reported. "Aww shit! Chip light! We're going down!"

The helicopter lurched upward briefly as Moss traded air speed for position. Boucher and the men could hear a loud *thunk* that was accompanied by the shuddering of the helicopter's entire airframe as Moss disengaged the engines from the transmission. Next he shut down the engines as he prepared to auto-rotate the truculent, heavily-loaded helicopter into a safe landing. Moss skillfully allowed the Boeing 234 to descend faster than normal before yanking back on the stick. For Boucher and his men in the cargo bay, this sensation was like riding an elevator down from a tall building and feeling it rapidly decelerate at the last moment. Moss held the heavy helicopter in a momentary hover before it slammed into the ground several feet below.

"Wow!" Moss yelled into the intercom. "Cheated death again! Survived another controlled crash! Son of a bitch, we made it to Echo!"

Boucher unbuckled and stood. His men followed.

"Wait for the rotors to stop spinning before we debark," Boucher shouted. "When you hit that hard they can sometimes break off while they're winding down and if you happen to be standing under one of 'em, it's really bad for your health."

The pungent smell of hot hydraulic fluid mixed with jet exhaust filled the cargo area. Everyone knew they had been lucky.

Moss remained in his seat, slowly unbuckling his safety harness.

"Dick, go see how Mossman is," Boucher commanded.

Llina grabbed his medical kit and went to Moss's side. After a quick examination of his two wounds, Llina returned to the cargo bay with Moss a few steps behind.

"Frag wounds, Boss. I dug one out of his shin. The one that hit him in the shoulder sliced clean through. I put a butterfly on it. He'll be fine as long as we can prevent infection. How's your head, Commander?"

Boucher put his hand on Llina's shoulder in reassurance.

"I'm fine. Just another knock on the head. Thanks Dick, you're still the best corpsman the Teams ever had."

It was still three hours before first light. Boucher opened the side door and stood peering out through his NVGs. He could see a rusty, old, fuel truck parked on the north edge of the tree line and a small, tin-sided building on the east side. There were no lights. This was nothing more than a clearing in the jungle next to the Mekong River with a narrow asphalt airstrip that paralleled the river's shore. They had chosen this field as a refuel point precisely because it was remote and just inside the Vietnamese border. Moss joined Boucher as the other men stepped off the helicopter.

"Alright everyone," Boucher said as the men gathered around him. "We're on the ground safely, thanks to Mossman. The helo is tits up, so we need to think through this and weigh our options to get out of here. Mojo, I want you to take a look at the boat option. Pat and Mossman, I want you to take a look at the air option. Billy, I need you to look at the land option. Thane and Johnny, you guys check out the E and E route. Everyone else, find cover and set up a security perimeter. We still have a few hours of night left and we need to take advantage of it while it lasts. We'll brief here, in the back of the chopper, in one hour. Let's go to work."

American Embassy, Bangkok, Thailand

Dwight Howe entered the Chief of Station's office with Richard Gunn following closely behind. Brown swiveled away from his desk to face the two men now standing on his right side.

"What the fuck went wrong?" he angrily demanded as he leaned toward Howe. "You were supposed to stop them and recover what they found! Your rules of engagement did not include getting into an aerial dogfight with them! Damn it! I ought to…"

Howe interrupted Brown in mid-sentence. "They splashed Stowell's bird in the river."

"And Stowell? Is he…?"

"Yes," Gunn replied faintly. "We broke off the chase and returned to the crash site. Couldn't find anything but an oil slick."

Brown angrily stood up as he spoke. "But I thought you said their helicopter wasn't armed?"

Gunn shook his head, "It wasn't."

"Then how the fuck did they out-fly and out-shoot your two birds?"

"Stowell got a little too close and they took advantage of it."

"Stowell got too close and they took advantage of two armed helicopters? You gotta be shitting me! We now have a bird down and some American bodies on the bottom of a fucking river in a country we had no permission to overfly! This is a damn mess! Dwight, I need you to personally develop a cover story that will hold up. I don't need this kind of shit to deal with!"

Howe straightened his posture before replying. "Yes Sir, right away Sir."

"And you, Mr. Gunn. You find out where that bogie helo you were chasing landed. I want those guys stopped—now more than ever. And I want what they recovered from that jungle crash site even more! Now get on it!"

Gunn nodded without saying anything as both he and Howe hurried to the door.

"One more thing, Dwight!" Brown demanded.

Howe cringed as he stopped short of the door, already knowing what Brown was about to say. He held up an open hand and closed his eyes as if to fend off the oncoming words as Brown angrily unleashed the warning.

"You better not fuck this up!"

CHAPTER 16

Point Echo, Vietnam

Y ou know what, Jake?" Patterson casually asked.

"What?"

"It's almost poetic justice that a bunch of old broke dicks like us are sitting here in a situation like this. We made it through Tet and a whole lot more after that, only to almost pull off the biggest operation we ever dreamed of. We got the gold like we planned and beat the odds, only to end up with a helicopter that's tits up and no way to haul off the loot."

Boucher slapped his old friend on the shoulder. "Maybe, but we still all have each other and that's what it's still all about."

"Yeah, you're right. How's your head doing?"

"Shit. Might have knocked some sense into me."

Both men chuckled.

"Hey Pat, look across the river. What do you see?"

"I see a bamboo pier and...holy shit! ...a plane!"

"Yeah, that's what I see too."

"Can you make out what kind of airplane it is?"

Patterson squinted into the darkness. "Jeez Jake, it looks like an old Grumman Albatross. I knew a few of them were still flying in the Caribbean, but I didn't think they were still being used over here."

"Okay. Since I'm not a flyboy, I have to ask the obvious question. What the fuck is a Grumman Albatross? I figure it's probably just another excuse for you flyboys to put a metal stick between your legs to make up for your lack of a real stick. Right?"

"You know dickhead, your metal stick joke is getting really old," Patterson scowled. "Anyway, as I remember, they were built in the late forties for the Navy as a patrol and rescue airplane. You know, they could land on the water and rescue us flyboys who got shot down trying to protect you dumbass ground guys. They were used extensively in Vietnam because they were amphibious. I'm surprised you never saw one during your deployments."

"Well I didn't, and SEALs aren't ground forces! Guess they weren't flying them much after dark, huh?"

Using his index finger, Patterson marked an imaginary score card and made the shape of a large number one.

"Okay snake eater, you got me on that one. So maybe we're looking at a sky fossil, but if it's flyable it could easily carry all of our bounty and us out of here. The Albatross was designed to be a kick-ass cargo hauler and long-range patrol plane. Maybe it will still fly. Maybe it won't. Depends on its condition. What do you want me to do?"

Boucher sat back and momentarily contemplated what Patterson had just told him. "Check it out and see if it can still fly. Take Mossman with you, swim over there and stay in radio contact. I want to know if someone farts on that side of the river. Got it?"

Patterson smiled back at his old friend. "Roger, Commander. By the way, are there sharks in this river?"

"Sharks? Pat, you are still an astonishing moron! The river is fresh water, dumbass! Sharks don't live in freshwater. They live in the ocean. So there ain't no friggin' sharks. Just probably a few crocodiles and snakes for sure. Probably some big-ass fucking snakes!"

Patterson smiled and went in search of Moss.

"I fucking hate snakes," Boucher muttered as he turned away and began walking back towards the helicopter.

By the way, Pat," Boucher growled back at his friend, "do you think you could fly that bird out-a-here?"

Patterson stopped with his back to Boucher.

"Does Wonder Woman have tits of iron? It has wings, not rotors, remember? Besides, if I can't fly it, Mossman or Jack probably can."

An hour later the men assembled in the helicopter's cargo bay for Boucher's briefing. Boucher switched on the red interior lights revealing a ragtag group of very tired, but determined men.

"Alright, here's the situation," Boucher began. "We're at Point Echo, about sixteen miles southwest of the C-130's crash site we left earlier. Somebody doesn't like us and they have some pretty darn high-tech capabilities. They're not indigenous, that's for sure. Our helo is tango uniform and down hard. We need an alternate means to get all of us out with as much of the gold and cash as we can bring along. Okay Mojo, what do you got?"

Lavender inserted a fresh dip of snuff between his lip and gum before replying to Boucher's question. "I got a motorized sampan about two hundred yards up river. It's big enough to carry all of us, but not our loot. It has two ten-gallon gas tanks and both are full. Probably give us a range of three or four hours. I figure ten knots max speed, so maybe thirty or forty miles."

Boucher nodded. "Thanks Mojo. Billy, what's the E and E picture look like?"

The ever stern, always professional Reilly began by holding up two fingers. "We have several options for escape and evasion, but only two seem reasonable. First and foremost, don't think we're safe just because we're not in Cambodia. If we get caught here in Vietnam, we're looking at a trial and probably some jail time and that's if they don't shoot us first. That said, we can E and E as a group with a larger detection signature, or we can split up into smaller elements and go out separately in twos and threes to reduce our signature. We carry out what loot we can on our backs."

Boucher frowned. "Billy, what are your proposed routes?"

"I think the overland option across Cambodia is the highest risk and it will take the longest. I think we should look at Mojo's sampan as a way out first. We follow the river as far as we can, then we make a run for it overland toward Thailand, further down the river."

Yellowhorse suddenly appeared from the darkness at the open tail ramp with a man and women in tow whom he had blindfolded and bound.

"Hey boss, these two were walking along the runway and would have compromised us."

Boucher walked back to Johnny and looked at the two trembling prisoners. "Jeez, just what we fucking don't need!"

Yellowhorse pulled his Emerson folding knife from his hip pocket and snapped the razor sharp blade open with a quick twist of his wrist. "What do you want me to do with them?"

Boucher shook his head no. "Put your knife away, Johnny. We're not going to hurt them. Put them in the chopper's cockpit and tie them into the seats."

Suddenly Boucher's radio crackled with a friendly voice. "Jake, you read me?"

"Yeah, hear you lima charlie. Go."

"Jake, we're onboard the plane and it looks airworthy. I opened both wing fuel tank caps and they look nearly full. There isn't anyone around. Everyone's in their hooch sleeping. You want me and Mossman to give it a try starting her up?"

"Hold what you got, Pat. I want to consult with the others."

"Roger. Standing by."

Boucher looked around the small cargo bay and into the eyes of each of his men, one at a time. Each nodded their consent. No one spoke because they all knew what they had to do.

"Alrighty then," Boucher said aloud, smiling. Raising the radio's handset to his mouth, he pushed the transmit button and spoke into the mic. "Pat, can you and Mossman paddle the plane away from the shore and get her out into the river?"

There was a pause and some radio static before Patterson answered. "I suppose so."

"Then I want you to get her out into the river as far as you can. I'm gonna have Mojo come and get you in a sampan and tow you over here. We'll beach the boat and use it as a pier to load the plane."

"Roger, WILCO, out."

Boucher squinted through the small cargo bay fuselage window toward the river, attempting to collect his thoughts before turning back to his men.

"Okay, it's worth a try and it seems to be our best option. Anyone disagree?" He paused, allowing a moment for any objections. "Alright, Mojo, take Dick with you and get the sampan. You know what to do. Put it in here, bow first, hard in the mud. We'll use it as a pier for the plane. As soon as the boat arrives, we'll begin loading it with the loot and transfer everything we can over to the plane. Billy, see if you can get that old fuel truck started. We'll use it to tow the helo over to water's edge so we don't have to carry the gold as far. It will speed up the transfer. If we get any visitors, we'll deal with it as best we can. Keep your weapons handy, but only engage as a last resort. I know we're all running on adrenaline, but there is no other way. We need to be out of here by daylight. Any questions?"

There were no questions. The men all snapped to their various tasks without hesitation. Only a few minutes had passed when Boucher heard the fuel truck's engine crank over a few times and spring to life. Reilly backed the truck up to the front end of the helicopter, where Yellowhorse and LeFever attached a chain bridle to the helo's front landing gear and shackled it to the truck's rear bumper. Reilly shifted the truck into low range and slowly towed the heavy helicopter along the narrow, asphalt runway toward the river shore. As the truck reached the closest possible point to the water's edge without getting stuck, Reilly skillfully turned away so the helicopter's tail ramp was facing the water. A few minutes later, Boucher heard the sampan's motor approaching from down river. Standing on the helo's open tail ramp, he strained to see the white froth of the boat's bow wake and the advancing ghostly silhouette of the seaplane lashed next to it.

Mojo was towing the plane by its starboard pontoon that he had secured along the boat's port side. This gave him excellent maneuverability and kept the plane in his total control. Mojo turned the boat and plane toward the riverbank, directly behind the helo's open cargo ramp. Running at full speed, Mojo rammed the bow of the boat into the soft mud of the river bank leaving only a distance of about twenty feet between the back of the helo and the boat. The rest of the men immediately formed a daisy chain between the boat and the helo and began passing the gold bars to the boat. From the boat, the bars were handed inside the plane through its open side cargo door. Inside, Mojo and Jackson stacked them on the deck along the plane's cargo area. Moss and Patterson began meticulously examining the plane's engines and navigation instruments.

The men had been working feverishly for several hours. Boucher was inside the helo's cargo bay unloading the last of the heavy, wooden crates when he heard the Albatross's first engine sputter, then start. The second engine followed shortly behind. Boucher thought to himself, *The cat's out of the bag now!* He'd hoped that they would have the time to load all of the gold onto the waiting plane before daylight, but it was not meant to be. There were still several gold bars left in the bottom of the crate and first light was upon them. Reilly appeared on the helo's tail ramp behind Boucher.

"It's time to go, Boss," Reilly urged. "Minutes count and daylight is not our friend."

"Yeah, you're right, Billy. Give me a hand with the rest of the cash and we're out of here. We'll leave the rest of the gold here for our two friends in the cockpit."

Reilly and Boucher passed the last of the cash-loaded backpacks outside and followed. Boucher stopped on the tail ramp for a second, then ran back inside the now empty cargo area up to the cockpit. First he cut the bonds holding the man, then he returned outside carrying the four OPLAN 5000 volumes in his arms. Reilly reached down and grabbed a handful of Boucher's shirt, helping him balance as he climbed into the awaiting Albatross. Boucher glanced forward into the airplane's cockpit and saw that Patterson and Moss were manning the pilot and co-pilot seats.

Boucher made his way through the cramped plane, stepping over gold and men to the cockpit. "Will this thing fly?" he yelled over the engine noise.

Moss turned toward Boucher with one of his characteristic "give-a-shit" grins plastered on his face. "Got gas, got engines, got balls...I reckon we're gonna find out."

Even though he knew that Moss had been a risk-taker his entire life, Boucher couldn't help but wonder how he had lived this long. He figured that Moss was either just the luckiest man on the planet, or he was just so damn good he made his own luck. Either way, Boucher was thankful the gifted pilot was on the team.

Moss shouted one final comment to Boucher as Patterson revved the plane's two powerful Wright 1820-76 main engines to full power and cycled the propellers to check hydraulic pressure.

"Didn't exactly have time to do a weight and balance on this load. Hope we got it all at the right spot or we're gonna nosedive into the river. Tried to load her keeping the floats level in the water. I guess it oughta be close enough. Hold on!" Moss flippantly directed.

Patterson slapped Moss on the leg and the two pilots taxied the heavily laden plane out into the middle of the river. Patterson brought the engines up to full power and the plane began to sluggishly pick up speed. Boucher watched as Patterson held the plane's nose level, enabling it to gather speed.

Moss was calling out the air speed. "Forty-five, fifty, fifty-five, sixty, sixty-five. Rotate, rotate."

Patterson pulled back on the yoke with both hands, but the heavy plane didn't leave the water.

"Son-of-a...we're so damn heavy we can't break suction!" Patterson yelled over at Moss.

"You see that boat up ahead?" Moss yelled above the engine noise.

Patterson nodded his head yes.

"Run up his wake and rotate when you cross his stern wave. We'll bounce this tired old bitch into the sky! I'll give you some help on the yoke."

Patterson turned the plane's heading a few degrees to the left and aimed the nose right at a sampan crossing the river about a quarter of a mile ahead of the plane. Once again, the plane began to build speed as he continually corrected the heading so that the plane would pass just behind the sampan where the boat's wake would be largest.

To the two unsuspecting people in the sampan it looked like the plane was going to drive right into them. They panicked as it approached and turned the sampan down river in an attempt to avoid what seemed to them to be an imminent collision. When they saw that the plane continued toward them they dove over the side, leaving the sampan's engine at full throttle and no one steering the rudderpost. The sampan began a slow, arcing left turn.

"We gotta hit that boat wake. Stay left!" Moss shouted over at Patterson.

"Yeah, but he's turning left! We're gonna hit'em!" Patterson shouted back.

"No we're not! We're gonna pass right behind him and bounce this bucket of bolts into the air! The wind line will be perfect. Stay with it!"

The sampan continued to slowly turn back toward the oncoming Albatross. Patterson kept adjusting the plane's course so it would pass just astern of the sampan.

Moss was again calling out the air speed with an eerie calm in his voice. "Fifty, fifty-five, sixty, and sixty-five."

Boucher glanced out the windshield and all he could see was the blur of an approaching sampan. Collision was imminent. Moss had his left hand behind the plane's two throttles, blocking any motion by Patterson that would retard them. Moss's right hand was lightly gripping the plane's yoke, just in case Patterson needed his help. The plane was now only yards from the sampan and it looked like they were going to plow straight into it.

"Stay with it, Pat!" Moss shouted. "You're line is perfect!"

Boucher closed his eyes as Moss shouted, "Rotate! Rotate! Rotate!"

Both men pulled back on the plane's yoke at the moment the plane crossed the sampan's stern, barely missing the boat by inches. The plane lurched upward into the air a few yards above the water. Patterson pushed the yoke forward, slightly dropping the plane's nose to take advantage of the ground effect and build air speed.

Moss turned toward Patterson shouting with delight, "Now that's what I'm talkin' about! There's pilots and there's sky gods! Yeeeehaaaaa!"

Boucher opened his eyes and blew out a slow breath as relief flooded over him. Patterson followed down the river for several miles holding the plane at treetop level, then began climbing several hundred feet and turning on a southwesterly heading back into Cambodian airspace.

The sun's red glow was just now reflecting along the edges of rain clouds in the eastern sky. Ahead, the sky was still black. Large raindrops were beginning to pelt the cockpit windshield. The cloud bottoms were only a few hundred feet above the plane.

"Check it out," Moss yelled, smiling back towards Boucher. "Another shitty day in paradise."

Boucher leaned forward, slapping both Patterson and Moss on the shoulder. "Just keep us flying."

AWACS – call sign Bull Dog, Gulf of Thailand, the same time

"Crimson Sky this is Bulldog, authenticate bravo six two fife, over."

"Bulldog, Crimson Sky, authenticate as zebra three fife one, report over."

"Crimson Sky, authentication positive. Bogie in sector fife heading two zero niner at two-hundred feet. Speed niner zero knots. Range two-hundred miles. Designated as target Delta Two. Over."

"Bulldog, Crimson Sky, copy Delta Two. We hold target on our screen. Good job, Bulldog. Maintain Delta Two over-watch as first priority."

"Bulldog, roger out."

CHAPTER 17

Onboard the Albatross

About two hours had passed and the melodious drone of the plane's twin engines had taken its toll on the tired men. Everyone was asleep except Patterson, who was at the controls fighting to remain alert. Mossman was slumped slightly forward in his seat, only restrained from falling into the control yoke by his seat harness. Suddenly a warning horn that was located above the cockpit instrument panel blasted loudly, providing an abrupt adrenaline rush for Patterson, Moss and Boucher. Had his seat safety harness not restrained him, Moss would have leapt out of his seat. Boucher went from a dreamy sleep to complete readiness in a fraction of a second. Both Patterson and Moss were now wide awake and frantically checking the instrument clusters in front of them to determine what the problem was.

"Not again!" Moss yelled over the noisy cockpit as he pointed to a temperature gauge on the panel before him. "Number two is overheating!"

Patterson leaned forward and peered through the cockpit side window at the engine above the right wing.

"Mossman, can you see smoke?"

Moss strained forward, trying to see.

"No, it looks fine," he shouted back.

A second warning light began to flash.

"Low oil pressure on number two engine. How close are we to Point Charlie?" Patterson shouted.

Boucher leaned forward between Patterson and Moss and watched Moss quickly transcribe the lat/long numbers off the antiquated navigation computer onto a chart. Drawing a line from that point to a small island about a half an inch straight ahead of their current position, he crudely folded the map's scale up beside the line he had just scribed. Holding it up for Boucher and Patterson to see, he shouted, "About twelve miles to Point Charlie."

Patterson patted the Albatross' dash as if it was a live pet. "Come on, old gal. Don't quit on us now."

Moss watched as the oil temperature gauge for number two engine continued to climb at an alarming rate.

"We're gonna have to feather number two before it catches on fire," Moss called over to Patterson.

"Roger."

Moss reached for number two throttle and pulled it back. The plane lurched violently to the left, but Patterson quickly countered the movement with a hard push on the rudder pedal that corrected the plane's course. Patterson carefully pushed the number one throttle forward, increasing power to number one engine to help maintain the plane's altitude. Even so, the old plane was so heavily loaded that it almost immediately began to gradually lose altitude.

"This can't be a good thing," Boucher proclaimed.

Suddenly the plane was over water. *Lots* of water. Boucher could make out a small island far ahead, barely visible on the horizon. He quickly estimated the distance to the island and compared it to the crippled plane's rate of descent. He realized they would fall short; probably several miles short.

Patterson tapped the gauges on the instrument panel cluster, again focusing on the oil pressure gauge on engine one. It seemed to be holding steady, even though the engine temperature was slowly rising. Moss sat coolly as he searched the sky around the plane for other aircraft. He would occasionally look inward and scan the instruments, then return his complete attention outside.

Boucher couldn't fight the temptation to ask any longer. He had to know. "Mossman," he shouted, "are we gonna make the island?"

Moss smiled without answering and continued scanning the sky forward and above the plane.

"Damn it, Mossman, are we gonna make the island?"

Moss cocked his head slightly in the direction of his friend. "Not in the air," he responded impassively.

Boucher pinched Moss's left shoulder in a powerful grip. "What the hell does that mean?"

Moss, still smiling, turned toward Boucher. "Relax, Jake. This here is a seaplane, remember?"

Boucher rolled his eyes and sat back with a growl.

The plane continued its gradual descent toward the small island, now looming several miles ahead. Boucher stared down, studying the sea below. The water seemed relatively calm and appeared to be a deep sapphire blue with occasional patches of whitish-green. He reasoned that it was deep enough to support a safe landing and there were no shoals to run aground on, but that didn't help to relieve his anxiety.

Patterson pulled out the landing checklist and waved it in front of Moss. "It's in English."

"Okay, Pat, let's get this old gal ready to go swimming."

Moss began running down the landing checklist.

Boucher estimated their altitude was about twelve-hundred feet when the low oil pressure warning horn sounded. Surprisingly, neither Patterson nor

Moss seemed very concerned. He watched as Patterson tapped the throttle back on engine one, slowly reducing its RPMs. Then he ran the plane's flaps down twenty percent. At the same time, Moss was rolling the trim wheel forward to keep the plane's nose at the proper angle so it wouldn't stall. The heavily-laden plane was now on a steep, thirty-degree, nose-down glide slope. Boucher nervously watched the altimeter unwind as the plane plummeted toward the water.

Boucher had experienced the sensation known as "ground rush" numerous times during his SEAL Team career while HALO jumping. He flashed back on one particular hair-raising parachute jump with Johnny Yellowhorse. High-altitude, low-opening jumps (HALO) are designed for tactical insertion. The SEALs typically jump from an altitude of fifteen-thousand feet or higher and freefall to a parachute opening altitude of twelve-hundred feet. This minimizes the chances of being detected by a ground observer and reduces the SEAL's vulnerability to ground fire, if detected, because they are only under their parachute canopy for a few minutes.

But the training jump Boucher remembered nearly killed both him and Yellowhorse. The SEAL platoon left the tail ramp of an Air Force Special Operations MC-130E, cruising at twelve-thousand feet above a small drop zone named "Canary" at Camp Lejune Marine Corps Base in North Carolina. The DZ was so named because it was just slightly larger than a football field and surrounded by 80-foot tall southern pine trees. Boucher and Yellowhorse were practicing relative work and quickly joined hands after getting stable. They were perfecting a stable vertical descent while wearing full combat equipment–not easy. The rest of Boucher's twelve-man platoon joined around them, using him and Yellowhorse as the base of the falling formation. Even in a daylight jump of this type it is somewhat difficult to perform this maneuver successfully because the combat equipment the SEALs wear is cumbersome, especially when falling at a velocity of one-hundred-twenty miles per hour.

This particular jump went well until the breakaway. At around three-thousand feet, the SEALs at the outside of the formation let go and began to track away from the others. This opened the configuration and reduced the chances of someone colliding with someone else's parachute during opening. As the formation opened, the plan was to have Boucher and Yellowhorse open their chutes first to be followed by those around them. This technique kept all the SEALs at roughly the same altitude when they opened, but vertically spaced a few hundred feet apart to reduce the chances of collision. From there, using their steerable, para-commander parachutes, they would remain in close proximity all the way to landing. Once on the ground they would hide their chutes and patrol to the objective.

The falling formation separated as planned. Yellowhorse and Boucher nodded and Yellowhorse pulled his ripcord and disappeared. Boucher waited for a moment and pulled his ripcord, but nothing happened. He rolled his right shoulder forward and peered backwards to see his pilot chute flapping a few feet above on its tether, but it wasn't pulling the main chute into the wind stream. He glanced back at the ground, which he was now rushing toward at a velocity of one-hundred-twenty miles per hour. At an altitude of twelve-hundred feet, he was dangerously low. He rolled sideways in an effort to allow the wind stream to grab the pilot chute, but the maneuver didn't work. At this point he only had one option and that was to first release the two capewells on his shoulder harness that fastened his main parachute to his harness, and to then deploy his reserve parachute which was worn in front, low on the chest. He deliberately put himself into a feet-down fall, released the capewells, and pulled his reserve parachute.

He was now at about eight-hundred feet and had no time to slow his descent velocity before opening his parachute. The last thing he saw was the ground rushing up at him. He yanked the rip cord, and then he saw stars.

The opening shock of his reserve parachute was so severe that it felt like a truck had hit him. He was dazed, but understood he was now sitting under a perfectly good twenty-four-foot-diameter, reserve parachute canopy. His life had been spared, but the ride was not over. The reserve parachute was not designed to give its user a soft landing, especially if he was heavily laden with combat equipment. It was only designed to save the user's life. It had done its job.

This was the first time Boucher ever had to actually use his reserve parachute. He knew from the stories he had heard from his fellow SEALs that the landing was going to be painful. As he oscillated to and fro, he unsuccessfully tried to slip the canopy toward the small DZ and miss the eighty-foot-high pine trees that bordered it. But it was not meant to be. He drifted with the wind into the top of a pine tree, landing squarely in the middle of its top branches. His equipment immediately snagged on the branches and there he hung, upside down, eighty feet above the ground as the parachute canopy gently collapsed over the entire treetop.

The rest of his platoon landed on the drop zone as planned and soon rallied beneath the tree where Boucher was hanging. They quickly got the tree-landing rescue equipment and Yellowhorse strapped on a pair of lineman's pole climbers. Boucher recalled that it took Yellowhorse nearly half an hour to climb the tree and cut him free. Then there was the ribbing he took from his men who lay on the ground below, telling jokes and yelling insults as they watched Yellowhorse rescue their helpless boss.

Boucher realized he was smiling as his attention flashed back to the present. It was ground rush all over again, only this time he couldn't pull a reserve parachute. Strangely enough, he didn't feel any panic. Patterson and Moss were calmly working their piloting magic and were in control. Boucher turned to peer back at his men. Some were still asleep. Those who were not were calmly sitting there, courageously ready to react to whatever situation they were handed. After all these years, Boucher was still just as proud of these men as ever.

Glancing forward again, it looked as if the plane was going to nose dive into the sea. Patterson pulled the control yoke backward, skillfully bringing the nose up into a flair for landing. Boucher could feel the plane's air speed bleed off as it leveled and slowly pitched nose upward. The plane seemed to float on a sponge, just above the water, for an abnormally long time. Then it settled into the sea with a gentle surge forward before being captured by the surrounding water. The sensation was like an amusement park water slide ride when the boat hits the water at the bottom of the flume.

Moss let out one of his famous "yeehaaa" howls and slapped Patterson on the shoulder. "Now that's some great flying!"

Patterson merely smiled as he quickly powered up the engine and steered the plane toward the island, about a mile and a half ahead. "Hey Jake, where you want this thing parked?"

Boucher turned the chart he was holding toward Patterson and Moss so they could see it. "Put her in this cove around the east side," he said pointing to a spot on the chart.

"Roger that," Moss replied as he took the chart and held it up in front of Patterson.

The lumbering Albatross plowed through the rolling sea toward the cove, occasionally dipping deep into a swell. Moss pointed toward the island that was growing ever closer. "Hey Pat, you see the cove over there?"

"Yeah, I got it."

"Okay. I'll spot for you. Let's take her in."

The cove had a narrow entrance that was protected by a shallow coral reef. Waves lapped at the reef from the seaward side, occasionally washing over the top of it and surging into the cove. Patterson guided the plane around the reef's left edge and then skillfully turned a hard left, putting the plane's nose directly in line with the middle of the channel leading into the cove. The entrance was so narrow that Boucher thought each wing would scrape the rocky beach. Moss was leaning forward in his seat keeping a close eye on the plane's wing tips.

"Come about six feet to the right, Pat," Moss calmly advised.

Patterson nodded and made the delicate course change.

"Good. Looking good!" Moss encouraged. "Over there Pat, next to the pier," he said pointing twenty degrees to the right.

"Got it. I'll put us nose in."

Boucher sat quietly watching as Patterson pulled the power back and slowed the plane, turning it toward a small motor-sail junk tied to a dilapidated bamboo fishing pier. Patterson steered the plane toward a sandy beach area at the foot of the pier that gently sloped up out of the water like a ramp. When he was lined up perfectly with the ramping beach, he ran the throttle up to full power. The plane surged forward with a slight burst of speed. Just prior to hitting the beach, Patterson pulled the plane's nose up like he was taking off. The plane skidded up the sandy beach and came to a resounding halt as its belly lodged in the soft sand. Moss quickly killed the engine. There was dead silence. For more than a minute no one spoke, or even moved.

Boucher leisurely unhooked his seat belt.

"Thanks Pat!" he exclaimed, slapping both Patterson and Moss on the shoulder. "Okay guys," he said in a commanding voice as he turned rearward, "let's get off this plane and see what Haus has for us to eat."

The SEALs opened the rear side door and slowly disembarked the plane, assembling on the white, sandy beach beside the wing. Boucher, Patterson and Moss were the last to appear.

The other men turned and began applauding and chanting, "Hooyah! Hooyah! Hooyah!"

Boucher flashed a wide grin and raised his hands to silence them. "Okay guys, thanks, but we're not home yet and we have work to do. For a starter, let's get some camouflage on top of the plane."

AWACS Bull Dog, Gulf of Thailand, the same time

"Crimson Sky, this is Bulldog, authenticate lima two fife two, over."

"Bulldog, Crimson Sky, authenticate as gulf fife one niner, report over."

"Crimson Sky, authentication positive. Delta Two target in sector four has landed. Current position is lima alfa tango, one fife two one six three, lima oscar gulf zero one eight six six niner. Over."

"Bulldog, Crimson Sky. Copy lima alfa tango one fife two one six three, lima oscar gulf zero one eight six six niner. Well done, Bulldog. Interrogative, can you get a visual without compromise?"

"Crimson Sky, Bulldog. Unknown. Will attempt visual."

"Bulldog, Crimson Sky. Maintain surveillance of Delta Two until relieved. Under no circumstances can you be detected by Delta Two.

"Bulldog, roger out."

In the AWACS's cockpit, Pilot in Command, Lieutenant Colonel Kratzenberg, sipped from a cup of hot coffee he had just been handed.

"Pilot," the Electronic Warfare Officer reported from the rear of the plane through Kratzenberg's headphones, "steer heading three one zero. Climb to level four three thousand."

"Roger, three one zero at forty-three-thousand," Colonel Kratzenberg replied.

"Delta Two must be something very important to tie us up like this," he commented, glancing over at his copilot.

"Yes Sir," the officer replied. "The Navy has a whole damn carrier battle group headed toward that contact."

"Jesus! You gotta wonder who these guys are or what they've done to warrant that kind of attention!"

CHAPTER 18

Point Charlie

The SEALs quickly threw sand onto the plane's wings to make it appear the same color as the beach when looking from above. Others cut jungle foliage and positioned it beside and on top of the plane's fuselage and wings. They knew it was a haphazard attempt to camouflage the aircraft and that it wouldn't fool a professional, but it only had to work for a few hours. Darkness would soon arrive and they would be gone by mid-morning.

Boucher strode over to a small camouflage canopy the men had strung between four coconut palms about thirty yards away. There he found his old friend Haus Quicklinsky sitting in an aluminum lawn chair. He was wearing his signature Hawaiian shirt and smoking a fat cigar.

"Fancy meeting you here, Sir," the retired SEAL Senior Chief said gruffly with a note of sarcasm in his voice.

"Hi, Haus. I was counting on it."

Both men chuckled as they shook hands.

"Good to see you made it, Jake."

"Good to see you too, Haus. You have any problem getting here?"

"None. But I guess you can't say that or you wouldn't be here."

"Yeah. Just thank God for Plan B!"

"Where did you get that old plane? It looks like a friggin' museum exhibit!"

"Now Haus, don't be talking bad about that old girl. She just saved our asses and made you a rich man."

"You have a point!" Quicklinsky chuckled.

Boucher turned and called to the rest of the men. "Gather round!"

It was like old home week as the old warriors shook hands and hugged their former platoon Chief. Boucher patiently waited for the excitement to subside before addressing the group. "Okay men, listen up. We've come a long way but it ain't over until the fat lady sings, and there aren't any fat ladies on this island that I know of. When I realized we weren't going to make it out in the chopper, I put Plan B into motion and Haus came in here to exfil us. We're all worn out and hungry. Haus has brought us food and water and a floating ticket out of here. We picked this island as an exfil location because it's uninhabited. Since we're the only ones here, I see no immediate threat to our welfare. I want everyone to eat his fill and get some rest. We're gonna have a cold camp tonight. I don't want to attract any attention with a fire." He pointed at the plane and then to the boat by the ramshackle pier. "At first light we'll transfer the gold from the plane to the junk and sail off into the sunset. Any questions?"

There were none.

Boucher joined Quicklinsky, Moss, and Patterson under the canopy and sat down on a driftwood log. The rest of the SEALs sat around them eating MREs and carrying on soft-spoken conversation. Only an occasional chortle rose out of the monotone voices. Everyone was exhausted, Boucher included. He could barely remain awake to finish eating. He forced a final gulp of water to guard against dehydration and rested back on his driftwood pillow. As he drifted off into a deep sleep, all he could think about was retirement.

USS John Stennis, Carrier Battle Group Five in the Andaman Sea

It was nearing last light. Complete darkness would be upon them within thirty minutes. Except for their red, white, and green nighttime navigation lights, the five ships comprising Carrier Battle Group Five observed strict darkened ship procedures. It was standard operational procedure throughout the entire U.S. Navy when underway at sea.

"Admiral," the messenger of the watch said as he handed a clipboard to Rear Admiral Simon, "an op-immediate, Sir."

Simon, the commander of Carrier Battle Group Five, was seated in his Captain's chair on the port side of the Flag Bridge onboard the USS Stennis. He never seemed to leave that chair. He napped there and ate there. Now awakened by the messenger, he straightened up a bit and took the clipboard from the young sailor.

"Thank you," he replied without ever looking at the man.

He quickly flipped up the orange cover sheet marked Top Secret SPECAT, exposing a hidden cable beneath, and began to silently read it.

"Officer of the Deck," the Admiral commanded, "inform the Group that we will be launching a reconnaissance mission in two hours. Get the SEAL Task Unit Commander up here ASAP."

CHAPTER 19

Point Charlie

Three hours before first light, Boucher awoke with a headache and a stiff neck from using that driftwood for a pillow. He carefully felt the scabbing wound on his head. It was tender.

"Damn," he mumbled to himself as he painfully got to his feet.

Glancing around the makeshift camp he could see his men sprawled in various forms, sound asleep. He stared across the black water of the small cove toward the ocean. The sky was starlit and strung with low-hanging clouds on the horizon. A warm breeze rustled the tops of the palm trees and seemed to pull playfully at his camouflage BDUs. He extended his arms skyward and then slowly bent down, stretching his back in an attempt to work the kinks out of his stiff, fifty-nine-year-old body. Now completely bent over and peering backward between his spread legs, his attention went to the beached seaplane a short distance away.

His mind flashed on the previous day and, for some reason, on the box of top-secret documents they had recovered along with the gold. Boucher casually walked over to the plane and went inside. Using a flashlight, he located the Plans. The orange covers of the top secret volumes read, OPLAN 5000. He sat down and began to read the oldest one first.

SEAL Team One, Echo Platoon

The battle group was still out of range to utilize its ships to carry Lieutenant Jim Murrant and his SEALs to within insertion range of the small island. There was only one alternative. That was to use the two Marine CH-53 helicopters, each carrying an internal, deck-loaded, auxiliary fuel tank, and conduct in-flight aerial refueling to extend their range for the round-trip flight. Because of the size of the auxiliary fuel tank, there would barely be enough room inside each helicopter for the SEAL's seven-man element and their rubber raiding craft. Murrant had split his fourteen-man SEAL platoon into two seven-man elements, Blue and Gold. The plan was that his assistant platoon commander, Lieutenant Junior Grade Bart Morgan, would lead the Blue element ashore on this operation. Murrant planned to remain in the second helicopter as a backup should Morgan's helicopter develop in-flight problems and have to abort the mission or run into trouble on the island and require reinforcement.

121

The CH-53s would overfly Thailand just north of Surat Thani, cross the Gulf of Thailand toward Vietnam, and drop off Morgan and his men over the horizon well seaward of the target island. Once at the drop-off point, the Marine Corps CH-53 carrying Morgan's SEAL element would hover just above the water with its tail ramp fully open. Morgan and his six fellow SEALs would push their inflatable, combat, rubber raiding craft (CRRC) off the tail ramp into the sea, start the silenced outboard motor, and ride the boat to the far side of the target island, arriving at midnight. They would hide their raiding craft in the dense, near-shore foliage. Then, Morgan and his men would follow the perimeter of the small island, remaining concealed just inside the tree line along the beach, until they could gain a secure position from which to observe the target. They were not to make contact, vigorously strive to prevent compromise of their presence, and positively avoid getting into a gunfight. Once Morgan was ashore, the two CH-53s would head for Thailand and remain on standby at Utapao, an old U.S. B-52 bomber base used during the Vietnam War that was now maintained by the Royal Thai Air Force. The plan seemed simple enough and, while prepared for the worst, the SEALs didn't expect a gunfight.

So far all had gone according to plan. Blue element was on time and on target. Lieutenant Morgan activated his throat mic. "Blue on target."

He recognized Murrant's raspy reply through his earpiece. "Roger, Blue. Good luck."

Morgan's men slowly fanned out in a line arching perpendicular to the beach. From this position they could safely observe the junk tied next to the small bamboo pier and the beached seaplane. They strained through their night vision goggles to identify the location and number of subjects. Morgan noted the faint glimmer of a flashlight coming from the open door of the beached plane.

"Blue at O. P." Morgan reported into his throat mic.

"Roger, Blue."

Morgan carefully scanned the area, counting those he could see before reporting.

"I count seven sleeping. Possibly one additional inside a beached seaplane. All armed with AK-47s. Fishing junk is tied to small pier. No life onboard observed."

"Roger all," came the reply.

...

Sitting inside the seaplane, Boucher was now completely absorbed in reading the OPLAN. He was so astounded by what he was reading that hours had gone by without him realizing it. The OPLAN was like a road map into history.

As first light broke Patterson entered the plane, startling him. "Whatcha doing, Jake? Been looking all over for you."

"Damn it, Pat! You just scared the hell out of me!"

"Sorry. Just thought you might want some breakfast before we transload the gold over to the junk." He handed Boucher an MRE and a liter bottle of water.

"Thanks, Pat."

Boucher tore open the MRE and began to eat it cold. After several bites he pointed with his plastic spoon at the open pages of the OPLAN, resting on the ammunition can in front of him.

"If I hadn't read it here for myself, I would have never believed it."

Patterson knelt down beside the plan. "What's so unbelievable?"

"As far as I can tell, there's been a well-orchestrated...jeez, I guess for lack of a better word, conspiracy, by the U.S. military going on since 1954."

"What do you mean 'conspiracy?'"

"Well, according to this, the Korean War and the Vietnam War were undertaken for the ultimate purpose of defeating the Soviet Empire."

Patterson sat down next to him with a puzzled look. "Huh?"

"You see Pat, when you connect the dots it goes something like this. We fought the Korean War using mostly leftover, worn-out equipment from World War II. The reason we fought it wasn't to secure a democratic nation for Korea, or to stop the communists in the north from imposing their form of government upon those in the south. We sacrificed all those American lives for one reason. To buy us time."

"Time for what?"

"We needed time to build a modern carrier and submarine fleet that could win in a war against the Soviet Union. And the U.S. government knew that making that a reality would take a bunch of years, lots of money, and the political resolve to follow through. Remember the post World War II time frame. Japan and Germany had fallen only a few years earlier. During World War II Japan had decimated the Korean peninsula, and a good deal of Asia for that matter. Japan stole most of its resources to keep the Japanese war machine fueled. China faired a little better than Korea at the mercy of the Japanese onslaught, only because of its size and geography. General MacArthur recognized that the future threat against the free world was the Soviet Union and maybe, ultimately, China. That meant, for a starter, we had to contain the USSR."

"Contain both the USSR and China?" Patterson questioned.

Boucher took another bite of his cold MRE and carefully chewed it as if it was a gourmet meal. Patterson was consistently amazed by how his friend seemed to always find delight in even the most mundane things.

"Good shit, right Jake?"

"The OPLANs?"

"No. The MRE!"

"Hey, I like the little things in life. You want to hear about this or not?"

"Yeah, sorry. I'm just messing with you. Go on."

Boucher swallowed and took a sip of water, seemingly undeterred. "So, how do you tell the American public and the politicians that we need to take and hold several sovereign nations because we need to use their real estate to win a war against an enemy we may never actually have to fight? How do you tell the American public something as abstract as that? What do you say to make your case? Sorry folks, it's gonna cost a lot of your son's lives, but it's necessary. You'll understand in about sixty years. Just trust us. Obviously no one would buy that, so you have to demonize something or someone that everyone would recognize as evil. Communists attacking a bunch of poor helpless nations would nicely fit that requirement and that would drive us and our allies to come to the rescue to stop the spread of Communism."

"Wait a minute, Jake," Patterson interrupted. "Are you suggesting that General MacArthur was part of some grand plan that continued for sixty years?" Patterson wrung his hands. "That's some pretty heavy analysis, Jake. It sounds like revisionist history to me."

"I haven't even started, Pat. You gotta ask yourself why the Korean peninsula was so important."

"Okay," Patterson asked, "Why was it so important? By the way, there's one-hundred-thousand dollars in each of these bundles. I figure we're sitting here on at least ten-million in cash."

Boucher cleared his throat. "You want an answer to your question or not?"

Patterson nodded as he started packing cash bundles into his backpack.

Boucher watched intently as he continued. "China had a huge army, but no way to project its power. China didn't have a navy and the only way they could bring the necessary resources south for a major invasion into Korea would have been on narrow, undeveloped roads. These roads weren't capable of supporting a major assault or the necessary follow-on logistical support required for an invasion force. That put North Korea in the obvious position to become the aggressor."

Patterson interrupted again. "But I thought they invaded the south because that's where the Korean agricultural and industrial base was?"

"We supported a democratic south and the communist north was thrust back to the thirty-eighth parallel in a bloody war labeled a police action. We occupied South Korea with a standing army, developed the deepwater ports from Bukbeyong to Chinhae, and gave them a small Air Force and Navy of their own. We even brought in our nuclear weapons and kept an active stockpile there, just in case."

"Okay I get that part, but where does the USSR fit into it?" Patterson questioned.

"It fits perfectly. Remember, we occupied Japan at the same time. If you look at a map of the Pacific and keep in mind the strategic location of the Japanese Islands and the Korean Peninsula, it should fall into place. The only warm-water port the USSR had in the entire Pacific Theater was Vladisvostok which, as you well know, is located about fifteen miles north of the North Korean-USSR border. During the last few days of World War II the USSR, acting as our ally, seized the southern-most Japanese-held Kuril Islands: Kunshiri and Iturup. By seizing these two islands, the Soviets gained control of all the sea passages between the Kamchatka Peninsula and Japan's northern-most large island, Hokkaido. Grabbing Kunshiri and Iturup gave them control of the two deep-water channels that ran between those two southern Kurils, providing the Soviet submarines a submerged shortcut from the Sea of Okhotsk into the North Pacific and ultimately, a straight shot across the Pacific to Alaska, Canada, and California."

Patterson leaned back against a stack of gold bars and picked one up, examining it closely. "I think I see where you're going with this, but I still don't see where Korea fits into the scheme."

"Okay, maybe this will help," Boucher replied patiently. "Let's go back to the post-World War II map of the Pacific again. This time, visualize the Korean Peninsula. The east side of the Korean Peninsula borders the Sea of Japan's west side. Looking north we have Vladisvostok, the only major Soviet naval base in the region. Looking east across the Sea of Japan we have the Japanese Islands, which the U.S. already occupied at the end of the war. Remember, this is post-World War II. Since, in effect, we control one side of that pond by occupying Japan and the Soviets own the other side, the only way to control the Soviet ships and subs coming and going from the Sea of Japan and Vladisvostok is to control the Strait of Korea. Remember, Vladisvostok is the only warm-water base that they can launch at us from in the Pacific. By securing South Korea, we effectively control both sides of the Strait of Korea, which is the single gateway into the East China Sea."

Boucher took another bite of his MRE, savoring it as before.

Patterson thought for a moment, as he tried to visualize what Boucher had just explained.

"Alright, I understand the significance of the Straight of Korea, but what about the Strait of La Perouse between Hokkaido and Sakahlin Island on the north end of the SOJ?"

"That's a fair question, Pat," Boucher said, as he swallowed his last bite of MRE. Remember, we're buying time to build a Navy that is capable of winning against the Soviet Navy. Since we didn't have enough carriers and warships to maintain sea control, or sufficient long-range fighter-bomber aircraft to win in a war against the Soviets, the only quick thing we could do as a substitute was to build airfields. The way we controlled the Strait of LaPerouse was through the use of land-based patrol aircraft and strategically-based, short-range, attack aircraft launching from airfields like the Misawa Air Force Base, four-hundred miles north of Tokyo. It was far cheaper for us to patrol these critical sea passages using land-based aircraft instead of carrier-based aircraft. Even so, that was still only a temporary fix because the land bases were vulnerable to Soviet missile attack. We had to be able to provide sea control using these land bases until we could build a six-hundred-ship Navy with fifteen carrier battle groups."

"But how does China fit into this?"

"Actually, China may be a junior varsity player when it comes to world domination. Granted, they have the largest standing army of any nation on this planet, but they don't have any way to move all those troops outside China to fight. Hell, China has never really been interested in world domination. China is the 'world,' according to China. Expansionism is not in their cultural vocabulary. They're not seen as a threat to the West for that reason. Sure, they have nukes and ICBMs, but they won't shoot first. The threat against the West, following World War II up to 1992 when they went out of business, was the USSR."

"I guess I never thought of China like that," Patterson commented. "Do the plans cover how we would have responded if the USSR had attacked our forces in Japan and Korea?"

"Big time! Our standing forces in Japan and Korea would have attempted to repulse a land invasion of Soviet forces, but you have to keep in mind how hard an attack like that would have been for the Soviets to pull off without early detection. They would have had to come by sea and amassing the number of ships, landing craft, and men required, without discovery, would have been impossible. We would have had plenty of indicators and warnings and we would have had the time to preempt it, or maybe even stop it, before they could have pulled it off. The Soviets knew that and that's why their first option would have been to use nukes and simply eliminate our capability to control their breakout through the Strait."

Patterson appeared troubled. "So you're telling me that both South Korea and Japan were basically target sacrificial lambs in the event of a nuclear war with the USSR?"

"Ahh-ha. It sure appears that way—and the Philippines and Taiwan as well. Our interest in those two was as a supporting element of these plans and that led to our occupation of Vietnam and why we fought the war there."

Patterson was now half laughing. "You know what, old buddy? I gotta hear this one."

"No shit, Pat, it's true. I told you this was a conspiracy. And there's more. I'll tell you after we move the gold over to the boat."

...

Lieutenant Junior Grade Morgan and his men studied the strange band of men stirring about forty yards in front of them. It was now first light and the subjects' camp was teeming with activity. The unknown group of men before them was clearly American and all around the same age—late fifties something. Morgan noted that they acted in a very military manner. They never strayed too far from their weapons. They were disciplined, situationally-aware, and rarely spoke to one another aloud.

They formed a line from the beached plane's side door to the boat and began passing what appeared to be golden bricks from the plane to the boat. *No, it couldn't be!* Morgan thought. But as he and his men watched, they saw dozens of these golden bricks passed down the line, man to man, and loaded onboard the boat.

When Morgan was given the surveillance mission, his orders were to observe and not make contact. He was to report anything abnormal via SATCOM and take digital pictures of the subjects in question. He was then to send that imagery back via the satellite. Between Morgan and his men, they had all but two of them photographed and the imagery they had taken so far was ID quality. Morgan gave his radioman a nod and handed him a memory stick containing the imagery file. The radioman inserted the memory stick into his computer and compressed the file. Several keystrokes later, the file was flashed to the military communications satellite in high geosynchronous orbit and relayed on.

Morgan continued to study this odd assemblage as they quietly worked. When they did speak, it was in low, almost inaudible voices. Morgan and his men needed to get closer to hear what the men were saying. While getting closer was risky, he felt that the information he might be able to collect from hearing their dialog was worth the risk. Besides, he had a fully-armed SEAL element on target, ready, willing, and able to fight their way out if need be.

Morgan and his men inched forward. About forty-five minutes passed.

They were now in position close enough to hear most of the conversation of those they were observing.

"Hey Chief, where you got the nav charts stashed?" Boucher asked Quicklinsky.

"I got a set under the chart table next to the helm. Where else do you keep nav charts?"

Morgan saw the two men smile at one another as the big one who asked the question disappeared below the boat's open hatch. A second man appeared, walking from the plane toward the boat, carrying a stack of four binder-like volumes in his arms that were all marked with the characteristic U.S. military Top Secret orange cover sheet and bookend marker. This man spoke to another man standing on the boat's deck, who was passing the gold bars down into the open hatch.

"Hey Billy, tell Jake we have about another hour to go. Ask him if he wants to hold the cash for last."

Morgan had, at this point, already transmitted pictures of the seaplane, junk, and every one of the men they were observing, but getting a picture of this guy with the Top Secret material would certainly be a prize. He snapped several digital pictures and passed the memory stick over to his radioman for immediate transmission. It was time to request further direction.

Pressing his throat mic he whispered, "Gold actual, Gold actual, this is Blue. See imagery just sent. Interrogative additional tasking, over."

Morgan heard some static followed by Murrant's characteristically raspy voice, "Roger, Blue. Wait, out."

That meant Murrant didn't have the answer and would have to see what higher authority wanted him and his SEALs to do. For now, Morgan would sit tight and continue to observe the peculiar band of unshaven men before him, who had to be either bank robbers or treasure hunters. Whatever they were, they were very rich men. About fifteen minutes had gone by when Morgan's earpiece crackled to life.

"Blue, this is Gold. Take subjects into custody if they attempt departure from island. Avoid, repeat, avoid engagement. I'm on my way to you with Gold. ETA two hours."

Morgan smiled, his white teeth flashing through his green-and-black, camouflage face paint, obviously pleased. "Roger, copy all. See you in two hotels. Out."

It was apparent to Morgan that the men he was observing were nearing completion of their loading task. They were now passing large ammunition cans that clearly didn't contain ammunition. He heard several of the men refer to the cans as "the cash." Morgan passed the word to his fellow SEALs to move forward to the edge of the tree line. Once in position, they would assault forward and take the unsuspecting men into custody at gunpoint. He ensured that all his SEALs knew the rules of engagement—shoot only in self-defense.

As Boucher and his men finished loading the final can, Morgan made his move. The SEALs assaulted forward across the narrow beach, catching Boucher and his men completely by surprise.

"Hands up!" Morgan shouted. "Don't anybody do anything stupid!"

Boucher slowly raised his hands as his men followed suit.

"Who the hell are you?" Boucher asked Morgan.

"I am Lieutenant Junior Grade Morgan. We are United States Navy SEALs and I am under orders to take you all into custody. Who's in charge?"

A bewildered Boucher looked around at his men then back at Morgan.

"You're shittin' me son, right?"

"No Sir. I'm serious as a heart attack."

Several of Boucher's men chuckled aloud at Morgan's response.

Lowering his hands, Boucher slowly stepped forward toward Morgan smiling. Morgan cautiously pulled his assault rifle up to the ready.

"What team are you in, son?"

Morgan seemed briefly taken aback by Boucher's calm question. "We're in Team One."

"Who's your C.O.?"

"Ahh, Commander Thomas."

"Would that be J.J. Thomas?"

"Yes, how do you know his name?"

"And tell us Lieutenant, what was your BUDS class number?"

"Class 256, why?"

"Cause you're an FNG! That's why!"

Boucher's men laughed. Morgan and his men all looked confused.

"Who are you?" Morgan asked Boucher.

"I'm Jake Boucher, UDT-R class 38, and that would be east coast training class 38."

Morgan stared momentarily, as if he was seeking some kind of divine inspiration. "You're the Vietnam SEAL who saved a POW and won the Navy Cross?"

"Yeah, something like that and," Boucher turned pointing to Patterson, "there's the pilot we saved."

"Holy shit!" Morgan said, lowering his gun barrel to the ground.

"It gets better," Boucher said pointing. "That guy over there is Mojo Lavender. You ever hear any stories about Mojo? And that guy is Billy Reilly.

He's probably killed more men than years you're old. That guy over there is Senior Chief Quicklinsky. He got the Silver Star for single-handedly rescuing Ramirez—who's standing over there—from capture after he got shot in the chest. You see Lieutenant, with the exception of Patterson and Moss over there, all of us are SEALs." Boucher smiled. "Now what in the hell are you boys doing in a place like this?"

Morgan glanced at his men. "Aaah, we were sent here to observe you and report on your actions. We've been watching you since 0400. When it looked like you were making preparations to get underway, I was ordered to take you into custody."

Boucher smiled at the young SEAL lieutenant again. "Okay, you have us in custody. Now what?"

Morgan fidgeted. "My orders are to hold you here until relieved by my platoon commander."

"And tell me Lieutenant, who would that be?"

"Lieutenant Jim Murrant."

At this point Ramirez spoke up. "You gotta be shittin' me! He's been over to my house for dinner. He's one of my son's best friends. Ohhh...my son is Josy Ramirez, Team One."

"Your son is Josy Ramirez?" Morgan asked. "He went through BUDS in the class ahead of mine."

"Yeah, small world, ain't it?"

Boucher brought everyone back to reality. "Like I asked, Lieutenant, what now?"

"Well Sir, I suppose we'll have to wait for my boss. He should be here in about eighty mikes."

Boucher's face hardened as he looked away. In a voice audible to everyone, he pronounced, "Sorry son, we have a date to keep. We haven't broken any U.S. laws, so we're going to go now. If you have a problem with that, I guess you'll just have to shoot us."

Morgan and his men immediately brought their guns up to the ready.

"I'm sorry Sir, but I'm going to have to ask you and your men to stand clear of your weapons and the boat."

Boucher nodded to his men, who all stood their ground. Suddenly, a voice that Boucher knew well came from the jungle behind Morgan and his men.

"Hey Lieutenant, if I was you I would tell my men to drop their weapons. Oh, I almost forgot to mention, I got an AK-47 aimed right at the back of your FNG head and it ain't no friggin' blank I got chambered!"

Morgan seemed uneasy but didn't budge.

"Hey Lieutenant. I wanna revise my point of aim. Sucks, 'cause you know I couldn't kill one of my own. I'm now holding a bead on your balls. You ever wanna get laid again, I strongly recommend that you and your boys put down your weapons."

Morgan slowly turned towards the mystery voice. He seemed to evaluate his position momentarily, then nodded to his men. Without looking down he carefully laid his assault rifle on the sand. His men followed.

"Now," the voice ordered, "I want you all to take two steps forward toward Commander Boucher and away from your weapons."

Morgan and his men complied.

"Okay, Jake. They belong to you!" the voice triumphantly proclaimed.

Boucher motioned to his men, who quickly confiscated the weapons.

"You said your boss was going to show up in eighty minutes, right?"

Morgan nodded yes.

"Okay boys, here's the plan. Offload fourteen bars of gold. Mister Morgan, I'm going to leave you and your men a little party fund. No one but us will ever know. You can take the gold with you or bury it here for later recovery. You can make up a story about how we gave you the slip. I don't give a shit! But here's the catch: if you tell anyone what you've learned and it compromises us, I'm going to tell the world that you robbed us before ratting us out. It will be the word of a bunch of FNGs against that of a bunch of old warriors. You'll be just as screwed as us. So that's your option, Lieutenant. You and your boys will leave here, either rich or broke. Take a moment and consult with your men. Tell me if you're in or out. Either way, me and my guys are out of here."

Morgan huddled with his men and soon gave his reply. "We're onboard, but not because of the gold."

Boucher had fourteen gold bars thrown onto the beach next to the bamboo pier.

"Okay, Johnny," he yelled toward the jungle, "it's time to go."

Moments later, a single figure emerged from the jungle behind Morgan and his men with an AK-47 slung over his shoulder.

As he passed by Morgan and his SEALs, he chuckled. "Next time you boys do a sneak and peek, you need to keep track of them ones who wander off. After bein' out there on guard all night, I was just finishing up squeezing out a massive MRE turd when you all moved in close and then I couldn't stop without a hangfire. I was wait'n to see what you were up to. Figured you'd find me from the stench. Next time you boys are on an OP you need to pay better attention to the smells around you."

Yellowhorse strolled onto the bamboo pier smiling and climbed onboard the boat. Morgan walked over to the gold bars lying half-buried in the soft sand. He looked down and kicked several of the bars.

"Hey," he yelled to Boucher. "Where are you headed?"

Boucher and his men had thrown off all the mooring lines and were in the process of backing the junk away from the pier. The boat's small auxiliary diesel clamored as it strained to pull the heavily laden boat out into the small lagoon. Boucher looked back over his shoulder at Morgan and held up his index finger, waving it from side to side while shaking his head no.

Morgan smiled and called, "Would your man behind us in the jungle really have shot us?"

Yellowhorse stepped into view and took aim a foot to the left of where Morgan stood. Morgan instinctively stepped back. Johnny adjusted his aim slightly and fired one shot that kicked up the sand next to Morgan.

"Nahh," Yellowhorse yelled as he leaned his AK-47 against the pilothouse. "I was just funnin' with ya."

"Would you have shot us?" Boucher yelled back.

Morgan drew his pistol from his leg holster and took aim towards Yellowhorse, then moved slightly to the left. He fired one shot that struck the wooden stock of Yellowhorse's AK-47, splintering it into toothpicks.

"Probably not. That would be like shooting dinosaurs."

Both men laughed and each held up an open hand to the other.

...

Occasionally puffing on his cigar, Quicklinsky skillfully eased the large junk into the mouth of the small lagoon and headed toward the open sea. Just before the boat disappeared beyond the protected lagoon, Boucher turned for one last look at the seaplane. He could make out Morgan and his men moving around the plane. The sun was now high in the morning sky and the breeze was perfect for using the sail. There was still one thing that bothered Boucher. How did the SEALs know where he and his men were and why was Morgan ordered to take them into custody? Boucher got everyone together.

"Okay gang, the boys on the beach said they had a helo inbound with an ETA of eighty minutes. That was about twenty minutes ago, so I figure that helo is only about an hour out by now. This boat does about 10 knots on a good day, so we're only going to be about ten miles away by the time the helo lands to pick up Morgan and his guys. Assuming that he will stall them a short while we might get a few miles further, but not far enough. If they come looking, they'll find us. The Chief brought some paint and other disguising materials along just in case we needed to give this baby a facelift in a hurry. We have one hour to make this junk look like a different boat. Let's get to it."

The men opened several boxes that were tied to the gunwale on deck and began removing paint, rollers and brushes. Others hoisted the boat's fishing nets and swung the booms outward into the ready position.

"This is a fishing boat," Boucher announced loudly. "Make it look like one. If we get any nosey air traffic, I want everyone below except for Johnny and Haus. They will be dressed in costume and act the part. We're making a run for the Spratlys."

CHAPTER 20

USS Virginia, South China Sea, eight hours later

"Captain on the con," The Chief of the Boat announced as Commander Dave Galloway stepped through the hatch into the submarine's cramped control room.

"OOD, what ya' got?"

Lieutenant Tim Cutler was standing the last hour of his six-hour watch as the Officer of the Deck. Cutler had just received an encoded message from SUBPAC headquarters in Hawaii. To Cutler, the new orders seemed odd. The USS Virginia was the Navy's most advanced fast attack submarine and sending her to a new patrol location to find a junk didn't make sense.

Cutler had read the orders over and over.

Locate High Interest Vessel believed to be a fishing vessel. Once HIV is located, maintain surveillance on same without being detected. Do not make contact of any kind.

Cutler was a veteran of three submarine patrols onboard the Virginia and these orders seemed very strange. Very strange indeed.

"Sir, it's about our new orders," he answered Galloway.

Galloway studied his lieutenant and realized he owed the young officer an explanation. "I've been in submarines my entire career and this is a first," Galloway commented. "However, orders are orders." Galloway put his hand on Cutler's shoulder. "You were right to summon me to the bridge." Galloway stepped closer to Cutler. "The battle group lost contact with this HIV about two-and-a-half hours ago. I guess we're going looking for a fishing junk, Mr. Cutler. You got an ETA to the new patrol area?"

"Yes Sir," Cutler replied. "ETA is nine hours forty-three minutes, if we maintain current course and speed."

Galloway turned toward the periscope. "Lieutenant, make your depth two-hundred-forty feet. Come left to new heading and steer course two seven five degrees. Ahead full."

"Yes Sir."

Galloway nodded. "That will put us in the general search area around daybreak. What's the weather doing in that area?"

"There's a large tropical depression moving in, Sir. I suspect it will sock us in for the next few days and make finding a boat that small pretty challenging."

"Damn!" Galloway replied, clenching his fists in front of him. "Alright, I want to ensure we arrive before daylight. I want you to shave off some time on our ETA. Give me best speed."

"I can probably get us an hour, maybe more, Sir."

"Excellent, Mr. Cutler. Also, have the COB and the XO meet me in my cabin in five minutes."

"Aye, Captain," Cutler replied.

Galloway briskly departed the control room for his cabin.

Onboard the Junk, the same time

The seas were becoming confused as the small, wooden vessel gradually made its way eastward. Chief Quicklinsky was marking the updated GPS location on the navigation chart. He smiled to himself as he glanced below deck. His teammates were sprawled in various positions in an attempt to find comfort and everyone was asleep. Redirecting his attention to navigating the small junk, Quicklinsky listened intently to a weather forecast on the radio. He didn't like what he heard. The seas ahead were forecast to build to massive, encompassing waves and wind that could compromise the small junk's seaworthiness. The wind was expected to shift from behind, to a fast-moving, northeasterly blast that would hit them from the quartering bow. In a few hours the easy ride would be over. He anticipated that they would have to change course and either head into the seas bow-on, on a northeasterly heading, or run from the storm and sail due south. Either option would delay their arrival in the Spratlys. He needed a decision from Boucher because he had to make the course change now.

Boucher was lying on his back on top of some sail canvas, just inside the access hatch to the main cabin. Quicklinsky hated to wake him, but it was necessary. He gently placed his hand on Boucher's arm.

"Jake, wake up. I need your help...Jake."

Boucher slowly opened his eyes and sat up calmly. "What you got, Haus?"

"Sorry to wake you, but we have a situation. We're heading into a typhoon. Weather report says we can expect state-3 seas. We need to change course so we don't get the shit kicked out of us."

"What are our options?"

"We can either head into the seas and ride out the storm and then run southeast back to the Spratlys after it passes, or we can turn south now and try to avoid it. We'll only lose about half a day if we ride her out. If we run south, we'll lose a day. Probably more."

Boucher slowly got to his feet. "What do you recommend, Haus? You think this old girl will stay together if we run her into the storm?"

"Yeah, I think she'll make it just fine. It's our guys I'm worried about. No one here is under fifty, remember?"

"Your point is well-taken Chief, but if we wanted it to be easy we would have all joined the Air Force. Right?"

Quicklinsky laughed. "I haven't heard that line since I retired. Guess I'm just damn proud to be a frogman. The only brothers we got who like it more miserable than we do are the Marines. I say we head into the storm."

Boucher chuckled. "Okay Chief, turn this mother into the seas and let's go for it. We have a date in Palawan and I don't want to be late."

Quicklinsky slapped Boucher on the shoulder and returned to the helm.

Boucher was now fully awake. He got up and poured himself a cup of coffee and opened an MRE. He grabbed OPLAN 5000 and went to the galley table. He opened the volume to the page he had folded to mark his place and began to read as he ate.

American Embassy, Bangkok

Melvin Lewis Brown paced the floor of his office in front of his desk. Dwight Howe, his Deputy Chief of Station, sat on a couch a few feet away flanked by Richard Gunn from the CIA's covert operations branch.

"How did you let those pirate, terrorist bastards slip through your fingers? That's what I want to know! They pull off the sloppiest operation I've ever seen and they get away! How the hell do you explain that?"

The two men sat quietly without comment as ML continued his rant.

"Who the hell are these guys anyway? We think we might know who some of them are, but we're not really sure. They got to be either the golldamn luckiest bastards on the planet or the smartest! Your guys couldn't stop them in Cambodia. The SEALs couldn't catch them on that shit-ass island where they crash-landed that golldamn, antique seaplane they stole! Now they're somewhere in the South China Sea on a fishing boat that just happened to be visiting that damn island the same time they were. And now AWACS can't even find them in the sea clutter from that fucking typhoon. Their last known position was when they sailed that junk off into the sunset! We have the most technically advanced submarine the fucking Navy owns headed their way. The problem is that the storm is bearing down directly on the entire area and it's going to make their detection difficult, even using state-of-the-art stuff like that sub has. This is a damn cluster fuck, gentleman, and I want it unfucked! Do you realize what's at stake here?"

The men continued to sit in silence. ML stopped pacing momentarily and pounded his fist on his desk.

"Now find those assholes and get those plans!"

Onboard the junk

The junk gracefully cut her way through the mounting swells with her wooden plank hull occasionally groaning and creaking from the strain. Quicklinsky checked the GPS again and recorded the position on the navigation chart, along with the time. Nearly eight hours had passed since they'd left the island. Quicklinsky judged that they were still about twenty hours from their rendezvous at the Spratlys—a conservative estimate, assuming everything went according to plan.

...

Boucher was still reading the plans. The rest of the men had awoken and were eating or attending to some other form of creature comfort. Lavender went topside to relieve Quicklinsky on the helm. Ramirez followed.

"Haus, we'll take it for the next four."

"Thanks, Mojo. Mind your heading. This storm will be on us like stink on shit in another hour. Keep her bow to the seas and we'll be fine. I'll check up on you later. Just yell if you need anything."

"Roger, Haus. We've all been through this kind of shit before. No big deal."

"Hey Mojo, you remember that op in 1976 when we were inserting into Beirut? Now that was some serious sea state!"

"Yeah. I remember how we almost lost it when that monster wave washed over us. Come to think of it, maybe we ought to tie ourselves fast when we're on the weather deck, just in case."

"That's probably a good precaution. Sure don't want to do donuts in this sea state trying to find somebody's dumbass that got washed overboard."

"Hey Haus, you got any dip? I'm out."

Quicklinsky pulled a tin of snuff from his shirt pocket and handed it to Lavender.

"Here you go Mojo, keep it. I got another two logs below."

"Thanks Haus. I sure don't want to be getting seasick."

"High seas—no dip? Yeah, I know where you're comin' from."

Quicklinsky went below and closed the hatch behind him, sealing the junk's interior from the outside weather. Lavender and Ramirez each tied a line around their waists and fastened the other end to a sail shackle next to the helm. It seemed that the storm's strength had increased a magnitude in just the time it took them to tie themselves fast. The tops of the waves were now breaking off in wind-blown, white water foam and beginning to plunge into the advancing trough ahead. Waves would occasionally break over the junk's bow and wash aft along the wooden deck, frothing white foam around their feet. Both Lavender and Ramirez knew this was a sign that there would soon be a test of the seaworthiness of the small junk they were piloting.

CHAPTER 21

The USS Virginia

"Dive, make your depth seventy feet. Raise scope," Lieutenant Cutler commanded. He was nearing the end of his six-hour watch and was tired. Nonetheless, he was intrigued by the events unfolding. He made a quick, three-hundred-sixty-degree sweep of the ocean's surface around the submarine.

"No shapes or shadows, Sir," Cutler reported to his commanding officer as he stepped back from the periscope.

"What is the current heading of that contact, Mister Cutler?" Galloway asked.

"Sonar has unidentified, intermittent contact at zero six seven degrees, range one-thousand-three-hundred yards. It looks like it's submerged, Sir."

Galloway rotated the periscope a quarter of a turn to his right and attempted to focus it. "Damn weather! I can't see shit out there using thermal or night vision."

"Aye Captain, the sea clutter swallows up a vessel as small as the one we're looking for."

"Yeah, I was afraid of that. Give me sonar range again."

"One-thousand-two-hundred yards at zero six seven degrees, Sir."

"Very well. Close contact to five-hundred yards on the starboard side. We'll attempt visual ID from there. It will be daylight in about thirty minutes. I want a positive ID before then so we can drop back into a position to tail and surveill."

"Five-hundred port side. Aye, Sir."

Galloway stepped away from the periscope and folded the handles inward.

"Lower scope," Cutler ordered. "Maintain depth at seven zero feet. Helm, come left to new heading zero six eight degrees, ahead two-thirds."

Cutler reached up and keyed the mic on the sub's intercom. "I intend to put us off the contact's starboard side at a range of five-hundred yards. Once there, we'll attempt a visual identification of the contact. Sonar, stay on the contact and advise any change in course and speed. Everyone else, stay alert."

Galloway and Cutler stood silently as the mammoth submarine changed course. They could occasionally feel the submarine shudder slightly from the storm, knowing full well the sea state above had to be extremely heavy in order to cause turbulence seventy feet below the ocean's surface. While neither of the two submariners had ever been onboard a surface vessel in such a storm, they understood what those onboard the contact vessel they were following were experiencing. It didn't matter what they may have done, or why the Navy was so interested in locating this vessel. Both men knew the meaning of the prayer engraved onto the brass plaque on Galloway's stateroom door. It was a simple prayer, but nonetheless shared by every sailor.

Oh Lord, this sea is so large and this ship is so small. Please watch over us. Amen.

"Captain, ETA nine minutes."

"Very well, Mister Cutler, make the ship's depth sixty feet."

"Aye, Sir. Depth sixty feet."

"Raise scope."

As the periscope locked into the up position, Galloway opened the handles. He made a quick three-hundred-sixty-degree sweep as he peered through the optics in search of the mystery contact. "You hold a sonar contact?" he asked Cutler.

"Sir, we hold an intermittent sonar contact bearing two seven three degrees, range five-hundred-fifty yards."

Galloway adjusted the periscope. "I got her. Looks like a cork bobbing in this sea state. I don't know who's crewing that thing, but the poor dumb bastards have balls. That damn boat they're riding is underwater more than above. Here take a look."

Lt. Cutler stepped up to the periscope and peered into the eyepiece. "Holy shit! That boat just took green water from bow to stern! I see one man on deck by the helm. They've reefed the sails. Must be running on their auxiliary engine. I'm going to shoot some video. I still can't make out any identifiable characteristics. The darn thing just doesn't stay visible long enough. Wooh! They darn near flipped over backwards on that wave! I got it on video."

Galloway considered the situation before giving his next order. "Alright, I want to close to three-hundred yards on the port side of the contact. I want some good photo data that I can send to SUBPAC for analysis."

Cutler pulled away from the periscope in surprise. "Sir, isn't that a bit risky?" he asked respectfully. "I mean, in this sea state, what if they see our periscope?"

"Noted, Lieutenant. They have one man on deck and he's holding on for his life. I think the odds of him looking out into the darkness and spotting our scope are slim."

"Aye, Sir," Cutler replied.

On the junk

Seawater occasionally flooded into the hatch, as waves continued to wash across the deck of the small, wooden vessel. Quicklinsky was back at the helm, skillfully keeping the junk aimed into the seas. Reilly was tied to the post beside him. In addition, they had tied themselves together with a buddy line. Neither man intended to be washed overboard without a swim buddy attached to him.

Below deck, most of the men were asleep. Remarkable as it seems, it is far easier to sleep through this type of storm than to try to maintain a conscious effort of balance. Fortunately, the boat's diesel engine and automatic bailing pumps were working normally and keeping up with the demands of the storm. Boucher had wedged himself into a corner, still absorbed with reading the OPLAN, when Reilly called down to him.

"Jake, get up here! You gotta see this!"

Boucher marked his page with a half fold and pulled himself over to the hatch. He carefully timed opening it to coincide with the brief period when the boat was poised at the top of a wave. Promptly at that moment, he threw open the hatch and left the safety of the cabin for the exposed weather deck. As he emerged, the bow of the boat crashed down and passed through the next wave, nearly knocking him off his feet. Clutching a lifeline to keep from being thrown overboard, he made his way over to Reilly.

"What you got, Billy?" he yelled above the sound of the storm.

Reilly pointed to his right. It was now first light and while the storm's black, water-heavy clouds had obliterated the sun, it was still light enough to see about two-hundred-fifty yards. Boucher turned and squinted into the direction Reilly was pointing.

"You see it?" Reilly shouted over the noise of the storm.

Boucher wiped the stinging seawater from his eyes and continued to look in the direction Reilly was pointing. "See what?"

"That pole sticking out of the water about two-hundred yards off our beam."

Boucher wiped his eyes again and tried to shield his face from the pelting spray using his hands. "Jeez! That looks like a fricken periscope!" he yelled to Reilly

"Yup! The Chief and me thought you oughta see it for yourself. You know… kinda makes it easier to believe."

Reilly handed Boucher a pair of binoculars and pointed at it again. Boucher peered through the eight-power binocular tubes in the direction Reilly pointed, scanning out to the visual limits allowed by the storm. He suddenly stopped and focused on a single point. He could see an exposed periscope mast in the trough of every passing wave. The periscope seemed stationary because the submarine was apparently matching the junk's course and speed.

After observing the periscope for a few minutes, Boucher angrily shoved the binoculars back to Reilly. "You got to be shitting me! Back in Cambodia we had a Global Hawk overhead *watching* us. Then we had a couple of little birds *shooting* at us. Then the SEALs show up on a no-name island and try to *arrest* us, but don't know *why* they were sent, and *now* there's a fricken submarine on our ass. What the hell is so damn important about us? It can't be the damn gold! If they wanted the gold they could have easily taken it!"

Reilly shrugged at Boucher. "The Chief and me were just saying the same thing and it beats the living shit out of us!"

Boucher shook his head and made his way back to the hatch. Before going below he glanced back at Quicklinsky and Reilly. He took pride in his two old friends and the many hardships they had endured together. This was little more to them than another notch on their pistol grip—just another among many—but there was a difference. This time, they were here for themselves. This was their last hooyah together. The gold would make them all rich men, but it really wasn't about the gold. It was about the kinship they shared as warriors. It was about the privilege of serving beside each other and accomplishing a common goal against overwhelming odds. Above all, it was about the SEAL brotherhood and their life-long obligation to one another.

Before closing the hatch, Boucher again turned his attention to the periscope. He searched the sea, but the periscope had vanished as mysteriously as it had appeared. He shook his head in disbelief and went below.

Boucher grabbed Moss and the two made their way to where Patterson was sleeping. "Pat, wake up," he said in a low voice as he shook his buddy's shoulder.

Patterson awoke in a startle. "Damn it, Jake! Can't you see I'm trying to sleep?"

"Yeah, but we have a problem."

"Like this storm that's beating the hell out of us?"

"No, like a submarine is following us and I just saw its periscope off our port side."

"A periscope?" Patterson questioned as he sat upright.

Boucher opened the navigation chart and spread it out on a box top beside Patterson. Moss held the chart open with one hand and shifted his position a bit to prevent casting his shadow over it.

"Here's our current position," Boucher explained. "Here's where we're headed. Here's our track."

Boucher ran his fingertip along the pencil line on the chart.

"Okay Jake, I got it. So what the fuck?" Patterson asked.

"We got to lose that sub while we're in this storm and make it so he can't pick us back up when the storm passes. We're about half a day away from the Spratlys. What do you think about making a run northeast with the storm?"

Patterson wiped the sweat off his forehead as he contemplated Boucher's proposal. "Let me get this straight, Jake. You're suggesting we intentionally stay in this storm and use it as cover?"

"Yeah, that's what I'm suggesting. The brunt of this storm is upon us. If we track our course along with the storm, there is no way in hell that sub will be able to stay with us. If this storm continues its current track and speed, we could ride it almost as far as Palawan."

"What about the Spratlys option?"

"We'll persevere like we always have."

For the first time ever, in all the years Boucher had known Moss, he saw concern on Moss's face. "Mossman, what are you thinking?

"Well, Jake, you know I'm not prone to getting overly excited over the small shit, but I don't like it."

Patterson shook his head, "Me either, Jake."

Boucher looked at his two trusted friends as if he was trying to read their thoughts, but couldn't. "Okay, why not?" he asked.

Moss ran his finger along the pencil line on the chart. "This is our intended course to the Spratlys. These position hacks represent our modified course, because of the storm. We chose to modify our intended course so we would have a better ride in the storm. If we continue on this heading we stay in the storm and use it for cover. You're suggesting we pop out up here, somewhere close to Palawan. You're gambling that the storm continues to track on this heading. You're also gambling that we will be able to keep our act together once we're at Palawan and that we'll find a way off that island, right?"

Boucher snorted, "Yeah, that's pretty much it."

Patterson now took the floor. "What if we turn now and make a run to the Spratlys? We're a hell of a lot closer to the Spratlys than we are to Palawan and we have everything in place at the Spratlys."

Boucher evaluated the idea before replying. "Two points: One, we'll be moving out of the storm, making it easy for the sub to track us and two, we'll be taking the seas from our beam, which is just begging for trouble in a sea state like this."

Moss put his finger back on the chart at their current position and began to run it toward the Spratlys. "As we approach the Spratlys, the sub will have to break off because of the reefs and shoals. She won't have enough water under her keel to be able to safely operate submerged. If we continue northeast for another couple of hours, but slow our speed to the bare minimum required to maintain navigation way in this sea state, the brunt of the storm will pass by. After it does, we cut a line hard east to the Spratlys and we take our chances with the seas."

All three men sat quietly staring at the navigation chart before them.

"You know what?" Boucher said. "You guys are pretty smart for a couple of flyboys. I'll run this by Haus and Billy and we'll make it so."

The USS Virginia

"Officer of the Deck, Sonar. Contact is changing course to an easterly bearing."

"Roger, Sonar," Lieutenant Cutler replied. "Report contact's new course when steady. Navigator, maintain same standoff distance. Diving officer, make your depth eighty feet. Raise scope."

Cutler waited until the sub ascended past ninety feet then flipped the handles down on the periscope and peered into the eyepiece. He made a rapid, three-hundred-sixty-degree sweep of the surrounding ocean to check for shapes or shadows that could threaten the submarine before returning to observe the junk. It was now daylight and he could easily see the junk being hammered by the heavy waves. Some of the waves were so steep that the junk appeared to literally leap out of the water as the waves passed by them. Others caused the junk to dive through the approaching wall of water. He could not make out any distinguishing feature on the junk that allowed for a positive ID. There were two men on deck at the helm who looked like they were hanging on for their lives. Cutler shot a few more strings of video, trying to capture clear views of them to aid in their identification.

"Sir, when you get a moment take a look at this," the Chief of the Boat requested.

Cutler pulled away from the periscope and sternly ordered, "Lower scope." He then stepped over to the chart table and joined the COB. "What you got, COB?"

The grizzly old Master Chief pointed to the navigation chart. "Well Lieutenant, we're going to run aground in about eight hours if we stay on this heading. Looks to me like they're making a run for the Spratlys."

"The Spratlys? But there's nothing there except for a Chinese lookout post."

"Beats the shit out of me, Sir. Just thought you might want to know, Sir."

"Yeah, thanks Master. I better let the Captain know."

"Yes Sir, Lieutenant. That would be the right thing to do. Oh, Sir, did you get any feedback from COMSUBPAC on the video we sent them earlier?"

"All they've told us so far is that this is a priority 1-A mission. It sure baffles me what's so important about that junk. The last time I ever heard about a mission like this was a few years back when the USS Marshall was tasked to track a Korean ship thought to be carrying nuke weapons to Iran. Have you ever been involved in something like this before?"

"Yes Sir, that I have, but we weren't tailing a surface contact through a typhoon."

CHAPTER 22

American Embassy, Bangkok, Thailand

"Trudy, get Director Thompson on the secure line for me please."
Thompson was the CIA's Director for Covert Operations and he reported directly to the DNCS at CIA headquarters in Langley, Virginia. Moments later, the red call-waiting light atop Melvin Brown's secure-voice telephone flashed.

Brown put the phone to his ear. "Rene, ML. I got a situation you need to know about. I just got a report that our High Interest Vessel has changed course and now appears to be headed to the Spratlys."

Brown listened for a moment. "Ahh, yes, but they're operating in a very severe storm." Brown paused to hear the reply. "No, I can't take further action until it's clear where they're heading. If it is the Spratlys, the only way we can get there is by sea, maybe seaplane, weather permitting."

This time Brown listened at length. "Okay, I understand how important it is, but these guys are good. We've already lost a helo and some good men because of them. I urge caution. We could..."

Brown was cut off in the middle of his sentence by Thompson and couldn't get a word in until Thompson was finished.

"Yes, I completely understand. I'll handle it."

Brown hung up the phone, took a deep breath, sat back in his leather-covered executive armchair and exhaled slowly. Offhandedly, he pushed down the intercom button.

"Trudy, please have Mr. Howe come to my office."

"Yes Sir," a woman's voice crackled over the speaker in terse reply.

Shortly after there was a knock on Brown's office door. Dwight Howe entered the room. Brown motioned for Howe to sit on the couch in front of his desk.

"Dwight, I just got off the phone with Langley. I've been instructed to pre-position a team in close proximity of the Spratly Islands."

Howe straightened up when he heard that. "The Spratlys? Why the Spratlys?" he questioned his boss.

"We got a SPECAT report from Naval Intelligence a short while ago saying that the vessel turned onto an easterly heading and is believed to be heading for the Spratlys. Langley wants our guys to be there waiting for them so we can recover the precious cargo. We just have one huge problem to contend with."

"What problem?"

"One mother of a tropical storm that is fringing the general area of operations as I speak. It's a slow-mover and it could stall in that vicinity, making insertion of our team next to impossible. Langley feels the risk is worth the price, so I need you to get with Gunn and come up with a workable plan. We need to launch this operation ASAP."

Brown observed Howe's uneasy body language in response to his ASAP order. "Dwight, I know it sucks, but we can't let these guys slip through our fingers again. National security is at stake here."

Howe stood and looked down at his boss. "I understand and I'm on it."

With that, Howe left the room, leaving Brown staring at a map of the Pacific littoral that he had taped onto the door covering his whiteboard. Brown slowly stood and walked over to the map, placing his finger on the Spratly Islands.

"Got you bastards this time!" he whispered.

Onboard the junk

Lavender and Jackson were taking a turn on the helm while Reilly and Quicklinsky rested below deck. Their new heading was difficult to steer because the quartering waves kept pushing the boat off course. The ride below deck was even more difficult because the boat was now rolling, as well as pitching up and down, not to mention the sheer, deafening roar of the storm. It was the absolute worst boat ride Boucher could ever remember. He couldn't even begin to sleep, so he decided to keep his mind off the circumstances by reading the OPLANs. He had already finished reading the earliest-dated volume, and was nearly through the succeeding one, which was dated June, 1958.

Boucher found this volume to be intriguing, not only because he was a history buff, but because it was written during his first tour in Vietnam. For the first time in his life, he finally understood the real reason he had gone to Vietnam. It was all there in front of him, revealed in the Plan. Reading these plans sequentially provided Boucher with an evolutionary perspective of U.S. policy from that time up to today. It was an uncensored, untouched, agenda-free account of our key plan to fight an all-out war in the Pacific against the Soviet Union. It detailed how many ships, planes, and ground units would be required, where they would be positioned for engagement, and what they would be expected to achieve. It described what countries the U.S. would consider sacrificial as well as those countries we considered strategic and intended to fight for.

He actually found the information both satisfying and troubling. It was satisfying to know the truth. The truth about why the United States fought the Korean War and the Vietnam War. It was satisfying to finally understand the true strategic value to U.S. security of countries like Japan, Korea, the Philippines, Taiwan, Indonesia, Thailand, Malaysia and Vietnam. He was finally piecing the puzzle together and connecting the dots. He wished he could tell all the Korean War and Vietnam War veterans about it because it was so revealing.

At the same time he was troubled by what he was learning. He was troubled because the cause and justifications sold to the public for going to war in Korea and Vietnam by the U.S. government were far from the truth. What Boucher had just learned was that neither of those two wars was about stopping communist aggression in those countries. Neither of those two wars was about democratizing the southern half of those countries so those poor, backward third world people could flourish in a free, democratic society. What he had learned from reading OPLAN 5000 was that the U.S. government had a sinister and far-reaching strategy in place for more than forty years. He had learned that every American President of that era continued the covert campaign of giving the U.S. public misinformation to justify the underlying truth for the real reason the U.S. fought two wars and for the sacrifice of so many of its sons. Boucher now understood the big picture and as he continued to read, the picture grew larger and more encompassing.

Most of the men were now awake and stirring about the cramped cabin, trying to get something to eat. Several hours passed as he read, but Boucher didn't notice. Patterson sat down next to him, bracing himself against the pitching boat. Moss joined them. Patterson passed a canteen cup of lukewarm coffee to Boucher, nearly splashing it on him as the boat pitched downward.

"Thanks for the java, Pat."

"You're always welcome, Jake. I'm just damn glad to be here to offer it to you."

Both men smiled at one another.

"Hey, you've been stuck to that OPLAN for hours. You learning anything?"

Boucher closed the Plan and placed it on the deck beside him. "Pat, this is some of the most informative historical reading I've ever done."

"You started to tell me about some of it when we were back in Cambodia, but I guess I really wasn't paying much attention. I think you told me that this explains why we fought in Vietnam—or something to that effect."

Boucher repositioned himself. He looked at Patterson and then at Moss. "You wanna hear what I've learned?" he asked them.

Moss shrugged and readjusted his DILLIGAFF hat. "Well, what the hell! We can't dance 'cause there ain't any Marines travel'n with us. Hell, there ain't anyplace to go drinking for the next few hours either."

Boucher smiled. "Okay, Mossman. Let me start at the beginning. Pat, I told you some of this before, but this time I can put it in perspective. These war plans are a sequential account of U.S. policy and detail exactly how we intended to fight a war in the Pacific theater against the Soviet Union. I've read two of the four Plans so far, and I'm about halfway through number three now. Each plan is an updated version of the previous one. I'm reading chronologically, starting with the first one dated February 1950. I don't know if the basic Plan was written prior to 1950 or if it was first formally classified on paper as a Plan in 1950. I suppose it doesn't matter."

Moss interrupted. "We got four Plans from that crash site, right?"

"Yes, four."

"What do you suppose they were doing on that airplane?"

"My guess is that they were probably part of the CIA's classified library at the American Embassy in Saigon and rather than destroy them unnecessarily, someone chose to fly them out on the Air America plane along with the gold. At any rate, there must have been a classified record kept of the cargo manifest. They just didn't know where their plane went down or the disposition of the crash site until we came along."

LeFever and Doyle, still munching on their MREs, joined the group. Boucher attempted to sip his coffee and spilled some down the front of his shirt as he did. "Friggin' weather!" he mumbled as he wiped his hand across his chin.

"Okay boys, I'm going to take you back to 1945 and the end of World War II. If I recall my history of that period, General Patton wanted to invade Russia since he was already in Europe with his army. Patton knew Russia was close to building its own nuclear weapon and he recognized he had an opportunity to nip it in the bud. He and MacArthur saw Stalin as a crazy man who had every intention of conquering post World War II Europe at any cost. General MacArthur wanted to nuke the Russians. The reason he wanted to do that was because he recognized them to be the only future, global, superpower threat to the United States. At the time, we were the only country in the world that possessed nuclear weapons and we had produced a few spares that we didn't use on Japan. MacArthur correctly reasoned that if we used them in a devastating surprise attack on Russia, we would eliminate Russia as a threat to the U.S. and the rest of the free world for the next seventy-five to one-hundred years."

LeFever interrupted, "Yeah, but Truman was President and saw Patton as an unguided missile and MacArthur as a serious Presidential hopeful. Right?"

"Absolutely!" Boucher answered. "President Truman wouldn't allow that on his watch because it was politically out of the question to attack Russia, even if it did make military sense. So MacArthur devised a plan to keep Russia in its box, but he had to make it sell politically. Since the U.S. was already occupying all of Japan and several other strategic locations throughout the Pacific as a result of the war, he reasoned that we would need to develop a containment strategy to first, buy time, and then to ultimately defeat the Russians should they decide to take us on militarily."

LeFever interrupted Boucher again. "Why is the Pacific so important? There's one hell of a lot of ocean between the east coast of Russia and California!"

Boucher gave him a thumbs-up. "Exactly! If Russia launched an attack against us, she would have had one hell of a logistics' problem re-supplying her forces. It would have required that Russia take and hold many of the same key islands and peninsulas that Japan used as bases to fight us in World War II. Russia would have needed to employ much of the same strategy Japan used in the Pacific."

LeFever interrupted again. "But Jake, what about ICBMs?"

"You have to remember the time period, Thane. It's post-WW II. The only guys who had any serious, guided-rocket technology were the Germans, and their V-2 rockets and buzz bombs weren't even close to being capable of intercontinental flight, much less sub-orbital ballistic flight. In fact, if you recall, when Germany surrendered both the U.S. and Russia raced to claim Germany's rocket scientists for themselves and that was the reason why. Both the U.S. and Russia realized that the next war would be fought using rocket-delivered nuclear weapons. That's probably why Russia was so interested in the space race and getting Sputnik in orbit."

Doyle chimed in. "So MacArthur had already figured it out for himself?"

"Yup," Boucher answered, "sure does seem to be the case, Jackie, and it gets a whole lot better."

Ramirez, who had been listening on the periphery, now joined the group along with Dick Llina.

Boucher continued. "You see, MacArthur realized that our military equipment was largely worn out following World War II and that we couldn't really succeed in a protracted, conventional war against Russia using that old equipment. We needed time to modernize our tanks, our planes and build a 600-ship-strong, modern Navy based on fourteen state-of-the-art carrier battle groups. We also needed a means to contain the Russians until that could be accomplished, because he knew that the American public and our allies had no stomach for more war after defeating Germany and Japan, and they had no intention of investing in a major military modernization program. So that brings us to the Korean War." Boucher took another sip of coffee and continued. "What was the one word we all grew up hearing that would catch the attention of every real American liberal or conservative? What was the one word that would rally the free world to take action? Can anyone tell me?"

"Communism!" Moss answered.

"Bingo," Boucher replied, slapping Moss on the shoulder. "You see MacArthur knew that the free world needed a rallying call. Now all he needed to do was focus that call to arms where it would buy us some time and serve to contain the Russians. And, my friends, that place was Korea. Korea had been devastated by Japan only a few years earlier, during World War II. Japan had essentially carted off most of Korea's resources, ranging from clear cutting their forests to make charcoal and construction timber, to stealing their gold, both privately-owned and the government reserves. Following World War II, Korea was broke and the Korean people were starving. The majority of the food grown there was in the south. The best deepwater ports were in the south and what little industrial base that was left following the war was in the south. So the south had it all, or at least most of it."

Yellowhorse spoke from across the small cabin. "But Jake, I thought China was behind the Korean War?"

"Well, they were a factor in it and here's why," Boucher answered. "During World War II Japan had also invaded China and had raped, pillaged, and plundered their way from north to south. They left the southeast portions of China as depleted as they had left Korea. Southeast China was starving, just like much of Korea, and for the same reasons. China and Korea had a two-thousand-year-long history of tribal warlord rule and friction between those rulers was the norm, not the exception. It was a feudal system, plain and simple. But, what's the closest system to the feudal system today? Socialism, a.k.a. Communism."

Boucher shifted his position slightly and carefully took another sip of coffee, wincing from the foul taste. "So here's the deal. Both China and Korea were recovering from World War II. While Korea was seen as a sovereign country by the rest of the world, the Chinese and Korean warlords didn't know that and didn't give a shit. They were only interested in restoring their individual empires and regaining what they had prior to Japan's invasion during WW II. But MacArthur needed an excuse to occupy Korea and he knew that stopping the communist-infested north from invading the peace-loving free people of the south would sell politically and militarily to everyone that counted at the time. What was never stated was that the real purpose for invading Korea was to take and hold the deepwater ports located on Korea's east coast, and to gain control of the Strait of Korea and Sea of Japan. MacArthur knew that if he could successfully pull that off, he would be able to contain the Soviet Navy based in Vladivostok, the only warm-water port they had in the Pacific, while at the same time denying them access to the closest, land-accessible, deepwater ports in Korea. It was a brilliant strategy."

"But I don't understand how that contained the Soviet Navy?" Ramirez asked.

"Fair question," Boucher responded. "If you picture the Sea of Japan, it's bordered by the Japanese Islands on the east. To the north, you have the Strait of La Perouse, running between Japan's Hokkaido on the east side and Russia's Sakhalin Island on the west. Farther west, you have Russia and the deepwater port of Vladivostok. Moving south along that coast, you have about twenty-five miles of China-owned real estate and then you hit North Korea. MacArthur knew we didn't have enough ships to control the Sea of Japan and keep the Russian fleet in check. He also knew that if Russia was to successfully launch an attack against the U.S. west coast from Vladivostok or other ports in the nearby locale, like those in Korea, they would have to be able to support such an attack logistically. That meant the U.S. had to have positive control of the Japanese Islands to prevent Russian ships and submarines from freely sortieing between the islands, and also control the southern Korean peninsula to prevent the Russians from running the Strait unchecked and breaking out into the South China Sea and beyond. MacArthur knew he had to devise a way to keep them bottled up inside the Sea of Japan and make it extremely costly for them to attempt break out."

Doyle scratched his head quizzically and seemed to search for the right way to frame a question. "Okay Jake, I understand what you're telling me about the importance of Korea and the Japanese Islands and about catching the Russians at the chokepoints between the islands and at the straits where they're most vulnerable. What I don't understand is where you're taking all this!"

Boucher went to take another sip of his cold coffee and stopped short, remembering his last taste minutes earlier. "It's actually somewhat abstract and that's why MacArthur needed something everyone would understand and rally behind. Getting the American public and most of the post-World War II allies behind defending South Korea from a communist invasion from the north is understandable. Trying to explain to the public what I just explained to you would not fly. It's too complex. MacArthur had to have realized that telling the American public the truth about the strategy he was putting in place wouldn't be understood, much less accepted. Think about it. This was a far-out strategy that would span several decades and would eventually lead to the demise of the Soviet Union in the distant future. Americans are simply too impatient to contemplate a long-term strategy like that, and they definitely wouldn't support it with money and their sons' lives. Nope. He needed a clear enemy that we could fight to provide the illusion of a conventional conflict where the good guys wear white hats and the bad guys wear black hats. And that was to invade South Korea, while all the time it was really about securing their deepwater ports and the Strait of Korea so the Russians wouldn't get them first. MacArthur just never told our citizens what it would cost in terms of lives. But, these Plans clearly lay out the strategy, and they don't deviate from it right up through the war we fought in Vietnam."

Patterson chimed in. "That's interesting, Jake, very interesting, indeed. But how do you tie all that to the Vietnam War?"

"I'm not done reading this Plan and I'd only briefly perused the last one when we were in Cambodia, so I'm not sure I can give you a blow-by-blow on that yet. It's sure pointing in that direction, though. What I have read so far explains how we would have responded if the Soviets had attacked us."

"Well shit, how about sharing," Doyle pleaded.

"You guys really want to hear more?"

"Hell yes!" was the resounding answer.

"Okay," Boucher smiled. "Where was I? Oh yeah...our response to a Soviet attack. Let me set the stage again. You now know why we fought the Korean War and the strategic importance of Korea and Japan. You also need to understand the importance of our continued occupation of the Philippines, long after World War II, and why we secured operating bases in locations like Taiwan, Hong Kong, Singapore, Thailand, and Malaysia, to name a few. I want to also explain their strategic importance to our being able to defeat the Soviet Union. That will take us up to the Vietnam War."

Moss picked up Boucher's coffee cup. "Refill?" he asked.

Boucher shook his head no and continued, unfazed by the tumultuous rise and fall of the junk amidst the raging storm. "Following World War II, we remained as an occupational force in Japan. MacArthur waged another war shortly thereafter and we became an occupational force in South Korea below the 38th parallel, where we agreed to go no further north and the North agreed to come no further south. That was great; the U.S. had liberated South Korea from the communists. We had established a DMZ based on a shaky truce with the communist North and that provided an acceptable justification to maintain a large, standing, U.S. military force in South Korea. It gave us the seaports and air bases we needed to launch a counterattack against the Soviets in the event of war, while at the same time providing a tripwire should the Soviets decide to go to war with us or attack one of our new allies in the region, such as Japan or Taiwan. Have you ever wondered what strategic value Taiwan offered? Remember how pissed off most of the conservatives were when Jimmy Carter withdrew our forces from Taiwan? Did you ever wonder why he did that? Most people thought it was to appease the Chinese, but maybe that wasn't why."

"Well Jake, why did we leave Taiwan?" Llina demanded. "The damn suspense is killing me!"

Boucher chuckled. "I'll tell you why, Dick. It's because by the time we left Taiwan we didn't need it anymore. We were only there to buy us some time to build that fourteen-carrier battle group Navy and modernize our military."

"Okay, I got that, Jake. Why did we need it in the first place?" Llina asked.

Boucher formed an imaginary map using his open hands and extended fingers to create a shape representing the Sea of Japan. "Go back to the Sea of Japan and the Soviet break out scenario that I just explained. Like I said, MacArthur was trying to plug all the holes and prevent the USSR's war ships and submarines from breaking out of the SOJ. He wanted to make it as costly as he could for the Soviets if they tried, but he knew that we would take losses and that many of the Soviet war ships would likely make it through to the relative safety of the Pacific Ocean expanses. He also knew that once they made it that far, they would have the freedom to attack our fleet and ultimately the coast of California, Canada, and Alaska. But the Soviets had an Achilles heel. They had a long transit and they would have had to utilize the same sea-lanes every other ship used. They only had two viable options after breaking out of the SOJ. The first was to sail north, along the Japanese Islands, for a run through the Strait of Alaska. The drawback on that option was that it did not offer them any in-route resupply or repair capability should they be attacked and depending on the time of year, it was weather dependent—as in frozen solid. The second option was to head for the South China Sea. This was a warm-water transit, with numerous ports along the way, offering both repair and resupply options should they be necessary. That route would take them by Hong Kong, Taiwan, the Philippines, Vietnam, and through the Strait of Malaysia that is bordered by Singapore and East Malaysia. Again, MacArthur recognized that if he could secure these strategic points along this critical route, it would also put the Soviets at risk from our maritime patrol aircraft and short-range attack aircraft operating from shore bases along the way. It would buy the U.S. time to rebuild our military. So you see, we had to occupy those places as a means of denying the Soviets the use of them as bases and to keep them under check so we could track their every move."

Moss slapped his knee. "I gotta hand it to you, Jake. That's about the most in-depth briefing I've ever had on this shit. I can't believe it's actually in the Plan."

"Well, Mossman, there's more, but I need to finish reading the other volumes. I can probably finish both in a couple of hours. If you guys want to convene later, I'll tell you the rest of the story, just like Paul Harvey does. I'm actually getting a little burned out from doing all the talking."

Moss smiled. "Hey, you mind if I start reading the first Plan?"

Boucher reached into the corner and passed the volume to Moss.

"Help yourself, Mossman. You might catch some stuff I missed. But be forewarned, there aren't any pictures and we all know that's an attention-sustaining handicap for you flyboys."

"Eat shit, knuckle dragger!"

Boucher smiled and headed for the deck to check on their progress.

CHAPTER 23

USS Virginia

Commander Galloway entered the control room and joined Cutler at the flat-screen chart display. Cutler pointed to the sub's position.

"We are currently here, Sir. We have been running about five-hundred yards astern of the HIV for the past seven hours. The seas remain state-3. As a result, we have been unable to successfully ID the vessel. We did record some still and video imagery of the HIV and attempted to capture ID quality imagery of those men on deck, but it has been pretty much useless because of the sea state and storm conditions above. Unfortunately, we have no better idea now who these guys are or what they're up to than we did twelve hours ago. As far as we can determine, they are mystery men on a mystery mission. We're now approaching the Spratlys and the bottom will be coming up under us. We're going to need to break off the pursuit very soon or risk grounding. Sorry, Skipper. What are your orders?"

Galloway contemplated what he had just been told by Cutler. "Lieutenant, exactly when do we need to break contact?"

Cutler touched a point on the electronic chart. "Providing the HIV maintains its current heading…here, Sir. We can safely go no shallower than this point right here."

"Very well, Mister Cutler. Proceed to that point before breaking contact. Once contact is broken, return ten miles seaward and assume patrol posture Charlie. We'll await further orders from COMSUBPAC there."

"Aye, Sir."

Galloway remained at the chart studying it. "Mister Cutler," Galloway asked his young Lieutenant, "if you were the guy in charge on that boat, which island in the Spratlys would you be going to?"

Cutler studied the chart again. "Well Sir, I know where I wouldn't go. I wouldn't go to this one," he said pointing to one of the largest of the many, "or even anywhere close to it."

"And why is that, Mister Cutler?"

"Well Sir, there's a fortified Chinese outpost on that one. They built it back in the eighties to intimidate all the other countries that lay claim to Spratlys Islands ownership. I've seen the overhead imagery on it and it's bristling with artillery and ground-to-air missiles. I guess it kind of resembles a concrete battleship of sorts."

"So you would avoid that atoll and any others close by?"

"Yes, Sir."

"Would you sail north or south of it?"

Cutler put his finger back on the chart. "I'd stay to the south. The water is a whole lot shallower and more dangerous to navigate, but it would provide some protection from a Chinese intercept should they be in the mood to come after you in one of their high-speed patrol boats."

"Interesting reasoning, Mister Cutler."

"Thank you, Captain."

"One more question. Based upon your scenario, do you see any way to put us into a position to cut them off on the other side?"

"Sure do, Sir. We certainly have enough water under us to maneuver on the other side. But what are you thinking, Captain? Are you thinking that we should continue surveillance on them or surface and take them down at gunpoint?"

"I'll let you know when the time comes, Mister Cutler. For now, I want you to plot a course around the other side to the point you just showed me. Plan on making the transit at three-hundred feet and best speed."

"Would you like me to inform COMSUBPAC?"

"Of course. We're trying to reacquire a lost contact."

"Yes, Sir," Cutler said, bracing to attention.

American Embassy, Bangkok

"Mr. Brown, Mr. Thompson is on the 'green line' for you."

Brown leaned forward towards the secure voice telephone to reply.

"Thanks, Trudy," he said in an uncharacteristically congenial voice.

. . .

Trudy, Brown's secretary, never knew how he would react to even the simplest of messages. Sometimes Brown would explode in anger for no apparent reason, and other times he would show no emotion at all. Trudy, a CIA office administrative employee for almost eighteen years, had worked for many bosses. She understood that his behavior was simply something she had to tolerate. After all, Brown was the CIA's Chief of Station in Bangkok. He was the top spy in the area, and men like him didn't ascend to lofty positions like that without knowing their stuff. But Brown's background was questionable. He'd spent most of his previous years at the CIA Headquarters in Langley, Virginia as an analyst, not as a Case Officer in the Operations Directorate. He was the product of the analytical culture, not an experienced operations planner or director. His skill-set ill fit the job he held. He was a Washington political hack who knew how to schmooze his superiors, not how to conduct covert operations. But over the past fifteen years the CIA culture had eroded to the point where face time at headquarters was rewarded with promotion and risk-taking was seen as a negative attribute for senior managers. Trudy reasoned that was probably the basis for some of his unpredictable behavior. He was not a risk-taker himself, and was always uncomfortable around those who were. He never missed an opportunity to take advantage of their successes or their failures. He had a well-refined talent for always coming out smelling like a rose.

Brown picked up the phone. "Rene, how are you this fine day? What can I do for you?"

Brown doodled on a note pad in front of him as he listened to his boss, Rene Thompson, the CIA's Director for Covert Operations.

"Yes, I dispatched a team to Manila several hours ago on our G-4. They're going to link up with some of Tom Miller's guys from our Manila office and head out to the Spratlys on a charter boat. That storm has us socked in, so using a seaplane is a non-starter." Brown listened. "I anticipate they will be on target by this evening, perhaps as early as 2100, weather permitting."

Brown began to scratch some notes.

"Yes, I have Dwight Howe leading the operation himself. Yes, I understand how important it is, but I don't know about using a seaplane to get out there faster. Okay, whatever you say. I'll pass it on to Howe...I will, thanks." He hung up the phone and sighed.

Brown pressed the intercom button. "Trudy, please get me a secure line to Tom Miller in Manila."

"Right away."

A few minutes later his phone rang. "Brown," he answered.

"Mr. Brown, Mr. Miller is on line one—secure."

"Thanks, Trudy."

Brown punched the flashing button. "Tom, I just got off the phone with Rene. We've been directed to have our guys fly out to the Spratlys and rendezvous with a submarine—the USS Virginia. They are to board the sub and go from there. Looks like we'll need a seaplane instead of a charter boat."

Brown paused to listen to Miller's reply.

"Look Tom, I know it's dangerous, but orders are orders. Yeah, I know who's in charge of the operation and I know I can run it as I see fit, but I'm using ML's rule of three. As long as it's legal, safe, and it gets the job done, it's a go."

Brown nervously shifted in his chair.

"Now Tom, I disagree with you. It's not bullshit! Rene says we can do it and we will. It's not any more risky than a boat transit to the same location and no, I have never personally landed in a seaplane on a stormy sea, but that is not the point."

Brown shifted his position again and propped his head up on his fist.

"Tom, don't raise your voice to me. I am only following orders and that is what you need to do as well."

Brown slumped forward on his desk as he listened.

"Look Tom, you can refuse to send your guys along. That's certainly your prerogative, but Howe and my other guys are going with or without your help!"

Brown began massaging his forehead with his free hand.

"Well, whatever! Rene says he needs to recover the precious cargo on that boat! Look Tom, I don't appreciate the words you're using and I don't think Director Thompson would either."

Now exasperated, Brown slouched down in his chair.

"Well, you can't expect to talk to me this way without Director Thompson knowing about it, now do you?"

Brown pulled the phone away from his ear. "That SOB just hung up on me!" he growled to himself.

Brown's anger blazed as he pressed the intercom button.

"Trudy, get me Director Thompson and do it now! I'm so damn pissed off I can't see straight! That SOB Miller thinks he has his shit together and that he can act anyway he pleases. I will not tolerate that son of a bitch! He's in the way! Get Thompson on the line now!"

"Yes Mr. Brown, right away."

On the junk

Lavender interrupted Boucher who was almost finished reading the last OPLAN volume.

"Hey Bossman, we're about an hour out. We're taking the southern passage to the east side. We should get some protection from the seas once we're inside the chain. I figure it'll take us a couple of hours to get through to the other side. Sure don't want to run this tub aground."

"Excellent, Mojo. How are you holding up?"

"Awh shoot. I've felt better on the mornings of my worst hangovers, but I'm okay I reckon."

"Yeah, I hear ya. None of us are getting any younger and we have been taking one hell of a pounding over the past few days. I am looking forward to a hot shower, an air-conditioned room, a soft bed, and a warm woman..."

Boucher laughed. "Amen! I heard that!"

Lavender became dead serious. "Jake, you got any idea why that sub was following us?"

"That's the six-hundred-forty-million-dollar question. My guess is that we've been under near constant surveillance since we started this operation. At first I figured it was about the gold, but now... now that I've read the OPLANs, I'm almost positive it's about them. That information is so revealing, I guess it could cause a loss of trust in the U.S. government if it were publicly divulged. I can just visualize it: documentaries, made for TV movies, talk shows and talking heads all discussing and spinning the facts to fit their own agendas. It could be devastating to national security.

On the other hand, there would be guys like us who would appreciate the genius in it. Think about it. How could General MacArthur have known? Better yet, it has got to be the best-kept secret the U.S. government ever had. Think of all the different Presidents who must have known and supported the grand strategy. While the documents are classified Top Secret, they are also marked Special Category code word. A SPECAT document requires exclusive access. It's need-to-know, and over the years only very few have had that need. So it's my guess that there were only a handful of high-ranking officials who were ever given the access to read the entire OPLAN 5000 document. Even at that level it would have been compartmentalized. A number of people would have had access to certain parts of the document, but not to the entire OPLAN. To understand the big picture you have to read it all from cover to cover."

Mojo smiled. "Yeah, I know the deal on the big picture. That's what generals, admirals, and politicians all have. I hear that when you become a flag officer they take you into a special room where they cut off your balls. Then they make you breathe chicken shit gas until you can't tell the difference between it and regular air. Then they show you the big picture. Problem is you ain't allowed to ever tell no one about it."

Boucher laughed at his friend's comments. "Well, that's probably pretty close to the way it is, Mojo. I'll tell you what really amazes me about this. We have four versions of the OPLAN that span about twenty years, from the beginning of the Korean War well into the Vietnam War. I know for a fact that when a revised version of an OPLAN is put out, the old version is destroyed. Why the first three volumes weren't destroyed beats the living shit out of me. I'm guessing that since the Plans were onboard a CIA Air America airplane, they must have come from the CIA's station within the American Embassy Saigon. The night we saw that plane streak overhead in flames, we were in the middle of the Tet offensive."

"Yeah. That was the all-out NVA assault against Saigon, and they damn near succeeded," Lavender commented.

"You're right, Mojo. I figure that the CIA ordered their Saigon office closed. These documents had to be shipped out of Vietnam before it fell to the NVA. Because of their sensitivity, the Plans were packaged as securely as possible. Casting them inside concrete seemed pretty secure at the time and I guess it worked—until we came along."

"So Jake, you think the CIA is still trying to find their lost documents after forty years?"

"Well, it sure seems like somebody is trying to get a hold of them. The more I think through the events of the past week, I think it has got to be about the OPLANs. The problem is that they're on to us. They're assuming we have the Plans because they know we have the gold. We have to figure out what that means to our future."

Mojo chuckled and stroked his silvery white beard. "Another fine mess you got us into. We are probably some of the richest men on the planet and we can't spend our money because we're carrying some super secret baggage that the government wants to recover. You suppose they see us as the good guys or the bad guys?"

"At this point I'm unsure. The important thing to remember is that we know the difference. We haven't broken any U.S. laws. We've recovered some gold from a location not under U.S. jurisdictional authority. The gold we recovered belonged to a government that no longer exists. Okay, we crashed a plane or two along the way, but tough shit. We had a shoot out and won, but we have the right of self-defense and they shot first. Would any of us ever shoot at our own countrymen or willingly do anything to endanger our government? We all know the answer to that question."

USS Virginia

Commander Galloway hadn't been able to sleep. He had just finished reviewing the sub's weekly status report. It was due at COMSUBPAC by the end of the day and there were some discrepancies in main engineering concerning the sub's nuclear reactor that concerned him. That, coupled with the new orders he had just received from COMSUBPAC, made his head hurt.

Lieutenant Cutler knocked on Galloway's stateroom door. He heard his commanding officer call a forceful, "Enter."

Stepping inside, Cutler braced to attention.

"Sir, reporting as ordered."

Galloway read from a clipboard covered with a red paper stamped "Secret."

"We just received orders to rendezvous on the surface with a seaplane at point Hotel. The LAT and LONG are provided here. We are to transfer three passengers aboard. A Mr. Howe will provide amplifying orders once onboard." Galloway pounded his desktop. "This smells like a CIA operation and I don't like it! Most of the CIA weenies I've ever known think they're all James Bond and that submarines are built by some guy named Q."

Cutler nodded but remained silent.

"But enough of my opinion," Galloway said changing his tone. "We're submariners and we'll support them as professionally as we possibly can. My calculation puts Point Hotel about two hours east of our current position."

Galloway handed Cutler the clipboard. Cutler studied the new position coordinates.

"Yes, Sir. It's southeast of our current posit. I recommend that we remain submerged as long as we can, Sir. In this sea state a pax transfer will be extremely dangerous, both for our guys and theirs. I recommend we use our OE mast to locate the plane. Once we see them on radar and they're close, we can surface. Getting a boat inflated and launched is going to be very dicey for our guys on deck."

"Concur. I'll join you in the con in a half hour."

"Aye, Sir."

On the junk

Boucher had completed reading all four volumes of OPLAN 5000. Included at the bottom of the last volume, he discovered and read a draft contingency plan that was titled CONPLAN 5028. It provided a detailed overview about what the U.S. intended to do in the event China entered the war as a Soviet ally. Boucher now understood the importance of these documents and what they meant to national security. Moss and Patterson were the first to notice that Boucher had finished the last volume. He had moved over to the chart table and was now reviewing the navigation chart that Quicklinsky had so diligently maintained with up-to-date position plots.

"Hey Jake, we still have a couple of hours to go. How about we continue what we started about the OPLAN this morning?" Patterson asked.

Boucher turned towards his two friends. "I suppose we could do that."

Moss sat on a stack of gold bars quietly munching on an MRE dessert pack. His attention was entirely focused upon another pile of gold bars a few feet away.

"Whatcha thinking about, Mossman?" Boucher asked.

Moss maintained his gaze as he swallowed a mouthful of chocolate fudge.

"Staring at all this gold is kinda like watching a dog take a shit; you just can't stop lookin' and you don't know why."

"Listen up! Jake is gonna continue the OPLAN briefing for those interested," Patterson announced for all to hear.

The men casually gathered around Boucher and made themselves as comfortable as they could under the stormy circumstances.

Patterson nodded to Boucher. "Okay Jake, take it away."

Boucher began where he left off.

"Well gentlemen, I told you that I would explain how the Vietnam War factored into our strategy to defeat the Soviet Union. I will now explain that and bring you up to speed on the China connection.

"You may recall that in the early 60's the U.S. began sending Army Special Forces Green Beret military advisors to South Vietnam to help train their military forces. At the time, South Vietnam didn't really exist as a sovereign breakaway, independent from the north. The North and South had been fighting a civil war against each other for years, and once again it was mostly based on an antiquated feudal system of government that involved class warfare. There were very rich and there were very poor people, but little-to-no middle class. The majority of Vietnam's food was grown in the south and private land ownership was virtually non-existent. The rich owned the land and the poor toiled on it. You guys picking up on any Korea parallels in what I'm telling you?"

Some of the men nodded agreement. Others stared at Boucher impassively. Everyone was captivated.

"Anyway, Vietnam had been embroiled in its civil war for years. The French occupied the country throughout the fifties and fought in that civil war on the side of the South. Why the South? Well, for the same reason we supported the South. We needed access to the seaports along the Mekong and as far north as Hanoi. The difference was that the French were a colonial power in the region. We were not there to colonize and open trade. The French suffered a series of stinging military defeats during their occupation of Vietnam and finally left with their tails between their legs. By this time it was the early 60s, the Korean War was over, and General MacArthur passed the OPLAN 5000 baton to President Kennedy. He needed Vietnam for seaports and airbases to control the west side of the South China Sea, but he couldn't just send our forces in there and take it. He needed both political and public support and a compelling reason to occupy Vietnam. Since it worked so well in Korea, the big C-word was introduced once more. Yep, it was those damn Commies again, trying to invade another small helpless nation of freedom-loving, harmless people."

Boucher paused momentarily to better brace himself against the tossing boat.

"So, first we sent in our military advisers. When they were regularly getting whacked on combat missions, President Kennedy sent in reinforcements, and when Lyndon Johnson became President after Kennedy's assassination, Johnson invaded. The first thing our guys did was to build numerous airbases and improve the deepwater harbors like Cam Ran Bay. Since the NVA didn't want us there, we had a real fight on our hands. Did you ever wonder why the President never took our gloves off and let us really kick the shit out of the North? Well I'll tell you why—we didn't need the North's real estate to achieve the Soviet containment strategy goals. If we had simply gone in there and kicked the livin' shit out of those assholes and achieved a clear victory, we would have had to reduce our standing force and leave the country in a matter of a few years."

"Wait a minute, Jake!" LeFever cautioned. "Are you telling us that our government intentionally prolonged the fight so we could base our forces in Vietnam under the pretense of a war to liberate the South from Communist aggression from the North?"

Boucher sighed. "Thane, I suppose that's basically it. You can read the Plan and connect the dots for yourself if you don't believe me."

"Jeez, Jake!" Patterson blurted out, sounding more like a cough than a statement. "So you're saying that all that sacrifice, all those guys killed, was really a delaying action and winning would have been contrary to the Plan because we would have had to take our toys and go home?"

"Yes, Pat. We never intended to win that war! We needed to occupy it to buy time to build the fourteen carrier battle group Navy and all the new B-1 bombers and the like."

Patterson shook his head in disbelief. "That was the carrier Navy I was part of?"

Boucher nodded. "We left Vietnam in 1975 because we didn't need to stay any longer. It had served its strategic purpose and it no longer mattered whether the NVA and the communist regime took it or not. We didn't quite have everything we needed to keep the Soviets in check by then, but we did have sea control. We had enough super carriers. We had enough long-range bombers. We had the air mobility and sealift capability to move our forces anywhere in the world we wanted on short notice. And we had a standing active duty military force that totaled more than three-million men in uniform. There was only one superpower left to threaten us and that was the Soviet Union."

Doyle raised his hand. "What about China. Didn't they have a huge army?"

"Good question, Jackie. The answer is, yes. China had and still has the largest army in the world. There's just one major point everybody seems to forget about China's military—it's a defensively equipped force. It lacks the capability for inter-continental mobility which means China can't project its military power further than they can march. Besides, if you take a really hard look at China's history over the last two-thousand-plus years, China has never postured militarily to project power. It has always largely been a closed society. But I will say that today the issue of Taiwan's independence is in jeopardy and that ties directly to the U.S. What do we really know about them?" Boucher asked as he rubbed his chin. "China is very much a wild card. Hell, they own over forty percent of our debt. We default and they own us! That's extraordinary power!"

Doyle raised his hand again. "So why did we need all those ships and airplanes during the Cold War? How does nuclear deterrence factor into all this strategy shit you're talking about?"

"Another good question, Jackie. You see the one thing that General MacArthur and the other framers of the containment strategy couldn't anticipate was how fast the rest of the world would develop their own nuclear arsenal. It didn't take the Brits very long because we shared our warhead design information with them. The Soviets didn't waste any time because they had captured a bunch of German physicists during World War II, just like we did. And their German scientists knew about as much about heavy water and yellow cake as the scientists we captured. The difference was that we dedicated a huge amount of our natural resources to the Manhattan Project with the single-minded goal of building an atomic bomb. The Russians were fighting the Germans and had neither the resources to dedicate nor the national focus required to build an atomic bomb."

"But after World War II, that all changed," Moss interrupted. "The Soviets raced to build a bomb of their own because they felt threatened by the U.S. in the belief that someone, like our friend General MacArthur, would use one on them and they wouldn't be able to retaliate. Right?"

"You're right, Mossman. I guess in hindsight, they weren't that far off. Anyway, the Soviets built their nuclear program largely through a successful espionage effort that targeted U.S. bomb design. I guess spying worked for them because once they started, they developed their bomb in record time and that's when the nuclear arms race started."

Everyone nodded in agreement.

"After the Soviets had the bomb, we entered a race to build bigger, more lethal bombs and, naturally, we all believed that the guy with the most toys and bombs wins. Even though we each had thousands of warheads, more was better. I remember as a kid, wondering how many times each country could totally kill every living thing on this planet in an all-out nuclear exchange. As I recall the answer was several hundred times, but that's what nuclear deterrence was all about. You couldn't resort to a nuclear war like that because no one would win. But a conventional war was feasible, especially if it provided a means to invade smaller, weaker nations that didn't have the bomb and couldn't adequately defend themselves militarily. I think it's probably fair to say that following World War II most of the small nations making up the Pacific littoral fit that description. They were ripe for the plucking. They were ripe for Soviet expansionism and we couldn't let the Reds have them. And that, my friends, is what OPLAN 5000 is all about. Now you need to hear the rest of the story because it gets a whole lot more convoluted. I just learned that part in a CONPLAN that was attached to the bottom of the last OPLAN volume I read."

Everyone just sat quietly for a few moments, and then Moss began to clap. Everyone joined in. Boucher felt embarrassed, but the men truly appreciated the insight he provided.

Doyle waited until the applause ended to ask his question. "So Jake, what do you think these guys who've been after us intend to do with the OPLANS if they get their hands on them?"

CHAPTER 24

Vicinity of the Spratlys, nine hours later

A veteran CIA pilot, Tim Dunkin from the Manila office, was piloting the seaplane carrying the two CIA operatives. He was an experienced pilot who knew the Philippine Islands like the palm of his hand. While he had over-flown the Spratlys Islands several times before, he had never landed there. It was a very dangerous day to fly anywhere, much less that far seaward. The visibility was about a quarter mile in the driving, tropical rain and the ceiling ranged between five-hundred to eight-hundred feet above the angry sea below. Dunkin was flying a straight south westerly line to the Spratlys at an altitude of four-hundred feet. He hadn't filed a flight plan or declared his position using the plane's transponder. This was a typical CIA clandestine mission. He would land on the sea, rendezvous with a U.S. submarine, transfer his two passengers and reappear back on the mainland without anyone being the wiser. But Dunkin had no idea what he, Howe, and Gunn would truly face this day.

"We're about an hour away," Dunkin reported to Howe, who was sitting in the co-pilot's seat.

"Good," Howe replied. He was plainly on the verge of becoming airsick from the turbulence that was bouncing the small seaplane beneath the rain-laden, cumulous clouds. "I'll be happy when this ride is over."

"Yeah, can't argue with that. It doesn't get much worse than this," Dunkin said as he forced a smile in Howe's direction. "Open your air vent further. Maybe that will help."

Even though he was feeling nauseous, Howe forced a smile back at Dunkin and nodded.

USS Virginia

Cutler clicked the intercom mic open to the Captain's stateroom. "Sir, inbound RADAR contact bearing zero niner three, one-hundred and six knots at four zero zero feet, ten miles, not squawking IFF. It's got to be the seaplane."

Commander Galloway rolled out of his rack. His splitting headache hadn't subsided, even after taking 600 milligrams of ibuprofen thirty minutes earlier.

"Damn!" he mumbled to himself as he flicked the intercom mic open to reply. "Very well, prepare to surface. I'm on my way."

On the junk

Boucher went topside. The seas had flattened somewhat because the junk was passing between the Spratlys Islands, which provided some protection. The rain continued its torrential assault, but the ride was definitely better. Boucher approached Quicklinsky who was expertly navigating the small junk between the numerous islands, shoals, and reefs that surrounded them. It was dangerous water to navigate on a clear, calm day, much less in the midst of a storm.

"How you holding up?" Boucher asked.

Quicklinsky wiped the water off his face before answering.

"Okay, I guess. I haven't had this much fun since '71, when we lost our engine off Cuba in that broke dick boat we borrowed from the Marines in Gitmo. You remember that night?"

Boucher put an arm around Quicklinsky's back and patted him.

"How you doing?" he asked Lavender, who was at the helm.

"Oh, I reckon I'm okay, Jake, but I'm running low on dip."

Boucher slapped him on the shoulder. "I'll see what I can do. How much further do you figure we have until we break out on the east side?"

Quicklinsky put his finger on the chart for Boucher to see. "Here's where we are. Here's the other side. I figure a few more miles to the deep water, providing we don't hit something first."

Boucher nodded.

It was then they heard the drone of a plane's engine approaching. All three men turned to the direction of the sound and searched the sky beneath the clouds. Then it appeared. The small seaplane was descending in what appeared to be a landing attempt. Quicklinsky quickly checked his navigation chart and looked back at the plane. A look of horror came over his face.

"That guy is going to smack into a reef if he lands there!"

The three old SEALs stared in silence as the plane continued its approach. The plane touched the surface of the water and vaulted across several wave tops before plunging through the next two. Suddenly, the plane flipped nose first onto its roof, coming to rest on a barely submerged coral reef.

There was no sign of life on the plane. Waves were breaking over the plane's wings and shoving it toward the edge of the reef where it certainly would slide off and sink in the deeper water.

Boucher acted quickly. In what seemed like two gigantic strides, he made it to the hatch leading below where the rest of his men were. He threw open the hatch.

"I need you boys on deck! A plane just crashed off our port bow!"

As the men assembled on deck, Boucher barked orders. "Launch the Zbird. Billy, I need you to drive. Johnny, you're with me. Get your jungle boots on so we can walk on the coral. Bring your swim gear."

Patterson stepped up to Boucher. "Not without me, good buddy."

Boucher nodded his consent.

The men quickly launched the Zodiac as Quicklinsky held the junk with its side against the seas to create a lee to make the launch safer. Boucher and his three men jumped into the inflatable boat and started the thirty-five horsepower outboard. The motor roared to life and they sped off toward the plane. Reilly skillfully maneuvered to bring the Zodiac bow-first into the seas and then cautiously toward the shallow reef. The boat came to a sudden, grinding halt as its bow grounded on the coral.

"Let's do it!" Boucher shouted as he leaped over the side onto the reef.

Patterson and Yellowhorse followed on his heels.

The plane was steadily being washed across the reef toward them every time a wave hit it. There was still no sign of life when Boucher opened the upside down door located behind the wing. Boucher climbed into the plane and directed Yellowhorse to remain outside where they could recover survivors. He waved to Patterson to follow him. Immediately, Boucher noted that there were three men onboard the plane. Everyone was dressed in black battle dress uniforms and armed with FN Five-Seven pistols and P-90 sub-machine guns. *CIA standard issue,* Boucher thought to himself.

The pilot and the man in the co-pilot's seat both looked dead. They were dangling upside down, suspended from their seats in chest deep water. Boucher quickly unbuckled the pilot's seat harness and pulled him from his seat, passing him over to Patterson. Patterson grabbed the lifeless man by the collar and dragged him back to the open door where Yellowhorse took him. The co-pilot was next. As Boucher passed the man to Patterson he noticed that the man had severe head lacerations that ran from ear to ear across his forehead. He also had a compound fracture of his right wrist.

"Don't grab his right wrist, Pat!"

"Roger!"

The man in the rear seat fared a little better. He was unconscious but didn't appear to be severely injured. As Boucher un-strapped the man, he groaned in pain and had trouble breathing.

"This guy's got a crushed chest," Boucher shouted to Patterson. "Watch how you hold him."

At that moment, a mammoth wave broke over the plane and pushed it another ten feet toward the abyss that was to be its inevitable end.

Yellowhorse shouted to Boucher and Patterson. "One more like that and you boys are gonna need SCUBA! It's time to go!"

"Okay Johnny, we got one more coming your way."

Boucher attempted to shove the man to the safety of Patterson's waiting hands, but the man's foot was wedged beneath the rear bottom of the front seat. Patterson reached through the plane's small door and grabbed the man's arm, holding him above the rising water. Boucher shifted himself completely into the rear of the airplane and was now attempting to free the man's foot. Another wave struck the plane, knocking Boucher off balance and washing Patterson into the sea next to the boat. Yellowhorse grabbed Patterson's leg and was able to hold on just long enough to allow him to regain his hold on the plane's wing strut and work his way back to the open door. The situation was becoming frantic as the men strained to rescue the plane's remaining survivor.

USS Virginia

The Virginia had surfaced about a quarter of a mile from the coral reef in deep water as it waited for the plane to arrive. Six crewmen were on deck in a fight with the sea, attempting to inflate a rubber raft to use for the personnel transfer from the plane to the sub.

"Captain!" the starboard lookout shouted. "Starboard lookout, contact at zero niner zero, eight-hundred yards. I see a junk attempting to maneuver and a small airplane upside down on a submerged reef...looks like there's a rescue underway."

Commander Galloway focused his binoculars in the precise direction the lookout had just reported. Galloway pulled his binoculars down and made a brief call into the ship's intercom.

"Man overboard! Man overboard! This is not a drill! This is the Captain speaking. We have a situation off our starboard side. It appears that a plane has crashed on a coral reef and that there is a small vessel present attempting to rescue survivors. Rescue swimmers on deck. Make ready and launch the inflatable boat."

"Captain!" the lookout yelled again. "It looks like that plane is being pushed off the reef by the waves and it's beginning to sink!"

Galloway yanked his binoculars back up to viewing position and stared as he watched the plane slide off the reef. It almost looked surreal to him. The plane slowly settled nose first and then flipped tail up. The wings disappeared from sight as seawater flooded into the plane's interior. A small, inflatable boat circled the plane. Just as the tail sank beneath the surface a man popped up next to it. Galloway gasped as he saw the man pull another man up next to him. The rubber boat approached and the men in the rubber boat pulled the two men who had just surfaced aboard.

"How much longer until we launch the boat?" Galloway shouted.

"We're ready now, Captain."

"Launch the boat and get over to that crash site as fast as you can! Ensure our men are armed, just in case."

"Aye, Sir!"

The submarine's rubber boat was slid into the water and the four sailors manning it were off in the direction of the coral reef.

On the junk

Boucher's entire crew was on deck watching the rescue. They were also watching the submarine that had surfaced about one-thousand yards seaward of their position and they saw the small, black, rubber, inflatable boat from the submarine, plowing its way through the heavy seas toward Boucher's Zodiac. Boucher's boat was now overloaded because of the additional three bodies they had pulled from the downed plane and it was taking on water. While it was in no danger of sinking because it was inflatable, all the additional weight made the going very slow.

Moss jumped up on the pilothouse behind Quicklinsky. "Chief, can we go get them?" he shouted.

"No way! If I take this tub any closer to that reef, we'll end up like that frickin' plane did! All I can do is try to hold her here in the channel and wait for them to come to us."

"Okay, I got it, but that boat from the sub is gaining on them."

Quicklinsky coolly surveyed the situation and then took charge.

"Alright everyone, listen up! I want four automatic weapons men positioned on the side I bring to bear. Doc, I want you and everyone else ready to receive casualties and recover our guys. Once they're onboard, I want the Zodiac tethered from the stern. We're going to turn now and get ready to make a run west back through this channel. Any questions?"

There were none. The men went about their tasks with classic SEAL efficiency. It was at this point the submarine began to send a signal to the junk in international Morse code, using a flashing light.

"What's the sub sending?" Ramirez mumbled.

"Shit, I haven't used any Morse code in twenty years. I don't have a clue," Quicklinsky answered.

"I can read it," Moss declared. "He says he's the USS Virginia. He's ordering us to come about and stop. He says we're going to be boarded."

"Yeah, boarded my ass!" Quicklinsky exclaimed. "Who the hell does that cockbreath think he is? We're in Vietnamese waters! He doesn't have any authority to order us to do shit out here! Anyone have a flashlight?"

"Yeah," Blum said. "I got my Surefire with a button on it. Here."

Moss took the light and pointed it in the direction of the sub.

"Okay, here goes." Moss verbally spelled out the reply as he flashed it in Morse code. "F...O...A...D."

Everyone began laughing. The message Moss had just sent to the submarine was a well-known Navy acronym meaning, fuck off and die!

Boucher's Zodiac was now about one-hundred yards astern of the junk. The sub's rubber boat was about three-hundred yards behind Boucher and gradually gaining on him. The rain had subsided and visibility was improving somewhat. The seas were still extremely rough, but the numerous reefs and islands comprising the Spratlys did provide some protection from the storm-driven seas. Boucher's men lined the junk's rail cheering him as he approached. Quicklinsky skillfully began turning the junk sideways to the incoming waves, creating a lee to give Boucher's boat some protection. Klum threw a line over the side to Boucher. Boucher quickly secured the line to his boat and steered next to the junk. Boucher and Patterson began passing the three injured men up to waiting hands and they were brought aboard. The transfer only took a few minutes, but that was enough to put the pursuing rubber boat from the submarine within a hundred yards of the junk.

It was at that point that Quicklinsky sounded the alarm.

"They got guns in that boat!"

"Looks like M-16s and a shot gun!" Klum shouted.

The men all crouched behind the junk's heavy wooden gunwale. The four SEALs Quicklinsky had armed now aimed at the submarine's approaching rubber boat. Boucher kneeled next to the injured men as Dick Llina examined them and conducted triage.

"How bad?" Boucher asked Llina.

"They all need a doctor, not a corpsman. This one needs surgery to fix his compound fracture. This guy needs oxygen. Probably has a punctured lung, judging by the frothy red blood he keeps coughing up. This one has a severe head injury and a broken leg, maybe a broken pelvis and internal injuries as well. They all need medical help way beyond anything I can give them."

Boucher sneered.

"Mossman," he yelled, "send a light to the sub. Tell them we're going to transfer three seriously injured survivors from the plane crash to them. Tell 'em these guys are in bad shape and need immediate medical attention."

Moss began to flash the submarine.

"Mossman, tell the sub we will transfer the injured to their rubber boat, but I want them to throw their guns over the side."

Moss nodded and continued to send the Morse code message using Blum's flashlight. The submarine's rubber boat was now about fifty yards from the junk's side when it stopped. The four men in the boat brought their guns to the ready position. As they did, the sub replied to Moss's flashing light with their own. Moss deciphered it and read the message aloud.

"Unidentified vessel, you are ordered to lay down your arms and be boarded."

Boucher stood upright and faced the submarine.

"Boarded my ass! What the hell are they thinking? Mossman, send them this reply: We have recovered three seriously injured men from plane crash. Two have life-threatening injuries. Propose we immediately transfer them to your boat under flag of truce. Have your boat crew unload their weapons and immediately make my lee side."

Moss sent the Morse code message and they all waited silently, watching the sub's crewman in the rubber boat. Boucher broke the silence.

"Haus, hang something white over the lee rail so they can see it."

"I got it for action," Yellowhorse announced as he stripped off his white t-shirt and draped it over the rail.

Another few tense minutes passed. Then the submarine began to flash its signal light again.

"We accept terms," Moss said. "Unload weapons."

Boucher turned to his men. "Okay boys, unload 'em and put them on the deck. Let's get the injured ready to transfer."

With that, the SEALs spun into action. The sub's rubber boat maneuvered alongside the junk. Boucher and Patterson watched with concern as the men began passing the injured carefully down to the sub's crewmen in the rubber boat.

"You got a doctor onboard that sub?" Boucher shouted to the crewman in the boat below.

"No," one of them replied, "only a corpsman."

"The guy coming down now needs surgery. He's in a bad way. So is the next guy."

"We'll do what we can for them. By the way, who are you guys?"

Boucher smiled. "We'll leave that one unanswered because it doesn't matter. Besides, I got a feeling the injured men we're passing down to you already know who we are."

"We saw you save these men from the plane crash. That was one hell of a rescue, Mister!"

"No, it wasn't. We just happened to be at the right place at the right time."

The sailor in the boat shrugged back at Boucher. The last injured man was safely handed down and put into a life jacket, as the others had been. The sailor sitting on the boat's bow feebly saluted and the boat motored away from the junk making a straight line toward the submarine.

Patterson clapped Boucher on the shoulder.

"Nice work old buddy. You always did have a soft spot when it comes to lifesaving."

Boucher made a comical face at his friend and smiled.

"Let's get this tub headed away from here and put some distance between us and that submarine."

Quicklinsky turned the junk back into the narrow channel and revved up the diesel auxiliary engine to its maximum RPM. Boucher, Patterson, and Moss stood on the junk's stern watching the rubber boat approach the submarine. Sailors were on the sub's metal hull waiting to transfer the injured men. Boucher grabbed Quicklinsky's binoculars, squinting into them as he observed the men on the open bridge atop the submarines sail. To his dismay, he saw that he was being photographed through what looked like a powerful telephoto lens.

American Embassy, Bangkok

The intercom chirped, startling ML Brown out of a daydream and back to the present. It was his secretary's familiar voice.

"Rene Thompson is on the green line for you, Sir."

"I got it, thanks."

Brown quickly placed the top-secret crypto card in its slot on the phone and punched the secure button. Soon the LCD window displayed the identity of the caller. "CIA Covert Operations," blinked across the small screen and switched to "top secret."

"Rene, ML here. I hold you TS. What do you have for me?"

"ML, we have imagery with a positive ID on our mystery men. Seems we have a situation that significantly complicates things. As you know the USS Virginia recovered your three guys from the seaplane crash site. They're all injured, but they're going to make it. Seems it wasn't the Virginia's crew who rescued them. It was our mystery men. The Virginia's CO himself saw them pull your guys from that crashed airplane as it was sinking. He said it was the damned most courageous thing he's ever witnessed. He said your three guys would have been shark bait if it weren't for our mystery men. Apparently, those men did a heck of a triage job on the two most seriously injured and then turned all three of them over to the Virginia under a flag of truce."

"Yeah, that's what I hear. But who are they?"

"You aren't going to believe this. The Virginia shot some really good ID quality imagery of these guys from the rescue to the turnover. We ran their images through our ID library and had the FBI and DoD do the same. They're almost all a damn bunch of former Navy SEALs. The big guy who pulled your guys from the plane crash as it sank is retired Navy SEAL Commander Jake Boucher. He's a damn hero! Navy Cross winner, Silver Star, two Bronze Stars, two Purple Hearts, Cross of Gallantry, etc., etc. The big black man who helped him is a recently retired FBI Supervisory Special Agent. He headed the Hostage Rescue Team for years and was the Unit Chief for the FBI's Critical Incident Response Group when he retired. The little guy driving their inflatable is a former SEAL by the name of Johnny Yellowhorse. He was awarded the Silver Star, Bronze Star, and Purple Heart. In fact, every one of the guys we identified were all in SEAL Team Two and they were in the same platoon. According to the Navy's records, they were in Vietnam together during the 1968 Tet Offensive and they operated in the vicinity of the Parrot's Beak. There's one other man with them we couldn't positively ID. We think he's the pilot who leased the Chinook that the group abandoned at that remote airfield in Vietnam."

"Well, it's starting to make sense. These guys must have seen the C-130 go down. How else would they have known where to search for it? When NSA gave us the heads up on the FBI requesting the Cambodia imagery and DMA did the geospatial analysis, we never put two and two together. They really covered their tracks and did their homework. Looking back on it now, knowing what we know, I'd say they were after the gold. There's no way they could have known about the Plans. The question now is have they read the Plans, and if so have they made sense of it and realized the significance?"

There was a moment of deafening silence.

"Yeah, I hear you," Thompson replied. "Okay, it comes down to this. We need to recover those Plans and destroy them. If they know what's in them, we need to ensure that they don't spill the beans. If they don't know, they can keep the gold and no one will be the wiser. But, we need to gain control of those Plans. If they got into the wrong hands it could bring down the Secretary of Defense, the CIA, and the entire intelligence community—maybe even the Office of the President. That's what's at stake!"

Brown could feel the acid forming in his stomach and his blood pressure climbing. "What do you want me to do?"

"At this point I don't think there's much you can do. You've lost two men and a helicopter in a crash. You lost a seaplane and you have three men seriously injured. Our former SEALs know someone is after them. They are not stupid people and may have figured out who it is. They have the gold and they have the Plans and they have disappeared from the radar screen again. Unless you know where they're heading or have a stroke of brilliance, it would seem to me that there is little else you can do, save staying out of the way."

Brown scowled as he sat back in his leather, executive armchair. "They have to be heading back to Thailand," he said after a heavy pause.

"What makes you believe that?"

"Because it makes sense. They launched this operation from there and I think they are logistically linked there. They've been passing coded messages to someone there, so that has to be where their support is coming from."

Thompson interrupted Brown. "What about the messages that were passed to Palawan? What about the replies that came from Puerto Princesa?"

"I don't know. The replies might have been a deception. Look Rene, I don't much give a shit. I'm telling you our boys are making a run for Thailand. That means they'll be crossing a few hundred miles of open sea and that makes them vulnerable to detection and interception."

"But what if they are headed for Palawan? We can't afford to gamble. We can't get air surveillance over them because of the storm. We can't effectively track them on the surface for the same reason. There's got to be another avenue we haven't explored."

"If we can locate them in the open ocean, we could have them boarded."

"Yeah, we could, but the key is still locating them in a storm. Even if we successfully board them, there is still no guarantee we'll get the Plans. No ML, we need to completely eliminate them and the Plans."

"But what about the gold?"

"Screw the gold! We need the Plans recovered or destroyed and a guarantee that our hero friends will never divulge their contents. We need to keep this in-house and there can be no trace. ML, do we understand each other?"

"Ahhhh...yes, I understand."

Brown winced as he heard the sharp crack of the phone being slammed down by Thompson. As he replaced his handset, he looked up and his eyes fixed on a wall map of the South China Sea.

CHAPTER 25

On the junk

"Tahnite, this is Jake. *Saw wa de cup*. I need your help," Boucher said into the Iridium satellite phone.

Patterson, Moss, and Quicklinsky were huddled next to him, listening intently. Boucher looked up and smiled confidently at them as he listened to Tahnite.

"Yeah, don't worry my friend. We're all fine but we have a bit of a problem. We're coming back to your location. We need to rendezvous at Point X-ray in seventy-two hours. And Tahnite, we're going to need a five-ton truck and a safe house for a few weeks."

Boucher patiently listened to Thanite before replying. "Okay, my old friend, I'll call you when we're five out and confirm rendezvous. See you in about seventy-two hours. *Saw wa de*."

Boucher pushed the off button on the satellite phone and handed it to Patterson.

"Thanite says no problem. Haus, plot us a northerly course to X-ray that keeps us running along the skirt of the storm. The ride will suck, but we need the cover. I want to brief our guys below in five minutes. Pass the word."

USS Virginia

The sub's leading petty officer in communications approached Lieutenant Cutler. "Sir, we just received a flash message."

"Let's see what they want us to do," Cutler replied as he took the envelope from the petty officer's hand.

Cutler removed the folded page stamped SECRET/SPECAT at the top and bottom in bold, red print and began to silently read it.

"Shit!" he mumbled under his breath.

"Sir?"

"That was not directed at you." Cutler keyed the intercom to engineering. "Engineering, OOD. Is the Captain still there with you?"

"Engineering, aye Sir."

"Please put him on."

"This is the Captain."

"Captain, OOD. New orders. Request your presence in the con."

"I'm on my way."

Moments later Commander Galloway stepped through the hatch. "What you got Lieutenant?"

"Well Sir, we have some new orders that are rather interesting."

Galloway took the cable from Cutler and carefully read it. "You gotta be shittin' me! They want us to rendezvous with a helo from Carrier Battle Group Five northeast of Kota Baharu tomorrow morning and transfer our casualties. A SEAL team element accompanied by some CIA weenies will cross deck to us from a Navy helo. Then we are to find that damn mystery junk again and have the SEALs board and apprehend the crew. Says here they are suspected terrorists."

Cutler shrugged in frustration. "Yes Sir, but terrorists don't save drowning men from certain death like we saw these guys do."

Galloway sneered. "You know what, Lieutenant? You're right! This doesn't pass the bullshit test, but we're going to execute our orders. Plot a direct course to the rendezvous point and make flank speed. I want to get these casualties offloaded for proper medical attention. Once that's done we'll deal with the junk and the boarding issue. The South China Sea is a large body of water. Even a submarine as advanced as ours can have difficulty finding something as small as that high interest vessel in a storm."

Cutler smiled at his CO with pride. "Aye, Sir!"

On the junk

Boucher slowly paced the deck, squinting into the stormy sea around the junk.

"You think they're going to follow us, don't you Jake?"

"Yeah," he replied curtly to old his friend Patterson. "We have been relentlessly pursued since we started this thing."

Patterson wiped the salt spray out of his eyes. "It's the Plans! It's the fucking Plans!"

Boucher nodded in agreement. "Yeah, I know. But they're history!"

Patterson shivered as he spoke. "Sure they are, but they reveal a trail of deception and conspiracy at the highest levels of the U.S. government. You said so yourself when you briefed us on them."

"Okay, Pat. Let's assume it's the Plans they want. Why would they commit all the resources they have just expended to recover some history books that weren't even history when they were written?"

"You know what, old buddy? You really are a dumbass bubblehead! It's simple; the U.S. government misled the American people to justify going to war in Korea and Vietnam. If you look at the reasons why we went to war with Iraq, there are similar parallels in the overarching strategy."

"What are you getting at, Pat?"

"It's simple. The Plans laid out an abstract strategy that ultimately led to the demise of the Soviet Empire in 1992. You told us that the Plans basically recognized the need to seize and then hold Korea and Vietnam until our Navy could be modernized and grown to sufficient strength where it could threaten the Soviets into an arms race. The arms race was designed so it would ultimately force them to spread their limited resources so thin that they would go bust. We needed sea control to bottle them up and we didn't have a sufficient number of ships to make it happen, so we took and held strategic land and sea bases from which we could launch an attack. Vietnam was key to control the South China Sea and its adjacent chokepoints. Those Plans revealed that we needed the use of Vietnam until we could build a fleet of six-hundred ships with enough carrier strength to replace the land bases. Right?"

Boucher began to stare at the stormy horizon. "Yeah, that's pretty much it."

Patterson walked up beside Boucher and put his hand on Boucher's shoulder.

"So, it's almost forty years later. The Soviet Union is out of business and no longer a threat. We're now deeply embroiled in Iraq and Afghanistan in a war against terrorism. The American people are skeptical, just like they were in Vietnam, but this time we're not up against an enemy like the Soviet Union. We're not fighting an enemy who has borders or who wants to expand its state control over other nations by conquering them like Hitler and Japan wanted to do in World War II. This war is not about turf. It's a war about ideology. Those radical Islam fuckers want to kill us because we don't believe what they believe. They want the world to return to the seventh century. They want us all to be wiping our asses with a handful of sand and to be living in a three-sided tent bowing to Mecca on our knees!"

"Pat, Pat, Pat...I don't disagree with anything you're saying, but what does that have to do with the Plans?"

"Jeez, Jake! Don't you get it? The bad guys aren't the Iraqis or the Afghanis! The bad guys are the terrorists who used Iraq and Afghanistan as a place to hide and train."

"I get that. Trust me! I just don't get the parallel you're trying to draw between Vietnam and the war in Iraq."

"Alright, fair enough! Let me put it this way. What if Iraq and Afghanistan aren't really the objective of the war? What if the real objective is abstract? What if the real objective is Iran or even China for that matter? According to what you said, the OPLANS revealed that the USSR was the real objective of the Vietnam War, right? We used Vietnam as an abstract means to contain Communism. What if we're using Iraq and Afghanistan as a means to contain

Iran as the heartbeat of radical Islam and the U.S. is labeling it as a fight against terrorism?"

Boucher contemplated Patterson's point for a short time before responding. "Okay, Pat, walk me through this."

"Sure!" Patterson smiled and put a dip of snuff in his lower lip before going on.

"Let's start with the political-military situation leading up to the second war in Iraq. Let's go back to the first Gulf War. Remember "Operation Earnest Will," when the U.S. re-flagged the Kuwaiti oil tankers as our own? That was around 1987. The USSR was weakening and on the verge of going out of business. Iraq was still our ally and Iran was our enemy. An Iranian ship, the Iran Ajar, was caught in the act of mining the Persian Gulf. The TF-160 helicopter guys gunned it and the SEALs boarded it and took prisoners. You remember that?"

"Yeah, I remember, but what does that have to…"

Patterson cut him off. "It's important from a political-military perspective because that was a little known operation that led to some incredible intelligence about Iran. The interrogations of those prisoners revealed that Iran had a nuclear weapons program. I read the intel report myself when it reached the FBI. So here's my analysis, old buddy. The President knew we couldn't wage war on Iran and have a reasonable chance of decisively winning a land war and then successfully occupying Iran, largely because of the geography. That meant that the only option was to contain Iran."

Boucher kicked the gunwale and held up his hand to stop Patterson.

"Jezz, Pat! You're making my head hurt. Since when did you become such a frickin' pol-mil expert? What ever happened to the dumbass flyboy I used to know and love?"

Patterson had to laugh. "Okay, you wanna hear why I think these guys are after us or not? If you do, shut the fuck up and pay attention. If you don't, I got places to visit and money to spend." He spat brown tobacco juice, accentuating his statement as it splattered on the deck a few inches from Boucher's bare feet. Boucher smiled at his friend and grabbed his arm.

"Let's go below." Turning, he yelled back to Quicklinsky, "You got the helm, Haus. We're going below."

Quicklinsky gave Boucher a thumbs-up and nodded. Boucher returned the thumbs-up gesture and the nod and disappeared through the hatch behind Patterson. Both men proceeded to the galley where Patterson poured himself a cup of coffee. LeFever, Jackson, Lavender, and Reilly were sitting around the galley table engaged in a quiet game of poker. Boucher scanned the small, dimly lighted cabin, noting that all the others were sleeping.

Boucher hoisted himself up onto the galley countertop next to Patterson and leaned back against the bulkhead. "Alright, Pat. Where were we?"

"I was explaining why we needed to contain Iran to check their nuclear weapons program and stop their support of terrorism, and how we were going to achieve that without going to war with them."

Reilly threw down his cards. "Sorry boys, but I gotta hear this."

Lavender, Jackson, and LeFever followed and sat back, giving Patterson their undivided attention.

Patterson peered at his newly found audience, sipped his coffee and continued.

"Okay boys. I think there's a link between today's war on terrorism, the Plans we recovered from the crash site and whoever it is that's after us. I think I've figured it out."

CHAPTER 26

The USS Virginia, many hours later

Commander Galloway stepped through the hatch into the control room. Cutler announced, "Captain on the bridge."

Galloway went directly to the sonar operator and bent down to view the digital display on the panel facing the sonar man. "Whatcha got, Petty Officer Johnson?"

"I hold an unidentified surface contact bearing two seven three degrees at nine-thousand yards. He's making about ten knots, Skipper. It sounds like a small, single-screw craft."

Galloway patted his crewman on the shoulder. "Very well. Stay on him."

Galloway turned toward Cutler. "Bring the ship up to periscope depth. Raise scope."

Cutler repeated his commanding officer's order and raised the sub's periscope. Galloway peered through the scope and made a quick three-hundred-sixty-degree sweep of the surrounding ocean, stopping on the heading of the unidentified contact.

"Move us to within five-hundred yards astern of her. I don't want to be seen."

Galloway looked away from the periscope. "Mister Cutler, ask that SEAL Lieutenant we took onboard last night to come to the bridge."

Lieutenant Cutler nodded and dispatched the messenger of the watch to find the SEAL officer and bring him to the bridge. Minutes later, Lieutenant Jim Murrant stepped through the hatch onto the bridge.

"Lieutenant Murrant reporting as requested, Sir." He approached Commander Galloway.

Galloway remained glued to the periscope. "Lieutenant, I think we may have found our high interest vessel. If we can confirm it, you will need to board and seize this vessel." Galloway looked up at Murrant. "What do you need from me to make that happen?"

Murrant didn't hesitate. "I'll need time to surface launch my two combat rubber raiding craft. Since these guys we're up against are reported to be armed with automatic weapons, I would like to do the underway boarding under the cover of darkness." Murrant checked his Rolex. "It's 1900 hours now. It will take me and my guys about an hour to prep for this op. We'll need another twenty minutes after you surface to inflate our CRRCs and get

182

the outboards running. It will be dark by then, so how does a 2030 launch time sound?"

Galloway turned to Cutler, silently asking for his input.

"That will work, Skipper."

"Great!" Murrant said smiling. "Could you run us well ahead of the target vessel so we can catch her from the side, rather than having to play catch up from behind?"

"Okay, no problem," Galloway replied. "We'll run up about fifteen miles ahead of her, surface when you're ready, and put you in the water. We'll duck back under and wait until she passes over us. We'll stay in trail, close enough to maintain a periscope visual, in case you run into trouble. Once you're onboard her, you can pop a flare to signal us to surface."

"Thank you, Sir. That ought to do it. I need to get my platoon ready and briefed."

Galloway smiled at the SEAL Lieutenant and turned towards the Officer of the Deck. "Lower scope, ahead one-third to a point fifteen miles past the target ship. We'll get our SEALs in the water and then dive. Any questions?"

"No, Sir."

"I'll be in engineering."

"Aye, Sir."

...

At 2010 the USS Virginia slowly rose above the surface of the sea in a black, ghostly silhouette ringed by white froth. The wind had subsided somewhat and changed direction but the seas remained rough. Galloway stood behind a clear, plastic windscreen on the open bridge of the submarine atop the sail. The lookouts crowded the small bridge area around Galloway, continually scanning the horizon through their binoculars for anything that could endanger their ship. Galloway watched as the deck hatch opened and three lifejacket-clad crewmen climbed out onto the sub's wet, steel deck. They were followed by fourteen SEAL Team operators who were all dressed in olive drab flight suits, wearing night vision goggles, and armed to the hilt. All the men carefully proceeded to the sub's stern area where they opened a large deck hatch that usually contained the submarine's mooring lines and other deck equipment. When the SEALs were embarked, the same deck storage area carried their deflated, combat rubber raiding craft.

The SEALs withdrew two large, black, nylon bags, each containing a combat rubber raiding craft. They quickly unrolled the deflated boats onto the sub's deck. The SEALs pulled a cord on each boat releasing high-pressure canisters of compressed carbon dioxide. The boats instantly sprang to life. They morphed from what looked like a flat mass of black rubber sheet into the shape of a boat in a matter of seconds. The SEALs finished inflating the boats using a SCUBA bottle fitted with a hose adapter and carefully checked the rigidity of each section of the now fully inflated boats. Other SEALs simultaneously secured soft fuel bladders inside the boats and hooked up the fuel lines to the outboard motors. The boats were then loaded with several waterproof bags that contained boarding equipment, ammunition, radios and first aid materials. Murrant turned and looked up at Galloway, giving him a thumbs-up. Galloway, who was still peering down at them from the bridge above, returned the gesture.

Murrant checked his watch. It was now 2029. "Comms check," he directed pointing at his SEAL radioman.

"Roger, Sir. I read 'em lima charlie."

Murrant nodded, gesturing a thumbs-up approval. "Chief," Murrant commanded his platoon chief, "let's do it."

The SEALs slid their two boats into the sea and climbed in. The engines were started and they quietly disappeared into the darkness of the surrounding seascape.

Galloway watched from the bridge and nodded approvingly, as if the SEALs could see him. Before giving the order to dive he took a deep breath of fresh air and gazed up into the night sky. There were no stars. In fact, it was so dark he could not distinguish the sea from the sky. A horizon simply didn't exist. He smiled to himself as he remembered asking Murrant what he intended to do if he and his fellow SEALs had engine trouble or had their boats shot out from under them. He remembered Murrant's reply. *That's why they issue us swim fins, Sir.* Until this dark night, he assumed it was intended to be a joke. Galloway fleetingly contemplated the courage of the men that he had just dropped off, then gave the order to dive.

CIA Headquarters, Langley, Virginia

Vice Admiral Robert Sinclair was being briefed by the CIA's Director for Covert Operations, Rene Thompson. Sinclair was not happy about what he was hearing.

"You see, Admiral, we think that this band of terrorists has an Al-Qaeda link and that's the reason they are so intent on recovering the gold. That gold will be used to fund more terrorism against United States interests."

"Who are they?" Sinclair pointedly asked Thompson.

"We haven't confirmed their identity, but they appear to be some U.S. expatriates who have aligned themselves with the dark side."

"You didn't answer my question."

Thompson looked bewildered.

"Who are they?"

"Ahh, we think one of them is a retired Navy guy and another is a former FBI agent."

"Yeah, I read the Cane Pebble cable. The name of the Navy guy you reference is Jake Boucher. Is that correct?"

"Ahh, yes, but that's not confirmed yet," Thompson added nervously.

"The name of the FBI agent is Leon Patterson. Is that correct?"

Thompson swallowed hard before answering, "Yes."

"Do you have any idea who these two men are?"

"They are terrorists as far as we are concerned."

Sinclair showed no emotion as he stood up from behind his desk. His six-foot-five inch form was, itself, imposing enough, but when he bent forward toward Thompson the strength of his aura seemed to reach into Thompson's chest and steal the oxygen from his lungs. Thompson stared into Sinclair's steel gray eyes and felt the chill of death. He instantly knew that Sinclair was not a man to trifle with.

"I want to tell you who they are, Director Thompson. You will keep this in code word channels. They are not terrorists. In fact, they are quite the opposite. Jake Boucher is a former Navy SEAL and a Navy Cross winner. Pat Patterson, up until a few months ago, was the Chief of the FBI's Counterterrorism Unit. I know them both. Now, I want you to consider this a directive from the DCO. You are to determine exactly who all these men are and what they are doing. Once you make that determination, I want a complete briefing on this operation. I want to know what led up to it and what you intend to do about it. I want to know what our sister agencies are thinking and doing about it as well. You will ensure that no harm comes to these men and you will not run any further armed operations against them. Am I clear, Mr. Thompson?"

In his twenty-five years at the CIA, Thompson had never been spoken to this bluntly before. He didn't like the new DCO who had just put him in a box and he didn't like being told how to run his operations by a military officer, much less some Navy puke. Even though his compulsion was to tell this admiral to go screw himself, Thompson's political survival instincts ran deeper than his anger. He stared back at Sinclair for a tense moment before answering. As their eyes met again, Thompson knew Sinclair would only accept one answer.

"Yes, Sir," Thompson replied.

Without losing eye contact, Sinclair sat back down at his desk.

"Mr. Thompson, I expect that you will keep me fully informed. Is that clear?"

"Yes, Sir."

The South China Sea, the same time

Murrant and his men loitered in the area where the Virginia had dropped them off, waiting for the high interest vessel, an unidentified terrorist junk, to pass nearby. It was his plan to gradually close in on the target vessel as it approached. He would move in as near as he dared and remain undetected. He knew that his two boats had a nearly nonexistent radar signature, so they would be indistinguishable from the sea clutter to anyone but the most experienced radar operator, and even then he would have to be looking for them. The odds of being detected by the type of small, surface search navigation radar installed on vessels similar to the one he was about to board were astronomically small. He correctly assumed that if he could get close he could attack from a rear quarter aspect as the vessel passed. Even if his two boats were sighted, by the time the terrorists could react he and his men would already be upon them. Murrant and his SEALs had no intention of losing this fight. He was confident that if there was a fight, it would be extremely short.

Nearly an hour had passed by. Murrant was in a state of semi-conscious sleep when his radioman grasped him by the arm.

"Sir, the Virginia advises that the target vessel is three miles at zero niner eight. ETA our position is fifteen mikes."

Murrant jolted, fully awake.

"Advise the Virginia we're executing."

On the junk

It was now nearly 2300. At the wheel on the junk's helm, Mojo Lavender was fighting to stay awake. Sitting beside him, Risser Jackson was keeping him on course and keeping him awake. Both men were fatigued from the week's ordeal and less than alert. Jackson would occasionally check the junk's radar screen for any surface contacts and, using his binoculars, follow up with a visual scan of the horizon, or at least where he thought it should be. Everyone else was fast asleep below deck. Far out at sea on this very dark night, no ambient light existed. Except for the dim glow of their electronic navigation instruments, it was otherwise pitch black.

Jackson felt uneasy and he wasn't sure why. He just knew it was one of those gut feelings you get just before something happens. He again scanned the dark sea for any contacts. As he stepped behind Lavender to look directly aft of the junk, he thought he saw a familiar form looming out of the junk's frothy wake...a periscope? *No, it can't be! Not out here!* He squinted into the binoculars, but it was gone.

"Mojo," he yelled, "get Jake. I'm turning back to the islands!"

Mojo didn't question Risser's alarm. He flung open the cabin door and yelled for Boucher.

Boucher appeared on deck seconds later.

"What's up?" he questioned.

"That fucking sub is back!"

"Change your heading and make a run back into the Spratlys' shallows!"

"Already have and we are!"

By now several other men had come on deck to see what the alarm was all about. Boucher grabbed the navigation chart, probing it with his beefy finger.

"Go for the large island. That's closest and there are reefs all around it. Give me 2300 RPM's."

"Roger."

What Boucher and his men didn't know was they were heading straight towards the Island that the Chinese had fortified and occupied.

"How long?" Boucher asked Mojo.

"Two hours, maybe more, depending on this sea state."

"We need to lose that friggin' sub once and for all!"

USS Virginia

"Officer of the Deck, sonar. I hold an unidentified submerged contact, three-hundred yards astern of the junk. It's a submarine, Sir."

Galloway picked up his mic. "Sonar, can you ID that contact?"

"Skipper, sonar, it's a diesel-electric boat running on snorkel. Signature appears to be Chinese, Sir. It's a Kilo-class boat, Sir. Surface contact has turned northeast and has picked up speed, Sir. It looks like they're making a run back towards the Spratlys!"

Galloway studied the navigational chart for a moment. "Mister Cutler, rig for silent running. Once that Chinese Kilo is out of range, I want to surface and pick up the SEALs. Is there any indication that the Chinese boat knows we're here?"

"None so far, Captain."

"Sonar, track both contacts as long as you can."

"Sir, it looks like our surface contact has changed course and is now headed directly toward that Chinese-held island and that diesel sub is following right on their ass."

"Mister Cutler, get a flash precedence Cane Pebble off to COMSUBPAC explaining the situation. Tell them boarding was aborted and we are holding position awaiting further orders."

CHAPTER 27

Onboard the junk

Quicklinsky plotted an updated position on the navigation chart and checked the screen on his surface search radar. Boucher was peering over his shoulder.

"Haus, you think we lost that sub?"

"Yup, the bottom is coming up real fast. There ain't a U.S. sub skipper in the fleet that would risk grounding his boat by sailing into water as shallow as this."

Boucher ran his finger around the top of the larger island on the chart. It was in their path. "Haus, take the northern channel."

"Okay Jake, will do, but that's cutting it kind of close...don't you think?"

"Yes, its close but we need to get among all these reefs so the sub can't track us. In fact, we better turn off our radar so they can't track our emissions either."

"Okay, but navigation through this channel won't be easy without an occasional radar fix to guarantee our position."

"You're right, Haus. Use it when you need to, otherwise, keep it on the standby mode."

Moss, Patterson, and Reilly had quietly joined Boucher and Quicklinsky. Reilly continued to search the junk's wake and surrounding water for the periscope.

"Shit!" Reilly blurted out pointing astern. "That friggin' sub won't quit!"

All four men snapped their attention to the dark sea behind the junk's white, frothing wake. Reilly handed the binoculars to Boucher, who took a quick look and handed them to Patterson, who followed suit, handing them on to Moss.

"That can't be a U.S. sub!" Patterson exclaimed. "No fucking way!"

Reilly reclaimed the binoculars. "Who, then?"

"I don't know, but we're in ninety feet of water so I'm damn sure it isn't one of ours. We're still about an hour from our island passage. I don't like this! I don't like it one damn bit!"

Quicklinsky switched the radar back to active search and studied the screen.

"I know what you mean, Jake. Take a look at this."

All the men crowded around the small radar screen's digital color display.

"Here's the big island up ahead. Here are one, two, three atolls that correspond to the navigation chart. You see these small blips on the radar? Well, they're moving towards us. Unless I'm wrong, these blips are boats and they're headed straight at us. I count three of them. At the speed they're traveling, they'll be on us in about eight to ten minutes."

Boucher scratched his head. "Where the hell did they come from?"

"The only place they could have come from is the big island," Moss reported as though he had the inside track.

Boucher grunted. "Billy, get everyone armed and on deck. If they're pirates, we're going to shoot it out. If they're something else, we'll decide on our course of action based on the scenario we're presented. Just get everyone ready to do whatever is needed and tell them to keep their heads down."

Reilly half saluted and disappeared below.

"Okay," Boucher said looking at Moss, Patterson, and Quicklinsky, "keep this tub in the channel and at full speed. We have the edge!"

Patterson held out his open hand beckoning to Boucher. "The edge? What edge?"

"We have each other," Boucher confidently stated.

The SEALs took up defensive positions around the junk's deck, finding cover wherever they could. Boucher and Patterson checked every one of them.

"Haus, status?" Boucher shouted toward the stern.

"The sub has dropped off. I show three boats on radar inbound. ETA at current closing speed, eight mikes. You ought to be able to see them with the naked eye in a few mikes."

It was at that moment that Boucher heard the sound of three mortar rounds being launched from the darkness ahead.

"Cover everyone! Cover!" he shouted at the top of his lungs.

Moments later the first round exploded on the water about fifty yards off the junk's starboard bow. The second round detonated about twenty yards straight off the bow and the third detonated just astern, barely missing the junk. Hot shrapnel hissed by as the water geysers rose above the points of impact. Boucher saw Quicklinsky fall forward as the last mortar round detonated. He rushed aft to find Quicklinsky sprawled, face first, on the deck. Boucher rolled him over and cradled him. Reilly took the wheel. Quicklinsky was conscious, but confused.

"Haus, are you hit?" Boucher shouted.

"I don't know. I'm kind of numb all over."

Boucher yelled forward towards Llina, "Corpsman!"

Llina came running.

"Dick, take care of Haus!"

Boucher ran forward. What he saw was not encouraging. There were three heavily armed patrol boats emerging out of the darkness about three-hundred yards off the bow, bearing down on the junk. Boucher could see the largest of the three boats had a deck-mounted machine gun on its bow. The other two boats had soldiers with light machine guns and assault rifles at the ready. There was a second volley of mortar fire. Boucher determined that all three boats had launched a mortar. The SEALs all huddled as closely as they could next to something solid on the junk, anticipating the fragmentation aftermath. Suddenly the sky was lighted by millions of candlepower as three flares burning high above suspended beneath their small parachutes. Then there was a burst of machine gun fire from the lead patrol boat. The rounds ripped through the junk's wooden hull and gunwale like it was cardboard. Boucher knew they were out-gunned and that those shooting at them weren't pirates.

Then he heard LeFever shout, "Billy's down!"

"How bad?" Boucher shouted back.

"He took a round through his triceps! No broken bones as far as I can tell!"

Boucher quickly assessed the tactical situation. Yes, they could return fire with their AK-47s, but they couldn't expect to win a gunfight against three steel-hull patrol boats with mortars, machine guns, armed troops, and twice the maneuvering speed as the junk. The only thing he could do to save his men from certain slaughter was to turn on the junk's running lights, hoist a white flag and put down their guns.

USS Virginia

"Sir," Lieutenant Cutler reported to Commander Galloway, "we just intercepted an Iridium call that apparently came from the junk. They reported they're under fire from three unidentified patrol boats at this position." Cutler placed his finger on the navigation chart next to the big island.

Galloway studied the position. "It's got to be the Chinese outpost."

"Yes, Sir. What do you want to do?"

Galloway hesitated as he studied the chart. "We lost the Kilo sub contact here and haven't yet reacquired it. We can't risk detection this close to their waters. Inform COMSUBPAC. See if COMSUBPAC has any assets available that can get us some real-time imagery. Maintain depth at two-hundred-fifty feet. Slow speed to one-third. We'll sit tight until we hear otherwise."

On the junk

The largest of the three patrol boats reached the junk's port side and tied up. All the boats' guns were pointing toward Boucher and his men, who had stacked their AKs on a pile forward of the pilothouse in plain sight. Boucher had raised a white flag and all his men were standing in ranks. Llina was tending to Quicklinsky and Reilly. A Chinese officer, accompanied by two soldiers, stepped onto the junk and screamed in Chinese at the newly found captives. Boucher stepped forward, only to be rifle-butted in the stomach by one of the soldiers, and collapsed to his knees.

The officer yelled again in Chinese. Boucher tried to remember how to make his stomach hard as he gasped out a reply. "We are Americans. We mean you no harm."

The Chinese officer seemed to understand the word Americans and nodded to his guards, who kept their AK-47s leveled at Boucher's chest. He then returned to his patrol boat where he made a radio call. Shortly, one of the other patrol boats transferred a young Chinese officer to the large patrol boat and he boarded the junk.

The two Chinese officers spoke for a few moments before the newly arrived officer addressed Boucher.

"What you do here?" the young officer asked in a very thick Chinese accent.

Boucher looked up at him. "May I stand?"

The officer said something in Mandarin to the others and then nodded his approval to Boucher. Boucher slowly stood as the two soldiers maintained their cautious guard.

"We are Americans. We are treasure hunters and pirates were chasing us. We tried to lose them by sailing into these islands."

The officer translated Boucher's statement to his superior. The other Chinese officer laughed before he spoke to his fellow officer.

"My captain say you lie!"

Boucher tried to not show any outward indication that he was rattled. "I do not lie and I can prove my claim is true. Please have your men inspect the cabin of my boat."

The young officer again translated Boucher's response to his superior. The superior officer spoke again and several more soldiers boarded the junk and immediately went below into the cabin. Moments later they emerged, each carrying several gold ingots. They proceeded to the senior officer and laid them at his feet.

The two officers again conversed.

The junior officer turned to Boucher. "You have much gold. You are prisoner of Peoples Republic of China. You come with us now."

"Wait a minute! We have not broken any laws of the high seas! I have two wounded men who need medical assistance."

The young officer translated as before and then returned his captain's angry response.

"My captain say you invade China territory and you break China law. You China prisoner!"

Boucher leaned towards the captain. "I am a U.S. Naval officer. I have two wounded men who need medical assistance. Our two countries are not enemies. I respectfully request your courtesy."

Again the young officer translated Boucher's words. This time the Chinese captain's response didn't seem quite as abrupt.

"My captain say we tow you to outpost. Doctor there help."

Boucher nodded politely. "Thank you," he said softly.

The Chinese captain gave several orders to the soldiers, both on the junk and on his patrol boat, and the soldiers began to scurry. They quickly bound the Americans' hands behind their backs and then removed all the guns from the junk and put them on the patrol boat. The soldiers ran a towline from the junk's bow to the stern of the large patrol boat. Before casting off, several soldiers were left onboard the junk to guard Boucher and his men. They were ordered to sit on the deck, forward of the pilothouse, and not allowed to speak. The tow was begun as the sun's reddish-orange flames of morning's first light emerged beneath the underside of the clouds in the east. Boucher knew that they had been lucky...at least so far.

CHAPTER 28

EP-3 on routine patrol above the South China Sea

The Navy EP-3 spy plane had been on patrol for four hours. Home based in Okinawa, Fleet Air Reconnaissance Squadron One (VQ-1), or "The World Watchers," as they were nicknamed, traditionally provided surveillance of Russian and Chinese navy ship movements. But the War on Terror changed that and expanded VQ-1's mission to include suspected merchant shipping. The patrols were normally twelve hours in duration, but occasionally lasted a couple of hours longer if the pilot shut down one of the plane's four turbo-props to conserve fuel. This presents a risk because a successful, cold-engine restart while in flight is always an unknown.

Each member of the EP-3's twenty-person crew was at his station when the new tasker came in over the secure UHF SATCOM system from USPACOM Headquarters in Hawaii.

The EP-3's pilot, Lieutenant "Gordy" Gordon, didn't like it. In fact, not one of them liked it. The orders they just received gave them all a pucker factor. The pilots, navigator, and EWMC were already extremely concerned about over-flying any of the Spratlys or proceeding beyond the twenty-mile PACOM-defined limit of the hotly contested island chain. But this mission was different. They were to proceed to within nine miles of the Chinese-held island and provide digital imagery. After the Hainan Island incident several years earlier—where an EP-3 was held along with its crew after doing an emergency landing in North Korean-held territory—the crew knew 7th Fleet and the US Pacific Command would watch this mission very carefully. The possibility of being intercepted by any of the nations contesting the Spratlys area was an ever-present threat of immeasurable proportions. Nonetheless, orders were orders.

Lieutenant Gordon didn't want to take any more risk than necessary.

"Okay, you spooks in the back, listen up! NFO, I want a constant position double-check using multiple nav sources. I'll do a figure eight orbit to avoid making any turns towards any particular country. ELINT operator and Hi-band, stay on top of your game. STORY BOOK, keep looking over your shoulder. BIG LOOK, when we get down low enough for the big M&M, you're looking for a junk and a periscope. SEVAL and SPECEVAL, we need to know what they're talking about and get it out TACREPs. We're going in *rigging* and I don't want to hear about any *cowboys* back there! If anyone needs to *break the code* or *pile on*, now would be a good time!"

The crew all knew what a pain in the ass rigging was. When the EP-3 flew low over the sea, everyone had to put on their helmets, gloves, and survival vests normally only worn during take off and landing or bailouts. Off-duty crewmembers were placed in each observation window. Everyone had to remain strapped into his or her seat. "Cowboy" was the nickname given to those crewmembers that would defy the rigging order and take off their safety equipment. "Breaking the code" was the term applied to the first person that had to crap. Since there was no toilet onboard the EP-3, the crew had to crap in a garbage bag and then carry it off the plane at the conclusion of the mission. Worse yet, by tradition, the first code-breaker had to carry everyone else's crap off the plane along with his own, so there was a tendency to pile on after the first guy broke the code.

Gordon heard a nameless crewmember reply over his intercom from behind the cockpit curtain.

"No spooks, no mission."

Gordon smiled and replied, "No spooks, no problems."

The Spratlys, Chinese outpost

It was now daylight and the storm had passed. Occasional patches of blue sky showed through holes in the billowing, rain-laden clouds drifting above. The island was in sight. It didn't really even look like an island. There was no vegetation of any kind. It looked more like a concrete fort protruding from the sea surface. As the boats approached, they entered a small man-made lagoon that appeared to have been blasted out of solid coral and beach rock. Ahead, Boucher could make out a small pier with several boat slips. There were two other small patrol boats moored in the slips. The concrete walls that made up the outer perimeter of the fortress were forbidding. They looked kind of like an undersized version of a medieval fortress the Crusaders might have built. Only this fortress was built on top of a coral atoll in the South China Sea. The walls bristled with machine guns and artillery.

The patrol boat was skillfully brought alongside the small pier. Using lines, soldiers pulled the junk in along the pier directly behind the patrol boat. Boucher and his men were off-loaded and led inside the fortress. They were put into a spartan room that had several light bulbs glaring from the ceiling and three small wooden tables with two chairs each. The door was locked and all was silent. The windowless room smelled moldy. Air circulation, if it existed, was undetectable. It was clear to Boucher that this fortress was not equipped to hold prisoners.

Shortly, the young English-speaking Chinese officer came to the room accompanied by a medical officer. Guards opened the door and the officer spoke. "Doctor to see bad men."

Boucher nodded as his men stepped aside. Llina was still caring for Haus and Reilly who were both conscious. The doctor and Chinese officer pointed to the tables and had both wounded men lifted onto the tables where the doctor carefully examined their wounds. During the examination, the doctor appeared to be reporting his findings to the officer. After thoroughly evaluating each wounded man, the officer spoke again.

"Doctor say men need small surgery for get better. We take hospital and fix."

Boucher looked at Llina. Llina nodded his agreement.

"Okay, thank you. You may take my two men to the hospital. May my medical officer accompany you?"

The officer shook his head no. "You stay."

Boucher held out his bound hands. "Would you please release our hands?"

The young officer gave orders to the guards who immediately cut the restraints from Boucher's hands.

"Okay for you and other men," the young officer said.

As the guards helped Reilly and Quicklinsky out the door, Boucher nodded silently to them. They understood what he meant. The door was closed and locked and silence reigned again. It was unnecessary for Boucher to speak. The men untied each other's bounds and immediately began sweeping the room for listening devices. They found none.

"Alright guys," Boucher said in a low voice, "we're in a bit of a situation. I need some EEI's so when it's time to say goodbye, we are all singing from the same sheet of music. Here's what I have so far. If they wanted to kill us they would have already done so. They appear to be a regular Army unit and show military discipline. They have our boat and everything on it. The gold is one thing, but the Plans are another. We have two men down. Their wounds are not critical. We have been separated from our wounded and they are apparently in some sort of sickbay, receiving medical attention. The Chinese could not have had time to translate and read the Plans. Chances are, they haven't had time to even evaluate the wealth on our boat in terms of gold and cash. They don't know who we are, but they do know we were running from someone."

Ramirez spoke up. "They have a total of five patrol boats. One is heavily armed with mortars and a deck-mounted 7.62 machine gun. The other four are not. They are diesel-powered, single-engine boats, steel hull and slow by patrol boat standards. I'd guess twelve to fifteen knots max at full throttle.

Probably have a range of no more than one-hundred to one-hundred-fifty miles on a flat sea. Their boat comms are limited to VHF radio. I didn't see any antennas on top of this building other than an HF long wire. I'll bet they don't have any satellite link back to Beijing."

"The boat dock was only guarded by two soldiers armed with AKs," Klum added. They had a guard shack at the head of the pier. The pier ran east-west. Our boat is at the far west end of the pier and is too big to accommodate a slip. It's going to have to stay where it is if they intend to keep it. The channel to the pier is about twelve feet deep and about thirty feet wide. It has a sharp elbow to protect the boat slip area from the surf about two-hundred yards off the end of the pier."

Doyle raised his hand and stood. "The fortress is pentagon shaped and has gun emplacements that provide for overlapping fields of fire. The artillery I saw was about 90 millimeters in size, so they have some serious range limitations. There are heavy machine guns, probably 12.7 millimeter, mounted on each point of the pentagon that can effectively cover the walls in crossfire, and do the same seaward with an effective range out to about one mile. All but three of the guns were covered and there was no ammunition loaded in those three guns. I'll bet they rarely, if ever, shoot all those guns. Anyway, if all of them were shootable, I would estimate it would take about three men per gun to fight them and maintain them. So three men times twenty guns is sixty men to start. Add another thirty men to support the maintenance, logistics, patrol boats, etc., I'd estimate this garrison's strength at about ninety to one-hundred men."

LeFever spit his dip on the floor, getting everyone's attention. "The chain of command is rigid. None of these guys do shit without being told to do it by a superior. I figure if we cut the head off the snake, the rest of it would not know where to crawl. What the fuck, we're only outnumbered nine to one and they're inside here with us so we know where they all are. The odds are in our favor. All we need to do is grab a couple of AKs from the guards, go get Haus and Billy, disable the artillery, sink their patrol boats, and we're home free."

The men all chuckled.

"They must have a helo pad somewhere on this building because there sure ain't no room anywhere else," Lavender pointed out. "I'm guessin' they get their main resupply from ships. Did any of you boys see any sort of piles or anchoring buoys off shore during the inbound tow? There's got to be a deep water mooring point somewhere around this island."

"Yeah, I caught a glimpse of what looked like a white mooring buoy on the east side," Yellowhorse reported. "In fact, there might have been more than one. The sun was in my eyes. Hey, maybe the garrison isn't as big as we think. What if there's only a skeleton crew here to keep the place up and running and to make it look like they have a real military defensive capability? I didn't see any soldiers manning any of the guns on the wall. Did any of you?"

The men all shook their heads no.

Boucher stood and walked to the door. He checked the latch to ensure it was locked, and then turned to address his men. "My guess is that we've already met the only English translator they have. I concur with all your findings. Now let's put a plan together and get the hell outta here!"

All talk stopped at the sound of the door being unlocked. Two guards entered the room and motioned for Boucher to follow them outside the room. Boucher turned to his men and nodded. They subtly returned the nod. They knew what he meant. The door was closed and locked again. Boucher was led up concrete stairs to what he judged to be the ground floor because he passed several narrow windows covered with bars. He was led down a passageway and could see the ocean through the windows. He was taken to a small office that contained a small wooden table with two wooden chairs positioned on either side. A single light bulb dimly illuminated the unpainted concrete walls of the room. The guards ordered him to sit. Moments later the Chinese captain entered and sat across from him. The English-speaking officer followed and stood at his side. He translated as the captain began the interrogation.

"Who are you?" he asked Boucher.

"I am Jake Boucher. My men and I are Americans."

"Why you come to China waters?"

"We were being chased by pirates and we thought we could lose them in the storm by sailing into these islands and using them for cover."

"We search boat and find much gold and much American money. Where it come from?"

"I told you before, we are treasure hunters. We recovered the gold from a crash site in Cambodia."

"What are American secret documents you have?"

"We are unsure of their significance, but they are old U.S. war plans from many years ago."

So far, Boucher was pretty much telling the truth and he hoped that his candor would buy him some trust. All he needed was the right moment and he would act without hesitation.

He made eye contact with the captain. "What do you intend to do with us?"

The Chinese officer looked momentarily puzzled by Boucher's question.

Finally, he gave his answer. "You are prisoners of Peoples Republic of China. You invade China territory."

Boucher quickly replied, "No Sir! We are sailors who were lost at sea and stumbled into your waters seeking shelter. Your patrol boats attacked us without cause!"

Again the officer looked puzzled. "With so much gold you not innocent sailors."

At this point Boucher realized that the issue was about the gold, not the fact that he and his men had stumbled into this fortress. He felt that his only option was to make an offer.

"I will split the gold with you for safe passage out of here."

The officer laughed. "We will take what we wish. You are criminals."

"So what do you intend to do with us?"

The officer thought about his answer for a few seconds. "We turn you over our superiors very soon. Until then, you are prisoners here."

Both officers stood and walked unceremoniously toward the door.

"Wait," Boucher pleaded. "What about my two wounded men?"

The officer stopped. "They will be treated well, but you are prisoners."

"May I visit them to see how they are?"

The officers stopped at the door, consulting in Chinese. "Yes, but only for short time. Come now!"

Boucher felt relieved as he was led from the room at gunpoint by two guards. He was taken through a maze of corridors, but remained on the same floor level. Boucher surmised that he had been taken around the building to its opposite side. They arrived at a non-descript door with a guard sitting outside, and entered. The room was small, poorly lighted and smelled like disinfectant. It was the sickbay. There were only four cots in a row along the wall and Reilly and Quicklinsky were laying in the first two. The room was otherwise empty. Both men were bandaged and appeared to be sleeping.

Boucher sat on a wooden chair between their beds. He pivoted toward Quicklinsky and took his hand. "Haus, can you hear me?" he whispered softly. There was no sign that he was awake, but Quicklinsky squeezed his hand. Next he pivoted toward Reilly and squeezed his hand. "Billy, can you hear me?" Reilly squeezed back, but otherwise didn't move.

Boucher knew they were both waiting for the right moment to act. He patted both of them on the head. "Be ready and well my old friends. We await your speedy recovery and return to us."

He slowly stood and the guards escorted him back to the confinement room.

The English-speaking officer closely observed Boucher throughout, but said nothing. Prior to entering the passageway, leaving the confinement room, the young officer offered Boucher the use of a toilet room. Boucher went inside and the officer followed. The guards waited outside.

The moment the door was closed he spoke. "You have no chance to escape."

Boucher was surprised by the young officer's words. "What are you trying to say?"

"You need me help you."

"Of course, I would like you to help us. What do you want from us?"

"I want be rich. You take me with you."

Boucher knew if he played this young officer properly that he might have a ticket out. "Okay," Boucher replied, "I will take you with us and give you an equal share of the gold."

The officer put out his hand and Boucher shook it.

"Okay, you say in United Station, 'good to go,'" the officer said smiling.

Boucher flashed one of his infamous toothy grins. "Deal, good to go," he replied. "What now?"

"I contact you soon again. No worry."

"Okay. What's your name?"

"Name Chi, Lieutenant Chi."

"Okay, Chi, you're on the payroll. Lieutenant Chi, has the gold been unloaded from my boat?"

"No, only take important war plans."

"Do you know where those plans are?"

Chi smiled confidently. "Plans in radio room on second floor over medical room."

"What about us? What will you do with us?"

"China submarine pick you up tomorrow night very late."

"How many men do you have here in this garrison?"

"Have thirty-two only."

Boucher returned the smile and left the room for the walk back to the detention room where his men were. When he entered, he smelled food. The men were eating rice broth soup.

"Okay boys, listen up. I got the skinny."

The men gathered around Boucher.

"I saw Billy and Haus. They're both okay. They're gonna sit tight in sickbay until we get an opportunity to move on our captors. That English-speaking Chinese lieutenant got me alone and offered to help us break out of here. He wants a cut of the loot. I said okay. It sure can't hurt having someone on the inside. As I walked to and from sickbay I saw no evidence of a fully-manned garrison. Johnny, you were right. The lieutenant says this place only has a skeleton crew of thirty-two. That's just enough men to keep a presence, but not enough to be of much consequence in a surprise attack. I'm almost sure that they expect some sort of indicators and warnings leading to a hostility build-up that would allow them time to reinforce this garrison with a full complement of soldiers. So...here's what we have going for us. We have Billy and Haus in sickbay. One soldier stands outside a locked door guarding them. The door is wood and it's flimsy. Sickbay is located on this floor level on the other side of the building. We have a choo-hoi Chinese officer who speaks English and wants to become a Capitalist pig like us. He'll help us, but we don't know to what extent we can trust him. Pat, I want you on him like stink on shit. If he tries to fuck us on the way out of here I want you to take him out. He told me that our boat is intact and that the Plans have been removed, but not the gold or the cash. He said they intend to put us on a PRC sub tomorrow night. For now, we're together. We're being fed. We need to all be outta here by morning with the Plans. Any questions?"

The men sat quietly. Yellowhorse stuck a stained porcelain spoon into a bowl of rice broth and passed it to Boucher. No one spoke.

USS Virginia

"Captain, Bridge. SUBPAC reports that one of our EP-3's holds the PRC island fortress at nine miles visual and is streaming imagery. They are establishing a SATCOM downlink through our HDR terminal. Imagery should be on the screen in Combat momentarily."

"Roger, I'm on my way. Meet me there."

"COB," Lieutenant Cutler asked, "do you hold the imagery yet?"

"Yes Sir, it's coming through now."

The flat LED color screen came to life and flickered a few seconds before showing a real-time, crystal clear image of the island. The EP-3 was in low orbit at nine miles from the island and below detectable air search radar range. The EP-3 was using digital color and low light cameras mounted in the observation window.

Ever since the end of the Cold War, the P-3 squadrons that used to track Soviet submarine movements were increasingly transitioning from submarine hunters to intelligence gathering platforms. The EP-3 was a dedicated spy plane that carried powerful cameras capable of capturing crystal clear video at ranges up to twenty miles in almost any conditions. The EP-3 also carried a suite of electronic listening apparatus, radio direction finding sensors, and some electronic countermeasures equipment. Otherwise, it was a propeller-driven, slow-flying, unarmed aircraft capable of fourteen-hour, non-stop patrols.

The satellite data link it had established with the Virginia was one of the newer capabilities the Navy had that allowed the viewer to digitally manipulate and zoom the picture on their screen.

"Captain on the bridge," Cutler announced.

Galloway peered at the flat screen display, rubbing his chin in thought.

"Zoom in on the pier and tell me if that's our mystery boat," he commanded.

The petty officer operating the monitor screen clicked his mouse and a frame around the pier area appeared. He clicked the right button of the mouse and the framed picture enlarged to full screen. It showed the junk was moored directly behind a large patrol boat and had an open path seaward through the narrow channel.

"That's the target vessel, Captain," the petty officer reported.

"Okay, advise COMSUBPAC, unless otherwise directed we're going to take up patrol position twenty miles west of that island. I have a hunch the Chinese sub we detected is somehow involved in this operation. The real question is whether or not our mystery men are in complicity with the Chinese."

Cutler stepped forward to address his CO. "Captain, recommend we reacquire that Chinese Kilo-class sub ASAP."

"Good recommendation, Lieutenant. Make it so."

CHAPTER 29

The Spratlys, Chinese outpost

It was now 2300 hours and the sun had set four hours earlier on the South China Sea. Boucher and his men were awakened from their uneasy sleep by the sound of the door being unlocked. Chi entered the room alone.

Chi passed Boucher a Chicom 9mm pistol and an AK-47 as he whispered, "We go now."

Boucher passed the AK over to Mojo. Both men immediately did a quick press check to ensure the two guns had a round in the chamber. They then dropped the magazine to make sure it was loaded to capacity and quickly reinstalled them with a slap.

"Okay, what now?" Boucher whispered to Chi.

"Guards sleep. We go to doctor room and get friends."

Boucher stopped and turned toward Lavender. "Mojo, you, Mossman, Thane, and Jack make your way to our boat and make it ready to get underway. Eliminate any guards in your way. Spare them if you have a choice. We need to block any attempt by those patrol boats to follow us out to sea."

Mojo gave Boucher a thumbs-up. "Got it."

"Dick, Cherry, Bad Bob, Gabe, and Pat, you're with me and Lieutenant Chi. We're going to get Billy and Haus and then the Plans. Once we get Billy and Haus, I want Dick, Cherry, and Gabe to take them to the boat. Pat and Bob, the Lieutenant and I will go get the Plans. If shooting becomes necessary, try to avoid killing them."

Chi interrupted the conversation. "Only one guard on pier. Only one guard at hospital. Only two men in radio room. Captain sleep in bedroom. Other soldiers sleep in barracks room. I lock door from outside on soldiers."

"Good work, Chi. All we want to do is leave. If we can do that without burning the place down and killing everyone, then I will consider that an accomplishment."

Chi grimaced.

"We all rendezvous on the junk in twenty mikes and make a run seaward. Any questions?" Boucher paused. "Okay boys, let's get it done."

The mission was on.

Boucher and his team headed for the sickbay with Chi in the lead. The guard was sitting in a chair outside the door sound asleep. His AK-47 was leaning against the wall beside him. Boucher stopped his assault element about twenty feet away and cautiously approached the sleeping guard with his pistol at the ready. He quietly took the guard's AK from the wall and pitched it back to Gabe. In a singular rapid movement, he snatched the guard from the chair and cupped his giant hand over the guard's mouth from behind. The startled man had no chance to resist. The rest of the men approached and Chi quickly unlocked the door. Boucher dragged the guard inside. Gabe took up a defensive position just inside the door, watching down the passageway. Bad Bob grabbed the guard from Boucher and threw him onto a bed where he gagged and bound him. Klum quickly released the holding restraints on Billy and Haus.

"You boys alright?" he whispered.

"Yeah. What the hell took you so long? These stitches itch worse than poison ivy and I couldn't scratch 'em!" Haus replied in a low voice.

"Billy, you okay?"

Reilly was groggy but conscious.

"Haus," Klum asked, "can you make it on your own?"

"Yeah, but Billy is going to need some help."

Llina quickly checked Reilly's bandages and helped him to his feet. Reilly was shaky at best.

"Keith, give me a hand with Billy."

Klum and Llina grabbed Reilly around the back and sat him into the wooden chair next to the bed. They picked him up using the chair like a cradle and gave the ready signal to Boucher. Boucher looked back at the door. Gabe gave them an all-clear thumbs-up.

"Get Billy and Haus to the boat. Bob, Pat, you and Chi are with me. Chi, take me to the Plans."

Chi led the way to the radio room where the Plans were being held. The radio room was a secure room that had a heavy, steel door leading inside. The door had both a mechanical cipher lock and a conventional, high security key lock on it as a means to control access. Chi motioned for Boucher and Barns to stand out of sight along the wall down the hall from the door. While there was no sophisticated closed circuit TV camera and monitor that provided the men on the inside a view of those requesting access, the door contained a fish eye similar to those on hotel room doors, and a mirror on the opposite wall from the door. This allowed those on the inside a view of those desiring access, and the mirror provided a partial view of the surrounding hallway. It was a very effective low-tech means to ID and control entry.

Chi approached the door and stood a few feet in front of it. He casually pushed the ringer button next to the door. Boucher peered down the hall, watching as the heavy door was unlocked from the inside and slowly opened. As Chi stepped through the door, Boucher and Barns charged forward, pushing Chi through the open door and over the man standing inside. Barns snatched the unsuspecting man by the throat as Boucher rushed the man at the communications console, tackling him off his chair. It all happened so fast the man at the console didn't have time to sound the alarm. Boucher and Barns quickly bound and gagged the two men with tape and electrical wire.

"Chi, where are my Plans?" Boucher demanded.

"Maybe here," he said pointing at a closet that contained documents.

Boucher and Barns quickly searched the closet without luck. "No Plans, Chi. Where else could they be?"

"Maybe in Captain's room?"

Boucher didn't like that answer.

"Bob, Pat, help me disable the comms gear."

Barns, Patterson, and Boucher tore out wires and pulled radios from their mounts in an effort to break or disable as much radio equipment as they could.

"Chi, you take us to your Captain's room."

He nodded. They left the two bound men on the floor inside the radio room and pulled the door closed, engaging the cipher lock from the outside. Chi again led Boucher and Barns down the passageway where they came to a narrow stairs leading up to the next floor. He motioned for Boucher to follow more closely. As they reached the next floor, Boucher noted there were only two doors at the end of a short hall. Chi pointed to the door on the left and shrugged. Boucher pulled Chi in close.

"Do you have a key?" he asked pointing at the door.

Chi shook his head no.

"How do we get inside? Knock?"

Chi looked puzzled.

"Chi, how do you summon your captain when you need to awaken him in his quarters?"

"Only emergency."

"Well okay, I guess we'll have to make one happen."

With that, Boucher pulled Chi over to the door and began to kick it as hard as he could. He could hear Chinese angrily being spoken from inside and he found it almost humorous. Suddenly the door opened and there stood the captain in a white nightgown, pistol in hand. Boucher snapped the gun from the man's grip like it was a toy and pushed Chi inside. Barns followed them inside and closed the door. Boucher held his pistol on Chi to make it look like he was his prisoner and passed the one he had just taken from the captain to Patterson.

"Ask him where the Plans are!" Boucher demanded.

Chi translated Boucher's question. The captain smirked and replied in a long-winded sentence.

"He say you go to hell! He not take orders from American cowboy bandits."

"Really?" Boucher said under his breath. "Tell him I will kill you if he doesn't tell me where he has the Plans."

Chi relayed the threat, but the captain continued to refuse. Boucher pushed the captain backwards into a chair next to a small wooden nightstand and grabbed a chrome-plated bayonet that was being used as a paperweight.

"Bob, search the room."

Barns had already begun the search and was intrigued by two, two-foot-long ship models the captain had displayed on a table next to the wall. One was a container ship and the other was a Ro-Ro ship.

"Lieutenant, tell your boss that if he doesn't tell me where the Plans are, I will begin by cutting off his ears. Then I will cut off his nose and if he still won't talk, I'll cut off his balls! Tell him!"

Chi translated Boucher's threat, but the captain remained defiant.

"Hey Jake," Barns said, "take a look at these two cut-away ship models."

Boucher kept his gun on Chi and the captain as he stepped over to Barns. Barns pointed at the Ro-Ro ship model.

"This is one of those roll on-roll off ships that has the stern-carried ramp. This is what the Japs and Koreans use to carry cars and trucks around the world. I think the MSC and the Rapid Deployment Force even use this kind of ship. They're everywhere and China has a huge fleet of them."

"So what's got your attention?" Boucher asked.

"Jake, look at this cut-away. You see the inside decks of the ship?"

"Yeah, what about it?"

"Jake, it's a troop ship not a commercial Ro-Ro ship. It's just made to look like a commercial ship. It has huge troop quarters and has tanks and artillery in the ro-ro area. Now look at the container ship model. The containers are all interconnected with passageways. Look, here. There's berthing, galleys, sickbay, laundry. Jeez, that's a modular troop ship! It just looks like a container ship."

Boucher and Barns stood and looked at each other. "Oh shit...!"

Boucher returned his attention to Chi. "Where did these models come from?"

"Captain work for shipbuilder before this," Chi replied.

"How did he end up here?"

"He get caught with wife of boss."

Boucher, Patterson, and Barns chuckled.

"Who would have guessed that this ugly son-of-a-bitch was a Romeo," commented Patterson.

Together with his menacing body language, Boucher's next statement left no question as to whether or not he was serious. "Tell the captain that I will take him with me and claim that he surrendered to us if he doesn't tell me where he put the Plans.

Chi rattled off Boucher's threat and this time he hit a nerve. The captain blurted out a reply and was now acting scared for the first time.

"He say all Plans in lock box in office."

"Where's his office?"

"Office next door through door there," Chi said pointing.

"Let's go take a look."

Chi led the men through the door into a small office. There was a locked steel file cabinet next to the wall by the desk. Barns tried to open it, but the lock wouldn't budge. Boucher grabbed the captain and pushed him forward to the cabinet.

"Open it!"

His order required no translation. The captain opened his top desk drawer, cautiously reached beside the drawer and withdrew a key. Boucher motioned impatiently for him to unlock the file cabinet. Once he did, Boucher pushed him down into his desk chair and told Barns to tie and gag him. Boucher began to rummage through the top drawer and found nothing but files written in Chinese. The second drawer had two bound volumes with Chinese military insignia printed on the outside and a Chicom pistol. He passed the volumes to Patterson and stuck the pistol in his belt after checking to make sure that it was loaded.

"What are these about?" Boucher asked Chi as he pointed to the two volumes he had just passed to Patterson."

Chi looked down at the floor ignoring the question.

"Damn it, Chi! What are these documents about? If you're coming with us I need you to be honest with me! What are they about?"

Chi finally looked up and reluctantly answered, "It big secret war plan to fight United Station."

Patterson threw both volumes on the desk. "Why would a little shit-ass outpost like this have big secret war plans?

Chi shrugged. "Very important outpost keep oil for China, not Philippians."

The next drawer contained all four volumes of OPLAN 5000. He threw those on the desk next to the two Chinese Plans. The next two drawers contained personnel files and logistics documents.

"Bob, find a bag that will carry all this stuff."

Barns quickly searched the office closet and found a gray canvas sack that resembled a duffle bag. He quickly stuffed all four OPLANS and the two Chinese war plans into the bag and still had room to spare. Boucher motioned for him to take all the files in the next shelf, too. Barns tied the bag shut and threw it over his shoulder.

Boucher turned off the light and the three of them made their way back to the hallway. Chi took them outside on a narrow walkway that led to the pier. They cautiously passed the guard shack where they saw a guard laying face down on the edge of the concrete pier. He had been bound, gagged, and blindfolded, but otherwise looked unharmed. They continued to the large patrol boat where Mossman and Haus were cutting the mooring lines. Boucher saw what they were doing and hurried down the pier to the junk. As they boarded the junk, the auxiliary engine was started and the mooring lines were thrown off. Mojo was at the helm and immediately began backing the junk away from the pier.

Moments later, Boucher heard the throaty growl of the engines on the large patrol boat start up. Boucher's men took up defensive positions with AK-47s on the junk's stern gunwale. Mojo skillfully turned the bulky junk into the narrow channel and maneuvered seaward at best speed. The patrol boat followed with Haus at the helm. When he reached the narrowest point in the channel, Haus turned the boat perpendicular and dropped anchor. Moss went below to the engine room and returned on deck shortly thereafter. He threw two canister-shaped objects over the side. Mojo backed down, putting the junk's stern next to the port side of the patrol boat. Moss and Quicklinsky jumped onboard the junk and Mojo gunned the engine to full speed.

Boucher went to Moss's side and shook his hand. "What did you and Haus do to keep those patrol boats from following us?"

Moss laughed. "I took all the oil filters off their engines and opened the engine cooling water intake scuttle. If they start those boats up, they either burn up the engines or flood the engine compartment, whichever comes first. Sorry, Jake. It's all I could think of on such short notice."

Boucher clapped Moss on the shoulder. "Well done!"

Boucher went over to Llina who was caring for Reilly. Reilly was still groggy.

"How's he doing, Dick?"

"Looks like that Chicom doctor did a fairly good job stitching him up.

He'll have a few more scars to brag about, but chicks dig scars and Billy digs chicks, so I figure he'll call it a wash."

"Yeah, I guess you're right. The son of a bitch is too pretty anyway."

Reilly smiled half-heartedly as Llina and Boucher joked.

Patterson shouted, "Lights are coming on back there! They're on to us!"

The fortress' lights were indeed coming on around the perimeter walls. A searchlight atop the wall overlooking the harbor began sweeping the pier area, but hadn't found the slow-moving, seaward-bound junk. The junk had cleared the narrow channel, but was still only about five-hundred yards from the fortress. It was only a matter of time until they were detected and they were still well within machine gun and mortar range. Boucher could see soldiers rushing to the patrol boats. The sound of engines being started carried across the water through the night air. Then the searchlight hit them.

"Johnny, you think you can make that shot?" Boucher shouted at Yellowhorse.

"Can Superman jump tall buildings with a single bound?" Yellowhorse declared as he rested his AK-47 on the junk's wooden gunwale and carefully aimed at the light.

Yellowhorse's single shot was precisely placed and the searchlight blinked out.

Haus was the only experienced sail boat sailor in the entire group and he gave the next orders. "Raise every sail this tub has! We're going to run with the seas. Let's move it, boys! We need some serious legs to put some distance between us and them."

The men sprang into action and began hauling up the sails. One of the small patrol boats had made its way to the large patrol boat that was blocking the channel and had come along its side. Soldiers were uncovering the mortar tube and the deck-mounted machine gun on the bow. Neither Moss nor Quicklinsky showed any concern over this action, but Boucher wasn't going to sit by and wait for another mortar attack.

"Mossman," Boucher yelled, "you see what they're doing on the big boat?"

"Sure do," Moss yelled back as he tightened the main sail.

"Well, I don't like it!"

"It will get better in a minute, Jake," Moss coolly responded. "We're doing okay."

Boucher saw a soldier adjust the mortar's launch angle and prepare to drop a mortar down the tube. He couldn't help but hold his breath in anticipation of the telltale thud that would report the launch. When the soldier dropped the mortar, there was an explosion that illuminated the night sky. A resounding shockwave passed over the junk seconds later. The patrol boat was on fire and sinking. Soldiers were jumping into the water from the small boat and thick smoke was billowing from its fiery interior.

Moss wiggled his eyebrows at Boucher, who at this point in the unfolding drama, was speechless.

"I left them a little surprise just in case they tried to drop mortars on us."

Boucher shrugged as he held his arms out, gesturing Moss to tell him what he had done.

"Okay, I gotta fess up," Moss admitted. "I put a grenade in the bottom of the tube with the pin out. Kinda figured they would be in a hurry and not check to make sure the tube was clear first. Those little sons of bitches deserved it anyway after what they did to Billy and Haus!"

Boucher was still speechless as he turned back to see the patrol boat sink in the channel.

The fortress grew smaller and smaller as the junk proceeded further seaward. There was a gentle breeze that blew the black smoke from the burning boat directly between the fortress and the junk. It worked like a smoke screen. The breeze also kept the junk's sails fully inflated and allowed the auxiliary engine to be shut down. The only sounds now were those groaning noises the junk made under full sail.

Patterson put a reassuring hand on Boucher's shoulder. "We did well back there, Jake."

Boucher contemplated Patterson's words. "Yeah, I suppose we did, Pat... I suppose we did."

CHAPTER 30

USS Virginia

Lt. Cutler dialed his CO's stateroom. "Captain, there's been an explosion at the Chinese fortress and the junk is underway again. You might want to take a look at this. We recorded the imagery."

Commander Galloway arrived in the control room about five minutes later.

"Captain on the bridge," the petty officer of the watch loudly announced.

Galloway sat down in front of the screen without comment. The petty officer replayed the event.

"You see our mystery men coming from the fort onto the pier in twos, threes, and fours. One group goes right to the junk. A second group goes from patrol boat to patrol boat. Then they get the junk underway along with the largest of the patrol boats. Now watch this, Sir. They block the channel with the patrol boat and the junk proceeds seaward. The Chinese begin to pursue, and bang, the patrol boat blows up."

"Jeeeez…" Galloway hissed. "That's a damn international incident in the making, especially if our mystery men are Americans. How much time does our EP-3 have left on station?"

"The EP-3 advised that he's breaking off and heading home now, Sir."

"Do we have a fix on that junk yet?"

"No Sir, but they can't be very far ahead us. They're under full sail so they're not traveling very fast."

"Anything on that Chinese Kilo-class sub we saw yesterday?"

"No, Sir."

"Alright, maintain silent running and tail that junk. Get a message off to COMSUBPAC and tell them what we're doing. If that Chinese Kilo shows up, let me know immediately. I'll be in my state room."

"CON, SONAR," the intercom crackled. "Contact bearing two seven niner degrees, range twelve-thousand yards. It's that Chicom Kilo-class diesel-electric sub and he's running at periscope depth."

Galloway stopped in his tracks, then turned to revise his last orders.

"Lieutenant, maintain depth, course, and speed. I don't want our Chinese friend to know we're out here. Get a track on that sub ASAP. We need to figure out what his intentions are."

"Aye, Captain," Lt. Cutler replied. "SONAR, CON. Jonesy, what's he up to?"

"Ahhh…well, Lieutenant, it looks like he's coming about so he can get into a position perpendicular to our heading. If he knows we're here, it will offer him a perfect broadside torpedo attack against our port side."

Cutler briefly studied the maneuvering board and devised a solution that coincided with what Petty Officer Jones had just predicted. "Captain, recommend we come left to new course two four zero degrees and dive to three-hundred feet. That will put the Chinese sub above us on our starboard bow and allow us a clear torpedo shot from six-thousand yards."

Galloway considered Cutler's recommendation before issuing his orders. "I don't think he knows we're here. I think he's as interested in that junk as we are. I just don't know why. No Lieutenant, we're going to follow that diesel boat and I think he'll lead us to the junk. Maintain current course. Reduce your speed to one third. Make your depth three-hundred feet and I want it so quiet on this boat that if one of those Chicom crewmen farts, we'll hear it. Am I clear, Lieutenant?"

"Clear, Sir!"

"Alright, I'll be in my stateroom. Call me the moment anything changes."

"Aye, Sir."

On the junk

"Hey, Billy, how you feelin'?" Boucher asked his old teammate.

"Ahhh, a little stiff in the shoulder, but otherwise pretty good for a Monday," Reilly responded.

Both men chuckled.

"I was a little worried about letting you get cut by that Chinese medical officer, but I guess he did okay."

"He could have put the stitches a little closer together but WTF, I guess he closed me up and it works."

Llina looked concerned. "You have swelling, some infection, and a low fever, Billy. I don't like it, Jake. He could go either way at this point and if it's the wrong way, Billy's gonna need some antibiotics fast."

Billy waved, casually stating, "I'll be fine. It's just a scratch."

"Wrong!" Llina countered forcefully. "It's a scratch that took surgery to repair and eighteen stitches to close. You're not twenty-five any more, Billy! You're fifty-eight and you need to remember that, 'cause you don't take hits like you used to and bounce back the next morning!"

"Dick," Boucher cautioned, "none of us are twenty-five anymore. What can you do for Billy without antibiotics?"

"I can try to keep the wound clean, but it's draining. That Chinese doc must

either not have got all the fragments out or he didn't use sterile procedure…
maybe both. If it becomes more infected and the infection spreads, Billy is
going to need antibiotics or he could buy it!"

Billy patted his friend Dick Llina on the arm. "I'll be fine. All I need is
some rest."

Llina and Boucher's eyes met fleetingly.

"Sure you will, Billy," Boucher replied softly. "Sure you will."

Boucher called a quick team meeting to figure out what the options were.
Only Yellowhorse remained on deck at the helm. The men all gathered around
Boucher in the junk's cramped cabin area. Boucher made sure that Chi was
included.

"Listen up!" Quicklinsky shouted to quiet the individual conversations.

Boucher began, much as he always did, by reviewing their current
status. "Okay boys, we're haze gray and underway once again. We made
a good escape from our captors thanks to Lieutenant Chi's help, and it
appears that they haven't pursued us. We have put enough distance
between us and the fortress so they won't attempt to recapture us using
their patrol boats. Billy is down and requires medical care. His wound
is mildly infected, but if it gets worse we're going to have to find some
medical attention and antibiotics for him. We're about two-hundred-fifty
miles southwest of Puerto Princesa, which as you all know is where our
alternate plan C rendezvous will take place. If we can make it there, we'll
be pretty much home free."

"Jake, how about the good lieutenant?" Doyle asked motioning towards Chi.

Chi appeared nervous.

"Well, as far as I'm concerned he's on the payroll, and that's what I
promised him for our ticket out from that fortress. Chi, do you have anything
you want to add?"

Chi stood before speaking and bowed humbly to Boucher and then to
everyone else. "I not want to be Communist. I want go United Station, buy
Honda, go Hollywood, be cowboy, make blond girlfriend."

All the men laughed, which made Chi even more nervous. Boucher
motioned to Chi to sit down.

"Okay, Chi. You will be rich enough to do all that and more. You're now a
member of this team. All we want you to do is contribute to the team wherever
and whenever you can."

Chi smiled widely and again bowed respectfully.

"Alright, let's get some rest. Johnny will keep us on heading to
Palawan."

Chi bowed to Boucher before speaking. "I read China war plan for you."

Boucher was too tired to care. "Sure, Chi. You can tell me about it later."
Chi bowed again and opened one of the Plans.

...

Boucher dozed off into a sound sleep and didn't wake for almost two hours. When he did, Chi was still sitting at the same location reading the Chinese war plan. Boucher stirred and climbed the narrow cabin ladder to the main deck above to get some fresh air. The sun was shining and the seas were following and nearly flat. Yellowhorse was still at the helm and had been joined by Doyle who was navigating using the GPS as well as updating their position on the navigation chart.

"How we doing?" Boucher asked.

"We're making a good seven knots. Not that bad for this tub under sail!" Doyle replied.

"How about you, Johnny?" Boucher asked Yellowhorse.

"Well, I don't know about you and the rest of our crew, but I'm hungry enough to eat the ass out of a skunk!"

Boucher unbuttoned his pant's cargo pocket and pulled out an MRE. "Here you go, Johnny. I'll have the ship's room service deliver the red wine later."

"Keep your wine for yourself college boy. Us home folks drink beer."

"Okay, Johnny. I'll buy you all you can drink when we reach Puerto Princesa. You still drink San Miguel?"

Suddenly Yellowhorse yelled, "Periscope off our port bow—eight-hundred yards!"

"Shit!" Boucher yelled. "Is he inbound?"

The three men studied the wake behind the periscope for a few minutes.

"He looks like he's going to pass behind us!" Doyle shouted.

Boucher watched intently through binoculars. "No, he's gradually turning. It looks like he's going to fall in and follow behind us. I'm going below to get some help on deck."

Boucher went below and woke everyone up. Patterson was now at Boucher's side.

"That friggin' periscope is back! I need two men on deck to observe and back up Johnny and Jack."

Klum and Barns sprung over to the ladder and disappeared on deck. Chi was alarmed and began to fidget.

"Don't worry Chi; we'll handle it," Boucher assured.

"Chi not worry about submarine; Chi worry about China plan. Here," he said, holding it up for Boucher and Patterson to see as though they could read Chinese.

"Chi, I never asked you back at the fort. What did you do in the army?"

"I communications officer."

"Ahh, now I get it," Patterson commented. "That's why you speak English."

"Yes, me speak Vietnamese also."

"So what's the deal with these Plans?" Boucher asked.

"I not read Plan 0911 before. Only captain read. I think plan very bad to know."

"What do you mean by bad?"

Boucher stood and handed Chi an MRE and opened one for himself. Chi tore open the MRE foil and took a healthy bite of cold chicken and rice.

"China not have much navy but have very big army. China have nuclear missiles but not so many bombers. China have much industry, but not so many oil. China need many oil from Middle East, but U.S. control Middle East, but not Iran. China get oil from Iran."

"Okay, you haven't told me anything that isn't public knowledge."

Chi held up his hand in caution. "China container ships and Ro-Ro ships carry soldiers, logistics, even airplanes and tanks. No one know."

"Carry them where?" Boucher asked.

"Go United Station."

"Huh? The U.S.? No way!"

"For sure! Plan say it here."

Patterson butt in. "Let me get this straight, Chi. You're saying that China has a strategic war plan to invade the United States using container ships and Ro-Ro ships?"

"Yes! Only small time. Not invade big."

Boucher looked shocked. "Chi, you can't be serious? There is no way China would risk world war and its own economic disaster by making a dumb move like that."

Chi seemed confused by Boucher's words. "China make look like come to help United Station."

"Help with what?"

"Help after terrorist nuclear attack."

"What the hell are you talking about, Chi?"

"Iran have many terrorists. China give terrorists nuclear bomb. Bomb Chicago. Bomb New York. Bomb Seattle. Bomb Capitol in Washington. Many death. United Station need China help. China send many ships. Troops on ships invade."

Boucher and Patterson stared at one another. "Huh?"

"So here's the scenario in plain English, if I understand this correctly," Boucher offered. "A nuke attack against four or more major U.S. cities occurs. The sheer magnitude of that attack eliminates the vast majority of the U.S. infrastructure along with the U.S. government, pretty much in one fell swoop. The casualty figures are astronomical and completely overwhelm our emergency response and medical resources. The cities that weren't nuked are engulfed by huge swarms of refugees frantically seeking food and shelter. Police and social services are overwhelmed. Anarchy ensues. The U.S. Armed Forces are directed to keep control, but now since all the politicians are dead and the U.S. Federal Government effectively doesn't exist any more, the state governors are in charge. Can you imagine the cluster fuck? And, shit...China arrives with its armada of ships as humanitarian saviors and they are welcomed. They roll off in strength and establish several beachheads. They don't appear to be threatening, but they are there to stay."

Patterson pounded on the bulkhead with his fist. "Jeeezus, Jake! You gotta be shittin' me!"

Chi was clearly perplexed. "He not shit you! Me tell truth!"

USS Virginia

"Captain, OOD, that Chinese Kilo is running at periscope depth and is maneuvering behind what SONAR reports may be a vessel under sail." Cutler paused as he listened on the phone. "Yes, Sir," he replied. "We're well clear and he doesn't know we're on to him." He stopped to hear the reply. "Yes Sir, understand. We'll continue tracking both contacts and remain undetected. Aye, Sir. I will keep you info."

The Chief of the Boat (COB) stood by his side. "What are your orders, Sir?"

Cutler contemplated the diesel sub's position in reference to the Virginia's. "We'll, maintain range and depth. If that sub changes its course, speed, or profile, I want an immediate firing solution."

"Aye, Sir."

"OOD, Communications," crackled the voice over the speaker above Cutler's head. "The EP-3 is squawking mayday! Sir, the plane reports that it can't get one of its four engines restarted."

"Shit! It has three other engines...right?" Cutler blurted in reply.

"Yes Sir, but they're reporting low oil pressure in one of the other engines and they will have to shut it down before it overheats and catches on fire."

The COB stepped closer to Cutler to be more private. "Sir, that plane needs all four of its engines to get back to Okinawa."

The voice on the intercom broke in again. "The plane advises that it is too far from any field to land safely and will need to ditch at sea."

"Wonderful! Just fucking wonderful!" Cutler growled in a low voice as he keyed the intercom mic. "What's its current heading and position?"

"Sir, it's turning and heading toward the junk. The junk is the closest surface vessel and we are the only U.S. ship within range."

Cutler called Galloway's stateroom on the intercom and advised him of the situation. "Do you want to surface?"

"We can't surface with that Chinese Kilo sub out there! We don't know his intentions."

Onboard the EP-3

"BIGLOOK, pilot, do you hold that surface contact?"

"Roger, he's dead ahead—range four one miles—it's a large boat under sail."

Gordon opened the intercom. "Alright everyone, prepare the plane to ditch. Secure everything that isn't hard fastened. Ensure all crypto is zeroed. I'm going to set her down about forty miles ahead, next to the junk we were tracking. The USS Virginia is in the area as well. Between the junk and the Virginia, we should have a good chance. We're going to keep trying a restart on number two engine until final. I'll let you know when we're five out."

On the junk

Boucher put his partially eaten MRE down. He was suddenly no longer hungry. "Pat, I think we better give somebody an Iridium call and let them know about this Chinese Plan."

"Yup, but who?"

"Well, I have an old SEAL friend at the Agency. I could let him know we're coming in. How about the FBI on your side?"

"I could give the Director a call. I think he'd listen and probably even help when he understands what we know. What about Homeland?"

"This has got to remain very close hold. DHS couldn't find their way out of a wet paper bag much less coordinate an interagency response of this magnitude."

"Yeah, I hear you. So how do we get the word back to the right people and maintain OPSEC?"

Boucher thought about it for a moment and turned to Chi. "Chi, I need you to trust me on this. Would you be willing to testify and reveal what you know?"

"I not afraid. I tell truth."

"Good, thanks."

"Wait a minute, Jake," Patterson cautioned. "I think we need to think this through before we start making calls. It seems to me that we have more than just some Chinese attack plans in our possession. We have the OPLANs too. Every one of us knows what's in them and we know the grand strategy that MacArthur put into place that our government followed beginning with Ike. Do we now throw the OPLANs over the side and never tell anyone the truth about them or do we turn them over along with the Chinese plans?"

Boucher was always thoughtful as well as patient and he took his friend's questions to heart. "Well Pat, here's what I think. I think we are good Americans and former U.S. Navy SEALs. We need to always tell the truth, as we know the truth to be. That might not be the truth as others know it, but that's their problem. As long as we can swear on the good book and pass a polygraph when we tell what we know, it's the truth."

"Yeah, I agree. But don't we have to consider the damage we can do by going public with what we know about OPLAN 5000? I mean, shit!"

"Okay Pat, let's get the boys together and make sure everyone is onboard before we call Washington. It could cost us some of our loot."

"Yeah, I was afraid you'd say something like that!"

"It will be dark here in another ten minutes, which means that it will soon be morning in DC. We'll make the calls after the sun sets."

USS Virginia

"CON, SONAR, the Kilo contact is blowing ballast and appears to be surfacing about five-hundred yards abeam of the junk."

"Roger, SONAR, stay on him. Diving Officer, take us up to periscope depth. COB, summon the Captain."

"Aye, Sir," the COB replied.

A few minutes later Galloway appeared. "What you got, Lieutenant?"

"Sir, the Kilo sub is surfacing. SONAR advises that it's in close proximity of the vessel under sail. I took the liberty of coming up to periscope depth."

Galloway nodded approval and stepped over to the periscope. "Raise scope."

He unfolded the handles as they arrived in his grasp and quickly made a three-hundred-sixty-degree sweep of the Virginia's surroundings on the surface. He slowly spun back to the right and adjusted the focus by twisting the grip.

"Take a look at this, Lieutenant."

Cutler stepped in and pressed his face into the periscope's rubber eyepieces.

"Well Sir, night vision shows a junk under sail and...holy shit, Sir! I can see that Kilo boat's periscope and snorkel coming up their ass. I bet he's no more than three- to four-hundred feet behind them and closing fast. Here, take a look, Sir!"

Galloway wasted no time issuing orders as he took the periscope. "Plot a course that puts us eight miles ahead of that junk. Maintain periscope depth, ahead two-thirds. Get that SEAL platoon commander up here on the double. He and his men have been riding this boat for days. I think they need to start earning their room and board. Where's the EP-3?"

"Based on his last report, he's about twenty minutes out; still heading our way, Sir."

On the junk

Haus shouted the alarm. "That fucking sub is running up our ass! We need to get some guns on him!"

Everyone came on deck except Reilly. Boucher grabbed the binoculars and peered aft.

"That dumb bastard is going to run into us if he doesn't turn soon! Johnny, when he gets a little closer and you can get a clear shot at the glass on his periscope, I want you to put his eyes out. Maybe that will get his attention."

"Roger!" Yellowhorse shouted back.

"Everyone, if he surfaces, keep the crew pinned down. I don't want them launching any boats or shooting at us. Remember, that sub could be one of ours."

Patterson appeared beside Boucher and pulled him toward the bow of the junk.

"Jake, what about the phone call?" he asked holding up the Iridium phone.

CHAPTER 31

CIA Headquarters, Langley, Virginia, the same time

Rene Thompson entered Vice Admiral Sinclair's office waving a flash precedence Cane Pebble cable in his hand. "We got them, Admiral! That is, if we want them," he announced smirking.

Sinclair took the cable and carefully read it as Thompson stood in front of his desk.

"The Virginia reports there is an unidentified diesel sub in the process of surfacing in close proximity to the junk. They believe the sub is a Chinese Kilo-class diesel-electric boat. So just how do we have them if we want them, Mr. Thompson?"

"Well Admiral, we can't allow the Chinese to take them prisoner...can we? It would seem to me we should have the Virginia surface and beat the Chinese to the junk. After all, those terrorists on the junk have some very important national security documents that we must deny the Chinese."

"Says here thirteen men have been observed aboard that junk. Unless my memory fails me, the previous reports based on eyewitness accounts and imagery claimed there were fourteen. Which is it?"

"Well, who knows? The Virginia visually confirms only thirteen men on the junk."

"Says here there were forty gold ingots transferred from the seaplane to the junk. Imagery showed at least twenty times that amount of gold at the crash site. Where is the rest of the gold?"

Thompson felt his palms begin to sweat. "We don't know. We thought they had all of it with them."

Sinclair read on before commenting again. "Says here they are believed to possess four volumes of OPLAN 5000. Where the hell did they come from?"

"Sir, we have no cargo manifest of the plane at the Cambodia crash site. We think the plane was probably one of ours, but we aren't sure. If you recall, our investigation of the crash site revealed there were nine concrete blocks that had been blasted open. We found some U.S. dollars at the site strewn on the ground, but no gold. The OPLANs probably came from the crash site, but we can't confirm that until we capture and interrogate the terrorists onboard the junk."

Sinclair grumbled, raising one eyebrow. "Identification was positively confirmed on the suspects. Is that correct?"

"Yes Sir, that is correct. But that doesn't matter."

"How so?" the admiral asked.

"Well, we have been able to recover both cell and Iridium phone call records, all of which point to a sophisticated terrorist collaboration network supporting those now onboard the junk. We're checking into Al-Qaeda links too. Anyway, we should be able to piece it all together when we figure out who they were talking to and why."

Sinclair nodded and handed the cable back to Thompson. "Keep me informed."

"Yes, Sir."

As Thompson left Sinclair's office for his own he broke into a wide smile, feeling for the first time he was on his way to accomplishing his mission.

...

Sinclair waited a few moments after Thompson had departed before dialing his secure phone. The phone only rang twice before it was answered.

"United States Special Operations Command, Vice Admiral Thornberg's office, Staff Sergeant Neumann speaking. How may I help you Sir or Madam?"

"This is Admiral Sinclair. I would like to speak to Admiral Thornberg."

"Yes Sir. Admiral Thornberg is in his office. I will patch you through immediately. Please standby, Admiral."

Sinclair had served in both SEAL Team Two and SEAL Team Six with Jim Thornberg when they were both junior officers. When Sinclair was the Commodore of Naval Special Warfare Group Two at the SEAL base in Little Creek, Virginia, his friend Jim Thornberg was the Commodore at Group One in Coronado, California. They had each been promoted to admiral and ascended to their current three-star, flag officer rank within thirteen months of one another. Thornberg remained in special operations line unit command positions while Sinclair made his three stars in the intelligence community. They had been friends for nearly thirty years and held great mutual respect for one another.

"Robert, how are you my friend? How are Nancy and the kids?"

"Oh, I suppose we're all doing pretty good. How are things on your end at SOCOM, Jim?"

"SOSDD...same old shit different day. You know the drill."

"Yeah, I know the drill. Listen, Jim, I wouldn't bug you unless it was important but I need some help."

"Sure Robert, anything."

"You probably saw that flash precedence Cane Pebble cable that came in about a half hour ago."

"Yes, I read it."

"Well Jim, as you know, some of your guys are riding the Virginia. They're in pursuit of some suspected terrorists who are using a junk for transportation. I know this has been a CIA operation but something smells about it and I'm trying to ferret out what it is."

"What can I do, Robert?"

"Well, let me tell you what I suspect. Maybe then, together, we can figure out what I need your help with. You see, I don't think the guys are terrorists nor have any links to terrorism. I think they are mostly all our own guys."

"What do you mean?" a very surprised Thornberg asked his friend.

"You remember Jake Boucher, Jim? Well, he seems to be the ringleader. And, you probably remember the POW he saved, Pat Patterson, who later became an FBI agent?"

"Yes, I know them both."

"Well, Patterson retired from the FBI a couple of months ago and he seems to be in on it with Jake. In fact, as best as I can determine, I think Jake has most of his old SEAL platoon involved in one way or another."

"You're shittin' me! Right? What makes you think that?"

"Jim, this has to stay close hold between us."

"Of course."

"Well...I talked to Jake about ten minutes ago. He called on an Iridium satellite phone and told me he was on a junk headed to Palawan and a submarine was tailing them. He was very cryptic because he was non-secure, but he said he had a PRC officer with him and some PRC war plans that involved the nuking of several major cities here in CONUS and a follow-on invasion. He also said that he would turn all the documents over to proper authority."

"You really are shittin' me!"

"I wish I were, Jim, but it sure looks like Jake and his boys got themselves in some potential trouble. There's theft of classified documents involved, gold, and maybe even murder. They're being labeled as terrorists and you and I know there is no way Jake or his guys would ever do anything like that. I just don't know how much of a bullshit factor is in play at this point and I don't think I'm getting the straight skinny from the people here at the Agency who are directing the operation. You have some of your SEALs onboard the Virginia, correct?"

"Yes, a full platoon."

"So I was wondering if they could run a litmus test on these guys for me, outside official channels."

"Jeez, Robert! Even if I can make it happen, how do we get the info passed back to you without compromise?"

"It will need to stay in SOCOM secure code word channels. Strictly PERSFOR—no one else. Once you get a hard copy, you can fax it secure, directly to me. What do you think?"

"I think some of our guys need our help. Didn't you serve with Jake?"

"Sure did. We were swim buddies in UDT/R training and we did a three-year tour together in Team Two as junior officers. He was one of the finest officers I ever had the privilege of serving beside."

"Okay, Robert, I'll work it and get back to you when I have something worth passing."

"Thanks, Jim. I owe you. Out on this end." Sinclair slowly hung up the phone and whispered, "Thanks, old friend."

CHAPTER 32

On the junk

B oucher checked his watch and did a quick full circle search of the horizon to ensure there were no other vessels close by.

"Okay Johnny, take the shot and blind that son of a bitch! If you can, punch a couple of holes in his snorkel tube as well."

Yellowhorse steadied his left elbow on the junk's wooden gunwale and carefully aimed his AK-47 at the glass lens on the front of the periscope. The sub had been following about one-hundred yards astern of the junk, matching the junk's course and speed, for the past two hours. It would be dark soon and Boucher knew they couldn't win against the sub, especially if the sub rammed the fragile wooden-hulled junk from below. The odds had to be evened. Yellowhorse squeezed the trigger and fired. The AK-47s thirty caliber bullet did its job and shattered the lens. He repositioned the Chinese-Russian assault rifle slightly and took aim at the snorkel located a few feet behind the periscope and fired several more shots in rapid succession. Both the periscope and the snorkel soon disappeared beneath the surface of the sea.

Boucher was elated, waving his fist above his head. "Yes! Yes! Yes!"

The men on deck all cheered.

Patterson was less enthusiastic. "Okay Jake, we put their eyes out. Now what?"

"Ahhh, if they raise their auxiliary scope, we'll blind that one too!"

"Not that, dumbass! I'm talking about what happens after that sub disappears and we arrive at Palawan?"

"We'll execute the final phase of plan C and find a really good investment banker."

"Yeah, I know all that!" Patterson replied in frustration. "What if they're really on to us? I mean, shit, we must have pissed off that Chinese captain yesterday. We have one of his key officers and some of his most sensitive war plans. If he doesn't get his man and his documents back, he's toast and he knows it."

"Jeez, Pat! Why do you give a shit about some Chinese commie bastard who tried to hold us as his prisoners?"

"Well, let's just say I don't like having people with a vengeance looking for my white ass."

Boucher chuckled aloud. "That's the first time in all the years I've known you that I ever heard you refer to any of your body parts as white. I actually kinda like the sound of it...you know...black guy with a white ass. Hilarious!"

"Damn it, Jake! You know exactly what I meant! I would really appreciate it if you would get serious for a second or two and tell me what you're thinking."

Boucher hugged his friend. "We're in deep shit, Pat! That sub didn't just happen to be there. I really don't think it was one of ours, even though I wouldn't put it past 'em. This really isn't about the gold. It's about the Plans—both theirs and ours. But we're the only ones who know we have both. Until we get the Plans into safe hands, we're gonna get dogged by all sides."

Patterson put his hands into his pockets and looked down at the wooden deck.

"Jake, you think we'll make it to Palawan?"

Boucher turned away to watch the last beam of light disappear from the horizon in the west. It was now pitch black. "I don't know, Pat. We all need to get a few hours of rest while we can. Pass the word."

As he turned around towards Patterson, he came face to face with the muzzle of a gun held by a ghostly silhouette.

"Hands up! Say nothing!" the silhouette ordered in a low, barely audible voice.

Patterson slowly raised his hands. As he did, he could see several other dark forms swiftly moving towards the junk's cabin door hatch that led below deck. Lavender, standing to his right, was also at gunpoint with his hands in the air. Jackson immediately recognized the gun that was being pointed at him as the FN SCAR-light—the 5.56mm, silenced, close quarter combat variant of SOCOM's Combat Assault Rifle. He knew only U.S. Special Operations Forces carried these high tech weapons and the men holding them knew how to use them and would not tolerate any resistance.

Boucher was surprised by a loud whisper coming from the darkness a few feet away. "Commander Boucher?" the voice questioned.

"Who's there?" Boucher whispered back.

"SEAL Lieutenant Jim Murrant. Sir, I need to ask you some questions on behalf of Admiral Thornberg. Will you talk with me, Sir?"

Boucher hesitated a moment before answering. "Admiral Thornberg, huh? Yeah, okay, I'll talk with you."

Murrant eased closer to Boucher. "Sir, the Admiral wants me to confirm your identity and the identity of your men."

"And why would the good Admiral want that?"

"Sir, I don't know. He sent me a PERSFOR through codeword channels and asked me to confirm your ID. That's all I know."

Boucher leaned toward Murrant. "You're a platoon commander in SEAL Team One?"

"Yes Sir, I am. We were told that you and your guys are involved in terrorist activity. Are you, Sir?"

"You gotta be shittin' me, son! You can assure Jim Thornberg that I am still the same man I have always been. You can also assure him that with the exception of a Chinese officer, he knows everyone with me and we have not broken any U.S. laws or compromised our country's national security in any way."

"Yes, Sir. I'll tell him, but there is more. He specifically asked me to find out what the deal is on the OPLANs and the gold."

"Lieutenant, I'm not going to reveal any details to you about the contents of those Plans. Just suffice it to say we have them in our custody and they have not been compromised. Please tell the good Admiral that I will be happy to personally give him a full data dump to any level of detail he desires upon my return to the U.S. Also tell him I do not appreciate being treated like a prisoner when I have done nothing wrong."

"Ahh, yes Sir. But Sir, is the black man with you really Leon Patterson?"

"Yes, he's really Leon Patterson, alright? He's the flyboy we rescued during Tet in Cambodia. The rest of the guys here with me were there as well."

"Jesus, Sir, I've read the whole rescue account. In fact they still use it as a case study in BUDS training."

"Yeah, whatever. Just assure the Admiral it's us, not some terrorist cell."

Murrant stood at attention. "Aye, Sir. I'll pass it to him ASAP." Murrant paused and put out his hand. "Sir, I am really sorry about boarding your vessel and taking you guys down at gunpoint."

Boucher chuckled as he shook Murrant's hand. "Yeah, kind of ironic, isn't it... after all we've been through, a friggin' FNG takes us down. Do you have a good loyal platoon, Lieutenant?"

Murrant smiled. "The best, Sir."

Boucher replied softly, "Well that's what really counts when the odds are stacked against you."

Suddenly, they all heard a familiar sound coming from the dark sea about one-hundred yards off the junk's port side. It was the unmistakable hissing and bubbling sound that only a submarine makes when it surfaces.

Murrant shouted into his squad radio, "Sub surfacing on port side is not ours! Repeat, sub is not ours! COMMS advise the Virginia."

The junk's deck became chaotic. Murrant's SEALs were all wearing NVGs and each had squad radios linking them to one another. Boucher's men had nothing except their naked eyes and ears.

Murrant was barking orders to his men. "I want a Mark 46 and Mark 48 man fore and aft. I want AT-4 anti-tank rockets and SCARs with enhanced grenade launcher modules amid ship. Lieutenant Morgan, you're in charge here. Everyone in my element to the boats. We're going to be in position to board, fight, or sink that bastard. Whatever level of violence he chooses works for me, but he won't take this junk. Move it!"

In a blink of an eye over half the SEALs who boarded the junk were gone, disappearing silently into the darkness as quickly as they had first appeared from it. Boucher and his men were still a little bit overwhelmed. The Chinese sub was now breaking the surface squarely off the junk's port side. Boucher strained through his binoculars, but couldn't see any movement on the sub's deck.

"Lieutenant Morgan?" Boucher shouted.

"Over here," a voice replied from the darkness.

Boucher hurried to the voice. "Lieutenant, I think we met previously in the week. What's the plan here?"

"Murrant and the rest of my platoon are proceeding astern of the sub. They will trail it in their Z-birds out of sight. If we need them, they'll be in position to hand that sub Skipper his ass. They have AT-4s and 40mm EGLMs."

Boucher acknowledged with a slap on Morgan's shoulder.

"Where did you boys come from?" Boucher asked.

"We've been riding the Virginia following you for the last couple of days."

"The Virginia?" Boucher questioned in astonishment. "Isn't that a sub?"

"Sure is, Sir. We got the green light to take you down about an hour before dark. We launched off the Virginia from over the horizon about twelve miles ahead. We didn't want to get into a gunfight with you under any circumstances, so we figured we could board you without being compromised if we waited until after dark."

Boucher was astonished. "So one of our subs, the Virginia, is out there right now?"

"Yes, Sir. She's there alright."

"Holy shit! You mean that me and my guys are important enough to have a sub with an embarked SEAL platoon tail us?"

"I guess so, Sir. But we were under strict orders not to return fire against you unless it meant saving ourselves."

"Oh hell! That gives me a warm fuzzy! Nothing like a blue-on-blue shoot'em out. That's always a lose-lose scenario!"

"Yes Sir, sure is!"

Morgan hunkered down behind the gunwale with his SCAR assault rifle aimed into the darkness toward the Chinese sub.

USS Virginia

Galloway was glued to the periscope as he watched the Chinese sub surface beside the junk.

"Come hard left and steer new course, zero two one, maintain periscope depth. Hold your range to the target at four-thousand yards."

"Aye, Captain. Left to course zero two one, maintain periscope depth, hold astern of target at four-thousand yards," Cutler repeated.

Galloway watched as Morgan's two Zodiacs departed the junk and zoomed into the darkness astern of the surfacing submarine. He could clearly see the SEALs on the junk taking up defensive positions and the Chinese sub growing larger on the surface off the junk's port side.

"Standby for emergency surface on my order!" Galloway barked.

"Standing by for emergency surface on your order, Captain."

As he watched the events unfold on the surface, Galloway hissed through his teeth. "Shhhhiiiit! That damn Chinese sub is too close to the junk to torpedo on the surface. If we hit her there we run the risk of collateral damage to our guys on the junk. Why the hell did Morgan leave some of his men on that junk? He fouled my ability to engage!"

"But Captain, you sent them over there to board and secure that vessel! Right?"

Galloway went into a tirade at Cutler's comment. "Damn those SEALs! They have no respect for any other warfare specialty! It's always about them! They think all we do is provide taxi service... and when they get their ass in a bind, then we're expected to bail them out!"

"But, Captain, our ROE doesn't allow us to engage without express permission from NCA!"

"That's true Lieutenant, but if we are directly threatened we can defend ourselves and we have a crippled EP-3 inbound and it's preparing to ditch at sea. Get a flash message off to COMSUBPAC. Inform them we have visual confirmation. Contact in question is visually confirmed as a Chinese Kilo-class diesel-electric attack sub. Kilo is on surface in close proximity to high interest vessel. Kilo's intentions are unclear. We have SEALs onboard HIV securing same. We are in a visual monitoring position of both vessels. Request ROE in the event Chinese sub fires upon or attempts boarding of HIV."

"Aye, Sir."

On the junk

"I wish those bastards back at the fortress hadn't taken our NVGs. They had a boatload of gold and what do they take…our fucking NVGs!" Boucher was squinting through his binoculars as he muttered a string of curses.

Patterson and Moss were by his side.

"Hey, what makes you think we can see anything either?" Moss protested. "It's really friggin' dark out here."

Patterson laughed. "A fine bunch of all-weather night fighters you limp-dicks have turned out to be. I never heard you bitch before. I think you've been spoiled by modern technology and now you're handicapped when you don't have it."

Boucher put down his binoculars and turned to face Patterson. "You know what, Pat? You're absolutely right! We're no worse off than we've ever been. We can still carry the fight to the enemy! Nothing has changed! We still own the night!"

With that Boucher stood, then grabbed Chi and pulled him over to his side. "Chi, I want you to remain next to me within arm's reach no matter what happens."

Chi nodded.

"Listen up!" Boucher shouted for all to hear. "We have a PRC sub off our port side. We have an active duty SEAL element onboard and another astern of us in Z-birds. We're in good shape here. We need to find out what that sub wants from us. I think I know the answer, but we need to stall them and make them ask. Don't anybody shoot unless I give the order. If I do give the order to fire, I want you to project maximum violence on the objective for as long as we can sustain it. Haus, if the shooting starts, you break away with a hard turn to starboard and run a one eighty the other way. That will give our boys in the Z-birds an unobstructed field of fire on the sub's stern steering and propulsion area. One more thing. Lieutenant Murrant advised me that his platoon launched on us from the USS Virginia—one of ours. We don't know her current position, but I'll bet my share of the gold she's watching us at this very moment. If she surfaces, don't shoot the good guys. Any questions?"

There was only silence and the hissing sounds of the nearly fully surfaced Chinese sub, now awash off the junk's port side. Everyone onboard made ready to deal with whatever might come their way.

USS Virginia

Galloway was glued to the periscope for what seemed like hours as he watched the Chinese sub surface.

"The Chinese boat has surfaced. It looks like it's charging its batteries. I'm capturing imagery from this point on. Put it on screen in combat and stream it back to COMSUBPAC. Here, take a look, Lieutenant."

Cutler stepped up to the periscope and peered through the eyepiece. He could see the Chinese sub on the surface. The sub's diesel exhaust overboard discharge was spilling white, frothing water back into the sea. Then five men appeared on the top of the sail. Two were clearly wearing officer uniforms; the others were enlisted sailors. The three sailors were armed with AK-47 assault rifles. The deck hatch opened aft of the submarine's sail and six sailors armed with AK-47s and one officer appeared on deck. They knelt side-by-side in a line facing the junk, holding their weapons down in a non-aggressive posture. One of the Chinese officers on the bridge sail raised a bullhorn to his mouth.

"Captain Galloway, are you watching this on the screen?"

"Yes, I am."

"It looks like there's going to be a confrontation and maybe some automatic weapons' exchange. Shouldn't we try to maneuver into an attack position just in case?"

"And do what...torpedo a PRC submarine? No, Lieutenant. That would be an unprovoked act of war. That sub Skipper doesn't know we're here and I want to keep it that way. I don't think he has a clue who he's dealing with on that junk."

On the junk

"Chi, what's he saying?" Boucher asked.

"He say he want me and Chinese plans back or he shoot."

Boucher shrugged at Moss and Patterson.

Patterson pointed toward the sub. "I think we oughta tell 'im to go fuck himself!"

Moss chuckled. "Nahhh, let's just sink the son of a bitch! I got people to see and places to go and ..."

Boucher interrupted, "Let's see if we can bribe him. Chi, tell him we'll give him twenty kilos of gold if he goes away."

Chi yelled over to the sub in Chinese. The officer immediately replied over the bullhorn.

"He say you crazy stupid!"

"Tell him we'll pay him thirty kilos of gold."

Once again, Chi translated Boucher's offer. Again the reply came immediately.

"Captain say no to deal! He say he sink junk if stolen Chinese documents and me not go back now. He say he not play game. He say now or he sink junk! How you say…he no bullshit!"

The sailors on the sub's deck had all raised their weapons and were now pointing them at the junk.

"Chi, please inform the Captain that if he opens fire we will defend ourselves. Tell him to please stand down. We have no quarrel with him."

Boucher coolly prepared his men to engage. "Okay boys, be ready on my command."

The bright lights first appeared in the sky well above the horizon, distantly on the opposite side of the sub, but it became obvious that they were getting closer and growing brighter by the second. Boucher and his men could see that the lights would pass very close. Then they heard the unmistakable droning sound of an approaching airplane. The airplane's landing lights were silhouetting the submarine, making it an easy target.

Chi repeated Boucher's message to the officer on the sub. The captain's response was swift. The sailors on the sub's afterdeck opened fire in the direction of the junk.

What happened next surprised even Boucher. As Quicklinsky turned the junk's rudder hard over to the right, Morgan's AT-4 and 40mm grenade men let loose a salvo of deadly anti-tank and personnel rounds directed at the sub's side and sail area. At the same time, two of Morgan's SEAL machine gunners opened fire with their Mk-46 and Mk-48 machine guns, raking the open bridge and deck area. Boucher's men opened fire with their AK-47s, taking aimed shots at the exposed sailors on the sub's deck who continued to grasp their guns. The sub never really had a chance. It was all over in about twenty seconds. The AT-4 anti-tank rockets easily pierced the watertight pressure hull of the sub above the water line and the warheads' armor-piercing, hot plasma continued inward, slicing through machinery, piping, and electrical wiring.

Black smoke began to immediately billow from some of the holes that had been blasted through the hull. Then the sub's klaxon horn sounded. Chi's face went ashen.

"They going to dive!" Chi yelled. "They going to dive!"

"Wrong!" Mojo yelled, mimicking Chi from the darkness nearby. "They're going to die!"

The sub was making a crash dive. As it disappeared beneath the surface everyone stood by, silently watching. Murrant's two Zodiac boats appeared out of the darkness, remaining well astern of the junk, acting as rear security.

At that very second the EP-3 zoomed overhead, barely missing the junk's main mast. Everyone on the junk instinctively ducked. At the same time they could hear the plane's engines throttle back up to full power.

"Holy shit!" Boucher exclaimed aloud. "I never thought for a second it would come to that! That sub skipper boldly went where many men have gone before...to the bottom! What a poor dumb bastard!"

Lieutenant Morgan stood by Boucher's side. "That was pretty awesome. I always thought subs were hard to sink...guess I was wrong."

"No you were right, Lieutenant." Mojo said. "They'll float forever as long as you don't dive them with holes in the hull. We didn't kill those poor bastards; they committed suicide."

Onboard the EP-3

"Restart successful," Gordon announced over the intercom as he pushed all four engine throttles forward to maximum power. "Crew, we're aborting the ditch! I say again, aborting ditch, aborting ditch! We're going home!"

USS Virginia

"The Chinese sub is diving! Sonar, get a fix on him!" Galloway shouted. "Track him Sonar! I don't want to lose him."

"Captain, Sonar. He's accelerating descent and is in a steep nose down, dive angle. Passing two-hundred feet...two-hundred-fifty feet...three-hundred feet...three-hundred-fifty...four, still accelerating, Sir...four-hundred-fifty... five... Sir, he's breaking up! Sir!"

The dull thud of the hull imploding rang through the speaker in the USS Virginia's cramped sonar room. Galloway did a quick three-hundred-sixty-degree sweep on the periscope.

"We're clear. Surface the boat and hold position," he ordered. "Prepare to search for survivors."

CHAPTER 33

CIA Headquarters, Langley, Virginia

Admiral Sinclair pondered the flash precedence Cane Pebble cable he had just finished reading. The silence was broken by the voice of his secretary on the desk-to-desk intercom.

"Admiral, Admiral Thornberg, SOCOM, is on line one secure."

"Thank you, Marcy. I'll take it."

A few moments later Sinclair's STE rang. Sinclair loosely held the cable in his right hand. "Jim, I'm looking at the cable." Sinclair listened to his old friend. "We got who, the junk or the PRC submarine?" Sinclair listened. "What about the sub? Our guys sank a PRC sub? The Virginia reported there was a small arms firefight between our SEALs onboard the junk and the sub. The sub shot first. Our forces defended themselves. The Virginia captured it all on video."

Sinclair paused to hear the reply. "Yes, Jim. I agree we couldn't allow the Chinese to take them prisoner and risk the loss of our Plans. But what I don't get is how you sink a sub with small arms fire? It says here that the SEALs fired four AT-4s into that Chinese sub. The Virginia reports the sub did a crash dive in an attempt to disengage and then apparently suffered catastrophic flooding from the AT-4 hull breeches. We need a plausible cover story."

Sinclair began to doodle on the cable while he listened. "Well Jim, both the EP-3 and the Virginia agree the sub never reported any difficulty or sent a distress signal. So as far as China knows, their sub was investigating a junk with terrorists onboard. They were the same terrorists who kidnapped a Chinese officer from China's Spratlys fortress and killed a bunch of Chinese troops in the process. It seems to me that we can use that to our advantage."

Thornberg's response was abnormally long-winded. It was clear to Sinclair his old friend was upset.

Sinclair interrupted, "Jim, the Chinese didn't know the Virginia was in the area or that Navy SEALs were onboard that junk. We can craft our story so the Virginia just happened to be passing through the area. What we need to do immediately is to get all our guys off the junk and onboard the Virginia. We'll scuttle the junk, shoot some holes in it, and claim that it must have gone down with all hands as a result of the damages it sustained in the firefight with the sub. China will be none the wiser and we sidestep any complicity with the loss of the sub. It's our word against no one else's. What do you think?"

Sinclair scribbled himself a note along the cable's margin as he listened.

"Okay, that works for me too. We can deal with The Hill once we get them back here. We keep all conversation and correspondence in code word channels." Sinclair smiled. "Thank you, Jim."

Sinclair put the phone back on its hook and sat back in his chair. He rubbed his eyes and keyed the intercom. "Marcy, please have Rene Thompson come to my office in thirty minutes. He knows the subject."

The following day

Boucher and his men were unceremoniously transferred by helicopter from the USS Virginia to the aircraft carrier USS John Stennis. Shortly thereafter, COD aircraft flew them from the Stennis to Manila, where they were taken into custody by FBI agents. They were put onboard a waiting C-17 transport plane which flew nonstop to Andrews Air Force Base, located just east of the Washington, DC beltway. Following complete medical checkups, they were taken to the Marine Corps Base at Quantico, Virginia and held there under house arrest.

Book Three

CHAPTER 34

Dirksen Senate Office Building, Washington, DC, four days later

Boucher was jerked back to the present by an amplified female voice talking to him over the loud speaker.

"So," Senator Cummings concluded, "it was at this point that you and your men were captured. Is that correct, Mr. Boucher?"

Boucher winced and replied without looking up. "U.S. citizens were illegally taken prisoner on the high seas by the Armed Forces of the United States. There was no warning and there was no arrest. We were treated like combatants. The SEALs boarded our vessel, took control of it, and acted as the prize crew."

"Yes, and I understand a prize it certainly was!" Cummings smirked before loudly blowing her nose in a pink handkerchief. "You don't seem to get it, Mr. Boucher. This Senate Select Committee on Intelligence is intent on preserving our nation's security. Your direct implication in this potential terrorist act casts grave doubts upon your patriotism and just who you think you are. I, for one, believe you are a terrorist and that you should be treated no better than any other terrorist. The fact you once served as a member of our Armed Forces is immaterial to what you have become and are today."

Boucher coolly focused his steel-eyed gaze on Cummings. "You, Senator, are wrong! I will not sit here and be insulted by the likes of you!"

Two uniformed Capitol Police officers approached and remained standing behind him.

Cummings' mouth gaped open in insulted disbelief. She looked at her fellow members on the panel and then squarely at Boucher. Choosing her words carefully, she again began to speak.

"Mr. Boucher, you are no gentleman and you are not someone who this committee will believe as credible. Through your own actions you have demonstrated your contempt for the United States government and the distinguished members of this committee, and you have made it clear you are no more civilized than those terrorists who murder innocent citizens rather than respect the rule of law. Therefore, I have no further questions for you or your fellow conspirators."

Boucher silently shook his head in disgust.

Senator Rowland from Arizona, a Vietnam veteran and former POW, slowly leaned forward to his microphone.

"Mr. Boucher, I think this committee should understand that you are, by all definitions of the word, a hero of this country. You won the Navy Cross, this nation's second highest combat award, saving the life of the man sitting beside you. You also won the Silver Star, two Bronze Stars for valor, and two Purple Hearts. You were additionally awarded the Legion of Merit and Meritorious Joint Service Medal, not to mention numerous other medals awarded to you by our foreign allies, such as the Cross of Gallantry and the Victoria Cross. The man sitting beside you, Mr. Patterson, is a retired Supervisory Special Agent of the FBI. His career is equally distinguished. I therefore do not accept my colleague's characterization of you and your band of brothers as terrorists. The real issue here, and the focus of this committee, is to determine to what extent, if any, this country's national security has been compromised by your actions. Would you be kind enough to explain for the record, exactly what you were up to and why?"

Boucher stared at Senator Rowland a moment before answering.

"As I have stated previously, we were on a treasure hunt. We were attempting to recover some of the gold reserves that formerly belonged to the Government of South Vietnam from a 1968 crash site located a few miles inside Cambodia. We researched the crash site and believed we could find it."

Rowland interrupted, "And you did find the gold, correct?"

"Yes, Senator. We found some gold along with several old volumes of OPLAN 5000."

"How much gold did you find, Mr. Boucher?"

"We recovered about forty ingots."

"And that was the gold you had with you onboard your boat when our forces boarded you?"

"Yes."

"What about the top secret OPLANs?"

"Senator, those OPLANs dated back to the 1950s. They could not possibly still hold a top secret classification."

"Did you or any of your men read those Plans?"

"Yes. Most of us read them and those who didn't were present as we discussed their contents."

Senator Cummings interrupted. "I want you to tell the committee exactly what you learned from reading those Plans!"

Boucher squirmed slightly. "Senator, I will only discuss that behind closed doors in the appropriate security environment that protects that information."

Cummings blistered with anger. "Mr. Boucher, you continue to behave arrogantly and contemptuously toward this committee!"

"Wait a minute, Senator!" Boucher cautioned Cummings. "You're passing judgment without the facts! Even though those Plans may be outdated, they remain extremely sensitive and I am not about to discuss their contents in any forum that doesn't provide an ample security environment!"

It was at this point that a well-built gentleman in a dark business suit approached Senator Cummings, the committee chair, and whispered into her ear. Cummings held her hand over the microphone as she replied to the gentleman. The man whispered again in response. Cummings nodded back in agreement. Removing her hand from the microphone Cummings took the gavel in her hand.

"Members of the committee, this session will reconvene in closed chambers in one hour."

Cummings struck her gavel on the table and slowly stood to join the tall gentleman waiting behind her. Boucher instantly recognized the tall gentleman when he appeared, and felt a flood of relief. He and Robb Sinclair knew each other very well. As Boucher stood, Sinclair glared at him. Sinclair's stony faced glare was a little unsettling for Boucher, but nothing that he had not seen his friend give him many times previously across the poker table. Before turning away, Boucher politely nodded to his friend in silent acknowledgement.

Boucher was led out of the room by two uniformed Capitol Policemen and taken to a small office adjacent to the hearing room. As the policemen left the room, Admiral Sinclair entered.

"Jake, it's good to see you my old friend."

As the two men took each other's right hand they hugged briefly, slapping one another on the back.

"Thanks for coming, Robb. You can't imagine how good it is to see you."

"Sure do," Sinclair said smiling. "How you been, Jake?"

"Just great until I agreed to testify at this hearing."

"Let's sit," Sinclair said, motioning to the chairs around a small table. "I had you and your guys checked out and I don't think that they can charge you with breaking any U.S. laws. As I understand it, you boys went treasure hunting and had no prior knowledge you would discover the OPLANs. Correct?"

"Yes."

"So how did you know where to look?"

"That's kind of a long story, Robb. If you really want to hear it…"

"Jake, I need to know the whole story."

Boucher sat back in his chair and took a deep breath. "Well Robb, it all began the night I met Pat Patterson."

Boucher glanced to the window. A heavy rainstorm was raging outside. Raindrops were streaming down the windows. Lightning flashed, followed by a reverberating thunderclap.

"It was a dark, rainy night during the '68 Tet Offensive…" Boucher was now staring through the window at the rain and it was as if he was there again. "In the middle of the firefight, a C-130 went over our heads in flames and we saw it crash a mile or so away. Pat later discovered it was carrying the gold reserves out of Saigon. I got my guys together and we located the crash site and recovered some gold. We have been followed, shot at, and attacked ever since. We had no idea we would find the OPLANs. But I gotta tell you Robb, after reading those Plans I now understand their importance to national security. Do you have any idea what I'm talking about?"

Sinclair stared at Boucher searching for the right words. "I've read OPLAN 5000, if that's what you mean."

"No, Robb! I'm talking about over forty years of strategy to defeat the Soviet Union that tied directly to the wars we fought in Korea and Vietnam. I'm talking about General MacArthur's grandest accomplishment and the fact that every U.S. President, from Truman to Reagan, supported it without ever telling the American public about it."

Sinclair sat up straight in his chair. "What strategy is that?" he asked.

"Robb, are you sure you want to hear this?" Boucher patiently questioned his old friend.

"Jake, I have no choice. It appears the CIA has been involved in running unauthorized covert operations against you in an attempt to stop you, but I have not been able to get to the bottom of it. I need your help."

"Robb, you will always have my unquestionable loyalty. I will tell you what I have learned and what it has led me to now believe. My fear is this information will be leaked by some airhead, like Senator Cummings, and become public. In my opinion it could cause quite a public relations mess for the White House and your agency, and that would probably just be the tip of the iceberg. I give you my word; none of my men or I will ever spill the beans on those Plans. All we want to do is go home and spend the money we recovered fair and square."

"Don't worry. I have custody of the OPLANs, Jake."

"What about the two volumes of the Chinese plans we grabbed from the fortress?"

"I have those too."

"Robb, you need to get them translated ASAP. That's where your focus needs to be."

Sinclair stood and walked over to Boucher. He hesitated, and then put his hand on Boucher's shoulder.

"You touched on them in your Iridium call to me a few days ago, but I'm not sure what you were trying to tell me."

"I was trying to tell you that, according to those Chinese plans, there are at least four major U.S. cities that either have a terrorist nuclear bomb planted in them already or there is one on the way. The terrorists intend to detonate all of them simultaneously. All the terrorists want is to kill Americans and put us out of business in the war against them in the Middle East. Iran is behind the terrorists, but China is providing the nukes. After they nuke us, China is going to send us aid in the form of container ships and Ro-Ro ships, only those ships will contain troops. We will be too disorganized—reeling from all the death and devastation across America—to be able to stop them. That's why my guys and I allowed ourselves to be brought back here. I needed to tell you that in person. The Chinese officer I brought along is seeking asylum. He'll help you translate the plans."

Sinclair seemed almost weak-kneed as he headed back to the desk chair. "Jake...nukes pre-staged in our major cities? Container ships? Ro-Ro ships? A Chinese invasion? When is all this going to happen? Do you have any idea what you're suggesting?"

"No, I don't know when! But yes, I completely understand the magnitude of what I'm telling you. I think there are others who know about this as well, and they've tried to prevent me from revealing it to you."

"But why, Jake? Why the Chinese?"

"I don't know why, but I am certain they would have stopped me if they could have."

Sinclair shook his head in disbelief. Boucher sat quietly watching his longtime friend. Sinclair finally broke the silence.

"Jake, this is well above the both of us."

"What the hell are you talking about, Robb?"

"I was afraid this was going to go south when I first heard that you were involved, but I guess I never thought you would successfully find that crash site, much less recover the Plans intact along with the gold. We've been looking for that plane since the night it went down."

Boucher was stunned. "What the hell are you saying, Robb?"

Sinclair opened his suit coat and withdrew a Glock 30 semi-auto .45 pistol and snapped the slide back to ensure Boucher saw he had a live round in the chamber.

"Damn it, Jake! I've always liked you, but you just have a way about you that confounds natural death. You have got to be the luckiest son of a bitch I've ever known!"

"Robb, what the f..."

"Shut up, Jake! You and your band of merry men have used up your nine lives. This is not easy for me, Jake, but some things must go beyond everything else—even old friendships. You were right about MacArthur. He was a genius. He got it right over forty years ago. If Truman had listened to him, we wouldn't be in this pissing contest in the Middle East and we wouldn't be kissing China's ass in fear of economically defaulting on our loans because of the huge deficit our kids will never be able to pay back. No, Sir!"

Boucher's mouth dropped open in disbelief.

"Then you came along; my invincible old buddy, Jake Boucher. Your little treasure hunt put a wrench in the strategic gears that have been turning in preparation to defeat both China and Russia since the end of World War II. Did you really think we didn't know about China's plans? Are you so naive to think OPLAN 5000 just went away in 1968 with the volumes you read and wasn't updated to counter every new threat? It was our people who put those Plans on that plane out of Saigon and the gold was our bankroll to make the Plan a reality."

Boucher sat bewildered. "Huh? What the hell?"

"This country needs a wake-up call, Jake! We thought the 9-11 attack would do the trick, but it became clear that it was too little, too late. The American public... shit, the world for that matter, just forgot about it. No Jake, this time many more good Americans will be sacrificed, but it will not be in vain because afterwards we will be able to do what has to be done! We'll take out China and Russia and light up any country in the Middle East that rears its ugly head against us along the way. It's time we have a strategy which has our enemies fear us as a priority over having them respect us."

Boucher couldn't believe what he was hearing. "What's preventing me from going to the authorities and spilling the beans on you?"

"Nothing, except no one will believe you. Besides, I am that authority! We have ELINT on you and we have imagery. You stole and murdered your way to this point. I can prove it and have a record of it all. You, on the other hand, have nothing on me or any of my people. Remember, I have the Plans. I even have the Chinese officer in one of my safe houses. Who is going to believe a story like you're going to try to tell?"

"You're fucking crazy, Robb! You need to see a shrink!"

"Am I, Jake? Am I crazy? Or am I doing what's necessary to preserve this country's freedoms and sovereignty? Maybe I'm not as crazy as senators like your friend Cummings, who thinks the whole world was created to support her career path to becoming President. Or maybe not as crazy as Senator Rowland who is willing to compromise as long as it furthers his chances at becoming the President someday. No, Jake! There has been a core group of patriots in existence since before MacArthur's days, crafting this nation's strategy and ensuring its success. The good General MacArthur was just one of many in a long line. We have been the guardians of this country's freedoms and we have done whatever it takes to keep this country secure. My question to you is simple. Will you join us? Will you continue to help me to preserve this great country that we have served so selflessly our entire lives? You can join us, or you can die fighting us. But consider this. If you fight us you will surely lose, as many have before you."

Boucher was bewildered. "Robb, we've been through a great deal together over the years. I need some time... I need some time to think this through, because if I commit my loyalty to you on this, I must have no second thoughts."

Sinclair studied Boucher from behind his desk. "Very well, you have until tomorrow at this same time. You may bring as many of your most trusted men along with you as you wish. I will consider those who choose otherwise to be causalities of war."

Sinclair leaned forward and pressed a red button on the desk telephone. Two plain clothes guards entered the office and led Boucher to a holding area where Patterson and Moss were also being held.

"What did your old pal, the Admiral, have to say?" Patterson asked.

CHAPTER 35

Marine Corps Base, Quantico, VA.

Following the hearing, Boucher, Patterson, and Moss were unceremoniously taken by van from the Senate hearing chambers in the Hart Building, downtown Washington, DC, to the Marine Corps Base, Quantico in Virginia, about thirty minutes south. Upon arrival, they were ushered up to the 4th floor of the bachelor officers' quarters and assigned individual rooms. Plain-clothes agents, who presumably worked for the CIA, remained at the stairwell exits and elevators to control access.

Boucher assumed the rooms were bugged. He did a quick sweep of his room, and to his surprise found nothing. Next, he tried the door to his room and found that it was unlocked. He carefully opened it and peered up and down the hallway, catching a glimpse of a plain clothes agent disappearing behind the fire exit door at the opposite end of the hall. Boucher cautiously stepped out into the dim hall and was startled by a human form doing the same thing peripherally from his right. As he reeled in that direction he recognized the form to be Patterson.

"Jeez, you scared the shit out of me, Pat!"

"Yeah, you did the same to me! The guard just went through the exit door at the end of the hall."

"Yeah, I saw him. Keep your voice down. Do you know what room they assigned Mossman?"

"Yeah. They put him in 431, across from me."

"Let's see if he's there. We need to talk."

"I'll get him."

Patterson strode across the hall and tapped on the door.

Moss' muffled voice came from inside. "What d'ya want?"

"Mossman, it's Pat and Jake. Open up."

"Give me five minutes, would ya? I'm sitting on the crapper taking a massive fighter pilot."

"Yeah, okay. Don't forget to wipe your helicopter pilot when you're through. Then join us in the room across the hall."

"Roger."

"Don't forget to wash your hands!" Boucher whispered.

The men entered Patterson's room and sat down to wait for Moss. Neither spoke. Except for the sound of a Marine CH-53 heavy lift helicopter that was practicing touch-and-goes at the nearby airfield, the silence was deafening.

Patterson stood and began to pace as he watched the CH-53 fly over the BOQ and descend behind the tree line.

"Hey Jake, you have any idea what the fuck is going on?" asked Patterson.

"Yeah, I'm afraid I do."

Moss entered the room and quietly closed the door, latching it behind him.

"Okay Jake, what now?" Moss asked as he sat down on the edge of the bed.

Boucher was clearly troubled as he labored through his words. "It's not going to be easy."

"What's not going to be easy?" Moss questioned.

"Exposing the conspiracy and surviving its wrath in the process." Boucher's eyes welled up and he stumbled on his words. "We're going to have to... neutralize Admiral Sinclair."

"Well, WTF! That Senate Select Intelligence Committee is already claiming that we're thieves, murders, and terrorists. What's a little neutralizing going to hurt? I'm in!" Patterson replied.

"Me too," said Moss.

"Thanks guys, but like I said, it won't be easy. Sinclair has a network of both witting and unwitting accomplices. They all follow his direction and they're all patriots to one degree or another."

Moss cocked his head to the right. "Didn't Chi tell us that there are a bunch of nukes already hidden in four or five major U.S. cities?"

"Yes, that's what Chi told us the Chinese plans revealed. The more important question is when. When are they going to set them off? Chi never told us that. Maybe the execution date wasn't in the plan."

Moss had one of his cockeyed looks. "Didn't Chi say the plan's number was 0911? Nine-eleven, Jake. What if the execution date is the same? Another 9-11 attack? So how do we stop those nukes from being detonated and melting down our cities?"

"I don't think those nukes are all in place yet. I mean, think about it...if there was a working nuke already hidden somewhere in downtown DC, do you think Sinclair would be here? I don't think he would because he sees his role in successfully continuing this grand strategy as too critical to risk being killed."

Patterson interrupted, "But Chi told us all the nukes would be detonated simultaneously, or at least as close to simultaneous as possible, to create the maximum psychological effect and overwhelm our emergency response capabilities. It seems to me all we need to do is find the nukes that are already here and disable them. Then we can devote our resources to preventing others from arriving."

Boucher's head began to hurt and he had to force himself to focus. "That's a very tall order, Pat. Who do you do think might take that on? NEST? DoD? DHS? The FBI? Who? From my limited experience, the odds would be better of finding a rogue nuke in a city environment by tripping over it than of finding one as a result of actually searching for it."

"But can't our satellites detect nuclear bombs?"

"Yeah, for sure Pat, but only after they go off. Only Hollywood scriptwriters can devise the technology to detect nuclear devices from satellites. Just because you've seen it done in the movies, doesn't make it real."

"What about the Nuclear Emergency Support Team? Doesn't NEST have special helicopters that can find a nuke?" Moss queried.

"They do, but their ability to detect a shielded radiation source on the ground is limited by how effectively the radiation source is shielded. Besides, searching for radioactivity in a city environment is like trying to hear a fart in a diarrhea ward. There are so many naturally occurring radioactive sources, as well as manmade sources in a city, it would take months to locate them and check them all out. And, coming back to the shielding problem, that's assuming you can actually find them all. There will always be some you don't detect for whatever reason."

"What about DoD and DHS's detection capability?"

"They all use pretty much the same detection equipment which shares the same limitations. There is only so much that can be done with detection equipment before you bump up against the laws of physics."

Patterson stood and clapped Boucher on the shoulder. "I guess you should know what you're talking about, Jake. You were a trained and qualified NEST guy. Didn't you do some of your graduate study at Los Alamos under the tutelage of one of the original Manhattan Project scientists?"

"Yeah, Doctor Simon Barnhart. A great man and trusted friend," Boucher injected.

"Weren't you with NEST as part of the Atlanta Olympic Games security contingency?"

"I was, as well as a shit load of other national security special events over the course of several years."

"So what do we do, Jake? We need to find out where these nukes are hidden and work from there…right?"

"You're right, Pat," Boucher nodded, "but we only need to locate one nuke to confirm the credibility of our information. I think Admiral Thornberg might be able to help. SOCOM has a competent WMD detection capability that could supplement the NEST capability. All I need to do is find a way to explain the situation. We need to either visit Tampa ASAP or get the good

243

Admiral to come to us. We have another Senate hearing in two hours. This time it's behind closed doors. Maybe there will be an opportunity to disclose what we know. Sinclair will either be present or he'll have some of his goons there. We can't afford to give him more of an advantage than he already has. We'll have to be very careful who we talk to and what we say."

"Do you think that half-a-commie, Senator Cummings, will be there again?"

"Jeez, I hope not, but I suspect she will!"

Moss perked up, "Isn't Cummings from New York?"

"Yes, I think she is. Why?" Boucher asked.

"Well, don't you think she'd help if she knew that New York City was a target and probably already had a nuke hidden there?"

"She's certainly mercenary enough to do anything to become President. Actually, Mossman, she might just become our champion and take this on if we can reduce the political risk for her."

"But how do we get to her to take this on?"

"We don't need to personally get to her. I need to contact my friend, Dick Skinner. He's a former Delta Force guy turned lobbyist after retiring from the Army. I know for a fact he regularly works stuff through Cummings and her staff. She'll listen to him. Shit! Why didn't I think of that before? I'll prep the battlefield with her at the closed door hearing."

Patterson stomped his shoe on the floor like he was smashing a bug. "How are you going to get her attention?"

Boucher thought for a few seconds before answering Patterson's question. "I'm going to pass her a little love note if I get the opportunity. After this morning, no one will suspect that we might become allies. Even if she decides to play ball with us, we're still going to need some additional help. Did either of you hear where they're holding our guys?"

Patterson sat up. "They're here on Quantico over at the HMX airfield BEQ. I heard one of the MPs who drove us here say that he was headed over there to relieve one of their guards who had a family emergency. Shit, that's walking distance from here!"

"Mossman, you think you can fly a CH-53?"

"Is the Pope Catholic?"

"Okay, I figured as much. I just thought I would make sure. Here's our warning order. We're going to break out of here when we get back from the hearing. It will be dark by then. The guards only rove through this hall about twice an hour. Guess they think as long as they have the downstairs secured, we can't get out. We'll go out through the roof access hatch at the far end of the hall. I checked it out shortly after I got off the elevator and it's not locked. Once we're on the roof, we'll climb down the tree next to the building and make our way to the airstrip to get some transportation."

Moss clapped his hands like a kid. "That's way cool! They'll never know we've gone until it's too late!"

"Unless something has changed since I last used this airstrip while I was still in the FBI, it's only guarded by a roving patrol and they are armed with handguns," Patterson offered. "However, there's always at least one CH-53 parked out there and it's kept in a fully fueled, ready status to support the HMX mission in case it's needed on short notice. We should be able to easily reach it after dark, especially if we come in from the marshy area on the north side of the field."

Moss immediately stopped smiling and grew very serious. "Are there alligators in that swamp?"

Patterson and Boucher burst out with their reply simultaneously, "*Dumbass!*"

Moss laughed, but appeared puzzled. "Okay, I got it, Jake. But just where is it you want me to take us once we get the helo?"

"We're gonna break our guys out of the enlisted quarters from the roof. You're going to hover the helo with the rear wheels on the roof, tail ramp down, until we can get them all onboard. Then we're going to go visit Admiral Sinclair at his residence in Mount Vernon. His house is right on the water and there's plenty of room between the house and the Potomac River to set the bird on his back lawn. We'll snatch him before he knows what hit him, and then get the hell out of Dodge."

Moss scratched his head. "To where?"

CHAPTER 36

Senate Select Committee on Intelligence, the Dirksen Building, Washington, DC

The seven Republican and nine Democratic senators who composed the sixteen-person committee were all present, which was somewhat unusual in itself. The closed-door session allowed discussion of sensitive and/or classified subjects otherwise kept from the public. Boucher, Patterson, and Moss were seated side-by-side at a table in front of the panel. Senator Cummings opened the hearing again with a rap of her gavel.

"This hearing will come to order."

Everyone in the room became silent.

"At this morning's open session I was advised that the nature of the questions and answers that we were pursuing was swiftly becoming classified. We have therefore reconvened in a closed-door security environment. All members of this committee and all those present are reminded that this is now a classified hearing and that all subject matter, questions and answers by those testifying, is considered classified. And now, our esteemed senator from the great state of Pennsylvania, Senator Hopkins. You have the floor."

Hopkins was the senior senator from Pennsylvania and had been a Marine who served two back-to-back tours in Vietnam in 1968 and 1969. He was severely wounded a month before his second tour was to end and nearly died from his wounds. The reconstructive surgery he had endured for years left his face very scarred and one cheek still somewhat deformed.

"Thank you, Senator Cummings. I will be brief. As a follow-on to this morning's testimony—and I direct this at all three gentleman sitting before me—at what point did any of you recognize your actions would have national security implications?"

"Well Senator," Moss replied, "I suppose it was when the two little birds were shooting at us and one of them crashed into the Mekong River."

Patterson spoke next. "I guess for me it was when the SEALs tried to take us prisoner on that island offshore Vietnam. We hadn't broken any U.S. laws, we were on foreign soil, and Armed Forces of the United States were attempting to take us prisoner."

Boucher waved his hand. "I think both of those events were noteworthy, but being captured by the Chinese in the Spratlys and then escaping with the help of one of their officers was a major turning point for all of us. When that Chinese sub surfaced and opened fire on us we had no other choice but to defend ourselves. I knew the active duty SEALs on our vessel would end up sharing the blame with us, and I really didn't want to see that happen to those kids. The SEALs defended themselves, as we did. I attempted, unsuccessfully, to negotiate a peaceful resolution with the Chinese sub skipper. He chose to take us under fire and we handed him his backside."

Senator Hopkins cleared his throat. "That's interesting gentlemen, but it also suggests a rather sad commentary about your lack of judgment and conscience. I want to return to the little birds. Are you telling this committee you didn't recognize or even suspect the little birds were an American asset?"

"That is correct, Senator. Neither of the little birds had any markings of any kind indicating they were ours, nor did they identify themselves as friendly. The rocket fire they directed towards me and my men was not judicious. They were clearly trying to shoot us down and almost did!" Boucher answered. "There was no doubt in any of our minds about their hostile intent."

Hopkins interrupted, "But you shot first, didn't you? It says so right here in the official radio transcript that was collected by the NSA."

"Wait a minute, Senator. They attacked me and my men! They shot first. We returned fire and defended ourselves. They got a little too bold and we splashed the closest one. I don't know where that transcript came from, but we didn't transmit a single word during that firefight. We were too damn busy trying to evade them."

Moss and Patterson both sat there nodding their heads in agreement with what Boucher had just said.

Senator Cummings was red-faced and bristling with obvious anger.

"So you shot that helicopter down and killed three Americans in the process?"

"No, ma'am!" Patterson exclaimed. "He flew up our rear so close we simply threw a bunch of cash out of the back end of our helo and he flew into it. He ingested the bills into his engine intakes and the cash acted as foreign object debris. That caused his engines to choke off, and without engines helicopters only go one direction. You know, take-offs are optional but landings are mandatory."

Cummings impatiently tapped her fingers on the table.

"So, you saw the helicopter crash into the river but you didn't turn around and go back to look for survivors. Why not?"

Boucher took the question. "As I said previously, we were being chased and shot at by both little birds. The other little bird was still fully capable of shooting us down. Frankly Senator, I didn't think I owed that SOB a damn thing after he tried to kill us!"

Cummings rolled her eyes in disgust. "But none of you have articulated who was shooting at you or why they were shooting at you. Do you know why they were shooting at you, Mr. Boucher?"

"I didn't at the time, Senator, but I think I do now."

"Well, why not share that information with this committee and enlighten us as to why you stole and murdered your way across half of Southeast Asia."

Boucher felt his anger rage. Senator Cummings was one of those rare people that seemed to push his temper button every time she spoke. Hell, just the sight of her pissed him off. Boucher composed himself and took a long, deep, cleansing breath before continuing.

"Well Senator, even you probably remember the 9-11 terrorist attack on the World Trade Center and the Pentagon…"

CHAPTER 37

Marine Corps Base Quantico, Virginia, five hours later

"Let's do it," Boucher whispered as he stepped onto the ladder leading to the roof hatch above.

Boucher unlatched the hinge and pushed it open. He climbed out onto the flat roof and knelt on one knee next to the hatch in the darkness. Patterson and Moss followed. Moss carefully closed the hatch behind. The three of them made their way to the rear edge of the roof where a large maple tree hung over the roof. Boucher easily stepped from the roof onto the tree and began to climb down the limbs. The others followed.

On the ground, they casually strolled away from the building toward the north end of the airfield. They attracted no attention and no one was aware of their departure from the building. They slowly made their way through the swampy wetlands to the edge of the tarmac. There were three Blackhawks and two Cobras on the tarmac between them and the CH-53. The roving security patrol was nowhere to be seen.

"Okay, this is the moment of truth," Boucher whispered. "We're going to move to that 53 and use the other choppers in between for concealment. If anyone challenges us, we make a break for the 53 and get it buttoned up while Mossman turns her up. Then we fly over to that building." Boucher pointed to a barracks on the northwest side of the airfield. "We get our guys and we're outta here!"

Moss and Patterson both nodded. Moss grabbed Boucher by the arm. "You still didn't tell me where I'm taking us after we snatch Sinclair."

"We'll do a low level to the Baker facility in West Virginia."

Patterson smiled. "You're thinking about using Site Yankee aren't you?"

"Yup," Boucher replied.

Patterson filled in the holes for Moss who had no clue what Boucher was talking about.

"Site 'Y' is an old, deep, underground government facility located inside a mountain a few miles east of Baker along new Route 55. It should work just fine. It was built during the Eisenhower administration around the same time Greenbrier and Site-R were built as bombproof DUGs facilities where government officials could hide and survive in the event of a nuclear attack. It has been rehabilitated since the 9-11 attack and is now in a caretaker status just in case Greenbrier and Site-R can't handle the numbers. I participated in an interagency counterterrorism exercise at Site-Y a couple of years ago, and at the time FEMA was refurbing it with state-of-the-art communications. It has a four-spot helicopter landing pad right next to the main tunnel entrance that leads inside."

"How's the entrance guarded?" Moss asked.

"I don't know for sure," Patterson said softly. "I recall the facility had some lightly-armed guards manning a guard shack at the tunnel entrance adjacent to the landing pad."

"Not to worry, Mossman! We have the element of surprise working in our favor," Boucher stated. "When you set us down, put your landing lights on the guard shack. We'll run off the rear of the tail ramp and they'll never see us coming. All we need to do is get past the guard shack. Once we're in the tunnel, we'll close the outer blast door and secure it from inside. From that point on, we become completely self-sufficient. There's enough food and water stockpiled inside to support thirteen hundred people for three months. It has its own electrical generation plant, air filtration, and it's bombproof. It has a radio and TV broadcast studio and a complete communications' suite. We should be good to go for as long as it takes."

Moss gave a giddy chuckle. "Let's do it or screw it!"

Boucher clapped his hands and pointed at his two friends. "Hooyah! Let's do it!"

The three of them cautiously made their way from helicopter to helicopter toward the mammoth CH-53 parked about the length of a football field away. There were still no guards to be seen. Moss was the first to cover the last twenty yards of concrete tarmac and board the CH-53 through the open starboard side door. Patterson and Boucher followed immediately behind and pulled the door closed behind them, just as a roving patrol turned their police car onto the aircraft parking area. Moss made his way to the cockpit and quickly strapped himself into the pilot's chair on the port side.

"Pat," he yelled over his shoulder, "I could use some help with the checklist."

Patterson quickly joined Moss and strapped into the right side, co-pilot's seat. Moss flicked the main power switches and began the jet turbo engine start up sequence. Patterson followed Moss's directions and warmed up the radios and navigation equipment. The security truck routinely drove past the helicopter and circled back at the end of the flight line, stopping just outside of rotor range almost directly in front of the CH-53. One of the Marine MPs stepped out of the truck and stood watching, just as Moss engaged the transmission and the rotors began to spin. Moss knew the young MP had seen him, so he gave him an assuring wave. The MP returned the wave and got back into his vehicle, showing no alarm.

"What do you suppose that was all about?" Patterson asked.

"Beats me," Moss replied over the jet engine noise.

Boucher was standing between Patterson and Moss, just behind the radio and navigation equipment center console. "I think I know," he replied. "When the Marines do a start-up they always have a crew member standing outside in front of the helo. That MP isn't sure what the deal is because there's no crewman outside. He knows something isn't right. Mossman, how long before you can get this beast airborne and out of here?"

"I'm bringing number three engine online now. I need to check all the flight controls and run the engines up to full power."

"Okay. I don't want to die in a fiery helicopter crash tonight, but make it snappy. We need to get this bad boy airborne before our MP friend out there figures out we are borrowing his helicopter."

"I'm working on it, Jake. It won't be much longer."

Almost as if on cue, both MPs exited their truck and drew their side arms. One of the MPs moved directly in front of the helo and aimed his pistol at Moss. The other ran towards the side door and tried to open it.

Boucher shouted above the jet engine noise, "Now would be a good time, Mossman!"

Moss turned in his chair and gave Boucher one of those *aaaahh shit* looks only Moss could bestow and yelled, "Hold the fuck on!"

With that, he shoved the three engine throttles up to full military power and did a maximum performance take off.

The powerful CH-53 was famous for its ability to climb straight up for the first one-hundred feet and then sling-shot forward to two-hundred miles per hour, all in about four seconds. And that's exactly what happened. Both MPs were swept off their feet by the helicopter's tornado-like rotor wash. There was simply no way for them to remain standing in a manmade windstorm that ferocious.

Moss made a quick circle of the field and lined up for an approach to the roof of the enlisted quarters. Boucher retracted the tail ramp door's upper clamshell half and lowered the tail ramp. Moss made a perfect approach to the building and hovered just above the roof, positioning the open tail ramp a few feet above and approximately at the center of the roof expanse. Boucher jumped onto the roof and pried the roof hatch open with a fire ax from the helicopter's emergency escape kit. He disappeared below only to reappear a few minutes later, followed by his men. As they piled into the waiting helicopter, Boucher did a head count.

"Where's Billy?" he yelled over to Haus.

"Walter Reed Army Hospital…being treated for infection. He's in good hands."

Boucher gave him a thumbs-up as he grabbed the crew chief's headphone and mic from the bulkhead, linking him to the helicopter's intercom. When he was sure he had everyone onboard, he gave Moss and Patterson the all clear to go. Moss slowly brought the mammoth helo into a slow ascent. When they reached about one-hundred feet of altitude, he rocked the helo forward and ran it up to its maximum forward speed. He flew straight north up the Potomac River toward Sinclair's riverside home in Mount Vernon.

Boucher moved to the darkened cockpit and sat in the jump seat between Moss and Patterson. He could see the dimly lighted instrument clusters in front of both Moss and Patterson. Moss was flying the massive helicopter without the aid of night vision goggles, about thirty feet above the river at two hundred miles per hour. How he was able to accomplish that feat on a dark night using naked eyes was beyond Boucher's understanding.

Boucher keyed his intercom mic. "Mossman, Sinclair's house is on the right, just past Monticello. Look for a boat dock that extends about twenty yards into the river and has a small boathouse on the end. Sinclair's house is centered on a cul-de-sac. Look for a modern colonial white brick with a matching, detached, two-car garage. There's a small, kidney-shaped pool directly behind the house with a screened-in gazebo. The yard between the pool and the pier is about sixty yards long and fifty wide. Except for some trees around the perimeter of the yard, all the wires and obstruction hazards are in the front of the house. I want you to set this bad boy down with the tail ramp facing the rear of the house. This is a body snatch. We'll be in and out in less than three mikes. When we leave, take us back down the Potomac. You pick the point to head west to Baker. Just stay low and follow the terrain."

Both Moss and Patterson nodded. Boucher cuffed both on the shoulder and headed back to the helicopter's cargo bay to give the rest of the men a quick course of action briefing.

A few minutes later, Patterson's voice transmitted through Boucher's headphones advising that they were thirty seconds out.

Moss set the helicopter squarely in the middle of Sinclair's backyard with the front end facing the river. Boucher and six of his men scurried off the open tail ramp and exploded through Sinclair's back patio door. Sinclair was sitting at his computer in his first floor office, located in the front of the house. He was taken completely by surprise.

"Robb, we're taking you with us!" Boucher ordered as he burst into the small office.

"Jake? What the f…"

"Stand up, Robb. You're coming with us!"

"The hell I am!"

Boucher signaled Quicklinsky, Doyle, and Lavender to physically take Sinclair. Quicklinsky grabbed Sinclair from behind while Doyle and Lavender each grabbed an arm. Sinclair struggled for a moment, but he was overpowered. Lavender used duct tape he grabbed from the helo to secure Sinclair's hands.

"Robb, where do you have the Plans?" Boucher demanded.

"Fuck you!"

"I know you have the Plans here. Where are they?"

"The Plans are at my office in Langley!"

"No they're not, they're here! Now, where are they?"

Boucher observed Sinclair's eyes as he glanced several times toward his lower desk drawer. Boucher pulled the drawer open and saw a government lock pouch—the type used to transport classified documents. He pulled the pouch from the file drawer and felt the volumes through the fabric.

"I'll have your ass for this!" Sinclair shouted.

"Tape his mouth and put 'im in the helo."

Lavender and Doyle manhandled Sinclair out the back door to the waiting helicopter.

Boucher threw the pouch to Quicklinsky. "Let's find a knife in the kitchen to cut it open."

Both men ran to the kitchen.

"How did you know he had the Plans here at his home?"

"At the hearing he told me that he had the Plans. If he had them at work, he would have said that the Agency had the Plans. After all, I've known Robb Sinclair over thirty-five years."

Boucher grabbed two paring knives from a drawer next to the sink and he and Quicklinsky ran to the helicopter.

Just before he jumped onboard, Boucher looked back at the house. He saw movement inside the windows. Jane Sinclair had been awakened by the noise of the helicopter and the voices downstairs. Boucher had known Jane for over twenty-six years and was thankful that he didn't have to confront his old friend's wife. Snatching Sinclair was painful enough. Taking him from her didn't make it any easier for Boucher to live with. Jumping onboard the helicopter, he gave Yellowhorse a thumbs-up and didn't look back.

As Yellowhorse raised the tail ramp, Boucher took a quick headcount and spoke into the intercom mic linking him to the cockpit. Moss pulled pitch on the collective and the giant CH-53 quickly rose above the treetops before it shot forward at nearly one hundred knots air speed. Boucher checked his watch.

Ground time had only been two minutes and forty seconds. Boucher nodded to himself, acknowledging a sense of accomplishment. He had Sinclair. He had the Plans. No one got hurt in the process. Even so, his chest felt tight and he had difficulty getting Jane Sinclair out of his thoughts.

CHAPTER 38

Baker, West Virginia

Moss and Patterson conducted a low-level, terrain-following flight to Baker. Throughout the flight, Moss kept the CH-53 just above the treetops and took advantage of the masking effect of the high mountains along the way by staying low in their valleys. Flying without the helicopter's marker lights on made the helicopter nearly invisible. The weather was slowly deteriorating as well. A front was moving in from the southwest and the sky was becoming cloudy. A thunder storm was on the way. The Baker facility was now about five minutes ahead and Boucher was again sitting in the jump seat between Moss and Patterson.

Moss pointed ahead at some lights that appeared on the side of an otherwise completely dark mountain.

"I'm going to bring us straight in to the pad, flair in front of the guard shack with my landing lights on, and then spin the helo's ass in toward the tunnel so we can run off. I'm going to leave the engines running and the blades spinning. Are you ready?"

Boucher clicked his mic open as he disappeared into the cargo bay in the rear. "Is your dick small?"

As anticipated, the guards at the tunnel entrance were caught completely by surprise and overwhelmed by the bright lights, jet noise, and swirling rotor wash. The helicopter's million- power landing lights blinded them and the rotor wash created a high velocity dust storm. Instead of running out of the guard shack to challenge the unknown, the guards had little choice but to cover their eyes and protect themselves. Boucher and all his men were off the helicopter, past the guard shack, and inside the tunnel before the guards knew what was happening.

Once inside the tunnel, they closed the outer blast door and secured it from the inside. Then, they commandeered several electric golf carts that had been modified with additional seats to carry six people and drove further down the tunnel to the inner blast door. They shut that door and barred it from the inside and additionally sealed the access door next to it. That door provided alternative access for people to pass around the blast door via an airlock and decontamination area.

They were now secure from the east access tunnel.

Boucher called to Patterson, "Pat, take a couple of guys and go secure the west tunnel entrance."

Patterson jumped back into one of the electric carts with Klum and Doyle and disappeared into the tunnel.

"Listen up, everyone. We need to search this place and ensure we're alone. If you find anyone, we'll put them out through the DECON room airlock. Risser, find the comms suite and boot it up. The admiral and I will be there shortly."

The former SEALs went to work searching the interior buildings of the underground Baker facility. Two maintenance workers were discovered in the electric generation and pumping room where the facilities' three locomotive-sized diesel generators were located. They were escorted to the main access tunnel's decontamination room airlock and allowed to leave. Beyond those two, no one else was inside the facility.

...

About twenty minutes later, Boucher, Sinclair, and the rest assembled in the operations center. The communications control room was located on one side. Risser Jackson was in the adjoining room, hard at work, bringing the communications network online. Sinclair was placed in a chair at a small conference table. His mouth was still taped shut and his hands were bound. Quicklinsky placed the four volumes of OPLAN 5000 and the two Chinese 0911 war plans on the table across from Sinclair. Boucher assembled the men and sat down across the table from Sinclair.

"Okay Admiral, we're here in the operations center inside Site Yankee at Baker. Before you are six extremely sensitive war plans. The four OPLAN 5000s are ours. OPLAN 5000 reveals there was a grand strategy in place to fight a war against the Soviet Union and reveals the motivations behind entering into the wars in Korea and Vietnam. The American public was never privy to it. The other two plans are Chinese. According to Lieutenant Chi, the Chinese have provided perhaps as many as four nuclear bombs to Iran. Iran has given them to terrorists. These four nukes either already are, or will soon be planted in the four largest cities here in the U.S. While all this is very troubling to people like me, it has become obvious that this strategy has been orchestrated by some key people in high government positions since the end of World War II."

Sinclair fought to stand, but was pushed back down into his chair by Yellowhorse and Lavender.

Boucher continued. "Admiral Sinclair, you are one of those key people. You knew the attack was coming on 9-11 and you allowed it to occur, anticipating it would galvanize the American public on a path into war. But the tie to China was never made because they brilliantly covered their tracks using Iraq and Iran as surrogates.

You then decided to up the ante and invite nukes into this country. One might ask why you would do something so horrific. Your goal is to have China invade our shores in the form of offering aid following the attack. The Chinese plans reveal they have a fleet of roll on-roll off ships, as well as container ships that are configured as troop and military vehicle carriers. They will deliver the Chinese forces to our shores in the name of aid, then secure a foothold and remain. And you already know about it all and you are allowing it to proceed. Take the tape off his mouth," Boucher directed Yellowhorse.

Yellowhorse peeled the duct tape away from Sinclair's mouth.

Sinclair winced in pain, but recovered in a rage. "You bastards are a bunch of murdering thugs! You have killed three CIA agents and shot one of their helicopters down. You sank a PRC submarine and killed all hands onboard in the process. You stole a U.S. government helicopter and have brought me here against my will—that's kidnapping and transit across state lines! And *you* sit there and accuse *me* of conspiracy? I guess I misjudged you all these years, Jake! You and your boys here are nothing more than common criminals!"

Boucher sat there unmoved. "Admiral," he said unemotionally, "you are the criminal, not me. I do not deny the events you just accused me of, but they all resulted from your aggression. You directed those little birds to attack us. You knew full well we were headed for capture by the Chinese. It wouldn't even surprise me if you tipped them that we were headed their way.

You can't allow the truth to be known because the American public would unseat you, and those like you who think they know best and work outside our constitutional process. What you have done is a travesty to this country's system of government and its honor."

Boucher took a deep breath. "I would have taken a bullet for you!" Boucher paused again. "No Sir, it has been I who misjudged you all these years."

Sinclair laughed aloud. "Cut the crap, Commander! You and I both know it's only a matter of time before the authorities break into this facility and haul your asses off to prison."

"That might be true, but I have the Plans and once they are analyzed my men and I will be vindicated."

"You are a hopeless romantic to believe that you will be anything other than a convict making big rocks into little ones at a federal prison!"

Boucher stood and walked over to a wall size map of the United States. He stared at it for a few seconds before turning around towards the admiral. "Where are the nukes, Robb?"

Sinclair sarcastically laughed again. "What? You think I'm an idiot like you? Why would I tell you? Even if I knew, I wouldn't tell you!"

Boucher remained cool. "Well then let me help you. I think I know one of the target cities that doesn't have a nuke planted yet would be Washington, DC. You want to know why I think that, Robb? It's because you're still there. I think you consider yourself too important to this conspiracy to risk nuking yourself. But, you do intend to take out D.C....don't you, Robb? Those nukes are going to be detonated simultaneously when they're all in place. They're just not all in place, are they?"

Sinclair shifted in his chair. "Who's going to believe a shit bird like you?"

"Maybe nobody. Maybe somebody. Regardless, I'm not going to let this happen if I can prevent it. Now I ask you again, where are the nukes?"

"Fuck you, Boucher! What are you going to do, torture me?"

"Gee Robb, you said yourself we're a bunch of murdering, stealing, kidnapping thugs. What's a little torture added on to those other charges?" Boucher motioned to Yellowhorse and Lavender who grabbed Sinclair and yanked him to his feet. "Here's what we're going to do, Robb. We're going to read the Plans out loud, starting with the earliest one dated in the 1950s. As we read them, I will stop and provide my analysis and point out where you and your fellow conspirators have played major roles. As best as I can determine, primarily very senior military officers have carried out this conspiracy. Okay, I know there were probably a few exceptions. Like Eisenhower, who later became President, and some of our former military senators over the years. I mean, look at the key government positions retired military officers have held over the years...President, Secretary of State, Director of the CIA, Secretary of Energy, senators, representatives...shit, Robb, what a great opportunity to have it your way!"

"You're throwing a great opportunity away, Jake! I told you we'd rather have you with us. It's not too late for you to change your mind. Join us and help us cleanse this country's government and bring it back to the greatness our Founding Fathers envisioned."

Boucher walked around the table toward Sinclair. As he approached, he studied his old friend. "Robb, your offer is tempting but how do you propose to get us out of this DUG's facility?"

"Jake, I'm the Director of Clandestine Operations at the CIA. We have a new Director of Central Intelligence and he's a four-star general. That should answer your question. The President insisted on the new DCI, but not because he was the only man qualified for the job."

"Well, why did the President want this particular four-star? What's his name...Gardner, right?"

"The President doesn't really think for himself. Hell, everyone knows that! He takes recommendations from his most trusted inner circle and then makes gut decisions based on their influence. We put him in front of the President, and with the Vice President's help we got him nominated. We got the help we needed from the Hill to confirm him and voila, he's the DCI."

"You mean you guys got him planted because he's one of you?"

"Exactly! You see, our network of VIPs has permeated nearly every senior level of government. You and your men need to join us, Jake, not fight us."

Boucher mopped the sweat off his forehead with his hand and wiped it on his pants. "But what about the nukes, Robb? How do I know you're not going to send me and my guys into one of the target cities and melt us down along with everyone else?"

"You and your men are far too valuable to waste like that. Look at all you've been through over the past few weeks. You have kicked ass every single time when the odds were stacked against you. You and your warriors are exactly the type of men our new order respects and needs in key positions of leadership. There will be great opportunities for you and warriors like you."

"Robb, your offer is indeed very tempting, but none of us want to continue kicking doors in for a living. We still have a few million in cash and gold that we got at the crash site and we'd like to be able to spend it."

Sinclair was relaxing. The conversation seemed to be shifting his way. "Jake, will you cut my hands lose?"

Boucher nodded his consent. Lavender grabbed a pair of scissors from a nearby desk and cut the duct tape, freeing Sinclair's hands.

"Thanks," Sinclair said softly. "Jake, the money and gold you recovered from that crash site is yours. Money is not an issue to our movement. We have all the funding we need."

Boucher nodded slightly, subtly raising one eyebrow.

"Jake, I wouldn't presume for a second to have you and your men kicking doors in. We need you to lead the counterattack."

"What do you mean, counterattack?"

"After the cities are nuked and the Chinese land on our shores, we will be ready for them. They just don't know it. We'll either kill or capture their invading army for the world to see. Our allies will support us. We'll nationalize all the Chinese international assets and the allies will follow suit. It's going to be economic payback time."

"But what's keeping China from launching ICBM's against us?"

Sinclair gurgled out a sincere laugh. "Ahhh Jake, you don't get it yet. You wanna know why China or the Soviet Union never launched on us during all those years of Cold War?"

Boucher shrugged.

"It's because none of us ever targeted any of the others' capitol city."

"So???"

"Well, if they had taken out Washington and eliminated the government, that would have put our field commanders in charge. Our admirals and generals would have taken charge, melted their ass down and turned those countries into glass parking lots. That's why! So now you see why we have to sacrifice Washington. It doesn't matter which party has control of the government. They're all the same and they put their own petty politics ahead of the long-term security of this country. They have allowed our military resources to be used up faster than they can be refurbished or replenished in a protracted war with Islamic fascists that have no territories to defend and aren't afraid to die for their cause. The Muslims will never quit until we put them back in their box. China knows that and is fanning the flames. Russia could help the situation, but they see this as an opportunity to have the West fail and ultimately fall without having to invest or risk anything of their own. It has been a painful decision, but there is no other way to win the long-term strategy and put China, Russia, and the Middle East back into their respective boxes."

Boucher felt so lightheaded that he grabbed on to one of the chair backs beside him to steady himself. He composed himself and felt a tear run down his cheek. He slowly turned toward the adjoining communications room. "Haus, see if Risser got it."

Quicklinsky strode over to the room and cracked the door. Boucher could see him nodding as he spoke to Jackson. Quicklinsky closed the door and turned back toward the men in the room. He gave Boucher a thumbs-up gesture and remained by the door.

Sinclair didn't understand at first, but as it all sunk in he went ballistic, erupting in anger.

"You bastards! You fucking bastards! You recorded this, didn't you? You dirty bastards recorded this!"

Lavender and Yellowhorse restrained Sinclair in his chair as he raged on.

"That's why you brought me to this facility! So you would have a direct interagency video conferencing link! I'll destroy you! You'll never see the light of day when I'm finished with you bastards!"

"Tie him up and tape his mouth!" Boucher ordered.

As his men restrained Sinclair, Boucher walked over to the communications room. Patterson and Moss followed. Haus opened the door and stood with his back against it, holding it open. The room was brightly lighted. Inside, Jackson was sitting at a control console. To his front were three flat-screen video displays. The middle screen displayed a picture of the operations center conference table where Sinclair could be seen being gagged and bound. The screen on the left showed a live video link to the Senate Select Committee on Intelligence in the Dirksen Building's secure meeting room, where they had been only yesterday. Sitting in the middle was Senator Rowland and to his left was Senator Cummings. There were four other persons sitting at the table that Boucher didn't recognize. The screen on the right showed four men sitting at a small table. Behind them were the American flag and a large, circular wall plaque with the FBI emblem on it. Beneath the plaque a sign boldly read, "CIRG".

Boucher patted Jackson on the shoulder. "Did they see and hear it all?"

"Sure did, Jake. I backed it all up on the hard drive and disk as well."

"Thanks, Risser. Are you still online for video conferencing in the ops center?"

"Good to go, Jake."

"Put it on screen out there."

Boucher patted Jackson on the back of the head and walked back to the conference room.

By the time Boucher returned to the operations center, two large, flat-screen videos on the wall behind the conference table showed both the Senate and the CIRG conference rooms.

Boucher took a seat across from Sinclair. "Can everyone hear me?" he asked as he looked at the screens.

He could see one of the men sitting at the CIRG desk reach toward a small control panel and press a button on it. "Yes, we hear you," the man replied.

Boucher checked the senate room and saw Senator Rowland do the same. "Yes, we hear you too," he responded.

"Ladies and gentlemen," Boucher began, "I want to first apologize for having to employ these tactics to get this critical information to you in a timely fashion so you can take action. It was clear to me yesterday I was getting nowhere. I had to find another way. It has been my experience that more often than not, drastic times require drastic measures. I hope you will forgive my men for the methods we chose, but it was the only course of action we had available on short notice. Senator Cummings, I want to personally apologize to you for the language I used in yesterday's hearings. As things worked out, it became clear to me that you were perhaps the only person not implicated in the conspiracy that was just revealed to you. So please forgive me, Senator."

Cummings nodded and smiled curtly.

"Now, for the matters at hand. You have heard for yourselves there may be as many as four nuclear bombs here in the U.S. The targets are our largest cities. According to the Chinese Plans and Admiral Sinclair, those nukes will be detonated simultaneously. We still don't know the target date for the attack, but it would seem to me the Chinese plans' use of a 0911 number might provide a clue. September is fast approaching. There is much work to be done to locate those nukes and render them safe before this plan can be carried out. It would also seem to me that you have much work to do involving ferreting out those within your ranks and elsewhere who are associated with this conspiracy. You and I both heard the admiral hint about the offices and posts that are involved. We must work swiftly and we must be sure. There are undoubtedly innocent, unwitting accomplices involved. I may have killed some of them over the past several weeks. Again, we must be sure. We are a country that lives by the rule of law. We must insist upon that principle without deviation as we investigate this conspiracy."

Boucher stood, but remained focused on the small camera mounted on the wall in front of him. Sinclair sat impassively, bound to his chair.

"I will unlock the entrance to this facility when you have assured me that you are prepared to take custody of Admiral Sinclair. My men and I would like safe passage out of the country. There is one other thing I would like to request your assistance on. I would like you to grant citizenship to Lieutenant Chi, the Chinese officer who helped us to escape from the Spratlys fortress. If he hadn't helped us, we would not be aware of the Chinese plan or the nukes."

Senator Cummings mumbled something inaudible to Senator Rowland. He nodded in agreement. She opened her mic. "Mr. Boucher, when you passed me your note yesterday I was suspicious of your intentions, but I now have no doubt whatsoever that you and your loyal followers were looking out for the best interests of this country throughout most of your ordeal. What started out as a treasure hunt certainly mushroomed into a major national security issue and potential international incident. I commend you for the way you and your men preserved national security and risked your very lives in the interest of our country. In my opinion, you and your men are heroes."

Boucher nodded his thanks without comment.

Senator Rowland opened his microphone. "Gentlemen, I too wish to commend you on behalf of this entire committee. The matter of your safe passage out of this country will be unnecessary. We will need you to testify as we prosecute the alleged conspirators like the good admiral. We will also want to fully debrief you and your men. The knowledge you all possess is extremely sensitive, and if disclosed could damage national security."

Boucher interrupted Rowland. "Senator, we obviously would like to go home. We would also like to have the cash and the gold we recovered returned to us. Can you facilitate that, Sir?"

Rowland frowned. "I'm sorry, but that is an area this committee has no control over. Perhaps the FBI can help you with that."

Boucher scowled at Sinclair. "I bet Admiral Sinclair knows where it is, don't you, Robb?"

"I'm sure it will all wash out during the investigation." Rowland glanced around at the other committee members. "Alright, we'll get back to you ASAP and advise you of the next step. Until then, sit tight and don't try to leave."

The two screens went blank.

Boucher looked around at his men, then over to Sinclair. "Get his sorry ass out of my sight! Find a room and secure him."

Lavender and Yellowhorse grabbed Sinclair and shuffled him out of the operations center. Boucher was visibly agitated.

"What do you think?" Patterson asked Boucher. "It seemed to go pretty well from my perspective."

Devoid of visible emotion, Boucher sat staring at the table. "You know Pat, I just don't have a warm and fuzzy. I think Cummings was telling us the truth, but my gut feeling is that Rowland was not being up front. I've been thinking about what Sinclair told us. He said there were former military senators in the conspiracy. Rowland is certainly former military and I just got the feeling from his answers that he was giving me a hand job. I especially didn't like his answer about our cash and gold. I'm not ready to trust him yet."

"What if he's in Sinclair's hip pocket?" Moss speculated. "I mean...how do we know?"

"Shit!" Patterson blurted as he slapped the table. "What if Sinclair's in *his* hip pocket?"

"What if the *President* is in his hip pocket?"

The rest of his men joined Boucher and Patterson at the table. Boucher sat calmly and carefully chose his words.

"The only one we can be sure about who is not in anyone's pocket, as far as this conspiracy is concerned, is Cummings. She's such a blazing, liberal half-a-commie, no one as diabolical as Sinclair would ever allow her into the inner circle. Hell, she's one of the government people in Washington he plans on killing in the cleansing process."

"You think she's smart enough to figure that out on her own, Jake?" Haus asked.

"Yeah, I think she's smart enough. The question is, will she connect the dots fast enough to be able to make a difference."

Llina looked perplexed. "Hell, Jake, I'm having trouble connecting the fucking dots! I still don't understand why Admiral Sinclair, or any of the rest of his buds, would allow an attack on the U.S.?"

Boucher leaned back in his chair and took a deep breath before answering. "As far as I can tell, they see themselves as the saviors of this country. Some of them think they're saviors of the world. Regardless, they feel they are the guardians. Sacrificing a few hundred thousand American lives to cleanse this country of the political blight in Washington, and getting our government back on track the way the Founding Fathers envisioned it is a small price to pay. At the same time it puts China back in its box and prevents them from later defeating us economically and raping our resources. That's what OPLAN 5000 has been about from the get-go. You just have to see the Plan's evolution to understand it. OPLAN 5000 was first designed to defeat the Soviet Union, and it worked. We read it for ourselves in the volumes we found at the crash site. I guess I didn't get it either, Dick. I didn't realize, until we encountered Sinclair, that OPLAN 5000 continued on as a grand strategy. Only now it's focused on defeating China along with all the cats and dogs in between."

Lavender scratched his head. "So do we sit here and wait for the cavalry to come over the hill, or do we get this info to the public?"

Jackson raised his hand. "I can link us into any network or news feed you want. The communications capabilities this facility has are topnotch. Just give me the word."

"Risser, do you think you can raise comms on a land line for me with Senator Cummings? I need to talk to her."

"I'm pretty sure I can. What about the NSA monitoring our call?"

"That's another accomplice in all this I hadn't considered. I couldn't figure out why we were being followed during the planning stage of our operation last month. The NSA had to be monitoring our phone calls and providing the info to Sinclair. So much for the President's program for domestic wire tapping of American citizens. NSA and CIA must have known all along that we were on to the crash site. Those bastards just sat back and watched us do the legwork and then tried to jump on it like stink on shit because they knew we would likely recover the Plans along with the gold. Hell, they didn't give a shit about the gold and still don't. The gold was their cover to make us think that was the reason we were being pursued."

"Jake, we don't have the crypto card to go secure to Cummings. It's going to have to be an open call. If the NSA is listening they'll easily catch it all."

"I don't think it will matter very much at this point, Risser. Please get Cummings on the phone."

"I'm on it."

Jackson hurried back inside the adjacent communications control room.

"Everyone else, listen up," Boucher said as he looked around the table at his trusted men. "I fully expect they will make an attempt to breach the decon chamber blast doors on one or both tunnels. If I was planning the attack, I'd strike at us simultaneously from both ends. They'll have a mix of the FBI's Hostage Rescue Team and Joint Special Operations Command's Delta and SEAL Team 6 operators to do the breaching and assault into the facility to get Sinclair. They can't afford for us to do more damage than we already have done, so they won't take prisoners. It will take them a minimum of five hours to assemble all that firepower here at the site. That means we need to figure out what we're going to do and then get it done before daylight. Gentlemen, I need some COA's. Let's meet back here in thirty minutes and see what we can come up with."

CHAPTER 39

US Special Operations Command, Tampa, Florida

Vice Admiral Jim Thornberg, the Deputy SOCOM commander, was being briefed on an operational contingency tasking that he had a personal interest in. The FBI had requested DoD support in breaching a government-owned, deep underground facility in Baker, West Virginia. It was reportedly a hostage scenario that involved twelve to fourteen terrorists who were holding the CIA's Director National Clandestine Service. Thornberg knew the hostage only too well as his longtime friend, Robb Sinclair. He also knew the identity of the hostage takers, Jake Boucher and his old SEAL Team Two platoon. SOCOM's mission was to breach the massive blast doors leading into the DUGs facility, kill the hostage takers and recover the hostage. He didn't like what he was hearing one bit.

Interrupting the JSOC briefer, he looked over to his aide. "Tom, please get me a secure line to General Hines."

Brigadier General Louis Hines was the JSOC Commanding General. As the CG, he would lead the mission. The Joint Special Operations Command, located at Fort Bragg in North Carolina, was the SOCOM subordinate command that had direct operational control of all the Special Operations Tier-one forces like the Rangers, Delta Force and SEAL Team Six and specific responsibility for hostage rescue. They maintained a round-the-clock departure readiness status of four hours from time of notification, and were prepared to deploy anywhere, world-wide, with a specially configured fly-away package of men and equipment.

Thornberg's aide dialed the secure telephone unit on the table and handed the phone to his boss. "Louis, Jim here. I'm a bit perplexed over what your OPS briefer is telling me. I personally know everyone involved inside the Baker facility and I can attest that they are not terrorists. I note that the Chairman and SECDEF have approved this assault order. That would not be something that I would necessarily find surprising, since it is SOP, but I can't help but wonder why there isn't a concurrence on it from Justice. The FBI is involved, so where is the Justice chop? Listen Louis, I don't like it. I want you to move slowly on this." Thornberg listened briefly and interrupted Hines's protest. "Yes General, that's exactly what I want you to do. I want you to drag your feet. And, yes, you may write all the memoranda for the record you want in protest of my order. Just be clear... no assault until daylight!"

Inside the Baker Facility

Boucher and his men reassembled in the operations center's conference room. They sat quietly waiting for Boucher to convene the planning session. This sort of forum was the very thing that made these men follow Boucher. They had been in many tight spots together over the years and they had all survived it. Certainly there was some luck involved, but their strength was based on the fact that they all knew what each one was thinking. They planned their courses of action together and then executed them. In doing so, they could anticipate nearly any alternative, and when necessary quickly deviate from the original plan and adapt to the changing situation.

Boucher entered the room with Patterson by his side. Both men sat down at the head of the conference table. Boucher started around the room.

"Haus, whatcha got?"

Quicklinsky leaned forward, placing his elbows on the table and quickly glanced around the room. "Jake, I speak for us all. We have alerted both the Senate Intelligence Committee and the FBI about the conspiracy and the pending nuclear threat. We can't help them find the nukes, even if we wanted to. Jake, we've done everything we can humanly do. We think the only way out of here in the vertical position is to give 'em Sinclair and the Plans. We need to cut a deal that allows us to walk."

Boucher considered Quicklinsky's proposal. The telephone's intercom speaker crackled on the table in front of Boucher, startling him.

It was Jackson's voice. "Jake, Senator Cummings is on line eight. Push the number eight button and you're good to go."

Boucher pushed the lighted button down opening the extension and put the phone on speaker. "Senator Cummings, thank you for taking my call. Listen, Senator, I would like to make you an offer that, hopefully, you can't refuse. I think it's a win-win for us both."

"Mr. Boucher, you have my attention."

"Well Senator, it appears to me that Senator Rowland might also be involved in this conspiracy. That's why I'm talking to you and that's why I'm offering you an opportunity to demonstrate your leadership ability in resolving this matter. We propose that you come to the Baker facility immediately. If you leave now, you can easily be here in two hours. We recommend that you bring any fellow senators you wish with you. We want you to enter the main access tunnel where we will pass you through the airlock to the inner facility. Once you join us, we will give you custody of Sinclair, and we will also give you both the U.S. and Chinese plans. My men and I will agree to testify on behalf of the prosecution as you investigate the conspiracy and identify all those involved. In turn, we want to walk out of this facility free men with no charges pending against us. Finally, we want the cash and the gold we recovered at the crash site given back to us."

"Mr. Boucher, you know I don't have your gold and I don't know who does."

"Yes Senator, we recognize that you don't have possession of the money or the gold, but I bet Sinclair knows exactly where it is. How about the rest of the deal?"

"I don't think you have any cards left to play, Mr. Boucher. So don't dictate..."

"Wait a minute, Senator," he interrupted, "I have a number of cards left to play if I have to. You'll look like a hero if you do this and I'll fully cooperate. Like I said, it's a win-win."

"Well, you can't expect me to just drop everything. I'll need to prepare. I want hand-picked news reporters to film me inside."

"Senator, bring anyone you like but you need to be here within the next two hours. Go to the main tunnel entrance. I'll wait for your call when you arrive."

Boucher hung up the phone and looked up. "That woman has got to be one of the dizziest, most miserable bitches I've ever had the misfortune of dealing with in my entire life! We're offering her the chance to be a friggin' hero, and she wants all the glory too. She wants the press to accompany her inside and film it all. Can you imagine what it would be like waking up next to her every morning! Jeez!"

Boucher stood and pointed toward Patterson, who got up and retrieved a roll of facility blueprints that he had left by the door. He and Boucher pinned two of the three-foot by four-foot blueprints to the corkboard on the wall. Boucher grabbed a laser pointer and projected a red dot on the center of the left print.

"Okay boys, this is where we are on this print. Here's the main air intake shaft. It rises 326 feet vertically, almost directly above the HVAC room over here. Now check this out. Here are two other airshafts. Both of them are auxiliary air sources should the main shaft become fouled from debris above. Note that all three shafts are separated on the surface by several hundred yards and that all three have poppets covering their intakes at ground level."

Boucher observed his men were all beginning to smile and relax. He was a natural leader who was composed and conveyed confidence. There was a potential way out—a means to escape—and if it was possible, he was determined to find it.

"The poppets are these things, here, that sit directly over the intake and look like giant, steel mushrooms. They're designed to automatically drop and seal off the air intakes in the event of a nuclear blast above or they can be remotely activated and closed from here. The airshafts are cut through solid rock and each has its own filter located in the HVAC room. Now look here where I'm pointing. There is a shaft access door, located above the HVAC filter on each of the three shafts. The print shows that each shaft also contains a ladder permanently affixed to the rock that runs from the access door above the filter all the way up to the poppet on the surface above."

Yellowhorse butt in. "So all we need to do is open the access door, climb the three-hundred foot ladder in the shaft, open the poppet, and step out on the surface above. Piece of cookie, Jake!"

"Not so fast, Johnny," Boucher warned. "It's not gonna be quite that easy and here's why. The drawing on the right shows the poppet detail and it looks like opening it from inside the shaft won't be easy. If you look where I'm pointing, it appears the poppet mechanism and structure are welded onto a frame that is lagged into solid rock. The only way to remove it will be to use a cutting torch."

Doyle raised his hand. "There's an oxy-acetylene cutting torch in the maintenance room, but the hoses aren't long enough to reach three-hundred feet up that shaft to the top. That means that we'll have to figure out a way to hoist the torch and oxy-acetylene tanks to the top so we can cut the poppet off."

Thane LeFever joined the discussion. "Then we're going to have to push that heavy bastard off the intake so we can climb out. Once we do that, we'll need to cut a hole in the steel cage that's built around the poppet. That's gonna take some serious muscle and burn up some valuable time."

Ramirez jumped in to the conversation. "Why can't we extend the oxy-acetylene hoses using compressed air hoses, so all we have to carry to the top is the cutting torch itself? Instead of cutting the poppet, how about we just cut a hole in the side of the intake pipe? The print shows it extending about three feet above the ground surface. Cutting a hole in the steel ought to be fast and easy. We dress our torch man in firefighter's bunker clothes so he doesn't get toasted, and we have those clothes available at the emergency fore station in the main tunnel. By the way, I'll run the torch unless one of you losers thinks you can kick my ass. Once I'm through the side of the pipe, I'll lay a bunker coat over the hot metal so we can crawl over it. I'll crawl outside and cut the cage. The rest of us make the climb as a group and we all make a run for the tree line."

Boucher and the rest of the men thought about Ramirez's proposal.

"Why even mess with a torch?" Klum said. "The tool room must have a cut-off grinder. Why not just rig an extension cord to the top of the shaft and cut our way out using the grinder? Granted, it will take a lot longer than the torch, but the result will be the same."

"What makes you boys think they won't see the sparks and catch us? Shit," Yellowhorse said, "it's still dark up there!"

The men broke into multiple sidebar conversations. Boucher realized he needed to regain control of the discussion.

"Okay boys, quiet! Here's what we're gonna do." The room grew quiet. "Risser, can you do a live feed into each of the major news organizations?"

"Yup, can do, Jake."

"Okay Risser, I want you to set up this room for live feed. Gabe and Cherry, you two will use the torch and cut us an escape hole through the side of the poppet pipe and surrounding cage. It will have to be done fast. The grinder idea is out—too slow. When you're cutting the cage outside, use a bunker coat like a tent to conceal the sparks. Bad Bob and Dick, you support Gabe and Cherry. Let's go out from the south shaft. That one looks like it's only about fifty yards from the perimeter fence, so there will be less chance of compromise. The road that leads down to the main tunnel entrance is on the other side about four-hundred yards away. According to the surface elevation print, there's a building between the road and our airshaft. Haus and Johnny, come up with an E and E plan. I want all the guys to go in pairs. No two pairs will go the same way."

Moss interrupted, "Wait a minute, Jake. What about you?"

"I got us into this and now I need to make it right. I'll stay behind here and hand Sinclair and the Plans over to Senator Cummings."

"Like hell you will!" Patterson yelled. "If you stay, I'm staying with you!"

"Me too!" Moss added.

Quicklinsky stood and held up both hands to quiet everyone. "Okay Jake, you can stay back if you like, but that means we all stay with you. If that isn't acceptable, then you need to escape with the rest of us because we aren't leaving without you!"

Boucher looked down at the table and smiled. He slowly stood. "Okay guys, you're right. I'll leave with you, but I will have to be the last one up the ladder. I'll have to open the airlock for Senator Cummings, but I'll hit the switch and then make a run for the airshaft. I'll only be a few minutes behind the rest of you. Her arrival, along with her entourage, will create a major diversion and it should add just the right amount of confusion to give us the edge we need to escape successfully. We have about an hour left to get everything ready down here and get the escape route cut and cleared. If this is to be our last hooyah, let's make it a good one!"

The men burst into cheers and immediately set out to their tasks. Boucher grabbed Patterson and pulled him over to the adjacent communications room.

"Asshole!" he said to Patterson.

"Yup!" Patterson replied.

"Okay Pat, let's get Sinclair out here. I want him taped to a chair in full camera view.

Risser, open the live media feed in about thirty mikes."

...

About an hour later, an incoming call lighted a phone line on the communications console. Boucher answered from an office just inside the airlock.

"Hello...yes Senator, I am prepared to open the airlock."

Senator Cummings, accompanied by a bi-partisan entourage of five other senators, the Deputy Director of the FBI and three Supervisory Special Agents, the Assistant Attorney General and two Department of Justice lawyers, CNN, CBS, and NBC news crews entered the airlock and went on through into the tunnel leading to the operations center. Armed guards and Federal Protective Service bodyguards encircled the VIP's as they followed the yellow marker tape Boucher had strung along the tunnel, marking the route to the operations center. Strangely, no one spoke. Only the shuffle of their shoes echoed through the tunnel. Water dripping from cracks in the rocky ceiling above could be heard at places along the way.

As this strange group approached the door to the operations center, the guards lined up on either side of the door. With a consenting nod they burst through the door into the brightly lighted room. Cummings followed right behind the security force.

She immediately recognized the room from the one she had seen the morning before. Sinclair was sitting at the head of the table, duct taped to his chair. The tape over his mouth had been removed, leaving a red rash-like mark on his cheeks. Positioned on the table in front of him were four volumes of OPLAN 5000. The OPLAN covers all bore orange TOP SECRET coversheets and markings. In front of those four volumes were two others, nearly as thick as the OPLAN 5000 volumes. Their covers were marked in red Chinese writing.

Lying prominently in front of all the volumes was a DVD disk in a clear, plastic case. It was labeled in handwritten, red felt pen. Cummings turned it her direction so she could read it. The hand written label read, "Copy of Sinclair video conf. at Baker facility." She looked at the flat screens on the wall and for the first time realized the closed circuit TV was showing a live picture of her and everyone else in the room. She turned and studied Sinclair for a moment before addressing him.

"Admiral Sinclair, how strange it is to find you here. I believe you have a great deal of explaining to do."

CHAPTER 40

Off Shore Key Largo, Florida, months later

R eilly took off his T-shirt, revealing several ugly scars on his triceps.
"Hey Billy," Moss chided, "show us your scar. You know…chicks dig scars."

All the men laughed.

Lavender piled on. "You better come up with a really hot shit story about how you got it 'cause there ain't nobody gonna believe you got shot by some Chinese army maggot. I'm thinkin' some shark-bite, bullshit story or somethin'."

Yellowhorse and Reilly were fishing from the stern of Boucher's new luxury motor yacht. Below them, on the outer hull, the name "Hooyah" was painted in large, block letters. LeFever, Jackson, Lavender, Yellowhorse, and Quicklinsky were sitting in white, vinyl, upholstered chairs, drinking beer as they watched. Moss was standing behind Yellowhorse's chair, holding a nearly empty margarita glass. Doyle and Ramirez were inside the air-conditioned cabin galley, concocting a fresh pitcher of frozen margaritas in the blender.

"Hey Jake," Moss called up to the open bridge where Patterson and Boucher manned the controls.

Boucher turned and peered down at them grinning. "What, Mossman?"

"What do you think about a chick story for Billy's scar that goes like this? There I was, swimming along at thirty feet when a giant lobster attacked me. He damn near pinched off my triceps before I could stick my knife up his ass and gut the son of a bitch. Lucky for me my favorite helicopter pilot was passing overhead and saw me struggling, so he dropped his hoist down to me and yanked me out of harm's way just in the nick of time."

Boucher grinned widely, shook his head and gave Moss a thumbs-down gesture.

Patterson looked over at Boucher. "We did it, Jake. We actually pulled it off."

"Yup, we did, Pat. We all made it back."

"I just gotta know something old buddy."

"Sure, what?"

"If you had it to do all over again would you do it all over again?"

A commotion began on the deck below.

"Holy shit!" Haus yelled at the top of his lungs. "Billy has friggin' Moby tuna on his line! Look at the size of that fish!"

Reilly was fighting the fish with all his might, but was having difficulty reeling the fish in because his triceps was still under rehab therapy and not up to full strength. Klum spit a mouth full of beer mixed with snuff toward Yellowhorse.

"Yellowhorse, get a gun and shoot that fuckin' fish the next time he jumps. Reilly can't handle it by himself!"

All the men laughed.

"Fuck you, you bunch of assholes!" Reilly shouted. "Hey Klum, I got somethin' danglin' you can handle!"

Chi was already drunk. He was precariously poised next to the side of the cabin, pissing over the gunwale. "Billy not asshole!" he blubbered. "Billy love United Station too much! Billy number one for me."

Billy looked over his shoulder back at Chi. "You're okay, Chi, and I don't give a shit what the rest of these assholes say about you."

Chi frowned. "What they say?"

Everyone laughed.

"They say Chinese military officers have something that looks like a dick only much, much smaller!" Klum shouted.

"But who is Dick? I not know him." Chi asked as he lost his balance and almost fell overboard from a passing swell.

Everyone hooted in gut-wrenching laughter.

It was clear that everyone was enjoying themselves. Boucher turned back to Patterson.

"You know Pat, I love every one of those sons of bitches down there."

Patterson nodded. "Me too."

"At this point in my life I don't think I could deal with losing a single one of them."

Patterson nodded affirmatively.

"You know Pat, we're all going to have to watch our sixes for a long time to come—maybe the rest of our lives. I have no doubt in my mind that the Luminous will pay us back if we give them a chance."

"I know, Jake. They'll regroup and try again. You think President Knight is one of them?"

"I certainly hope not, but there's no way of knowing for sure."

"That's a pisser, because I actually like the man. I mean it was his intervention that got us our money back."

"That operation we just pulled off really tested our mettle. I thought I knew these guys before, but now…" Boucher hesitated. "Now we're truly family. I never had a brother. You're the closest thing I have to a blood brother, Pat. So you ask if I would do it all over again. The answer is yes. I would do it all over again without missing a heartbeat! So why did you ask? You have something in mind?"

Patterson smiled in admiration of his friend. "Well you know Jake, we still have over two-thirds of our gold just lying in the mud on the bottom of that canal intersection, right where we stashed it. I was just wondering if you're up for going back there and recovering it? I think we need a bigger boat."

Epilogue

The OPLANs were secured by the Justice Department. The CIA translated and analyzed the Chinese plans, which revealed the nuclear plot to attack major U.S. cities along the east coast followed by a Chinese Trojan Horse invasion, exactly as Boucher had warned. This information was held within special access program code word channels at the highest levels of the government, and as such was not released to those cities targeted, or the public in general. As part of a larger U.S. government strategy to put Iran on the blame line in the event of a terrorist nuclear attack, Iran was publicly put on notice to stop its uranium enrichment program. This has also served to divert public focus away from the Chinese. It has further isolated China from its ties to the already fragile trade imbalance between the U.S. and China, and the growing U.S. national debt. The Department of Homeland Security was assigned as the lead federal agency in the task of locating the rogue nukes, already believed hidden in four or more major U.S. cities. To date, none have been located or intercepted during transit. The search continues.

Vice Admiral Sinclair was tried by a military tribunal and given a thirty-year sentence in federal prison for conspiracy to commit treason. The trial was never made public. His CIA boss, General Gardner, was investigated but his complicity in the conspiracy could not be substantiated and no indictment was made. He voluntarily resigned his position as DCI two weeks following the conclusion of the investigation so he could spend more time with his family. Rene Thompson, the CIA's Director for Covert Operations, was indicted and found to be an unwitting accomplice in the conspiracy. Thompson quietly opted for early retirement and now teaches International Affairs as an adjunct professor at the American University in Washington, DC. Senator Rowland denied any wrongdoing, as did the Vice President. Both men faced a closed-door, grand jury investigation. Both were found non-complicit and were vindicated by the administration. They remain in power today. President Knight was not implicated and remains aloof to most of the details.

Senator Cummings is the front-runner for the Democratic Party's nomination for President in the next election. Senator Rowland, a Republican, has declared his intention to run for President and may be her only serious competition. Vice Admiral Thornberg retired as the Deputy SOCOM Commander and now works as a political-military consultant for FOX news. Commander Galloway, CO of the USS Virginia, was transferred nine months later to a staff position at COMSUBPAC and continues a successful naval career. Lieutenant Cutler, who was primarily involved in his duty position of serving as Officer of the Deck onboard the USS Virginia, resigned from the Navy one month after Commander Galloway was transferred. He is currently a student at Harvard Business School studying for his MBA.

Melvin Brown, the CIA's former Chief of Station in Bangkok, was reposted and now heads the State Department's Office of the Coordinator for Counterterrorism as the Ambassador at Large. Lieutenant Murrant, SEAL Team One, Echo Platoon Commander, was recently killed in hostile action in Iraq. His assistant, Lieutenant (junior grade) Morgan, was promoted to lieutenant and is now serving as a platoon commander in SEAL Team Four. Lieutenant Chi, the PRC Army officer who helped Boucher and his men escape from the Chinese Spratlys fortress, was granted full U.S. citizenship by an Act of Congress. He now works as an interpreter for the U.S. Department of State's Mission to the United Nations and lives in New York City. He is dating a blond woman from Sweden who also works at the UN. Tahnite, the former Thai SEAL commander, is a multi-millionaire and continues to run his family's rice export business in Bangkok. He regularly visits the U.S. on business and always spends time with Boucher. Expatriate Paul "Goodie" Goodman and wife, Tu, sold their hotel in Bongserrie. They now live in a mansion overlooking their private beach on Fiji.

James Ray, the former Air America pilot suffering from Alzheimer's, recently died. His death went without notice except for two well dressed, middle-aged men—one black and one white—who attended Ray's funeral at Arlington National Cemetery. They spoke to no one else and disappeared as mysteriously as they appeared after the closing prayer.

While they each quietly went their separate ways, Boucher and his men remain in close contact with one another. They are planning a reunion next summer onboard Boucher's newly purchased motor yacht, which he maintains in Baltimore's Inner Harbor at Fells Point.

THE END

FACT

U.S. Navy SEALs operated in Cambodia in the area of the Parrots Beak well before and during the 1968 Tet Offensive. President Johnson vehemently denied that any U.S. Forces were operating outside the borders of Vietnam. The CIA's Air America planes provided counter-insurgency forces supplies and money to fund the counter-offensive against North Vietnam. The gold reserves of South Vietnam have never been recovered. Some believe they were transported to the Philippines during the Tet Offensive, just in case South Vietnam fell.

OPLAN 5000 did exist as a top secret war plan that provided overarching strategy on how U.S. Forces would engage and defeat the Soviet Union in the Pacific Theater. The Plan was updated every couple of years with the old volumes destroyed. Japan, South Korea, Vietnam, the Philippines, Taiwan, Thailand, and Malaysia were strategically key to control of the critical sea lines of communication and to denying the Soviets additional warm water bases of operation beyond Vladivostok on the west shore of the Sea of Japan.

There are significant oil reserves beneath the Spratlys Islands, making the Spratlys strategically and economically valuable. China, Vietnam, and the Philippines dispute Spratlys ownership. China built a fortified outpost on one of the larger Spratlys during the 1980's to assert their claim to the islands. It exists today and is still occupied by a small Chinese Army garrison.

There is a "Luminous" group of behind-the-scenes people who steer the U.S. government despite the political party in power. From this secretive, elite, apolitical group, power is given or taken and direction is imposed.

Descriptions of hardware, equipment and capabilities portrayed in this novel are accurate.

GLOSSARY OF TERMS

ACP - Automatic Colt Pistol. Designed by John Browning at the turn of the 20th century specifically for his 1911 model .45 caliber automatic Colt pistol.

ALCON – Military acronym for "All concerned."

AWACS – Airborne warning and control system – specially equipped Air Force planes, used for detection of friend and foe and for battle space control.

BEQ – Bachelor Enlisted Quarters

BUD/S – Basic UDT/SEAL training. See UDT/R below.

Cast Zone – Area designated to drop boats or swimmers from a helicopter at low level above the water.

CADRG map – Compressed ARC Digitized Raster Graphics (CADRG) are digital raster representations of paper graphic products. CADRG files are physically formatted within a National Imagery Transmission Format (NITF) message. Because of their unique digital accuracy, CADRG map displays are used on command and control systems for mission planning systems and in aircraft cockpits.

CO – Commanding Officer

COA – Courses of Action – Term used by military operations planners.

COB – Chief of the Boat – The senior Chief Petty Officer crew member onboard all U.S. submarines is designated the COB. The COB is one of the CO's most trusted and knowledgeable members of the crew and holds an almost "god-like" position as the COB.

CON – Control room on a submarine – paramount to the bridge area of a surface ship.

CONPLAN – Contingency Plan – CONPLANS detail specific elements of a war plan not covered in an OPLAN. A CONPLAN, for example, might typically cover how the military would expect to fight against North Korea should the North violate the DMZ and invade South Korea.

Chip light – A warning light that automatically flashes on a helicopter's instrument panel when a piece of a transmission breaks free inside the transmission housing. This is one of the most dreaded warning lights for helicopter pilots because it indicates that he must land immediately or risk having the transmission blow up or lock up if the chip lodges in the wrong location or cause more fracturing of gears.

CIRG – FBI acronym for their Critical Incident Response Group that includes several tactical elements of the FBI, like the Hostage Rescue Team (HRT).

DECON (DECON room) – Decontamination room – Specially configured room with washing, scrubbing, and changing areas that are isolated from the rest of the facility to prevent contamination being brought inside the main facility. DECON areas/rooms typically have air locks on entry and exit sides.

DILLIGAFF – Military acronym for "Does it look like I give a flying fuck?"

DMZ – Demilitarized Zone – term given to an area considered neutral by opposing sides. Korea's DMZ still exists today along the 38th parallel separating North and South Korea. A DMZ was created during the Vietnam War between North and South Vietnam using Korea as a model, but it failed miserably and was dissolved upon the departure of U.S. troops in 1975 and the Communist reunification of Vietnam.

DZ – Military term for parachute "Drop Zone."

EEI's – Essential Elements of Information – critical to accurate and timely mission planning.

EGLM (40mm EGLM) – Enhanced Grenade Launcher Module – The EGLM mounts on the SCAR's (see SCAR) 6 o'clock Picatinny rail beneath the barrel. The EGLM fires conventional 40mm low velocity grenades accurately with an effective range out to 350 meters. The 40mm grenade warhead is a high fragmentation shaped charge effective against personnel and light armor.

ETA – Expected Time of Arrival.

FNG – Fucking New Guy – SEALs refer to any other SEAL who went through BUD/S (basic SEAL training) after them as FNGs.

FOAD – Fuck Off And Die.

Frag – Fragmentation from exploding bombs, rockets, mortars, or any other object that causes high velocity fragmentation.

FOD – Foreign Object Debris – term applied to any loose object or material that can be ingested into a jet air intake and potentially cause damage or engine failure.

Global Hawk – Highly sophisticated remotely piloted (unmanned) reconnaissance aircraft. In use by the U.S. military and CIA throughout the world today.

GPS - Global Positioning System

HIV – High Interest Vessel – Term applied to any vessel the U.S. believes may be transporting terrorists, weapons of mass destruction, precursor materials for WMD use, or any other high interest agenda outside the law.

HDR antenna/terminal – Provides modern submarines with a 16-inch dish antenna capable of satellite data rates ranging from 128 Kilobits per second (kbps) to 8 megabits per second (Mbps). It also accesses EHF Low Data Rate/Medium Data Rate (LDR/MDR) transmissions, SHF, and the Global Broadcast Service (GBS).

Howdy Doody – The name of a good natured, wooden puppet that appeared on a children's TV show in the late 1950s.

HRT's "Kill House" – FBI's Hostage Rescue Team practices their shooting techniques inside a specially built facility located at the FBI Academy in Quantico, VA. The kill house has bullet-absorbing walls and the walls are moveable so the HRT can rehearse multiple room entry techniques using live fire.

HVAC (HVAC room) – Heating, Ventilation, Air Conditioning – Equipment room containing HVAC equipment in virtually all modern, non-residential buildings today.

ID markings – Identification markings. Sometimes used only as ID.

Imagery – term applied to digital pictures taken from ground elements, aircraft, or satellites that provide sufficient detail and clarity so they can be used to detect and identify individuals, troop emplacements, structures, vehicles, etc.

LAT and LONG – Latitude and longitude.

LAW rocket – Light Anti-armor Warhead rocket – man portable shoulder-fired rocket from a one-shot, disposable, plastic launch tube.

LZ – Landing Zone. A designated area clear of obstructions, suitable for a helicopter landing. A "hot LZ" refers to an LZ that has enemy present and/or enemy shooting at the helicopter.

LIDAR images – Laser Imaging, Distance, and Ranging (similar to RADAR only this system uses a laser instead of radio waves).

Lima Charlie – Military phonetic alphabet for the letters L and C. Used in radio communications brevity to represent the words "loud and clear." Example: I hear you lima charlie.

MRE – Meals ready to Eat – prepackaged meals that can be eaten cold

Mic – short for microphone.

Mikes – Used in military communications brevity, meaning "minutes."

NCA – National Command Authority. NCA is composed of the President and the Secretary of Defense.

NEST – Nuclear Emergency Support Team – Department of Energy's highly classified premier operational radiological and nuclear counterterrorism asset consisting of about one thousand volunteer scientists, engineers, and technicians sourced from the National Laboratories (Los Alamos, Sandia, Lawrence Livermore). NEST has a global mission to locate and disable rogue nuclear weapons and radiological devices. They are the only people on the planet who run toward a working nuclear weapon. They may well be our last line of defense should terrorists attempt a nuclear attack against the U.S..

NSA – National Security Agency – NSA conducts technical intelligence collection.

NVA – North Vietnamese Army – regular conventional forces not considered rebels or guerilla forces.

NVGs – Night Vision Goggles – Magnify available starlight so humans can see in the dark.

OP – Operation – or OPS (Operations) is sometimes used.

OPSEC – Operational Security – Term applied to special care and handling of sensitive operations to prevent compromise.

OPLAN – Operation Plan – OPLANs are highly classified military war plans.

OE mast - Provides modern submarines radio frequency communications in HF, VHF, and L-band UHF for Link 16, Identification Friend or Foe (IFF) and Global Positioning System (GPS).

Pallets – The military stacks all cargo on pallets before loading the pallets into the cargo bay of transport aircraft. The pallets are made of approximately 1 inch thick aluminum plate and are 8x8 feet square. Cargo is typically stacked 8 feet high and then secured to the pallet with the use of a very robust nylon cargo net specifically designed for those dimensions.

ROE – Rules of Engagement – Strict standing guidelines for engaging the enemy.

Roger - Used primarily in radio communications brevity - meaning "I understand."

Ro-Ro ship – Roll on-Roll off ship- Very large ships designed with large ramps that can be lowered from the ship to the pier, allowing rapid loading and unloading of wheeled or tracked vehicles. Ro-Ro ships are commonly used by foreign car manufacturers to deliver thousands of cars and trucks to the U.S. Ro-Ro ships, because of their cargo capacity and inherent speed in loading and unloading, are also used by many militaries throughout the world to rapidly deliver military vehicles and troops.

PRC – Peoples Republic of China

SAC – Supervisory Agent in Charge

SAM – Surface to air missile. SAMs come in all sizes. SAMs can be fired from large vehicle-mounted launchers or shoulder fired from lightweight man-portable launchers.

SCAR-light – Special Operations Combat Assault Rifle chambered in 5.56mm (.223 cal).

SPECAT – Special Category – SPECAT is a designation given to need-to-know, very sensitive information. SPECAT designations are accompanied by a code word and require a "read in" to gain access to the information and a "read-out" when a person leaves the government or changes jobs that no longer require information access to a particular SPECAT program.

SCI – Sensitive Compartmented Information – SCI information is even more exclusive than SPECAT and like SPECAT, is kept within very exclusive code word channels. Many times SCI programs only have a handful of people (three or four) in them who have the total picture. Everyone else working within a particular program only has a fragmental understanding of a specific element or piece of the overall program. This system of information disclosure and control effectively prevents information compromise. Obviously, a person could easily be an unwitting accomplice to a much larger sinister plot and never know it.

SOCOM – Special Operations Command – located in Tampa, Florida.

SOP – Standard Operational Procedure

STE phone – Secure telephone equipment – a desk top telephone, not much different from a standard office phone, except the STE uses a computer key card (looks like a credit card) that is inserted into a slot in the side of the phone. This key card, once installed, allows the user to press a button and the phone will automatically scramble the conversation which can only be decoded on the other end by a similar STE with a key card installed.

SUBPAC – U.S. Navy submarine headquarters in the Pacific. Many times used as a shortened version of COMSUBPAC (Commander, Submarine Headquarters in the Pacific).

TACAN beacon - Tactical Air Navigation beacon. Used by all military aircraft to navigate. Also used by air traffic control.

UDT inflatable life jackets – Specially designed low profile inflatable life jackets, originally used by the Navy's famed Underwater Demolition Team "Frogmen," and now worn by Navy SEALs whenever they are operating in a maritime or riverine environment.

UDT/R – Underwater Demolition Team Replacement training. Prior to BUD/S training, it was called UDT/R. In 1983 the Navy's four remaining Underwater Demolition Teams were all decommissioned and then recomissioned as SEAL Teams. The UDT and SEAL basic training school name was changed to BUD/S.

WILCO – Military communications brevity for "Will comply."

XO – Short for "Executive Officer", the number two man in command behind the CO.

Printed in the United States
124886LV00002B/1-48/P

9 781595 94273